HERE
AND
AGAIN

Center Point
Large Print

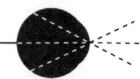

**This Large Print Book carries the
Seal of Approval of N.A.V.H.**

HERE AND AGAIN

NICOLE R. DICKSON

CENTER POINT LARGE PRINT
THORNDIKE, MAINE

This Center Point Large Print edition is published
in the year 2014 by arrangement with NAL Signet,
a member of Penguin Group (USA) LLC,
a Penguin Random House Company.

This is a work of fiction. Names, characters, places, and
incidents either are the product of the author's imagination
or are used fictitiously, and any resemblance to actual
persons, living or dead, business establishments, events, or
locales is entirely coincidental.

The text of this Large Print edition is unabridged.
In other aspects, this book may vary from the original edition.
Printed in the United States of America on permanent paper.
Set in 16-point Times New Roman type.

ISBN: 978-1-62899-261-8

Library of Congress Cataloging-in-Publication Data

Dickson, Nicole R.
  Here and again / Nicole R. Dickson. —
    Center Point Large Print edition.
      pages ; cm
  Summary: "Since her husband was killed in Iraq, Ginger Martin's life
has been fraught with grief and uncertainty. But a mysterious stranger
will help her come to terms with her loss and the necessity of change"
—Provided by publisher.
  ISBN 978-1-62899-261-8 (library binding : alk. paper)
  1. Nurses—Fiction. 2. Widows—Fiction. 3. Soldiers—Fiction.
    4. Large type books. I. Title.
PS3604.I328H47 2014b
813'.6—dc23
                                                    2014025779

For my grandmothers
Martha Dora Barnes Beebe
and my blue ribbon
Lola Virginia Swenson Dickson
and the magic of applesauce

ACKNOWLEDGMENTS

A path is best if shared. It becomes a journey where discoveries are made not only by what we individually take in, but more importantly what we learned through the experiences of others—to see the world and road through another's eyes. For this novel, I'd like to acknowledge those who walked this path with me and all the others I met along the way.

Thanks to my traveling partner, my daughter, Elspeth Rowan Dickson Bartlett, for quiet company walking through the battlefields of Virginia, Pennsylvania, and Maryland. I am grateful to Mary Hanes for driving the Shenandoah with me the first time and keeping us on the road when I first arrived at Harpers Ferry. Thanks also to my family, Laurel, Andrew, Amy, Emily, and Arden Dickson, for wandering with me through Petersburg and Appomattox.

I'd like to remember Boyd and thank Barbara Lyon for sharing so much with my family and for the use of their cabin so long ago, where I met the goat and learned a mighty lesson at Steep Ravine.

Thanks to Elaine Legg, RN, for her medical knowledge and discussions about her emergency room experiences. Scott Hanes—thanking him for general farming knowledge and equipment discussions. Also, appreciation to Meredith Scales for conversations regarding farming in rural Virginia and the nature of goats. Thank you, Kathy Green, for information on herdsmanship and for your patience as I worked through the novel.

Thanks to Susan Coulter for her first edit. To Christie Scott I owe gratitude for editing help and for working through specific plot points. Thank you to Merry Creed, Terrie Parrish and Denise Robinson for reading the first drafts of the book, adding commentary, and helping with the conversation guide.

I'd like to acknowledge the service of the park rangers in our national parks and the volunteers there, especially those in Gettysburg, Antietam, Manassas, Petersburg, Harpers Ferry, and Appomattox. Thank you also to the visitors' center in Lexington, Virginia, for information regarding Thomas Jackson, Washington and Lee University, and VMI.

Thank you to Claire Zion, editor, and my agent, Linda Chester of Linda Chester's Literary Agency, for support with this book.

Finally, I'd like to personally offer my gratitude and appreciation to all those in the armed forces, in this country and abroad, now as back then, and to their families who continue to give up all or part of their own lives in service to others. For my own family, I'd like to recognize my father,

William H. Dickson, my brother, Andrew A. Dickson, my uncles, Stanley Houghton and George Iaeger, and my cousins, Kathleen Iaeger Shroy, Lee Ann Iaeger, and Mike Carey. Love and thanks to all of you.

May 10, 18611
Laurel Creek

Dear Juliette,
When I awoke this morning, my body was wound tight like the string of a violin that awaits the bow. I wanted to go, yet Laurel Creek babbled softly to the birds singing in the tree outside my window. I could only think of home, spring, and the fields rising to flower. All was still in the house as I dressed. To my surprise, I found the buttons to Grandpa Samuel's uniform sewn onto my own. The dawn glimmered on them, causing me some difficulty securing my sword.

I walked from my room as quietly as I could, but found greeting me with murmured morning voices my father, my sister, Ann, and her husband, Peter. Their eyes were swimming and I could not long look upon them nor speak—so thick was my throat. I headed for the front door. Before I reached it, Ann stopped me, making small adjustments to the placement of the coat upon my shoulders. Her hands knew this uniform for from them it was made. She kissed my cheek with a God Bless and I thought that to be the end of it, but my father followed me to the creek. He was stumbling over the slippery rocks so much so that I had to help him back to the other side. When I return, the first thing I shall do is build a bridge over that stream—a bridge with a roof. It'll be the death of him if I do not. His final words to me were that the buttons would bring me home. They had kept his father's father alive through the last Revolution, so they should bring me safely home through this one. He took me in his arms, after which I, once again, crossed Laurel Creek. I looked back only once to ensure he had stayed on his side of the water. He had done, thus I headed for Jeb and Zachary's house.

I arrived in time for breakfast. Zachary was waiting at the door and when I walked in his mother shook me out of my coat like dirt off of a rug. Immediately, she tore off my brass buttons, replacing them with several mismatching ones from various coats of the late Reverend. Zachary said he could have shot me a mile off, the buttons shined so. No shiny target would I make, declared his mother. I did try to explain what my father had said, but she felt it superstitious and nonsense.

As Zachary and I ate in silence, his mother secured the orphaned buttons to my coat and I stole peeks through the window as Jeb said good-bye to his promised, Ruth. She wept as he kissed her cheek so softly. I thought of you then.

I have grieved with you, Juliette, in your loss

this last year. Charles was a good and honorable man and a true friend. If I had to lose your hand, it would not have been so easily endured had it been to anyone else but him. The four years since I left Lexington have been at once hollow and painful as you did not return with me as my wife. But, also, they have been joyous and without worry for I left you with a better man than myself. Only your happiness has helped settle me in contentment these last years.

Juliette, I have walked letter by letter with you down the widow's path. I would be nowhere else. My intention has always been to see you happy once more—to have you loved as you deserve to be loved once more. So I have received your last letter with both jubilant elation and unfathomable sadness, for in it I find words of love given to me. Oh, Juliette, I have loved and will love none but you. In the joy of receiving such a gift as your love, my heart weighs heavily. Duty calls me, Juliette, and I can only answer. War is come. I am a soldier. My duty takes me from you, and as I leave, I leave you free. I would not suppose to press my love for you until I can, with open heart and clarity of the future, ask for your hand if you would have me.

So, I shall take up the sword, and as I do, I feel your whispered breath upon my ear and your hair brush gently my neck as you rest your head upon my shoulder. So quiet and deep do I feel you, like the waters at the bottom of the river flowing over its bed.

Though I promised with this pen and paper to write home as often as I could, I think I shall write mostly to you. I shall send, also, one of my grandfather's buttons with each letter—a token of my family's past to one who, with hope, shall hold my future. Thus, when I return, you shall have and know all of me that you have missed and we can then speak only of you, whom I have missed, filling my mind and heart with you, having emptied both on the road of war. To return from war with a clear conscience is my most longed-for wish.

I must go now. Captain Tiffany calls a muster. Four years has it been since I have strayed from home and upon my return from university at Virginia Military Institute, I swore I should never leave again. But now, I can only say my heart is forever home with you—whether upon Laurel Creek or any other water beyond which I may find thee.

Your devoted,
Samuel E. Annanais

CHAPTER 1

THE COVERED BRIDGE

The afternoon was cold and as the school bus drove away the dark cloud of its exhaust drifted heavily behind Ginger Martin, following her up the lane. The snow on the top of her shoes had gradually changed from loose and powdery as she walked to the bus stop to dense and icy now on the return home. It had started to drizzle. Her feet were heavier, as was her mind, for this was a day unlike any other in the last year.

A long whine brought her attention from her feet to the road ahead, where her youngest, Oliver, was sinking into the ditch on the Creeds' side of the lane. He had slipped off the asphalt as he ran home and was being pulled from the hip-deep snow by his older brother, Henry. Hip deep to Oliver anyway, for he was the smallest in his kindergarten class. Now he was wet and the whine climbed an octave as he gazed down the road and found his mother's eyes on him. Quickly Henry silenced him and, with a backward glance at Ginger, dragged Oliver whimpering toward the house.

Usually on her days off she'd drive them to and

from school. Now, with finances the way they were, the family had had to choose between spending money on gas driving on these special days or keeping the satellite dish for the television. After very little debate, Ginger's three children agreed that they would keep the television—not a surprise. So this morning, just as they were now doing this evening, they had walked to the bus stop. Earlier, they had woken up, eaten breakfast, and headed out the door as if it was any other day of the week that she wasn't there. Like Grandma Osbee, whom they lived with, she could have stayed in the house and watched them make their way down the long road to where the school bus picked them up. But somehow that seemed unfair. It was cold; they were cold as they walked to the bus. In commiseration, she slipped into her husband Jesse's work coat and her rubber boots and made the trek with them.

At first, there had been a bit of whining in the morning from Oliver because the winter snow was at his knees in places on the road. But no whining had also been part of the agreement. Thus Henry, ten years old and her eldest, picked Oliver up along the way, just as he was doing now on the way home, where the drifts became a little too deep.

The true grace for Oliver this winter had been John Mitchell. The aging farmer came down the road with his tractor every few days, especially after the heaviest snowfall, to clear the asphalt. Ginger was incredibly thankful. Because Mr. Mitchell plowed, she could maneuver her truck down the drive every day without shoveling. Her children could walk to and from the bus without sinking into the fallen snow. There had not been one cold or flu in her house all winter, knock on wood. She shuffled to the right and actually did— she stopped and knocked on the Schaafs' white wooden fence to her right. Then she returned to the slushy road and continued home, trying to count how many dozens of ginger cookies she, Osbee, and the kids had made for Mr. Mitchell this winter.

He always came when the family was home, and every time she found his tractor slowly making its way up the road she'd turn the TV off and have her two sons comb their hair in the tidy, respectful fashion taught to them by their father. Her daughter, Bea, would, without a word, head upstairs and return with a blue ribbon. She'd hand it to Grandma Osbee, who quickly braided the little girl's dark brown hair and secured the bottom with the ribbon. Then the entire family would don their coats and meet the old man at the top of their drive with a plate of cookies and a cup of hot coffee.

As always, Mr. Mitchell ate almost every one. The rest he tucked away in his various pockets, remarking how fluffy and chewy they were—just as he liked them to be. Most of the time, he sipped his coffee, pondering why Jesse had pulled up the asphalt on their drive and paved it with gravel. No one really had an answer and the fact that there was likely to be no answer just made the kids fidget. Ginger usually smiled, shrugging away the comment the way she'd shrug off an unwanted arm wrapping around her shoulders in condolence.

After finishing his snack, Mr. Mitchell returned to his tractor and backed down the gravel drive. Only when he reached the asphalt road would Ginger release her children and they'd bolt back inside, strip off their coats, and land in a pile in front of the TV. At that point, right on cue, Oliver would whine that there were no more cookies, as John Mitchell had taken every last one. They truly were the old farmer's favorites. But Oliver didn't care nor did he realize that his bottom was dry when he boarded the bus because of the grace of Mr. Mitchell. His only concern was the lack of cookies.

That was what it was to live in this little hairpin curve of the Shenandoah River. Together, five farm families watched out for one another and the littlest ones were kept oblivious to cold and worry when possible. As Jesse and Ginger Martin's children were the only kids left on the road—all others having grown and moved away—it was mostly the other farmers who looked out for their brood. Henry, Bea, and Oliver were known in the area as the "Little Smoots," Henry and Osbee's great-grandchildren. When the Martin family moved to the Smoots' farm, every farmer became their other grandfather and their wives other grandmothers. These were Jesse's children and Jesse had pretty much grown up on his grandparents' farm himself.

Jesse's nature was not that of his father's people, the Martins from Richmond. His blood ran with the Shenandoah and with his mother's family, the Smoots. His mother and father raised their children in Richmond. During the summer, his brother and sister were sent away from the city to camps. Jesse asked to spend his vacation with his grandparents, and so he did. He farmed and fished, milked cows and planted flower beds. He crossed the river in a boat and climbed the hill beyond into the state park that was his playground. The winding water, which was a bubbling rapid to the south, looped around in a U-bend, becoming a smooth, glassy flow to the north. It was his playmate. It was his friend on lonely days. It was family.

So when Grandpa Henry passed on five years earlier, Jesse had to step in. There was great pressure put upon Grandma Osbee by her daughter, Ester, to sell the Smoots' forty-two acres of Shenandoah land. Osbee was too old to continue to farm it alone and the best option, according to Ester, was to sell the farm, put the money into a trust, and move Osbee closer to Richmond.

But Osbee didn't want to sell and leave her land. That would dishonor everyone who had held it since 1799. Though she was lonely and hurting, her weathered root was yet strong, deeply grounded in the land of her family. She knew who would always keep her on the land. She knew who would fight Ester, his own mother, taking his grandmother's side in all things. Thus the call came to Jesse and he answered it as he answered all calls to duty. Though stationed with the 16th Military Police Brigade in Fort Bragg, North Carolina, when not deployed, he sent Ginger and the children to live on the farm, coming home himself between deployments and on all possible leaves. Jesse Day Martin was bound to the farm just like his grandmother. So when it came time to pass on the land, Osbee would bypass her own children, knowing they would sell it, and leave the farm to her grandson Jesse, who would work it.

Ginger pulled Jesse's work coat tighter around her body, stopping as she reached the end of her drive. The Smoots' farm began where the road ended, the gravel drive climbing five hundred yards up a gentle-incline hill to a small white farmhouse rebuilt in 1866 after a fire had destroyed the original. To the left and north of the house sat a large, raw, unpainted barn built at the same time. It was home to Half-a-Penny (or just Penny) and Christian, two workhorses Jesse had brought home for his children to ride. Beau, their brown, tattered mutt, lived there also, along with Regard, the gray tabby cat.

Regard didn't belong to the family. He was a stray that stayed. As Ginger gazed around, she found him crouched on top of one of many fence rails that were strewn on both sides of the drive. It was rough-hewn locust wood and would have been part of the snake-rail fence Jesse had planned on completing last time he was home. His duty, however, had taken him away just as he finished sinking the posts into the soil, so all lay exactly as he had left it a year and, what? Nine months. It was forever since he had been gone.

As she kissed at the cat, Ginger surveyed what winter had brought to the farm. The property was the half-moon end of a loop in the north fork of the Shenandoah River. To Ginger's north and left was a wide, flat field that rolled down and away from the small rise of the house to a large stand of trees from which the snake-rail fence had been cut. A version of that same fence separated the horses' corral from the rest of the cropland. Jesse had finished that before he left. Now the field was covered with snow, its furrows hidden beneath the smooth blanket of white and winter wheat, undisturbed all winter by horse or human.

On Ginger's right and south was a pond that used to feed the springhouse by way of a stream. In times past, when there was no such thing as a refrigerator, such a springhouse was used to keep food from spoiling. It was a mystery to the Smoots why the pond no longer fed the stream, but it hadn't since the Civil War. So a small, dry streambed ran down to a copse of ash, hickory, and walnut trees. It was on this side Jesse had planted Ginger's apple and pear orchard eleven years before when they came to spend their honeymoon on the farm. They hadn't gone to Hawaii or Tahiti. Military people rarely find true rest anywhere but home, where they rarely are— or so Jesse had explained. The perfect honeymoon, therefore, was to be home together and home was the farm. Grandpa Henry had helped Jesse dig and plant for four days, getting the trees solidly set into the ground to help Ginger and her Northwest sensibilities find a root there, too. Ginger smiled as she watched Jesse in her mind's eye carry a tin bucket of McIntosh over to her.

"Make me a pie, woman," she whispered to the barren branches of her winter orchard.

Beyond the orchard and hidden behind the copse of ash, hickory, and walnut, the little streambed ran past the springhouse to the river and there Jesse had taught his children to swim and fish and find the magical, secret world of his own boyhood. He dreamed for nothing greater in life than for Henry, Bea, and Oliver to grow on this land and flow like this river. Though he was a soldier, the tender of his heart beat freely here, in his Shenandoah dream, with Ginger, his children, and his grandmother. He took it with him when he was deployed; he'd lock away his green, gentle heaven, keeping him connected to the subdued beauty and serenity of his valley home when in the omnipresent heat and violence of war's fury.

Ginger stood, listening to him tell her as much as he rested his head upon her breast the night before he last left. She sighed, her breath as white as the flat white sky above. If there was a sun up there, Ginger didn't see it nor did she feel its heat. She could go into the house now to be warmed by the cup of coffee she knew Osbee had waiting for her. Instead, she turned toward the pond. Between the orchard and the copse of trees, a covered bridge stood over the streambed. A covered bridge over a dried-up stream in the middle of a forty-two-acre farm in a hairpin turn of the Shenandoah—what use was that? It was the first question Ginger had asked of Jesse when he had brought her to the farm to meet his grandparents. In answer, he'd explained to her that it was there so someone could put a historic marker on Interstate 81 calling attention to it and people would exit, drive five miles of windy roads to the Smoots' farm, and give the people living there new faces to look at. She had laughed then. Now, eleven years later, the bridge seemed just as strange and out of place as she felt.

Heading in that direction, Ginger felt a longing for her home in Seattle. She wanted her parents and the city. She wanted lots of people and noise and traffic and large bodies of water everywhere. Ginger was born in 1972, the only child of Tim and Monica Barnes. It might have been 1972 for the rest of the planet, but for Tim and Monica it was still the sixties. They raised their daughter in a small flat above their retail store, the Ginger Moon, which they named after their daughter. The shop was a community fixture in the Fremont District. They sold brass Buddhas and silver dancing Shivas; tarot cards, hemp handbags, and cotton tie-dyed dresses were bestsellers. Patchouli was the first scent Ginger remembered smelling, and the sound of the sitar, the first music she heard. Her childhood was free and magical, full of raw milk and tofu and people from everywhere speaking many languages, most of which she did not understand. Yet all of their voices became the rich background music of her life. She wanted to travel one day and submerge herself in the deep water of the world of which Fremont was just a tiny raindrop.

That was what she said she wanted to be when she grew up, a traveler, and always she wanted to be a nurse. But art was everything to her parents.

When she began to show an interest in science, her father and mother, in absolute terror, fought back. They sent her to after-school art classes, drama classes, dance classes, and singing classes. Ginger enjoyed it all, but mostly her attention was drawn back to small things—bugs or moss or the soft brown feathers on the top of ferns. She liked microscopes because even tinier things could be seen—like bone tissue or liver cells. To Ginger, histology was art. So, loving their daughter as they did, Tim and Monica relented, falling back into the community of their store and letting Ginger pursue her nursing degree and then sail away from them into the waters of the world.

It was as a traveling nurse in an emergency room at a hospital in Fayetteville, North Carolina, that Ginger had met Jesse. He'd seemed cold that night, coming to collect two soldiers who were in her charge due to a bar brawl in town. Distant and aloof were not words enough to describe being in his icy gray gaze. When she'd enter the room to check on her two patients, the quiet murmurs of Jesse and his men would stop. In silence, she'd check an IV or administer a painkiller without looking at any of them and it wasn't soon enough for Ginger that the soldiers were released and headed back to Fort Bragg.

So it was quite a shock when she stepped out of the hospital, dawn just rising, to find Jesse in jeans and a sweater standing next to his truck, asking her out for coffee and maybe breakfast. He was not cold, but warm—not aloof, but more present than anyone she had ever met. He loved her full name, Virginia, for it was his home state, he said, which made them both laugh. They dated for three weeks, after which time Ginger's contract was up and she sat weeping on a plane back to Seattle. When she arrived, she stepped into the Ginger Moon and fell apart in her parents' arms, trying to understand the incredible emptiness in her body. Forever, she had been free, light, and airy, with no particular need to go any one direction or to be responsible to anyone but herself. But such freedom seemed now hollow; being without direction seemed suddenly pointless.

Ginger was a contract nurse who took assignments all over the country. Quickly she searched for contracts on the East Coast, but nothing was open in North Carolina. She could have gone to Virginia or Georgia, but what use was that? Her schedule would be erratic, as was always the case for a traveling nurse, and unless she lived closer to Fort Bragg, there was no guarantee she could get enough time off to drive there when Jesse had days free. So instead they talked on the phone. They'd call and talk for hours and as soon as they hung up Ginger returned to empty. It hurt so deeply—all her bone tissue, every liver cell. Being without him disturbed her peace so entirely that, soon, she wouldn't answer his calls anymore.

He was there and she was here and an entire country lay between them.

Notes stacked up on the counter at the Ginger Moon: *Jesse called at noon. Call Jesse. Will you PLEASE call Jesse. He's tying up our line.* But Ginger wouldn't call. She worked. Sixteen-hour days back-to-back in Seattle or in little rural hospitals to the east, blowing around the state of Washington like a tiny seed on the wind that never finds a place to root.

Then, late one night, as she shuffled out of Swedish Hospital absolutely exhausted, she found Jesse standing in his uniform next to her car. She said nothing. She cried and he took her in his arms, grounding her within his heart. They were married by the end of the week and she was on a plane to Fort Bragg, having kissed her mother and father good-bye.

"You will always be our Ginger Moon," she whispered, repeating her parents' words, her voice echoing in the hollowness of the covered bridge. As she stepped out, she sank ankle deep into the snow on the other side.

Looking to her right, she saw the springhouse looking lonely and abandoned. When the stream went dry, the springhouse lost its purpose. So it stood, forgetting what it was there for, becoming nothing more than a barrier that blocked the north wind from blowing across the Smoots' small family cemetery. The short, black iron railing seemed to have sunk deeper in the snow. Several crosses peeked out, dark and gray against winter's white mantle. Yet there in the snow, several vases of weathered but colorful flowers dotted the cemetery—Osbee's dutiful care for her husband and their mutual relatives.

Ginger wanted to go home to her relatives in Seattle, but she could not—for here were Osbee and the farm. The actual farming of the land fell now on the shoulders of John Mitchell, Solomon Schaaf, Todd Whitaker, and James Creed. These four men were working their own fields and farms each day, after which they'd come down the road in shifts instead of spending time with their wives. It was a team effort, keeping the Smoots' farm a going concern until Jesse returned. He had planted and was shortly thereafter deployed to Iraq. That was a year and nine months ago, in May.

The four farmers harvested that fall and set to planting the following spring, working the crops for Jesse until his expected return home this last June. But summer came and went without him. So they harvested once more and now it was coming on to planting time again. Ginger knew it was because John Mitchell had said so last time he plowed the drive. How could she ask them to plant once more? Especially Solomon Schaaf. He could barely sit his own tractor, he was so old. To have them plant again would continue to take them away from their own needs. She had tried to compensate them by paying them from the farm's proceeds, but they'd have none of it. Each of them knew she needed every cent to pay the taxes and next year's planting needs. Even when she kept all the earnings, it wasn't enough.

Thus Ginger stayed for Osbee's sake, continuing to work as a traveling nurse, picking up shifts throughout the valley and West Virginia from the nurse registry. When she wasn't working, she was bartering her skills to pay the deep debt she owed these farmers. With great care and sensitivity, she performed the service she was educated to do. Someone would twist their ankle, sure it was broken, or have a strange pain in their neck, convinced it was a heart attack, or catch a bad cold, positive they had the bird flu. Ginger was there to feel the ankle, never broken; review the neck pain, from being on the phone too long with a shoulder scrunched up to the ear; or prescribe cough medicine and a week in bed for a bad cold. Not only did Ginger save them the cost of going to the doctor, which all of them could little afford, but she also was the local medical practitioner whose advice was free to be ignored, which it usually was. Still the phone would be on the ear just as it always had been and a farmer couldn't stay in bed a week. Death would have to be knocking on the door for that to happen.

And Ginger would never allow that—death to knock on the door—ever, and this day could be like so many others lived these last eleven years. Jesse was simply gone on another deployment like the others before, leaving Ginger and his children on the Smoots' land, holding on to Grandma Osbee, clinging to his dream. It could have been and was until last March, one year ago to the day, when a car pulled up the gravel drive and parked next to the unfinished fence. Two uniformed men came slowly up the steps, their eyes sorrowful but steady. Had Grandma Osbee not held her hand that day, Ginger would have burst into ash and blown away. But Osbee was there then and Ginger was here now and so today could have been like so many others these eleven years—but it wasn't.

She stepped from the little wood of ash, hickory, and walnut and came to a tottering stop. No one, not Ginger, not her kids, not even Osbee had ventured beyond the copse of trees in the last year, for this was Jesse's spot, given him as a boy by his grandfather as his own private place. This was where the empty stream met the mighty river and a giant ash tree lent its trunk as a shoulder to lean upon for support. It was from here, near the ash on the river, where Jesse would float across in a little boat to the other side. Here is where he'd come to be quiet and hear the world and think and dream. Surely, if he was still around, here is where he'd be.

But he wasn't and she fell helpless to her knees. She wept quietly, disturbing neither the squirrels who busied themselves around her seeking nuts they'd buried last fall, nor the crows sleeping in the branches above her head. The river murmured as it flowed slowly by the snowy bank. The world was cold and quiet and pale as Ginger's grief fell heavily on the frozen ground.

She waited—waited for him, for anything. Just one more passing word, a touch of his hand on her hair, soft breath on her neck. Anything. Anything. A wind blew. It was a strange breeze—warm and moist, flowing down the winter water as if spring was just coming around the bend. Ginger felt it touch her cheek and ear and she closed her eyes, imagining Jesse sitting next to her near the river just as he used to do. The breeze turned cold again.

"Stay," she whispered.

"Good afternoon."

Ginger spun her head to the left and found a man standing on a fallen pine tree that spanned the river. Quickly she stood, wiping her cheeks. Jesse's ash tree had split and splintered across the small pebbly streambed. A massive pine tree had uprooted on the other side of the river and its top was just long enough to reach the ash, the two fallen trees forming a bridge over the river. Snow flittered around her like so many silent white flower petals and Ginger stared, dazed by the violet light of winter's coming eve and the darkness of the uprooted base of Jesse's tree.

"Afternoon," the man repeated as he stood perfectly still with his cap held in his hands. He was gaunt, about the age of thirty, with light brown tousled hair and a neatly trimmed mustache and goatee, and wearing a butternut-colored military uniform. She had seen uniforms like his before since reenactments of Civil War battles were year-round affairs in the Shenandoah. But this man's was dusty, the insignia worn, and it fit him loosely. Surely it was not his uniform; Ginger thought it must be borrowed.

"G-good afternoon," she replied hoarsely.

"A cold afternoon," he added.

"It is cold. You lose your regiment?" She tried to smile. Her cheeks stung with tears.

"Why, yes, I did." His accent was very Virginian. Not from Richmond. Not from the coast. Ginger was very good at placing Virginia accents because Jesse had a talent for mimicking them. This man's accent, though, was not one she had heard Jesse do. A tear escaped, rolling hot down her face.

"Why are you crying?" the man asked, gently.

Ginger looked away from him, shaking her head.

"It's personal," she replied, wiping the tear as she slid her gaze across the river, searching for more roaming Civil War soldiers in the woods. The man chuckled. Ginger flicked her eyes back to him, unclear why what she had said was at all funny.

"I apologize, but I have never cried a tear nor heard of one shed that was not personal," he said with a little smile. She cocked her head and smiled a little in return. His eyes were the color of his hair and soft and he stood so still, as if he yet waited for her to answer.

"My husband died," she whispered.

"I am sorry. Was it sudden?"

Ginger took in a deep breath and looked up at the soft purple-white sky above her, trying not to feel her hurt. It didn't work.

"He was a soldier, like you," she said, smiling back at him through her unwanted tears. "He died serving his country."

"It is an honorable death, then."

Ginger nodded quickly, pulling the sleeve of Jesse's coat to her mouth. Sometimes she could just catch his scent within the flannel lining.

"He's in a better place," the man continued.

Ginger's throat tightened.

"You know? I don't believe that," Ginger whispered. "A better place for him would be here. Planting his fields and mending fences and picking apples for pie and teaching the kids to ride horses and caring for his grandmother, who cared for him. What better place? Where is this better place? I sure don't see it!" Ginger froze; her voice had grown angry and her words tore the still air like the cawing crows that now lifted into the air from the branches above.

"I'm sorry," she said, shaking her head and covering her mouth. "I'm so sorry."

"It is all right," he replied, quietly, almost formally.

"Sorry," she whispered.

"It's personal," he said with a small smile.

Ginger nodded, wiping her face with Jesse's sleeve again.

"I should go. Um . . . you wanna come in? Osbee's probably made coffee by now and I can take you back to your regiment. I'm so sorry."

"We have already had forgiveness here. No need to apologize further. Who is Osbee?"

"Oh, uh, Grandma."

He nodded. "And you? What is your name?"

"Virginia."

The man smiled with a chuckle.

Ginger shrugged. "I know. It's your state," she said.

"No. It is my country," the man corrected.

"Oh, right," Ginger replied. "Fighting for Old Dominion." She knew those who had fought in the Civil War thought of Virginia as a country, a separate republic. So Jesse had said.

"Virginia what?" he asked.

Ginger's heart lifted a bit from her grief. This was her favorite question when asked by someone from the state.

"Virginia what?" the man pressed as he watched her face lighten.

"Virginia Moon." She grinned as a smile grew brighter on his face as well.

"Virginia Moon. I love your name!"

"Most people around here do," she replied, her head heavy again with cold and tears. "Where's your regiment? I'll take you back."

"No need. They are a ways away and I have to take care of a couple of things on that side of the river." He pointed to the woods of the state park. "But I thank you."

He turned and headed back across the river.

"Careful. There's snow on the tree," she said, imagining that, if he fell in, it would be a visit to the emergency room for sure. That was one place she did not wish to go today.

"I have waited a long time to cross this river. No slippery path shall take me down," he replied with his back toward her. "You go and be warm." The man stopped and turned back to face her. "And, Virginia Moon?"

"Yes?"

"A man is not dead if his dream yet lives. If his love lives."

Ginger gazed into his soft brown eyes, so far away. She swallowed hard.

"Think on that."

She nodded, watching him turn and cross back to the other side of the river. He jumped off the fallen pine and climbed up toward the wall of trees.

"Hey!" she yelled. "What's your name?"

"Samuel," he whispered. "Samuel Ezra Annanais."

Then he climbed through the trees and disappeared into the brush.

CHAPTER 2

THE JESSE TREE

Ginger stood for a while, waiting to see if Samuel would return. There were several cultural struggles she had to wrestle with when she moved from the West Coast to the East and even more so when she arrived in the South. The greatest of these was this courtesy right here. Samuel had said to go in and be warm. If she was in Seattle, that meant exactly that: go in, be warm. In the East, and in particular the Southeast, it may mean exactly that or it may have just been said out of courtesy. The expectation, of course, would be that she wait for him and, together, they would go in. Together they would be warm. Her needs did not supersede his. Her comfort was gained only when they both had comfort. "Together," in the South, wasn't an adverb or an adjective; it was a noun and a verb. It was being and action— belonging. *We are one together* and so she waited.

She looked up to the empty branches above her head and to the pale evening sky beyond. She leaned forward, peering south to see what, if anything, had changed around the river's bend. She examined everywhere but the fallen ash. Yet, if Samuel was to return, he would cross upon it, and so her eyes turned ever to Jesse's tree. The emptiness in her body was just like the earth there—a gaping wound left by a broken root. Shifting in the hollow cold with tears threatening again, she watched in her mind's eye as the two solemn men climbed the drive, and she decided Samuel was not returning. Quickly, she stepped away from the river and headed to the house.

The footprints she had made going down to the river were perfectly set in shape and form to her foot, and heavily she followed them back just to their right, measuring her stride as close as she could in order to create a second set of perfect footprints going in the opposite direction. It seemed to her that this was always how it had been with Jesse. He was going in one direction, she in another. But always they circled each other, being apart and then together—mostly apart. *Together* for them was not the Southern sense. It had part of that intense conformity from Jesse's Virginia sensibilities, but from Ginger there was her Western independence and liberty. The depth of their differences should have made for great conflict. But that was not how it was. Instead, he planted her in Virginia's soil where the roots of family obligation ran thick and many like the veins in an old man's well-worked hands. In return, she helped him begin his own family—less Martin, more Barnes. Together they made a new home on old land where their faith in each other was so bright, it burned straight through the body and lit all the dark places of the soul. And Jesse had dark places. War creates them.

She stopped, peering back to follow her footsteps coming and now going from Jesse's tree and the great, dark hole at the water's edge.

Ginger rested her head against the ash, her eyes closed in the lazy afternoon weight of Shenandoah's early fall. Henry's head lay across her thighs, his breath steady and even with sleep. The insects buzzed conversation about her head and as she rested, feeling the slight kick and roll beneath her belly button, she laid her hand there to soothe the child within. From out on the water, she could hear Jesse reading, his voice high and clear in imitation of a little English girl.

" 'WHAT'S that thing?' said Lucie—'that's not my pocket-handkin'.' " His voice changed to an old Englishwoman. "Oh no, if you please'm. That's a little scarlet waistcoat belonging to Cock Robin."

The buzzing of an insect grew nearer Ginger's ear and as she waved it away she realized Jesse had stopped. She opened her eyes. Following the rope that anchored him to the tree on which she rested, she found her husband lying prone across an inner tube floating in the river, with three-year-old Bea curled up on his chest, fast asleep. His nose was buried in the hair upon his daughter's head and his eyes were as fast closed as hers.

"She fell asleep? She never falls asleep to Mrs. Tiggy-Winkle," Ginger said. "I guess you are just not a believable little English girl."

"I think I'm a better girl than I am a hedgehog."

They both laughed softly so as not to wake the sleeping children. Then all fell silent, except for the insects. They stared a long while at each other, the small smile on his lips matching the smile on hers.

Jesse finally broke the silence. "What are we going to name that one?"

"Well, we're not calling it after any Civil War general," Ginger said adamantly.

"I think you need to reconsider that."

"I am not standing at the back door and calling, 'Thomas Stonewall Jackson Martin, come in for dinner.'"

Jesse snickered. "I wouldn't name him that anyway."

"Okay, well, I'm not calling, 'A. P. Hill Martin, your room needs to be picked up.'"

Jesse let his head fall back on the inner tube and he stared up at the sky. From behind Ginger, Osbee called, "Jubal Early Martin, your daddy's calling you!"

Jesse laughed.

"Exactly!" Ginger declared, turning her head and nodding to Osbee, who was away in the woods to the left, gleaning walnuts. Five-year-old Henry stirred on her lap. Jesse lifted his head, returning his gaze to Ginger.

"Well, I won't be back before it's born, so you'll have to name that little Thee-Me yourself."

"What if it's a boy?" Ginger asked.

"We're doing this by gender?" Jesse's eyebrows rose.

"You named Henry. I named Bea," Ginger replied.

"Oh—I thought we were doing every other one. I did the first. You did the second."

"Oh." Ginger giggled. "Hadn't thought of it that way."

"Gender, huh? Hadn't thought of it that way," Jesse said and laid his head back upon the inner tube again.

"Well, if it's every other, then it's your turn."

"I won't be home and if it's the last one, don't you want to do it?"

"We don't know if it's our last Thee-Me."

"I still won't be here."

"Then we'll wait."

Jesse lifted his head once more.

"Wait?" he repeated.

"Yep. I'll simply give the name Martin, and then when you get home, we'll see."

"Shouldn't a baby have a name at birth?"

"Why?"

Jesse rubbed Bea's head.

"So it can be called?"

"You'll be back on leave, what, nine months after it's born? We'll just call it Martin or Thee-Me and we'll wait."

"I don't know, Ginger."

"We'll wait."

They met each other's eyes, yet now there was no smile. There was dark silence in the sudden rain of golden red leaves set loose by a stirring wind.

I'll be back, he mouthed.

Ginger nodded. We'll wait.

Ginger wiped away a rogue tear.

"No, Samuel." She breathed.

A very loud meow drew Ginger's attention back toward the covered bridge and there Regard stood as a dark silhouette against the pale reflection of the violet sky upon the snow. Evening was pressing its shoulder on the day and the cat was hunkered down into a small, crouching ball, his fur puffed up in an effort to keep himself warm in the cold breeze that blew through the bridge.

"You following me, cat?" she asked. With one backward glance to Jesse's fallen tree, she scanned the other shore for Samuel just to be sure and headed toward the bridge.

Regard stood up, waited for her, and when she passed him, he trotted quickly after.

"And where will you go if we leave?"

He didn't answer, but ran on ahead, across the bridge toward the summer kitchen. Where would he go? Where would Beau go? And the horses? It would not be a day she'd like to live when she had to take her children away from their animals. Just the image of standing on the porch, kissing Osbee good-bye, and heading down the dirt drive to the asphalt never to return made her stomach churn. She even retched a little as she passed the summer kitchen. Following the cat up the back stairs, she opened the door to the sunroom and Regard bolted inside. She paused and gave a whistle at the barn. Beau stepped out, ears forward.

"You cold?" she asked. The dog ran across the snowy yard and trotted up the stairs. Ginger stepped in behind him and stomped her icy feet on the slate floor as the screen door slammed shut.

"Coffee's ready," Osbee said, poking her head out the kitchen door. Ginger could hear Henry arguing with Oliver over a pencil.

"Jesse's tree has fallen down," Ginger whispered, pulling off her right boot.

Several furrows rolled across the old woman's forehead, and as soon as they appeared, they disappeared.

"It was old," Osbee replied. "Been there since before I was born."

The old woman stood in her cornflower apron, white cotton sweater, and pull-on jeans. Osbee was not one to go to the beautician to have her hair set every two or three weeks like so many other women her age. Her hair was long and gray, forming a single braid down the back. It was thick near the roots and thinner at the bottom and, at the moment, there was a red ribbon tied to it. It had not been there when Ginger left to pick the kids up from the bus stop, and when she saw the fraying piece of satin wrapped tightly around the braid, her stomach dropped to her left knee. It only stopped there because she still had on her boot. If she hadn't, it would have hit the bottom of her foot for sure.

"You get a letter?" Ginger inquired, shrugging out of Jesse's coat.

"A call."

"They coming tonight?"

"Tomorrow morning. I was thinking of baking cookies. Oliver and Henry said they'd help. Bea— well, you know Bea."

With a deep breath, Ginger slid out of the left boot. Her stomach stayed in her knee. That was promising.

"Need a new ribbon," she said softly, touching the old woman's braid. Osbee winked.

Whenever her daughter came to visit after

Henry's death, Osbee tied a red ribbon onto the end of her braid. Once, Ginger asked why and Osbee's answer was not at all what she had expected. The answer, to be kept like a secret, was that it matched the color of her underwear. The real question was why she always wore red underwear, so Osbee had prompted. Of course Ginger had to know and she asked the question, the answer to which was quite simple. Mary, Queen of Scots, wore red undergarments at her execution, and every time her daughter visited, Osbee felt like she was going to her execution. It was a way to protest—to defy her daughter and that husband of hers. So here was the red ribbon and Ginger knew a conflict was brewing and Osbee was going to protest. She was formulating a dissent. Dissent was a sensibility Ginger felt she'd brought to the farm from Seattle.

"Nothing lasts forever. Not even mountains and trees," Osbee stated flatly. There was no emotion in her words, just as the pain of Jesse's fallen tree had been but a fleeting crease across the old woman's brow. So Southern. Ginger, however, had lived in Virginia long enough to know that, no matter how pleasant and normal the face and tone of a Southerner was, there were indeed deep emotions. Why there was all this hiding of them was yet a mystery to her.

"You want me to stay?" Ginger asked, not for the first time.

Osbee's brown eyes, as deep and endless as her root, revealed nothing, answered nothing. She frowned then.

"Why is that dirty dog in here?" Osbee asked, scowling at Beau. He sat promptly, hoping manners would get him through the kitchen door.

"Regard came in," Ginger replied, folding Jesse's coat over her arm. She nodded to the dog, who quickly rose and shuffled by Osbee.

"And?"

"Seems unfair to leave the dog out when the cat is in." Ginger cocked her head and followed Beau through the door. She tossed Jesse's coat on the back of an empty kitchen chair.

"Mom, Oliver stole my pencil," Henry said.

"Did not."

"That's mine," Henry said.

"Doesn't have your name on it," Oliver replied. He said it exactly in the same voice Henry used when taunting Bea. Little boys learn so much from big boys, but it always seemed to Ginger they learned the worst things first.

"Give Henry back his pencil and go get your own," Ginger said to Oliver.

"It's mine, Mama!"

"Oliver, your pencils always have teeth marks and you bite the eraser off. That pencil clearly has its eraser. Now give it back to your brother and go get your own."

Oliver slammed the pencil down so hard it

bounced off the table and hit Bea on the chin.

"Hey," Bea said quietly. "Watch it."

The little girl rubbed her chin and went back to her homework. She didn't even look up. Ginger pursed her lips and opened the refrigerator.

"I wish I could run away," Henry said.

"Wouldn't you be lonely?" Ginger asked as she surveyed the milk cartons for the open one.

"No. I'd be happy at not having to listen to Oliver whining."

"One time your daddy ran away," Osbee said.

"He did?" Ginger asked. She didn't know that.

"Yep. Crossed the river in his boat and wasn't coming back."

"Why?" Henry asked.

"Because summer was ending and he didn't want to go back home to Richmond," Osbee replied. "He got lost and he was missing for an entire night. It rained and thundered and worried me and his grandpa something awful. Then he walks back in the door the next morning and apologizes. Tells us he'll go home so he could come back. He realized if he'd have stayed away, his parents would never allow him to spend summers here again."

Ginger poured milk into her coffee and gazed over at Bea. The little girl didn't even appear to be marking the conversation.

"How did he find his way back?" Henry asked.

"A man found him and they camped together.

Then he helped your dad come home. He was very lucky to run across someone on that kind of night in the state park over there."

"You want some milk while I have it out, Bea?" Ginger asked, prompting some response from her daughter.

"No, thanks, Mama," she replied without as much as a glance in her direction.

"You, Henry?"

"No, thanks. I'll wait for dinner."

"Such nice manners," Osbee said, stirring the pot on the stove. "Sometimes, Henry, you have to think of others, not just what you want. What if you left? Bea would have to deal with Oliver all by herself."

Henry smiled over at his mother. Bea made no response at all.

"What's for dinner?" Oliver asked, returning from the other room and settling back into his chair. He had found one of his pencils. It was so ravaged, the lead was sticking out on one side where he had chewed all the wood away.

"Spaghetti."

"Again?" Oliver whined. "We always have spaghetti."

"Shut up, Oliver," Henry said.

"Don't say, 'Shut up.' Say, 'Be quiet,' " Ginger corrected as she put the milk away.

"You shut up," Oliver said. "I want some milk."

"You can wait for dinner."

"Why'd you ask *them?*" Everything was a whine.

"I can't hear you, Oliver," Ginger replied, stirring her coffee.

"Why'd you ask them?" he said, his whiny voice growing louder.

"She can't hear you 'cause you're whining," Henry shouted.

"Mom!" Oliver yelled.

"I can't hear you!" she yelled back. He looked up at her. She smiled.

"Why did you ask them?" he whispered, grinning back.

" 'Cause they eat their dinner when they drink milk. You fill up on milk and don't eat your dinner."

"Done," Bea said. She shut her workbook, returned her pencil into its spot in her plastic pencil case, and tucked it all into her backpack.

"You want me to check your work?" Ginger asked as she leaned against the counter.

"Nope," Bea replied, tossing the backpack by the sunroom door. "I need to check the horses."

"No, you don't," Henry said, sharpening his pencil.

"Leave her be," Osbee interjected. "Thanks for taking care of them, Bea."

The door opened and shut without another word. Peering over her cup, Ginger found Osbee looking at her. The old woman turned back and opened the oven.

"What's in there?" Oliver asked.

"Meatballs," Osbee replied, pulling them out of the oven and sliding them off the baking sheet into her bubbling pot of spaghetti sauce.

"Spaghetti *and* meatballs," Oliver said, smiling at his mother. "Not just spaghetti. I love meatballs."

"Yes, you do," she replied, placing her cup on the counter. "Finish your homework."

Ginger grabbed Jesse's coat again and headed for the door. Beau rose to follow but she shook her head. Lying back down beneath Oliver's chair, he let out a great breath of relief. Duty would have him follow her to the barn, but it was cold. Luckily, he'd get to stay inside.

Glancing back at Osbee, she winked and quietly left the kitchen. She gazed out the sunroom door, finding the yard washed in the lapis watercolor of early evening. The bare walnut tree that grew between the house and barn painted dark brown streaks of shadow across the snow. As she pulled her boots back on, she searched for Bea, but the little girl was nowhere to be seen. She had entered the barn already. Slowly, so as not to let the sunroom door squeak, Ginger stepped back out into the cold and tiptoed across the yard to the barn.

When she arrived, she could hear the murmured voice of Bea talking in the darkness beyond the closed barn door. Ginger bent and peeked through a knothole in the wood. In the back of the barn where shadows seemed forever, Henry's Child, as it was called, blinked at her in the fading light. The 1957 International Harvester 600 gas tractor had been purchased in 1966 and then doted upon ever since, first by Henry and later by Jesse. It was the first vehicle Jesse learned to drive and it was a favorite event for all three children to ride upon it into the hay and cornfields with their father. It was, though, Bea who rose at dawn every day with Jesse. Bea favored working with her father from the time she could sit up to any playing she could do elsewhere with any other. Bea was Jesse's child. Now Henry's Child, like the snake-rail fence on the driveway, sat exactly where Jesse had left it, for the tractor had blown a piston just two days before his deployment. He had to have parts machined for it and as there was no time to do so before he left, Jesse pushed the tractor into its spot in the barn, intending to fix it upon his return. There it remained, silent and still and visited now only secretly by Bea, for whom it was a tangible memory of her father.

So here she was, sitting on its seat, bouncing gently as if she rode upon it now. Bea had caused Ginger the most worry since Jesse's death. She had gone completely silent, neither weeping nor talking. What she had done instead was begin to leave the table after meals and come out to check on the horses. It had become her chore, so she said. Each night Ginger would follow her little girl, squatting down as she did now, her head resting against the wood of the barn with her eyes closed, listening to Bea speak with her father on the tractor as they rode together in the forever shadows.

"I think we gotta take down that tree on the far side of the field. It looks like it'll fall down with the next snow anyway and we gotta fix the fence," Bea said quietly. "Christian got out last month and went wandering over into Mama's orchard. He remembered there were apples and pears over there from the last time he kicked the fence down in summer. He ate half a tree before we got him. Man, did he have a stomachache."

Bea laughed. Ginger smiled at the memory herself as a warm breeze gently shifted her hair around her ear.

"I think he thought there were apples there. Horses aren't very smart, huh? There are no apples in winter and he walked all the way over there in the wind and snow for nothing. Mama says it served him right. But we gotta mend the fence."

"Good evening, Virginia Moon."

Ginger bolted to a stand. Samuel stood before her with his cap on and a bedroll on his back, secured diagonally across his chest with a rope. She shook her head.

"Is something the matter?"

"Shh," Ginger said, motioning him away from

the door. Bea laughed again. Samuel glanced over at the barn door and then back to Ginger.

"Is someone in there who should not be?" he asked in a low voice.

"No, it's my daughter," she whispered.

"You do not want to know why she is laughing?" Samuel tilted his head.

"She's riding with her father."

Samuel frowned, gazing around the barnyard. "He is not . . . gone . . . yet?"

Ginger stepped sideways toward the gravel drive. Samuel followed.

"She goes in there and rides with her dad—or the memory of her dad."

"Ah." Samuel nodded. "And you are spying on her. In her private moment with her father." Samuel's lip curled slightly.

"No, no," Ginger said adamantly. "Not spying."

"What do you call it?" He was staring at her now, his brown eyes shaded dark in the growing twilight.

"She doesn't really talk anymore. She completely shut down since her dad died. The school psychologist thinks she needs help—like, maybe medication. That she's not grieving her father's death."

"What is a school psychologist?"

"A busybody."

"Oh."

"She goes in the barn and this is where I can

hear where she's at, you know? How it is with her. I know she'll be okay because this is—it's how she mourns."

"Ah. So you tell the school psychologist this?"

"No. It's private," she replied, stepping back from Samuel. Why did she need to tell him any of this anyway?

"Well?" he pressed, his eyes growing darker.

Ginger shifted her feet. Night was coming on fast. "It's how I know the psychologist is wrong. Bea just . . . mourns privately. That's all."

"Bea. That is her name?"

Ginger nodded, thinking she should call her daughter because it was getting very dark.

"Grief is felt with the same depth as love, I think. To love someone wholly is to be entirely filled with them, and when they are lost—a gaping emptiness."

Ginger took a deep, cold breath through her nose. It had grown so black, so cold. She exhaled and, with it, emptiness passed her lips. She had no words. There was no light. There was only pain.

"So you stand out here to help carry the entirety of your daughter's loss while bearing your own."

Ginger nodded. She had no breath for there was no air. *I'm her mother,* she mouthed.

"You are a good mother."

Ginger shrugged, shaking her head.

"Yes, you are," he replied.

"Mama?" Bea's soft voice hit Ginger on the

back, forcing a gasping inhale. Samuel didn't move, but kept staring at her.

"Yeah, Bea," she replied hoarsely.

"Who's that?"

"Um, Mr. Annanais. Mr. Annanais, this is Beatrix, my daughter."

Samuel smiled at Ginger and turned toward Bea. "Well met, Beatrix."

"You in a Civil War play or something?"

"Or something," Samuel replied. Ginger watched him lean down and squint as he looked carefully at Bea. "You look very familiar."

Bea shrugged and stepped forward.

"Why are all your buttons different?" she asked, pointing to Samuel's coat.

"It is a long story and I need to make my way home."

"Oh," Bea said. She looked over at her mother and raised her eyebrows.

Ginger shrugged, breathing purposefully, counting the beats of her heart. "Would you like to come in first?" Ginger offered in nearly a whisper. "We're having dinner and then I can drive you home."

The sky had turned the shade of a fine, dark lapis. In all of Ginger's travels, only Virginia had a twilight sky so deep. She glanced around confused, for just a minute ago it had been as dark as dark can be. She blinked, gazing up at the North Star.

"No, but I thank you. I can walk home now."

"You sure? It's five miles on this road and it's going to be cold tonight," Ginger said, still staring at the lapis blue sky.

"I would like to walk. It was very nice meeting you, Beatrix."

"You, too, Mr. Annanais."

"Your daughter has nice manners."

"From her father," Ginger replied, returning her gaze to Samuel.

"And her good mother," Samuel added, staring back at her with deeper eyes. He bowed a little and walked by her, heading down the drive.

"It gets really dark on the road and slippery. You be careful."

"I shall," he replied over his shoulder, and as he walked he adjusted his bedroll on his back.

"Mama?"

"Yes, Bea?" she asked, looking down at her daughter. Her eyes were bright, reflecting the darkening blue sky above. Why was the light in her daughter's eyes so bright when Samuel's had been so shadowed?

"Where'd he come from?"

"I'm not sure. He was in some reenactment over the river earlier and then I guess he just came back across. Daddy's ash tree fell down and there's like a tree bridge over the Shenandoah."

Bea's forehead creased. Ginger winced. She should not have said that. Why had she said that? Ginger brushed her daughter's forehead, trying to smooth away her pain. The sunroom door squeaked and they could see Osbee peek out, the light from the house spilling out behind her.

"Dinner," she called.

"Coming!" Ginger answered.

"Hey, Mama?"

"Yeah?"

"Where did Mr. Annanais go?"

Ginger spun her head and gazed down the drive. He was not there nor was there any movement on the road. That was odd. It took longer than that to walk to the road. "I don't know," she replied with a frown.

"Maybe he's crossing the Schaafs' field. It'd be faster to the big road."

"Maybe," Ginger said, scanning the Schaafs' land for a shadow moving in the darkness. The trees were quite a distance from the road and she had no idea how he would have made it so far so fast.

"I'm hungry," Bea said, sliding her hand into her mother's palm. For a moment, Ginger froze. Bea never held her hand. Always, she was with her father—by the hand, in his arms, on his lap. It felt so awkward and yet the incredible emptiness in Ginger lightened a bit. Her throat tightened as she gave her daughter's hand a little squeeze.

"Me, too. Let's go in."

Gazing up at the sky, Ginger found the North Star twinkling in the clear Virginia heaven. It was a new moon and there would be no light in the dark places tonight.

"I hope he doesn't get lost," she murmured.

....

May 26, 1861

My dear Juliette,
Upon arrival at Harper's Ferry, I was quite surprised to find my professor of Natural and Experimental Philosophy, the now Colonel Thomas J. Jackson, as the commanding officer. He had come to Harper's Ferry two weeks prior, bringing with him cadets from VMI with orders to secure the town and organize the incoming militias. I remained quiet, but now and then I was greeted by a few of my old classmates with raised eyebrows. It was on all of our minds, those who attended VMI, how it was possible that a man who was so poor a teacher could lead our gathering militia to war. We will, however, keep our thoughts to ourselves. We shall perform our duty in obedience and if that includes following Colonel Jackson into the Valley of Death, then so be it. We are VMI and Virginia. No duty is greater.

With that, to my present location. I have been promoted and now am Second Lieutenant Samuel E. Annanais, tasked with relocating a locomotive engine to Staunton. When we arrived, Colonel Jackson had stopped all trains of the Baltimore and Ohio Railroad on the tracks that pass through Harper's Ferry. He directed us to take several locomotives to Staunton and so we did, running them down a spur line to Winchester. But the tracks ended there. It is twenty miles farther to Staunton. Just for a minute, we wondered if the Colonel was aware that the railroad line ended in Winchester. Then, in obedience, we followed orders and because it is our duty to follow Colonel Jackson, we are now hauling the locomotives down a turnpike. Not a few people have dropped a jaw as we pass by. We brightly smile, tipping our hats to the ladies on the road. What stories shall the little ones tell their grandchildren in some far distant future? The army of the great nation of Virginia rode by the town with locomotives and boxcars and not a track for miles. What tenacity and determination! Track or no track, we shall get these trains to Staunton as ordered. No mean feat, this.

But moving locomotives is heavy work and so we are at rest. I have here in my hand your last letter and have read it so many times now. I follow the curving lines of your words with my finger, touching the paper where I know your hand has touched. Your voice whispers to me as I read and my spirit ebbs and flows in the memory of its music. Nothing in the world would keep me from you but this duty I must fulfill. But once the war ends and I am granted the honor of your hand by your father, Juliette, I shall never leave your side again. I cannot replace Charles. No man can replace another. No husband can replace another. I will, however, be the man who loves you and the husband and father who serves you and our children. I wish nothing more, for there can be nothing greater.

So I sit here with your letter while the horses are watered in a small brook. They bluster now and then, speaking to each other in whispers only they can understand. I wonder if they speak of the weeping willow leaves that rustle as gently they brush the brook. I close my eyes and feel your hair loose, tumbling across my face. To take in its sweetness as the willow draws in the cool water—that is what I long for. I shall keep this thought in mind and heart until next I write. You are ever here, Juliette, with me.

Your devoted,
Samuel E. Annanais

CHAPTER 3

THE DROWNING

Ginger woke with a start. The alarm on her cell phone chimed quietly and she reached over, hitting the dismiss button. It was eleven fifty-six p.m., time for her night shift. Lying still, she could hear Beau snoring on the floor beside her bed and feel Regard curled up in the crook of her bent legs. All was still in the house and there was but a soft rustle now and then of snow falling from the branches beyond her window. Something felt odd, yet she couldn't quite place what it was. Slowly, Ginger slid her feet out of the blankets so as not to disturb Regard and sat up. She flipped on the light. There was no light. The electricity was out.

"That must be it," she whispered to Beau, who stirred at her feet. Opening the top drawer of her nightstand, she pulled out the flashlight and flicked it on. The light struck the darkness of her room and as it did, she found buried at the bottom of the nightstand drawer, the edge of a small yellowing envelope. It had been several months since she had touched it.

Reluctantly, she had emptied the contents of the closet and the drawers of Jesse's things. It had taken her nine months, and even now several boxes of his clothing and papers remained in the attic. She just couldn't see getting rid of him altogether. The one thing she had found and kept in her bedroom was this envelope. Pulling it out, she opened the end and let the key within slide onto the nightstand. It shined dully in the reflection of the flashlight, and with her index finger she moved it back and forth, flicking it gently to and fro and over and over. It was curious to her. She never remembered seeing it before his death nor did she recall Jesse ever mentioning it. But as she removed the last of his socks from his drawer, she had found buried beneath them this envelope with its small gold key. Searching through the entire house, she had looked for a lock that it would fit, but to no avail. It was a mystery like the gravel drive, and though she knew her husband intimately, she knew there was much she had not yet discovered about him. She was not done knowing him. In the last minutes of this dying March day, with its recollection of two men on her porch and becoming ash, she wished to have him here in bed next to her.

"Come home," she said.

At that moment, the flashlight's glare caused Ginger to gaze down at the yellowing envelope and there she found typed lettering appear through the paper. She'd never seen that before. Lifting the envelope, Ginger pressed on its edges and looked inside, where, at its very bottom, she found a tiny newspaper clipping.

"Huh." With her right index finger, she coaxed the small piece of paper out of the envelope:

Needed: Good home for two draught horses. Please contact Ed Rogers at 540-555-7957

"Ah! Christian and Penny," Ginger said with a half smile. Jesse had never told her where he'd purchased the horses; he just pulled up one day, coming home from Fort Bragg, towing a horse trailer. She had laughed until tears rolled down her cheeks as she stood on the porch watching Osbee trot quickly down the steps, waving her hands wildly and telling him to take them back. She had no wish to have animals again. This was strictly a corn and hay farm. Ginger straightened on the edge of her bed, gazing from the little ad to the golden key.

"Perhaps Mr. Rogers knows what the key is for," she whispered to Regard. There was a hope. She'd been without any hope for a year and nine months, and now that she had a small granule of light, her hurt eased a little. Sliding the key and the ad back into the envelope, Ginger stood, dropped it into her handbag sitting on her desk, and tiptoed across the wooden floor of her bedroom to the hall. No matter how quietly she walked, the floor squeaked and Beau lifted his head, yawning.

"Sorry," she said softly as she stepped into the hall. "Go back to sleep."

Quietly, she crossed to the bathroom, shut the door, slipped into her scrubs, brushed her teeth, and twisted her dark brown, curly hair around her fingers and clipped it into place. Then she shuffled into Osbee's room.

"Osbee," she whispered.

"I don't smell coffee," the old woman replied as she sat up in bed.

"No electricity. I'll get tea from the fridge."

"What time you off?"

"Two o'clock so I'll be home just as the kids come back from school. When're Mr. and Mrs. Martin coming?"

"In the morning. Hope the electricity comes on before they get here."

Ginger sat down on the bed, pointing the flashlight at the floor. She could just make out Osbee's red ribbon in the light.

"Osbee." She reached up and touched the ribbon. "Osbee—"

"There's no fighting this, my dear." Osbee brushed Ginger's cheek. "I'm not getting any younger."

"You are my fight," Ginger replied.

"Look, Ginger. It's planting time again."

"I know."

"There's no one to plant and we can't keep asking everybody to pull for us."

"I know."

"And you can't make enough money to keep this farm and the children—"

"I have Jesse's life insurance."

"That's for the children. A final offering from their father, the last he can give for his dream of their future."

Ginger nodded, glancing out the window. There was no hint of a new morning. "But their home is here. This is all they know."

"I've learned over the years that children are so resilient. They'll adjust. Lots to do and discover in a city. And you have your mom and dad, Ginger. You'll have more help. Maybe one day you'll meet a nice man. They need a father."

"They need *their* father," Ginger whispered, her throat tightening.

"He's gone. Still here in our hearts, but he's not returning."

Ginger looked at the old woman's face. Her wrinkles looked deeper in the glare of the flashlight.

"What will you do?"

"No need to worry about me. You need to think about you and Henry and Bea and Oliver."

That was such a Southern thing to say. She could mean exactly what she was saying but she could mean just the opposite as well. Separate parts of Ginger wanted both to be true.

"You come with me," Ginger said.

Osbee shook her head. "My home is here."

"If you sell the farm, what difference does it make? You come with me—to Seattle."

"What does an old Virginian woman need? What does a young Seattle woman need? You don't need an old woman to care for."

"I'm a young Virginia woman now."

Osbee smiled and wrapped her thin arms around Ginger's neck, pulling her into a hug. Though she was eighty-two years old, her arms were not frail. They were neither weak nor old. How long would she remain strong if she was taken from her home?

"Come with me," Ginger whispered into her lavender-scented ear.

"I can't and there is no fighting this, daughter. Things happen when they happen. You need to go."

Osbee released her and when she did Ginger felt like the ash she was, drifting away.

"You need to get going. It's an hour and a half to the hospital and the roads through the mountains will be ice."

"I love you, Osbee," Ginger whispered as she stood.

"I love you, too. Be careful driving."

As Ginger stepped out of Osbee's room, she found Beau standing at attention, swaying sleepily to and fro.

"Go lie down," she whispered, patting his head

as she passed. Carefully, she made her way down the stairs, listening to Beau's clicking toenails make their way across her bedroom floor and back to the rug on which he had been sleeping. By the time she reached the bottom, all was quiet again upstairs. Opening the refrigerator door, Ginger found the breakfast Osbee always made for her in its usual brown paper sack. After pouring herself some tea, she grabbed the sack, put on Jesse's coat, opened the back door, and made her way to the truck.

The sky was clear and the stars were bright and thick, as there was no moon to outshine them. There also was no new snow, which was a relief. Because it had not warmed up too much the day before and there was no new snow, the ground would be less icy than usual on the trip from the farm to Franklin, West Virginia. Her road would take Ginger through the mountains and she disliked driving on the windy back roads when there was ice. She could imagine herself sliding off into a ravine and no one would find her for hours. It had happened before; not to her but to several cases she had seen in ERs across the states. That was the problem with specializing in emergency room and trauma care. Every strange way of being injured or dying came through the door. Ignorance is bliss—the emergency room motto.

Turning on the truck, she checked the battery on

her cell phone in the lights of the dashboard. It was fully charged. She turned off the heater, as it was, at the moment, blowing cold air. Flipping on her lights, she crawled down the drive and, gazing to her left, found the pond an inky blot in the white snow.

Ginger sat hunched over the fire, the pear tree branches dripping melted snow on her head as the bacon popped and hit her hand. She winced and looked over at her husband, whose gray gaze peered across the fire at her with a small smile on his face. To his left, seven-year-old Henry sat board straight with his ramrod resting between his shoulder and ear, greedily watching the bacon fry in the cast-iron pan. Five-year-old Bea was rolling the tip of her ramrod in the brightly glowing embers of the fire. Two-year-old Oliver sat within his father's crossed legs, whimpering.

"Oliver doesn't like to camp," Ginger stated.

"We're not camping, Mama," Bea replied. "We're learning to bivouac."

"In Washington, we call it camping and we usually do it in the summer on a mountain or island where there are tents and bath-rooms and proper fire pits that won't burn down an orchard."

Oliver moaned and then sank deeper into his father's chest.

"We're here, Virginia, beneath the beautiful Virginia moon, to learn how to build shelter and cook something when shelter and food are scarce."

"What's 'scarce'?" Henry asked.

"There's not a lot of it around for people to use," Ginger replied, pulling the six slices of bacon from the frying pan and placing them on a tin plate. "Your father is preparing you for another invasion from the North."

"You're a Yankee, Mama," Bea said.

"She is not," Jesse declared. "Who said that?"

"Mr. Mitchell," Bea replied quietly, her shoulders slumping as if she had caused great injury to her father. Jesse reached down and rubbed her back.

"Oh. Well, it's a common mistake, but your mother isn't a Yankee. She's from the West."

"Which side did they fight on?" Henry asked.

"We didn't. We had no side. That's why camping for us is in warm tents with s'mores and salmon and guitars playing 'Kumbaya.' "

Jesse snickered.

"We having s'mores?" Henry asked with hope.

"We're having sloosh," Bea said.

"S'mores can't keep you strong and alive," Jesse said. "Sloosh can."

"According to current medical knowledge, though, eating bacon-grease-soaked corn-meal will cause several health problems after prolonged use—namely high blood pressure, hardened arteries, stomach disorders, bowel probl—"

"Thank you, Virginia, heart of my hearts. Please pour the cornmeal into the pan."

Ginger moved the pan on the fire and into the bacon grease she poured the cornmeal. It started to rain. Jesse and the children scooted back farther into the small shelter they had constructed before nightfall. They had gone out past the barn and fallow cornfields and picked up fallen branches and dead brush. After dragging debris across the fields and gravel drive, they built a little lean-to between two small volunteer pear trees close to the pond. It was where they were sleeping this evening. Ginger, on the other hand, sat across from them, out in the rain as she cooked. She pulled her hood over her head, stirring the cornmeal-grease mixture.

"Did you know, Bea, that some of the officers in the war brought their wives and children along?" Jesse asked. Ginger glanced over to him and he winked at her. Her hood shifted as she shook her head. He chuckled.

"I wouldn't have been a wife. I would've been a soldier," Bea said.

"Girls didn't fight back then," Henry said with a sneer.

"A couple did," Jesse corrected.

"Okay," Ginger said. "It's too hot for little hands, so your dad can make the snakes. Uh, have you washed your hands?" She looked at Jesse's hands from beneath her hood. She couldn't tell if they were dark because of shadow or dirt.

"Soldiers don't always have water to wash their hands," he replied, smiling at her. She sighed and with a quiet curse under her breath pulled a small portion of the hot cornmeal-grease batter out of the pan, quickly moving it from hand to hand as she rolled out a snake. It was sticky and gritty and when she thought it was long enough, she held it out to Jesse for inspection.

"Perfect!" he said. She pulled it quickly away from his outstretched hand.

"Hold out your stick, Bea," Ginger said. Bea pulled her ramrod out of the fire and Ginger leaned forward, wrapping the snake of cornmeal-grease batter around it.

"It's not a stick," Bea said and then held her ramrod with the sloosh over the fire to cook.

"Would you have gone with Daddy, Mama, if he was in the Civil War?"

Ginger sat back, pulling another handful of batter from the pan, and replied, "Yes, Bea. I would have done. For no other reason than to keep him from getting sick because he wouldn't wash his hands."

Henry giggled.

A lump of snow from the branch above hit Ginger on the head, and then it slid into the frying pan. The snow on the hot bacon fat exploded like a gun, sending steam and hot grease in Ginger's direction. Ginger flew backward and fell in the snow on her bottom, her hand held high, saving the sloosh within it from hitting the ground. Stunned, she looked over at her family, who sat wide-mouthed and wide-eyed.

"You okay?" Jesse asked, shifting Oliver toward Henry.

"Maybe, Bea, I would've stayed home," she said, smiling.

"I'd have never lasted if you had," Jesse said. Sliding Oliver over to his brother, he stood up and walked toward her.

"I saved the sloosh!" she declared as Jesse helped her up. Henry and Bea burst into applause. Oliver started to cry.

"S'mores?" Jesse whispered in her ear as he brushed off her back.

"No way! I just took a spill for this sloosh! What'd ya think? We give up when it's hard?"

Jesse looked at her and then kissed her cheek.

"You go sit in the shelter," he said, holding out his left hand. She gazed down. It was clean. Dropping the sloosh into his palm, she carefully made her way back to the fire.

"Maybe, Bea, I'd go with him after all."

As she climbed northwest out of Harrisonburg toward West Virginia and the town of Franklin, Ginger wished she could have gone with him. She wished she would have been there in that street in Iraq. Did he call for her? If she had been there and she had answered, would he have found a way to stay? Could she have helped them piece him back together? But even as she thought it, she knew there was no saving him. He was gone the moment he stepped into the street. If he had died any other way, she would now be filled with so much anger. Sometimes she wished he had. Surely filling with anger was easier to bear than emptiness.

"What'd ya think? We give up when it's hard?" she whispered. Her own words echoed back to her in her icy mountain ascent with memories of sloosh and laughter and lying together, all five of them hungry and freezing in the snow as they survived a winter's night with nothing but a bramble roof and each other for comfort and warmth. Ginger giggled watching herself slide whining Oliver next to his father for the night.

"Sloosh," she said. "Needed onion."

The road was curvy and white and it seemed to

74

Ginger that the sky darkened. The cab of her truck became suddenly colder and she shivered, flip-ping the heater on full. Leaning forward, she took the turns slowly and at a steady speed. A sign for Oak Flat winked at her as her headlights flashed across it, and as she came around the next hairpin curve a person jumped off the road just beyond the glare of her lights. Ginger slammed on the brakes, fishtailing slightly on the snowy road, and when she came to a stop, she looked just past the steady beam of her head-lights. There stood Samuel Annanais and he looked stricken. Shaking her head slowly, Ginger put her truck in park and opened the door.

"Samuel?"

"Virginia Moon!"

"Samuel, what are you doing out here?" She climbed out of the cab, staring at him in disbelief.

"There's a boy!"

"A boy?"

"Hurry. He's down here!"

Samuel motioned her to follow. Grabbing her flashlight, Ginger followed and there, in a small ravine, lay a teenage boy curled up near a deep root of a pine tree with half his face resting in a trickle of water. Sliding uneasily down into the steep ditch, Ginger touched his cheek. It was cold. Sticking her fingers into the neck of his coat, she found not only a pulse but heat.

"Samuel, we need to get him to the hospital."

There was no answer. Ginger stood and looked around. Samuel was nowhere to be seen.

"Samuel!" she yelled.

"I think I see another!" he replied, his voice echoing from deep in the darkness of the wood.

Ginger shook the boy. He stirred.

"Hey. Hey. Wake up."

Opening his eyes, the boy blinked away from the flashlight.

"I'm sick," he said, his breath smelling of whiskey.

"Yeah, no kidding." Ginger coughed. "Come on."

With effort, she helped the boy to his feet and, struggling, dragged him up onto the road. There, he promptly threw up.

"How much have you had?" she asked.

"I dunno." He retched. "I'm so tired."

"Don't go to sleep. Hang on. Samuel!"

"Coming."

Opening the back of her cab, she sat the boy down on her backseat.

"Please don't throw up in my truck."

"I don't feel good." He groaned and crawled farther inside, collapsing across the seat.

"Samuel!" Ginger yelled again to the trees.

"I am here, Virginia Moon."

Startled, she spun around and there he was on the driver's side of the truck.

"Wh-what happened to the other one?"

"He ran when he saw me coming."

"I have to get this one to the hospital. You climb in."

"I am going home."

"Yes, I know, and I have to go to work. Where's home?"

"Yet far from here. Laurel Creek. South."

"Well, get in and I'll drive you to Franklin. Can you sit with him? Keep him awake?"

"I cannot," was his reply.

Ginger blinked. She must have heard him wrong.

"Samuel. It's freezing out here and this kid has alcohol poisoning or hypothermia or both. I need your help."

"I have helped. I stopped you here. Now I must go." Samuel turned and walked to the edge of the trees.

"Samuel!"

"I am sorry. I cannot help more. I would if I could."

Then he was off, moving down into the ravine from which Ginger had just pulled the boy and disappearing into the forest beyond.

"Samuel!" she yelled. But there was no answer. Ginger looked around in the darkness and snow, her jaw moving up and down, saying his name over and over.

"What the hell?" she whispered and slammed the cab door. She came around the front of the truck and lifted her right foot to climb in. She stopped.

"Last call, Samuel! I'm leaving!" She waited, but there was no answer.

Pulling herself into the driver's seat, Ginger shut her door and shifted the truck into gear. The boy groaned.

"What's your name?" she asked.

"Jacob," he mumbled.

"Well, Jacob. We've got about fifteen minutes to Franklin. Please don't throw up in my truck."

"Okay." He moaned, and then he retched.

CHAPTER 4

SLOOSH

Ginger pulled up to the emergency room entrance at one forty-five a.m., climbed out of the truck, and with slippery steps walked to the glass door. She banged three times and as she waited for an answer she gazed at her reflection. Her ginger-colored roots were peeking out of her dark brown hair. She'd need to do something about that soon. A woman in her late fifties with close-cropped gray hair and pink scrubs poked her head out from behind the triage room wall.

"Morning! I got an inebriated teenage boy I found in a ditch," she yelled through the glass.

The woman stepped out from behind the desk, walking to the door. Her name badge read, "Margery T., RN."

"His name Jacob?" she asked with a scowl.

Ginger tilted her head. "Yeah," she replied.

Nurse T. unlocked and opened the door. "Let's bring him in," she mumbled, setting the door ajar. "I'm Margery Thompson."

"Virginia Martin," Ginger replied. "You know him?"

"This is only his fifth time here in as many

weeks," she said, following Ginger back to her truck. She opened the back door.

"*Eewwww-wee,*" Margery declared. "That's a mess."

"I know. And I gotta drive all the way home after it sits in here for twelve hours during my shift. I'm the new nurse," Ginger replied with a grimace.

Margery welcomed her with a wry smile. Together they lifted Jacob out of the backseat and dragged his dead weight through the small waiting room to the closest bed. There, they dumped his body.

"I'll call the doctor."

"Thanks," Ginger said and went outside to park her car.

Franklin District Community Hospital was like most rural ERs—small enough that its weekend and evening staff usually came from medical registries. It was a three-bed emergency room with five acute beds and an attached skilled nursing facility, which was staffed twenty-four hours a day with two LVNs and two nurses' aides. Major traumas in the area were medevaced to Winchester, Virginia. The usual patients in Franklin were small children with bad flus, broken bones of all ages, abdominal and chest pain of all ages. The care was basic emergency and acute care, and since it was such a small hospital, one nurse was on staff on the night shift to serve as triage, nurse, and even cook, if needed. There was one doctor, who generally slept on a bed in the day clinic across the parking lot until needed. The ambulance owner and driver lived in the house across the street.

Which was why, as she slipped across the vast patient parking lot, Ginger wondered how it was the medical staff parking lot was so far away to the left. After all, the ER could handle only one-fifth of the parking spaces allotted for patients. Cold and winded, she stepped back into the bright lights of the ER, locking the door behind her. She found the disheveled doctor scratching her head and yawning as she poured herself a cup of coffee. Her badge read, "Anna Maria D., MD."

"Nurse says he's been in here before," the doctor mumbled.

"She did say that, Doctor," Ginger replied, taking off her coat.

"You been here before?"

"This is only my third shift here. Last one was three months ago."

"So you don't know him."

Ginger shook her head as she stuck her hands beneath the warm water. It burned her frozen skin.

"You found him?"

"FFDID," Ginger said. ER term for "Found Face Down In Ditch." ER personnel had a very dark and dry wit, usually punctuated by acronyms.

ER speak, as Ginger called it, was a language unto itself.

"YPPA?" the doctor asked. "Young Practicing Professional Alcoholic."

"Seems to be," Ginger said, drying her burning hands.

"All right." The doctor yawned, putting down the coffee cup. With Anna Maria D., MD, leading the way, Ginger walked to where she and Nurse Thompson had dropped Jacob on a gurney. He was now without a coat, shirt, boots, or pants, lying beneath a heated blanket with an IV stuck in his arm. Taking the chart, the doctor checked the vitals, after which she handed it to Ginger, walked over to the sink, and washed her hands. Then she put on latex gloves, each one snapping into place. Placing the chart on the end of the bed, Ginger did the same. She always felt her snapping latex gloves had less of a commanding sound than the doctor's.

"Not hypothermic. That's good. Hey, Jacob. Jacob Esch."

"Huh," the kid answered. It was less a word than a grunt.

"Where you from?"

"Oak Flat," he replied. His mouth moved but nothing else did.

"You don't sound like you're from around here," the doctor replied. "Your chart says you're from Pennsylvania."

"Oh. Yah." He rolled over and retched. With the skill of a practiced nurse, Ginger grabbed the pink plastic container and caught his vomit in midair.

Gently the doctor rolled him over on his back, opened one of his eyes, and flicked her little light on his irises. Ginger could see that they were contracting in the light.

"Did you know, Jacob, that throwing up is the body's way of getting rid of stuff it cannot process?" The doctor was feeling Jacob's neck and down his chest to his stomach.

"Huh," was all he had as an answer.

"Did you know that if you drink fast enough, alcohol can depress the throw-up response and force your body to keep inside what it cannot process?"

He didn't answer.

"You're a very lucky young man that you are throwing up."

As she pushed on his stomach, he groaned, at which point the doctor rolled him on his side. Ginger caught the vomit in the dish again.

"I don't feel lucky," he muttered, drool oozing from his lips onto the gurney sheet. Ginger grabbed a paper towel and wiped his mouth.

"Well, you are. Now, we will just hope that no police come in here with an emergency tonight because it is also against the law for anyone under the age of twenty-one to drink alcohol."

"I'll pray," he whispered.

"You do that."

The doctor walked back over to the sink, removed her gloves, and washed her hands again.

"No need to call lab on the blood. Let him sleep a bit and then see if any one of his contacts can come pick him up. He'll be a real mess tomorrow."

With that, the doctor stepped away, leaving Jacob, Margery, Ginger, and the bowl of vomit alone in the quiet ER.

"There'll be no flower sign here," Margery said, walking toward the nurses' desk. "Flower sign" referred to patients who have flowers sent to them in the hospital and was ER speak indicating that the patient had someone who cared for them— someone who would come get them. Soon. Nurse T. seemed to feel Jacob was on his own.

"I guess, unless it gets busy, we'll just leave him?" Ginger asked, placing the bowl of vomit in the bathroom as she passed.

"That's what we've done the last five times he's been in. Real nice kid. Very apologetic. I think he'll feel bad about your car," she said, heading toward the acute care section of the hospital. "We've only got one other patient tonight. A regular by the name Jack Wolfe. Sixty-six-year-old white male. He's COPD, CHP, diabetic, non-compliant."

Before they entered the room, Ginger could hear

him. COPD meant emphysema. His breathing was indeed loud. They opened the door.

"Hey, you got a dollar, Marg?"

"Jack here wants a candy bar," Margery said with a false smile. "He wants to go down the hall and buy himself one."

Jack chuckled a little and coughed.

"But Jack has CHF—congestive heart failure—and cannot have salt and is diabetic. He's also noncompliant, which means he doesn't take his medicine and so he cannot have a candy bar."

"I'll get one when I leave," he said, winking at Ginger.

Jack was obviously the kind of patient who had lived on his own terms and, as he was coming to the end of his life, wanted to go out the same way. For nurses like Margery, her entire duty was to force compliance to medical orders. If the patient wasn't going to obey on his own, she would make him while he was in her care. But Ginger was a different kind of nurse. She understood that disregarding orders was a final act of humanity. Sometimes it was a form of dissent. Sometimes it was the right thing to do. For Mr. Wolfe, apparently, it was the right thing to do. Jesse had made the same decision a year earlier, so she winked back now to Mr. Wolfe.

Jack chuckled a little deeper and coughed harder, which caused Margery to glance over to Ginger. She shied away a little. Margery stared more forcefully at her, which then caused Ginger to smile.

"Hmm," Margery said, pursing her lips tightly as she headed out of Jack's room.

"The LVNs tonight are Janet and Debbie. Nurses' aides are Yvette and Brad. If an emergency comes through the door, make sure to get the EMT or police to stay and help until one of those four can come over."

"Okay," Ginger replied, following Margery into the nurses' station.

"Doctors switch at six a.m.," Margery said, reaching down to open a drawer. She lifted her handbag from within it and closed it again with her knee.

" 'Kay."

Turning to face Ginger, Margery squinted a little in the ER's fluorescent lights. "Mr. Wolfe cannot have a candy bar."

"I know." Ginger smiled again.

Placing her handbag on her shoulder, Margery walked to the ER doors.

"Has anyone talked to him about his drinking?" Ginger asked as she bent to unlock them.

"Who?"

"Jacob Esch."

"Oh, sure. But he's Amish. You know. They reach sixteen and they're allowed to go all wild. What's the word?"

Ginger knew what the nurse was talking about

but didn't know the word. She shook her head and opened the door.

"Well, he must have lost his way. He's eighteen and still drinking. Not even close to home. He's a mess. Good night."

"Good night," Ginger said.

With the door wide-open and winter crawling in like a lost dog, Ginger watched the woman slip and slide across the empty parking lot until she reached her car. Then, when the headlights flipped on and the car slowly started forward, she shut the glass door against the night and bolted it tight. She shivered.

"What in the world is Samuel thinking?" she muttered to the black beyond the door. He must have hitched a ride to get so far so fast, but why he wouldn't get in her truck made no sense. Surely it was darker and colder than it had been when he'd climbed into the car that drove him to Oak Flat.

Ginger stopped at Jacob's side and checked his IV. The boy snored softly through his whiskey haze. He didn't really look eighteen. His whiskers were yet soft as they grew in and his forehead and chin had acne. He had his whole life ahead of him. He could be anything. Yet already there was no flower sign. So young for no flower sign. She brushed the lock of brown hair off his cheek.

"I'm so tired," he whispered.

"Rest," she replied. As she left the ER, she

turned down the lights. Before she saw him, she could hear Jack Wolfe as she made her way back to acute care. He coughed as she came through his open door.

"You gotta dollar?"

"You shouldn't have candy."

"I love chocolate."

"So do I," Ginger replied.

"Haven't seen you around here before and I'm a regular," he said with a short laugh.

"This is only my third shift."

"What's your name?"

"Virginia Moon Martin."

Jack's eyes widened and he lifted his head off his pillow. Then he smiled the way they all smiled when she said her name. Ginger grinned back.

"You're not from around here, are you?"

"Nope."

He nodded and then dropped his head back onto its pillow, closing his eyes as he breathed in heavily. Ginger came into the room, took his wrist, and, looking at her watch, counted—one, two, three. How many times had these little beats coursed through this man's veins? How many times had someone held his wrist to check them? Ginger sighed and started over—one, two, three.

"Did you find it, Nurse Moon?"

Ginger looked up and found Jack Wolfe staring at her with a pop eye. "What?" she asked.

"My pulse?"

Ginger nodded and set his wrist back down. She gazed up at his drip.

"Good. You had me worried."

"Why?" she asked, turning the drip nozzle so it fed faster.

"There's a tear on your cheek and I thought I passed."

Ginger reached up quickly, wiping the tear. The little drop of water glistened in the overhead light. Where did that come from?

"Can I ask you a question, Mr. Wolfe?" she said, quickly diverting the conversation.

"Sure. I'm not sleeping anyway." He sat up a little in bed, his chest rising with the weight in his lungs as he struggled for air.

"You do know that candy bars are bad for you, don't you?"

"Yeah, well, most everything I've done in my life has been bad for me. I drank too much. I smoked too much. I had a great time doing both. I'd do both now if I could." He smiled.

"No regrets?"

"I had a good life. I had fun. I worked. I loved. What's to regret?"

"So even though you are stuck in this bed with no chocolate, you wouldn't change a thing."

"Not one minute." He chuckled. "And I only got no chocolate right now."

Ginger squinted at him.

"You gonna give me a dollar?"

She shook her head.

"I'm released tomorrow."

She grinned and turned to leave. "Well, Mr. Wolfe," she said over her shoulder. "Find a candy bar with less salt. At least try to give one of your ailments a break while overloading the other. And before you leave, we'll make sure your insulin levels are good, 'kay?"

"I like Snickers."

Ginger chuckled and shook her head again.

"Nurse Moon?"

Ginger stopped and looked over her shoulder at him.

"What was the tear?"

She hadn't even known she had a tear. She did, however, know why it was there and she also knew that she was a nurse and Mr. Wolfe a patient. She smiled and shook her head.

"Ah, come on. You can tell me."

"No, I really can't."

"Just me." He looked around the room. "No one will know."

She looked into his chocolate brown eyes and thought that, even though he looked tired and drawn, his chest heaving from working so hard to breathe, his gaze was so awake.

"It was my wrist you were holding, after all. Come on. I shared."

Ginger shrugged.

"Come on," he whispered. His eyes didn't move.

"I was just thinking—I was just hoping someone had hold of my husband's wrist when his pulse stopped."

Jack leaned his head to the left. "I hope whoever held his wrist held it as tenderly as you did mine," he replied.

Me, too, she mouthed and, flicking off his light, Ginger shut Jack's door. Taking a deep breath, she headed back to the ER and slid next to Jacob's gurney. He was shivering. Pulling out another warmed blanket from the cabinet, she laid it over the boy, tucking it under his legs and shoulders.

"You need to go home, Jacob Esch," she said softly.

"I know, Captain. But I can't," he replied.

Dear Juliette,

A queersome feeling awoke me at dawn this day. It is July and spring has ridden away; her vibrant colors and new green leaves scattered in her wake. Now the world is turning deep, lush, and thick, as is the nature of summer in Virginia. Do you remember summers here? There were dances lit by a full moon and lightning bugs. I see you still in your pale blue dress as we spun around in a waltz for the first time. Are you remembered of the night we first met? Do summer nights in Sharpsburg hold the ebb of lightning bugs and the memory of our first dance not so long ago?

The earth is always weighty as Virginia dons her summer shawl. Trees are heavy. Air is heavy. Yet I was light last night with the memory of you in my arms. But all levity vanished with the breaking day, for nothing should have been as heavy as it was this morning, which is what brought me from my blankets just before reveille.

It had softly rained the night before, the mist of which stood like a ghostly wall all round. It neither rose nor fell, but simply hung as if waiting for us all to stand and crawl on top of it. The sky was violet-gray but the mist reflected no light and I stood in the silence. That is unusual since I am now always surrounded by my regiment but even their breath was still. And in that silence, I heard a solitary bird singing, if a song is what you could call it. The sound was less trill and more whistle, a punctuating sound inflected up as if it asked a question of me—the same short question over and over. If I understood its language, perhaps I could have answered, but since I did not, I simply whistled back to it the same sound, the same question. As soon as I did so, the bird stopped and all was quiet and in that heavy stillness I heard someone calling my name. Not as if I was called to dinner or was needed for something, rather it was inflected up—Samuel? I turned around in the mist, seeking for the person, but could see no one. I answered—Yes? And then the bird sang again, posing the exact same query it had done so many times before. But now, in answer, the bugle struck reveille and a thousand men coughed as one, breaking the stillness. The mist stirred, twirling, falling, rising with the movement of men.

So I lie here now, resting in the evening after a day of marching. Colonel Jackson is now Brigadier General. As you may have heard, we destroyed many engines and railroad cars at Martinsburg. Now we move north as part of

General Johnston's army, our destination not generally known nor could I write it down here, lest my letters be accidentally misplaced and picked up by another. But, knowing where we go, I find this morning's event as heavy on me as was the mist at dawn—a wall beyond which I cannot see. What was the bird asking? Who is it that calls my name? Is it you praying for me, Juliette? I can only find peace when thinking of you, so there my thoughts have turned the entire day. The sky is a lapis stone as the sun just sets, clear of all trouble, and upon it the evening star shines brightly. I see it, a single bright point in the great lapis blue emptiness of the sky, and in it, I see you. I pray that I shall fall asleep quickly, with no bird and no mist weighing on me—just the light and brightness of you in my soul.

Your devoted,
Samuel E. Annanais

CHAPTER 5

MANASSAS

The early-morning quiet at Franklin District Community Hospital was broken by a howling two-year-old boy who arrived at five a.m. with a temperature of 103, chills, and a severe cough. As Anna Maria D., MD, and Ginger were working on him, the ambulance across the street screamed to life at five thirty a.m. and a telephone call came in stating a seventy-four-year-old man with chest pain was on his way in. He coded twice in the ambulance. There was no radio at Franklin District Community Hospital, just the phone, so as Anna Maria continued with the two-year-old's bronchitis, Ginger called into Winchester Medical informing them that they were likely to receive a new patient and to please send a helicopter. The ambulance pulled up to the door at five forty-five a.m. with the morning shift on its heels along with the arrival of Jonathan J., MD, and Everett K., RN.

Everett took the baby bronchitis as Dr. Anna Maria, Dr. Jonathan, and Nurse Ginger stabilized the heart attack. Not once but three times did Anna Maria D., MD, call out "NGMI"—"Not Going to Make It." Ginger could hear the helicopter land because a nearly severed finger and an asthmatic with the flu came in the door, followed by a winter morning exhale, which sent its great chilled breath blowing through the tiny ER. The heart attack stabilized and was rushed out into the cold, bright morning to the helicopter, which lifted off in the presence of what, to Ginger, seemed like the entire town. Anna Maria D., MD, left at seven forty-five a.m. and as Ginger went from heart attack to nearly severed finger to asthmatic flu, Jack Wolfe and Jacob Esch were released. Ginger hadn't really noticed exactly when they left. They, after all, had become Everett K., RN's patients, as all incoming patients were her triage responsibility. She simply found their beds empty when she went on break at ten a.m.

So the morning passed; the baby was sent home, as was the nearly severed finger. The asthmatic with flu was admitted. Two FABIANS ("Felt Awful But I'm Alright Now Syndrome"), a broken arm, and a "Two Beers" came and went. Two Beers was brought in by the local police, having slid off the road quite near to where Ginger had seen Samuel the night before. As always, though clearly drunk, he claimed to have had only two beers before his crash earned him his now broken collarbone. When the blood alcohol level returned with .08, his arm was placed in a sling, the typical treatment, with instructions to keep it immobile for four to six weeks. Then, without handcuffs, he was placed in the back of the police car and driven off for his DUI booking just as Ginger's shift came to an end.

Dialing home, she walked out into a clear blue and white day, her feet sliding on the icy asphalt of the parking lot.

"Hello?" Osbee answered the phone.

"I'm off. We need anything from the store?"

"Uh, no. No." Osbee's voice was quieter than usual. Ginger stopped.

"Everything all right?"

"Yes, yes. Uh . . . Ester and Hugh are still here. They are staying for supper."

"Oh." This was bad news. Ginger's body was still buzzing with adrenaline from the night's work but she knew by the time she reached home she'd be spent. If Jesse's mother and father were still there, she'd need to keep her wits about her.

"They brought presents for the children."

"That's nice," Ginger replied. That was her Southern way of having no opinion one way or the other on a subject.

"You working tonight?"

"No. My registry schedule is tonight off, then Friday and Saturday back up here in Franklin. Why?"

"Oh," Osbee said brightly. "Maybe you'd like to take some time for yourself. Go somewhere. A drive or something."

Though that did sound appealing from an

avoidance point of view, she felt it cowardly. Plus, she had no extra money for gas.

"I'll give you some cash when you get home," Osbee offered as if reading her mind.

"You've no money."

"Not yet, but I will."

More of Ginger went cold than just her feet and hands. "Osbee," Ginger whispered, hoarsely.

"Not to worry, Ginger, my dear. You go. Have a nice lunch. It warm up there?"

"Not really."

"Well, there's no new snow and it's relatively warm down here. Like spring is about to spring. Come down here. Drive the Shenandoah."

Ginger wanted to go home. She wanted to— to— She wasn't sure exactly. But she didn't want Osbee to be alone.

"Go for a drive. Have some mommy alone time."

Ginger sighed. It felt so wrong. It was as if she were surrendering before the battle even began.

"Ginger?"

"Yeah. Okay."

"Good. Be careful and call now and then so we know where you are."

"Okay," Ginger said again. Her stomach rose to her throat, threatening to empty its contents onto the snow.

"Not to worry," Osbee repeated. "Have fun."

"All right," Ginger replied. "Bye."

"Bye-bye." The line went dead.

"Shit," Ginger said, swallowing hard to avoid throwing up. She knew Osbee had signed papers. She knew Osbee was selling her home—her root. Unlocking the door, Ginger opened the truck and was promptly slapped across the face by the horrendous smell.

"For the love of Pete!" she declared, and covering her mouth, she opened all four doors to the cab of her truck. As she was the only RN on duty during the night and the ER had been so busy when the morning shift arrived, there had not been one minute for Ginger to deal with the mess in her truck. Now she left the vehicle open while she went back inside the ER, grabbed towels and a bucket, and returned to clean out the backseat. The smell was better but not completely gone, so she rummaged through her handbag, looking for the small bottle of perfume Jesse had given her three Christmases ago. She'd worn it only when she was out with him, and as he was now gone, she never had cause to use it. It was buried deep somewhere in the bottom of her purse, so she dug. Before she spotted it, she came across the little yellow envelope with its gold key.

"Aha," she said with a smile. "Hope."

Pulling the envelope from her handbag, she carefully extricated the newspaper clipping. Ginger held her breath and scooted into the front seat, engaging the engine to warm the truck.

Sliding back out again, she stood in the snow, dialing Ed Rogers. The phone rang four times, and as she was about to hang up, someone picked up the line. It was a woman.

"Hallo?"

"Oh. Uh. Hello. My name is Ginger Martin and I was calling for Ed Rogers."

"Martin, did you say?"

"Yes. Ginger Martin."

"Just a minute." There was a muffled cry from the phone with the woman yelling for Ed as she held her hand to the receiver. Ginger's heart sped up as she looked down inside the envelope at the little gold key. The phone rattled a bit on the other side and then a very Virginian man with an accent from the north near Richmond came on the line.

"Mrs. Martin? Are you Jesse Martin's wife?"

Ginger smiled, relieved. Ed Rogers was still at the same number and he remembered her husband.

"Yes, I am."

"It is so good to hear from you. How is your husband?"

Ginger stopped breathing. Of course he would want to know. How obvious. But she had rarely spoken to anyone regarding what was being asked of her now, for everyone she knew already knew. So, for the first time, she tried putting into words the truth of the matter. Her mouth wouldn't cooperate.

"Mrs. Martin?" The man's voice went softer and far lower.

"Yes?" Ginger whispered, tears rolling down her cheeks, causing the world to glisten in blue and white.

"I'm sorry. I'm so sorry," he replied.

"It's all right," she lied.

"No, it's not," he said.

Ginger let out a little weeping chuckle. "No, it's not," she agreed.

"I am sorry. I hadn't heard from him, so I thought he was still deployed. We often lost touch for a year or so while he was overseas. He was a good man."

"He was."

"Mrs. Martin? I have a couple of tractor parts he asked me to get for him. I was wondering if you'd like me to ship them to you."

"I—I have no money to pay—"

"Oh, he already paid. You want me to ship them?"

Ginger thought for a moment. She had nothing to do. "Where exactly are you, Mr. Rogers?"

"Call me Ed. I'm by Manassas."

Manassas was a three-hour drive. "Are you busy today?"

"No. No. Not at all."

"Well, I can be there at around five or six. Is that all right?"

"That's fine. You need directions?"

"Let me get a little closer if that's all right, and then I'll call to ask."

"Very good. See you soon, Mrs. Martin."

"Ginger. Call me Ginger. Ed?" She quickly climbed into her truck. The smell brought tears to her eyes. She was sure that's what was causing them now.

"Yes?"

"Do you know anything about a little gold key?" There was silence.

"Ed?"

"No. Not that I remember."

"Okay. It was just in an envelope with your number so I thought they went together."

"Sorry I can't help."

"It's all right. I'll be there in a few hours."

"Be careful, Ginger. Roads are icy."

"Yes. Thank you. Bye."

She hung up and as she put the truck in gear her entire body lightened. It was as if weight had shifted onto the seat next to her, and though she knew it would slide back eventually, she could at least feel a touch of the world as it was when Jesse was alive. She glanced up into the blue sky that sparkled as only the blue sky can when the earth is covered in white, filling her dark places inside with the blue-white winter light.

Jesse had Ginger's hand with his right and was holding two-year-old Henry in his left arm. It was steep from the bridge to the water and Ginger could barely see her feet over her very round belly.

"Be careful," Jesse said.

"Hard to be when I can't see where my feet are going," she replied. There was no sweat trickling anymore down her neck. Bad sign.

"Let's just get in the shadow of the bridge and out of the sun for a minute."

"You need to get the ranger to help," she said.

It was so humid, Ginger felt she wasn't even breathing. She had been fine as they walked around Henry Hill Visitor Center, and though Jesse liked the idea, Ginger decided she wanted to take the path to the stone bridge over Bull Run. It was, after all, July 21, the anniversary of First Manassas. She knew Jesse wanted to make the trek. He, however, wouldn't go without her and as he was not about to take her in Virginia's summer sun for a walk, or more like a waddle, to the creek, she had to just start heading that way without discussing the matter with him. There was, however, little silence on the way because he just kept repeating, "Ginger, we should go back."

Truly, they should have gone back. She was now dizzy and nauseated and though she had been absolutely convinced she couldn't get heatstroke in the two miles of path it took to get to the stone bridge, she was now not so sure. She needed to cool off. She needed to get out of the sun. So here she was, slipping down the steep embankment to the water, trying to get in the shade of the bridge on the east side.

"I'm so stupid," she said, her breath shallow.

"Sit." Jesse lowered her to the grass right next to the bridge. A small sliver of dark shade covered her head.

"Here, hold Henry. Let me get some water." Ginger leaned against the bridge, the stone still holding the heat of the noonday sun, which had passed two hours earlier. Jesse unbuttoned his shirt, pulled off his undershirt, and went down to the river, where he dunked it into the muddy water. Wringing it out into the grass, he first dripped a little of the water on Henry's head and then rubbed his under-shirt across Ginger's neck and shoulders. It was so cool. Her head was pounding.

"You need to go get help," she said.

"I can't just leave you."

"Take Henry and go back."

"Look. I'm not just going to leave you here. What da ya think?"

She looked up at him and found his gray eyes as unyielding as the day she met him at the hospital. She smiled a little.

"I say that—'What da ya think?' "

"Well, that's where I am with this. No argument."

"We need help."

"It'll come," he replied, sliding back into his shirt. Kneeling down in front of her, he moved his wet T-shirt from the back of her neck to the front while sliding a portion of it over Henry's head again.

"Jesse?"

"I'm not leaving."

"No, no—I'm sorry. I should've thought of Henry."

"Henry's not in trouble, Ginger."

"I know. But now we're here and we don't have his food or anything."

"Help will come."

"Are you sure?"

"This is the stone bridge at Manassas. It is July twenty-first. Help is probably approaching the bridge as we speak."

At that moment, Ginger heard a fife playing in the distance.

"See?" he said, grinning at her.

She closed her eyes, listening. The music grew louder and now there were voices— children and adults laughing and talking. They were yet too far for her to understand what was being said.

"Shouldn't you go get whoever it is?" she asked.

"Help always comes when you need it. Just have to sit still long enough."

"Shouldn't you go bring them here?"

"If you go and it comes, it won't find you."

The voices were very close but there were so many of them and her head hurt so entirely that she understood none of what was being said. Jesse burst out laughing.

"What is it?"

He couldn't stop laughing.

"Jesse?"

He took in a breath. "It's a Girl Scout troop." He bent down and kissed her head, chuckling still. "See? Help," he said.

"Can you ask them if they have any cookies?"

She wasn't sure exactly why her truck decided to take her there, but at four thirty p.m. she pulled into the Henry Hill Visitor Center at Manassas National Battlefield. The parking lot was covered with snow, as was the gentle rolling plain of the battlefield that surrounded it.

Ginger turned off her car, imagining summer and heat and cicadas singing with a fife. Opening her door, she climbed out, tucked her cell phone and car keys in her pockets, shut the door, and locked the truck. The path to the stone bridge was to the right. It looped around the parking lot and headed east and then north. Instead of heading in that direction, Ginger walked toward the Henry

House. She and little Bea had done very well that day waddling in that direction. Jesse had held Henry, talking with him about this and that artillery and regiment. Now, walking on the path with the world so quiet under its blanket of snow, she tried to remember his voice as he spoke with his boy—the manner of his walk, his back straight and shoulders square as he held Henry in his arms. Ginger stopped, closing her eyes at the memory of how beautiful Jesse was in that moment. She was so pregnant at the time, but her body stirred for him there, standing with little Henry babbling in his embrace.

She felt that same ache now—the ache that so often kept her awake at night. To avoid it growing stronger, she decided she should take a walk to the bridge, after all.

She opened her eyes. She froze. There on the far side of the Henry House she saw a lone man standing. His back was toward her and all of a sudden he jerked to a squat. Ginger frowned, standing on tiptoe as she gazed around looking for other people. There was no one else. There was just Ginger and the snow and the man squatting up ahead. Thinking she ought to check, for help always comes, she walked in his direction.

"Hello?" she called. In his crouched position, he slid to the left, ducking his head now and then like a frog crossing a lily pad.

"What in the world?" she mused, trotting now toward him. "Hey, are you okay?"

Suddenly the man stood, lifting a musket from the ground. Ginger stopped dead in the snow. He was wearing a butternut uniform and as he lifted the musket to his eye, he fixed its point upon something moving in the distance. He turned to the right, and as he came around, Ginger could now see the full profile of his face.

"Samuel?" she breathed. With a start, he pulled the musket from his eye and looked in her direction.

"Ma'am?"

Ginger jumped, spinning around to find a ranger standing at her back.

"Samuel," she said, pointing behind her. But when she turned around, she found the field empty.

"Uh, no. I'm Richard. I just came to say we're about to close."

"Did—did you see where he—he went?"

"Who?"

"Samuel. He—he was standing right there."

The ranger looked past her and then shook his head. "Sorry. I didn't see anyone come with you. I must have missed him getting out of the car. Is he a little boy?" The ranger stepped by her and headed in the direction Ginger was pointing.

"N-no. No," Ginger said, following the ranger toward the spot she had seen Samuel. "He must have been here. You having a reenactment?"

The ranger halted and turned around.

"A reenactment of what?"

"Of a battle here." Ginger sped by the ranger, coming at last to the front of the Henry House. Maybe Samuel had gone around the side of the building.

The ranger guffawed.

Ginger spun on her heel and looked back at him.

"There were two battles here, ma'am. The first was fought in July and the—"

"The second was August. August 28 to 30, 1862, to be exact. I am well aware of the battles here, Ranger Richard. Thank you." Ginger gritted her teeth, holding her next sentence behind them. What in the world was she so angry at?

"Sorry," she said, gazing back to the Henry House. "I just thought I saw someone I knew."

"No one is here but you."

"You sure? Maybe he walked here. Maybe he hitchhiked and was dropped off somewhere else in the battlefield."

"Ma'am, it is twenty-five degrees out here with four inches of snow. I'm pretty sure no one would be around the Henry House without driving in the entrance. No offense."

Ginger stared at the place she was sure she had seen Samuel. There were no footprints, no signs of him crawling sideways in a ducked position.

"Four inches of snow?" she asked quietly.

"According to the weather report."

Ginger stuck her hands in her pockets and gazed

up at the Virginia sky. It was coming on to sunset.

"It's about five o'clock, ma'am. The park is closing."

"You don't think he went in there, do you?" She pointed to the door of the Henry House.

"It's closed."

She sunk her hands deeper into her pockets.

"I swear he was standing right there," Ginger said, gazing at the ranger. The man shook his head, his brow furrowed in apology.

Slowly, turning now and then back to the place she was positive Samuel had been, Ginger made her way back to her truck. She opened the door. The smell of perfume, whiskey, and throw-up greeted her. She looked over at the ranger, who stepped back a little, his eyes squinting at her as he let go a small cough.

"Uh—not me. An Amish boy I found on the road."

The ranger nodded. "Drive carefully," he said.

"Sorry to have kept you out in the cold, Richard." She climbed into her fragrant truck.

"Thank you for visiting," he replied.

Engaging the engine, Ginger gave Ranger Richard an embarrassed wave and backed out of her parking space. She knew what he was thinking. She knew if she were in his shoes, she'd be thinking that same thing. But she hadn't been drinking and she had seen Samuel.

She stopped at the entrance sign to Manassas and dialed Ed Rogers for directions. As he read them off, she scribbled them down in a small spiral pad. As she wrote, she gazed back at the parking lot and the Henry House, waiting to see if Samuel would emerge from somewhere. He did not. Ranger Richard, however, did, walking hunched over in his coat toward her truck. Hanging up quickly with Ed, she made her way down the road to the left and watched Ranger Richard swing the gate to the parking lot closed. He locked it with a large, heavy chain; its gritty metallic clang echoed after her. She shivered and, with a little, nervous laugh, called, "Scroooooooge."

"You have labored on it since. It is a ponderous chain," she moaned, trying to create Jesse's ghostly impression of Jacob Marley herself. He had been so good at becoming the characters when reading at bedtime.

"He must think I'm nuts," she said to herself in her side-view mirror, and at the T intersection she took a left. As she drove, she ran Samuel's image through her mind—his ducking movement, his profile, his eyes turning in her direction. She had been so startled by Ranger Rick that now she could not even remember if she saw Samuel's entire face or if he had actually seen her. Having seen her, would he have not come over? And what was he doing at Manassas anyway? Last she saw him, he was in West Virginia, headed south to Laurel Creek.

She drove, wondering how Samuel could have been at Smoot's farm, Franklin, and Manassas all in one twenty-four-hour period. Her rumination was disquieting to her. After a while she decided that it wasn't Samuel at all at Manassas. It must have been someone who looked like Samuel. Ranger Rick was incorrect also. Some man was stealing across the battlefield in the snow. That's just how it had to have been. It made sense.

She had nearly convinced herself of it by the time she hit her right blinker and bumped off the road onto a dirt driveway that led to Ed Rogers's place. She stopped. Night was pouring across the sky at five p.m., the sun but a hazy pale blue-pink memory peeping through the trees to the west. The bare branches reached over the driveway, their spindly fingers shaking hands overhead. Shuddering, Ginger thought that maybe she should just turn around. Although winter solstice had passed two months earlier, she had neglected to remember that the days were still very short and that she would be heading to an unknown man's house out in rural Virginia at night.

"Mr. Rogers," she whispered. *Nothing bad can happen at Mr. Rogers's house.*

She smiled anxiously at herself in her rearview mirror, took her foot off the brake, and, as she crawled down the dirt road, dialed home just to let Osbee know where she was—just in case.

112

CHAPTER 6

MR. ROGERS

As Ginger drove from beneath the column of trees, floodlights switched on, bursting through her cab as if she were some secret service agent driving right into some great sting operation from which there was no escape. She pressed her brake and stopped the truck, blinking in the bright lights.

Placing her hand over her eyes, she peered out through the glare and found she was parked before a very large, old brick antebellum mansion. She was situated not at the front of the building but at its side. To her left, far over yards of trodden snow, she spotted two very large barns—one that seemed to date from the time of the house and the other much newer. Squinting, she could just make out a shadow passing between the older barn and the house. It was a golf cart and the person inside waved. As she flipped off her lights, several floodlights from the direction of the barns turned off. Now she could see that there, driving in the snow, was a woman clothed in a blue and white ski coat and a blue scarf. She waved again. Ginger turned off her engine and opened the door.

"Mrs. Rogers?" she called.

"Ginger!" the woman said, laughing a little as if the name tickled. "Ginger Martin. I am so happy to see you. Jesse spoke of you so often."

Ginger slid out of the truck and shut her door.

"Ed is in the barn. Are you cold? Hungry?" the woman asked, stopping the golf cart and climbing out. She walked up and shook Ginger's hand. "I'm Lorena. Would you like to get the tractor parts into the back of your truck first?"

"I grabbed Chick-fil-A on the way here, thank you. Um—maybe I should get the parts first."

"Good. Good. Ed is pulling them from his vast supply," Lorena replied, rolling her eyes. She adjusted the hood on her head and said, "Climb in."

"He has a lot of tractor parts?" Ginger inquired as she scooted onto the golf cart seat.

"Without the buildings hiding everything, we'd look like a junkyard."

Ginger laughed quietly, holding on to the side of her seat as they traversed the yard to the nearest barn.

"Ed was trying actually to buy that tractor from Jesse, you know."

"No, I didn't."

"My husband is a collector of farming equipment. Has been all his life. Now that he's getting older, he seems to be narrowing his assortment to mainly tractors. Miracle!"

She laughed as she veered left. "That one of

your husband's is quite a collector's piece," Lorena added.

"Is it?"

"Hmm. Ed was trying to exchange for it."

"Exchange what?"

The golf cart stopped. "Well, for one, the horses. Ed had those so he could use his horse plows. He's done with that, so we put an ad in the *Army Times* and here comes Jesse. VMI and everything." Lorena grunted as she slid out of the cart.

Ginger followed. "Ed went to VMI?"

"Oh, sure. And he teaches there now. Jesse and he loved to talk to each other in Latin. They'd talk up a storm when he'd visit."

"That was one of Jesse's favorite classes," Ginger said, wondering why she had never heard of Ed Rogers. "Was he a professor of Jesse's?"

"No, no. He was career military, actually. He didn't start teaching until 2000. After retiring."

"Ah," Ginger replied as she followed Lorena into the barn. Upon entry, Lorena came to an abrupt stop. Ginger nearly ran into the back of her. Peering over the woman's blue and white shoulder, Ginger's eyes widened. The barn looked like a huge bulk superstore, with metal scaffolding on both sides of a large dirt aisle. Stacked two high, various farm implements were displayed as if for sale. All was tidy and clean in the bright fluorescent lights overhead. Ginger whistled quietly.

"I know," Lorena whispered, gazing over her shoulder at Ginger. "It's an obsession out of control. This is just the equipment and parts barn. The newer one farther out is where he keeps his tractors." Lorena shook her head, her hood falling back to show her short salt-and-pepper hair.

"I suppose Henry's Child would fit right in here," Ginger noted.

"Who's Henry's Child?"

"Oh—the tractor. We call it Henry's Child. It was his baby."

"I bet. Very rare, that one. When Ed found out Jesse had it, he tried to give the horses away for free. Took him around the barn here. Showed him all the equipment that could be worked with the horses. But your husband said he only needed Penny and Christian for his kids and he couldn't sell the tractor."

"No, I suppose not." Ginger looked down at her toes, her stomach rolling as she thought of Osbee and Ester and Hugh and papers signing away her husband's dream.

"So, here we are—a barn half filled with horse-drawn farming equipment and no horses." Lorena giggled. "Story of my life."

Ginger didn't smile. She just kept thinking of Bea and the tractor and flying away to Seattle.

"Ginger?" Lorena touched her shoulder. "You okay?"

"Yeah. I think Osbee's going to sell the farm,

though, so maybe Ed will get Henry's Child, after all. I suppose Jesse would like that."

"What do you mean, sell the farm?"

Ginger started at the sound of the man's voice. It was gentle and very Virginian but something in its inflection made her straighten her back. Glancing in the direction from which it came, she found a tall, thin man in a black fleece coat, jeans, and black rubber riding boots. He was very tidy with silver hair and a square jaw and eyes the lapis color of Virginia's sky. She said nothing, finding her voice had completely surrendered and ran AWOL—taking up hidden residence in her left thumb under the intensity of those piercing blue eyes.

"What do you mean, please?" he repeated. In his hands, Ginger saw one large piston. She wished she could grab it and run.

"It's time to plant," Ginger said hoarsely. It came out sounding to her more like a cough.

"It is almost," he agreed. Not a muscle moved in his body—not even a twitch in his eye. Only his mouth moved.

"There's only Osbee and me and we can't farm. The other men in the area have been doing it for us since Jesse last left and—well, he's—" Her voice broke, but she did not look away. She couldn't.

"We're sorry for that," Lorena replied. "We feel his loss also."

The woman's arm wrapped around Ginger's shoulder. This time, she didn't shrug it off. Nor did she cry. She simply stood, held at attention before Ed Rogers.

"That land is for Jesse's children," Ed said quietly.

"I know," Ginger replied. "But Osbee has to make her decision."

"Did you tell her to keep it?"

"It isn't mine to tell her. It's hers to say, now that Jesse's gone. I have reminded her that he wanted his kids to grow up there. She just thinks it's time."

Ed looked down at the piston. Ginger let go a sigh of relief. Man, did he have a way about him. She was sure she wouldn't ever have passed any class he taught.

"I don't suppose you know how to put this piston in?" he said, musing at the little metal rings that encircled it.

"No."

"Well, I have always wanted to see it. I'd like to come get Henry's Child going again. Would you allow that?"

He gazed up at her, his eyes and demeanor having noticeably softened.

"I would be very grateful."

"Good. Let's get some coffee."

He motioned to the barn door through which she had just come, and together they all walked back to the golf cart. To Ginger's relief, Lorena drove, so it was next to her that she sat, with Ed very quietly facing the other way.

"Uh, how long have you lived here?" Ginger said, trying to break the silence of the trip.

"Since I was married, thirty-seven years ago. Ed's lived here all his life."

"My family's been on this land since 1799."

Ginger leaned her head to the left, looking back at Ed. "That's when Jesse's family settled where they are."

"Yes. Jesse and I spoke a great deal about that. It was quite far there, Prince William County to the Shenandoah in those days. We thought maybe they met each other in the war, but the Smoots fought for the North and my people fought for the South."

They pulled up to the side of the house and came to a stop.

"We didn't suppose our families knew each other." Ed slid off the back of the cart and walked to Ginger's truck.

"Come. Have coffee before you go. Sure you're not hungry?"

"Thank you. Just coffee."

Ginger followed Lorena in through the side door. The hall in front of her had high ceilings and a wooden floor, the planks of which were wide and obviously original.

"The kitchen is just here." Entering through a

door, Ginger found a large, very modern kitchen. It was obviously not original except for the huge fireplace that stood on the back wall. It held within it a small fire, but as Lorena poured coffee, Ed came in and tossed two logs upon it. They cracked and popped, firing shots of joy as they came to life.

"This used to be a back parlor," Ed said. "The original kitchen is downstairs, but Lorena refuses to carry the food up the stairs when we have dinners."

Lorena guffawed. "Milk and sugar in your coffee, Ginger?"

"Just milk, please."

"The kitchen, as he calls it, is a brick cave used in olden times. Who can cook anything in darkness? Besides, his mother never had to cook in it."

"Who cooked?"

"We had a cook," Ed said, unzipping his coat. Ginger thought him very handsome as he took the cup from his wife and handed it to her.

"I was so terrified when Ed brought me home to meet his folks. This house is so huge and imposing from the outside, but when I entered, it became so much smaller. There is such grandeur built into the outside of these old mansions."

"Architecture for another era, Lorena. It was meant to be imposing."

"I never wanted to live here, but Ed inherited

and so here I was. With a cave for a kitchen."

"So, if ever I was to eat, I had to build her this kitchen. And then we rebuilt it. And rebuilt it. And—"

"Stop," Lorena said, handing him a cup. Ed mouthed to Ginger, *And rebuilt it.*

Then he smiled and Ginger grinned happily back, for his was a small smile without showing any teeth, but warm and kind. She hadn't thought he ever smiled, but there, on his face, was clearly an event that must happen often as told by the lines about his eyes and cheeks. His demeanor, though, would not lead one to believe it was true.

"Cold and imposing, but welcoming and warm on the inside. Like Edward here," Lorena said.

"That's how I thought of Jesse at first, too. Cold and imposing," Ginger said.

"He saw your name badge and the freckles like stars on your face and knew he was going to ask you out," Ed said.

Ginger nodded, chuckling. Stars on her face. Stars all over her body. Why hadn't she heard of Ed Rogers if he had heard that of her?

"That's why I asked Lorena to dance, too."

Ginger furrowed her brow and sipped her coffee.

"Have you never heard that song?" Ed asked.

Ginger shook her head, having no idea what he was talking about.

He cleared his throat a little and began to sing:

"The years creep slowly by, Lorena. The snow is on the grass again."

His voice was tenor, every note hit true, and he finished a single verse, then stopped. Ginger wished he would finish, but thought his song, like his smile, seemed not to be given easily.

"That is a beautiful song," Ginger said.

"It has several verses. A very beautiful love song. I heard a friend of mine introducing Lorena to another man at a USO dance. There she was— the woman in the song—soft brown hair, soft brown eyes. My heart beat so heavily I couldn't swallow. It took me two hours to slide in beside her. She was dancing with everybody, but I finally saw my chance, took her hand that night, and haven't left her side since."

He touched his wife's right index finger.

"And rebuilt my kitchen?" Lorena asked, raising her eyebrows.

"Again and again," he replied, smiling once more. He gazed in Ginger's direction. There was a silence then. A quiet that seemed forever. Then, as if from a great distance, he said, "I have three daughters, Virginia, but if ever I had a son, I feel so surely he would have been like Jesse. He loved as I love. I feel your wound deeply just as I feel my own."

Ginger didn't reply. She stood holding her breath in the light of his smile. There were no tears to shed. There was not a cry peeling from her empty place. There were simply two souls sharing a loss. He looked down at his coffee. Ginger did also.

"I should be going," she said, breaking the solemnity of the kitchen. "I should try to get home before Osbee puts the kids to bed."

She placed her cup on the counter. "Thank you for the coffee."

"We are so happy to have finally met you," Lorena replied, slipping her arm inside the crook of Ginger's elbow. "When Ed comes to fix the tractor, may I join him? I'd like to meet Osbee."

"Please," Ginger said. "I'll be home tomorrow, but have to work the following two days. My next day off is Sunday."

"Would afternoon be all right?" Ed asked, opening the side door for them.

"Sure. Anytime," Ginger replied, stepping out into the snowy darkness.

"Very good," he said. Following his wife, who still held Ginger by the elbow, he came to the truck and opened the door. The smell drifted out. Ginger could smell it from where she was walking, but if Ed smelled it, he made no sign.

"I had a run-in with an Amish boy last night," she stated, though no one seemed to be asking. "On my way to work I found him curled up in a ditch, drunk and freezing. He threw up in my cab as I drove him to the hospital."

"Oh, is he all right?" Lorena asked.

"Well, he left, so I suppose so."

"How is an Amish boy in West Virginia?" inquired Ed.

"According to another nurse, he's on that teenage thingy the Amish do."

"Rumspringa," Lorena offered.

"That's it!" Ginger declared, climbing into the truck. "I've been trying to find that word all day."

Ed smiled as Ginger settled into her seat. She looked at him, waiting for the door to shut. He smiled ever so slightly more.

"Thank you for letting me get the doors," he said. Gazing into his eyes, which were as bright blue in the floodlights as they had been in the kitchen, she realized this had also been a discussion he must have had with Jesse.

"It seems important to y'all." She snickered.

"It is," he replied.

"You know, I once stood beside a door in Alexandria for five minutes straight, waiting for Jesse to go in before me."

"We know," Lorena said, chuckling.

"Then I gave up and went in. It was so uncomfortable."

"But he never held it for you in Seattle," Ed said.

"Almost never," Ginger corrected. "He just couldn't get past it."

"If a man does not hold a door for a woman

down here, it reflects on his mother," Ed explained. "Or grandmother."

"Yeah. Mrs. Schaaf, the farmer's wife who lives just up the road from Smoot's? She said the same after I waited for two men to come out of a coffee shop. They were on the inside and when we came to the door, the first one opened it. It felt so weird 'cause I would have to walk by his out-stretched arm to go in, so I waited for him to come out. Mrs. Schaaf whispered in my ear, 'Go in. The other one is watching.' "

Lorena laughed. "The one holding the door for you couldn't do anything else but wait for you to enter or the man he was with would think poorly of him."

"And poorly of his grandmother," Ginger added.

"And his grandmother," Ed agreed.

"Thank you," she said. That was the proper thing to do and only then did Ed shut the door. She rolled down her window as she engaged her engine. "Please come down Sunday. Osbee would like to meet you, I'm sure."

"We'll be there," Lorena said.

Ginger shifted into reverse, backed up, and headed down the drive, the branches making now what seemed a bivouac upon the road.

She hummed the tune to *Mr. Rogers' Neighbor-hood* and the lightness she had felt since leaving the hospital lifted slightly more. Henry's Child would be running again and would have a proper home when she left.

"One down," Ginger whispered. "Beau, Regard, Penny, and Christian to go."

She flipped on her blinker and climbed back onto the asphalt.

"And Osbee," she added to herself in the mirror.

As she said it, the weight that had been sitting in the passenger seat crawled back upon her lap as if for comfort. She rolled down her window further to smell Virginia's winter night. It was heavy and dry and cold comfort.

July 22, 1861
Manassas

Dear Juliette,
The ringing of cannon is yet in my ears and the glaring flash of musket has burned my eyes. I have not slept nor can I sleep and though the dawn rises I cannot feel its warmth. I feel my brothers fall. And then—they fall again. I cannot rise.

We thought the fight would be small and on the far right flank, away from us. It came instead from our direct right and left. We stood upon a hill at the northeast corner of a house, watching the chaos of battle below rage across a stone bridge. It built and grew, a writhing, horrendous violence, and it was on all of our minds to leave as it crawled inexorably in our direction. We were losing, backing up toward our position. Yet we did not leave. We did not flinch. For there, upon his horse, was Jackson, that queersome professor of ours—so odd, so cold. The butt of so many jokes. He gazed over to us, his eyes shining blue, and though we knew he looked on us, we could feel he looked elsewhere, some far ethereal place. In that moment, the battle crashed upon us like a great wave coming upon a seawall. But it could not breach us.

I fired. All was smoke and screaming horses and men yelling and where I saw blue I fired. I could not see their faces, so as I fixed aim I said a prayer for in that sea of blue somewhere would be Zach and Jeb—the loving sons of the late Reverend, whose buttons now secured my coat. They chose Union and never did I want to see them at the end of my bayonet. A cannon boomed and I, along with my entire division, hit the ground. The great blast tore a hole in the house next to us and, unbeknownst to us at the time, the invalid lady lying on her mattress within was blown to pieces. I stood, praying as I fixed my next target—praying that it wasn't Zach or Jeb.

Then all went quiet, like the morning mist days before, and I heard my name—Samuel? When I turned, I saw a shape in the cannon smoke. I shifted to see past the cloud, and in that second a minié ball nicked my left ear and killed Avery, who stood behind me. I watched the ball enter his eye and he fell. Jackson ordered us forward then, he told us to yell like furies, and I tried to scream, turning as ordered, advancing as I was taught to do, but all that came from my open mouth was a silent wail—the keening as my brothers fell around me—one and then another.

I could not tell when it ended. The dead lay

about the field, the screaming wounded. There, in the distance, all those fine women and men who apparently had ridden out from Washington to see the battle flew away, tangling themselves in their retreating troops and random musket fire. What did they think to see? A play? A Shakespearean narrator with mighty voice, marking the hour and minute as a bloodless sword fight ensued? Fools.

My regiment is three quarters gone. One battle and we are decimated. Our president rode past us at dusk, thinking we were stragglers and speaking words to us as if to rally us. Finally someone told him it was us who held the line—the seawall that was not breached. He left us, riding toward Jackson, and as I looked, there was the moon, rising full—pale orange floating away on a glowing cloud. I stood, fixed upon its cool, soothing face, and wept, for I wish now to return home. To return and find you and live as all my friends, dead around me, will never live. I wept until the rain started, and though there was great elation at our victory all around, I could not notice anything but the moon covered by cloud, my friends' absence, and the ache I have for you.

So here I have sat the night, what is left of our brigade to be enveloped in another. Some believe it is over, but I cannot see that. The blue sea has simply receded. Though they have lost this day, I know two officers yonder. They are in earnest.

I close with great pain. I have written here to empty myself to you but I am not empty. My mind reels with that voice—Samuel? My life spared by a voice from a silent cloud of cannon smoke and because of it Avery is dead. It is a burden I do not know how yet to carry. Can you help, my love? Can I ask of you to hold this thing so I can be empty? I no longer know if such a thing can be asked of another. Nor do I think I would have you carry it—my love for you is such that I would have you free of burden. Such is duty and this duty is mine to carry. If I may instead ask of you, Juliette, your arms' embrace beneath a pale orange summer moon one night, so lightness shall have hold of me within this weighty burden. Would you? I await that night.

Your devoted,
Samuel

CHAPTER 7

ELYSIUM

When she arrived home, the Martins' Mercedes was gone.

It was nine thirty and the snow covering the fields was pale but not bright in the moonless night. Ginger turned the car off, resting her head on the steering wheel for a moment. She was exhausted after twenty-two hours awake. Spent.

The warming weather in the valley during the day had melted the snow and now, with the temperature dropping, all was freezing to ice. She thought of nothing but the slippery asphalt and Osbee leaving the farm. In her mind, she saw images of Bea and Henry and Oliver seated in the back of the truck, weeping as they waved goodbye to their grandmother. They loved her parents and were very excited when they'd come to visit. But what was true, more true than Ginger wanted to admit, was what little Oliver had observed six months earlier as he and his siblings watched her parents' airplane take off from Dulles: Only Grandma Osbee gives love. Everybody else gives gifts.

Ginger had cringed at the comment. But to her

children, Jesse's parents and her own must have seemed no more than old people bearing gifts—Santa Clauses or wise men making great journeys to deliver this doll or that game. Neither set visited more than twice a year and Jesse's hadn't been by in two. So she wasn't unsurprised when she climbed out of her truck and found three brand-new bicycles leaning together on the porch for warmth.

"Merry Christmas," she whispered, shutting her truck door. The reverberation of it caused several balls of snow to fall from the eave just to her right. She quickly dodged them and skipped up to the porch. She slipped her house key into the lock. All was dark and quiet within, except a couple of giggles from the second floor.

"Ginger?" Osbee's voice floated down the stairs.

"It's me."

"If you want, dinner is in the fridge. Just put it in there. It's probably still warm."

She shut the door. Even though she hadn't eaten in twenty-two hours, she was too tired to eat.

"Thanks, but I'm exhausted," she said and climbed the stairs. Peering into her sons' room, she found them seated together under Henry's covers reading *Harry the Dirty Dog*. It was Henry's favorite story when he was smaller and was one Oliver always picked because Henry always agreed to read it.

"Lights out," she said, entering their room and kissing them both on the head.

"Awww," Oliver whined.

"Two more pages and we're done," Henry said, scooting deeper into his covers. Oliver scrunched down next to him.

"Two more pages and lights out."

"Yeah, yeah," Oliver whispered and smiled up at her.

She rubbed his strawberry blond head and stepped back into the hall. Opening Bea's door, she found the room dark and still. Tripping over a globe and an open atlas, Ginger caught her balance on the bed.

"Mama?" Bea whispered.

"Sorry, Bea. I can't see the stuff on your floor." The light on Bea's nightstand popped on. She sat straight up in bed and gazed wide-eyed at her mother. Ginger winced in the sudden light.

"What is it, Bea?"

"A ranger from the state park came by today."

"Oh?" Ginger responded, sitting down on the little girl's bed.

"Yeah. They need to come through our field to get the trees up from the river."

Ginger looked at her daughter. Clearly she was bothered by something. "What's worrying you, Little Bea?" She asked it just as Jesse had done and, in that instant, tried to swallow the words back. She knew the rule. Only Jesse was allowed to call her Little Bea. It was Bea's rule.

"I asked him about Mr. Annanais."

Ginger frowned and cocked her head. Bea hadn't noticed Ginger's infraction. That was odd. "What about him?"

"I asked the ranger what battle happened on the other side of the river and he said there was no battle." Bea stared into her mother's eyes intensely. Then she gazed at the window.

Ginger followed her eyes, her frown deepening. "Okay," Ginger prompted.

"I said that a man in a Southern uniform came over to us yesterday and then the ranger asked if his coat had mismatching buttons."

The world stopped turning. All Ginger could hear was her breath and Bea's breath and the rising speed of her own heart.

"I didn't answer the ranger, Mama," Bea whispered.

"Mr. Annanais left, Bea," Ginger said, quietly, keeping her own rising anxiety from her voice. Was Samuel a thief? A criminal? Ginger wished she had double-checked the doors downstairs to make sure they were locked. She cursed at herself as she touched Bea's hair. "I think he's a long ways off. Does the ranger think he'll be back or something?"

"Mama?" Bea whispered again, reaching over and touching Ginger's cheek.

"It's okay, Bea."

"He's a ghost, Mama." Bea said it so quietly that Ginger was sure she hadn't heard it correctly over the terror pounding through her ears.

"A what?"

"A ghost. The ranger winked at me when he said it." Bea looked down for a minute. "I don't like that guy."

"What do you mean, a ghost?" Images of Samuel flipped through her mind—standing on the fallen tree, his dark eyes by the barn, his odd behavior on the road at Oak Flat. Manassas? But—that wasn't him at Manassas.

"I hid behind Grandma 'cause I didn't like that ranger. He told Grandma the ghost helps people sometimes in the park. Sometimes people get lost and he helps them find their way out."

Manassas . . . the musket . . . a turning profile. It wasn't him; she was sure. She smiled.

"He's just pulling your leg, Bea," Ginger said. "Maybe that's why you didn't like him. Maybe you could tell he was just joking with you in that way adults do that you don't like."

Bea was a serious person. She meant business. Anytime any adult spoke to her in a childish way, especially in a joking fashion, she didn't like them.

"He wasn't joking."

"You and I saw Mr. Annanais, Bea. And I saw him up near my work on the road."

"You saw him again?" Bea's eyebrows knit together.

Ginger giggled, trying to lighten her daughter's mood. "Yes. He was going home to Laurel Creek, hitchhiking home. He's not here and he's no ghost."

"You sure?" She was serious.

"Positive."

"Where's Laurel Creek?" Bea asked, pointing to her atlas.

Ginger shook her head with a chuckle, her heart slowing down, and her world lightened again. Having seen Samuel up in West Virginia had convinced her that he was no ghost nor was he anywhere near the farm. Thank heaven Samuel wasn't a weirdo wandering around the state park. As tired as she was, that would have just pushed her over the edge.

"I think it must be in West Virginia because that's where I was working." Ginger reached down and pulled the atlas from the floor.

"Not Virginia."

"West Virginia," Ginger repeated, flipping to the index. She found West Virginia on page fifteen and Virginia on page twelve.

"Not even on the same page," Ginger muttered, turning to page twelve.

"What?"

"The states. Look. Here's Virginia and we are—" Ginger ran her finger down Highway 81 from Winchester, southwest and then directly east. "Here. Here we are."

She batted the pages with her hand until she was on page fifteen.

"Let's see. Laurel Creek. Where is Laurel Creek?" She followed the road from Oak Flat to Franklin and then south. She did not find Laurel Creek.

"He sure went way out of his way. Oh! Here, Bea." Ginger held her finger on the tiny dot of Laurel Creek.

"That's his home?"

"Yep. That's where he said he was headed."

Bea flipped the page back. "Not on the same page."

"Nope. Page fifteen. We're page twelve. So you just don't worry, Bea. Mr. Annanais is not a ghost and he's probably home with his family, watching TV or going to bed or reading atlases with his little girl."

Bea gazed up at her mother, her eyes slits. Ginger leaned forward, placing her forehead on Bea's forehead and grinned. Bea smiled too and lay back down in bed.

"I don't like that ranger."

"Well, you know who you like and who you don't, Bea. Sometimes, though, people don't know exactly who you are, so they make mistakes. Just meeting someone can be—awkward."

"Don't like people who wink."

"All right, Bea." Ginger flicked off the light, kissed her daughter on the cheek in the darkness, stood, and headed carefully back out the door.

"Mama?"

Ginger stopped as she entered the hall.

"Only Daddy calls me Little Bea."

"I know. It . . . just popped out. Maybe because I thought you were worried and it would help you feel him and be comforted. I'm sorry."

"It's okay," she replied.

Ginger stood still as if she had been handed a gift she had waited for all her life. "I love you, Little Bea," Ginger said.

"I love you, too, Mama. And I love Daddy."

"Me, too," Ginger whispered.

Taking the handle of the door, Ginger closed it halfway and walked into the bathroom. There she slipped out of her scrubs and, as she always did, hopped in the shower to wash the ER from her body. Anyone who works in an emergency room knows that there is nowhere with more germs on the planet. She knew showering when she got home wouldn't do much to protect her from catching something that had come in the ER door, but she always felt better if she bathed after work. She put on her pajamas, which were exactly where she had left them the night before, brushed her teeth, tossed her scrubs into the hamper, turned off the light, and shuffled to her room. There she found Beau and Regard exactly where she had last seen them.

"You guys do anything today?" They both looked at her and yawned. Beau wagged his tail slightly, just so Ginger could see a little effort at happiness on her return, and then his head went back on top of his paws. Wiggling her legs past Regard, who wouldn't move an inch from where he was lying, Ginger pulled the covers to her waist. She sat.

Looking past her curtains to the night sky, she saw the world was white and cold and still. Winter's heaven was transparent, like a window looking out onto Elysium, and the stars were but shards of glass from a crystalline goblet dropped by some great hero who sat at Kronos's table. Ginger half smiled, gazing up to the great fields of the dead. She lay down and as she closed her eyes a tear formed. Within it, she saw the reflection of a star falling from the sky above. It landed silently on her pillow.

A dim orange glow emanated from little Henry's room, and as she passed by in the hallway she could hear Jesse's voice whispering to him in the rhythmic manner that meant he was reciting. Ginger tiptoed into the room and stood next to the chair where Jesse sat with Henry on his chest.

"And our ghosts have been wandering in Elysium until we have learned to love the shade. We have no objection to revisiting the light." He stopped, tilting back and forth in the rocking chair, burying his nose in little Henry's scarce hair.

"What's Elysium?" he whispered to her. Ginger shrugged, her lip curling in anticipation of the comment that would now follow her silence.

"What kind of education you get over there in the West?" Jesse chuckled, kissing Henry's head.

"What're the islets of Langerhans?" she inquired.

He laid his cheek on Henry's head and shrugged.

"What kinda education you get at that military institute?"

They smiled at each other.

"Henry Adams?" she added.

"Our son's name is Henry Adams Martin," he replied.

"No, what you were reciting?"

Jesse nodded and dropped his head lazily on the back of the chair as he looked at her.

"I reckon you never learned about sich," Jesse whispered and buried his nose again in his little boy's hair. He closed his eyes and Ginger knew, by the weight of the room, he was moving his mind, making adjustments inside himself to leave home—to leave the farm.

They were young in their military life together, as this was their first vacation home from life in Fort Lewis. Jesse had been so care-free, wandering around the barns and fields with his new son, showing him all his boyhood haunts. Now was the time to head back to North Carolina, and the army and Jesse was shifting internally to do so. She imagined this was what he always had to do when leaving his grandparents, even as a boy returning home after each summer. She quietly crossed the wooden floor and put her hand upon Jesse's head.

"Not about sich or such," she replied.

"Elysium is the afterlife. The Elysian Fields are where all heroes of virtue go." He stood up.

"Heroes of virtue also come home and help their grandfathers in the cornfields."

Jesse deposited Henry into his crib, covering the little baby up with a purple crocheted blanket. He made no remark to her little jest as he gazed out the window.

"The sky is so clear in winter," he commented.

"It is," she replied softly, walking to his side.

"I was thinking that the winter night sky is so transparent, so clear, it's like we can see Elysium."

Jesse looked down at her, his eyes so

shadowed she couldn't tell if they were open or closed.

He said, "Tonight, I think the stars look like glass broken on the table of Kronos."

"Who's Kronos?"

"The king of Elysium."

She could see her husband smile. He pulled her into his arms, facing her forward to the window as he slid in behind her.

"The sky appears just so on the cold, moonless nights everywhere in the world," he whispered in her ear.

"Everywhere? How do you know?"

"Because the Elysian Fields roll across the sky and the sky rolls everywhere."

"I see," Ginger said, shaking her head. "Can we go to bed or was there further edification for me tonight?"

"Shh. Listen. Wherever I am deployed, Ginger, remember—I send to you love across Kronos's table."

His head lay upon her left shoulder now and she turned, taking the full of him into her arms. "Is that how the glass was broken up there on his table? Someone sending love without a 'Please pass this' to the next person seated at the table?" she asked, gazing up into his shadowed face.

"I said that's what it looks like to me."

She kissed his neck quickly, sliding out of

his arms and grabbing his hand. "Come on. Time for bed."

"Is everything all right, daughter?" Grandpa Henry called from downstairs.

"What are you doing up?" Ginger asked.

"He wanted a piece of your apple pie." Osbee's reply came from the direction of their bedroom.

"Doesn't anyone sleep in this house?" Ginger inquired, shoving Jesse into their room. "Good night to both of you." Before either Henry or Osbee could answer, Ginger shut the door.

"In bed," she ordered, and obediently Jesse climbed in. Shuffling in the darkness around to the other side, Ginger pulled the covers down and crawled beneath them. The bedsheets were cold.

"If you had gone to bed, the covers would be warmer," she noted with a shiver.

"Come over here," he said, his arm slithering through the blankets and wrapping around her waist. He pulled her beneath him, leaning his face closer for a kiss.

"We're going home to Fort Bragg and then we'll be back here next vacation. And this Kronos person and his table can just do without you 'cause that corn is gonna come up and Grandpa Henry will be waiting for help." She waited.

"Okay," he replied.

"Fine," she said, turning to face him. She found him hovering over her, staring at her through the shadows.

"I will always return here," he said softly.

She touched his cheek.

"To my orchard," she whispered. She couldn't hear it, but she knew he was laughing quietly as he kissed her neck, for his body gently quaked in her arms.

"And Henry," she added.

"And Henry and your orchard and the corn," he agreed, and then she kissed him.

There was no alarm. There was the smell of bacon and a door opening. It was just light outside and without so much as a courtesy to Regard, Ginger flung the covers off and jumped out of bed.

"Wait!" she yelled.

"We're gonna miss the bus," Bea called up the stairs.

"I'm coming," Ginger replied, shimmying into a pair of jeans and sliding a sweatshirt over her head. Quickly, she grabbed a pair of socks and stuck her feet into them as she headed down the stairs.

"Don't kill yourself, Ginger, my dear," Osbee said. The old woman appeared at the bottom of the stairs holding Jesse's coat and her rubber boots.

"Why didn't you guys wake me up?" she asked, pulling on her boots.

"You didn't sleep at all yesterday," Osbee replied, offering the coat.

"Yeah, but we're together on this. *We* have to walk to the bus." Ginger put the coat on and stepped outside. Though she was shocked by the cold, having just flung herself out of bed, Ginger had a sense that it had warmed up a bit from yesterday. Henry and Oliver were waiting for her on the porch, looking at their bikes. Bea was already down the drive.

"Wait, Bea!" Ginger called and, motioning to her sons, skipped down the front steps. They had to walk briskly to catch up to her daughter.

"You see my bike, Mama?" Oliver asked, his backpack bobbing up and down as he trotted to keep up.

"I did."

"Grandma and Grandpa brought each of us one. Mine and Bea's have the training wheels."

"I saw that."

"I don't need training wheels," Bea announced over her shoulder.

"Yeah, you will," Henry said, adjusting Oliver's backpack a little so it would stop bouncing so much.

"Will not," Bea replied.

"We'll see when the snow clears a little more," Ginger said. "Maybe she'll need them. Maybe she won't."

"I need mine," Oliver said, taking his mother's hand.

"Yes, you do. So, what's your favorite part of *Harry the Dirty Dog?*" Ginger asked, looking down at her youngest. She knew, of course, that Oliver's favorite part of that story was lying in bed with his brother, having it read to him.

"When he slides down the coal chute," Oliver said.

"That's a good part."

"I like that his name is Harry," Henry said. "Harry can be my name, too."

"Henry is not Harry," Bea said.

"It is, too. Daddy said King Henry was known as King Harry, too."

"But Henry's your name and you are not a king," Bea replied.

"But I can be called Harry just like you're Bea and Mama's Ginger."

"Oh." Bea stopped.

As they passed her, Ginger looked back. Her daughter's eyes were closed.

" 'The gentler gamester is the soonest winner,' " she said and, opening her eyes, began to walk again.

"Yep," Henry said.

Ginger shook her head and gazed up, wondering if Jesse was sitting at Kronos's table laughing at all this. Most kids could quote *Harry the Dirty Dog* or some other children's story at eight years old. Ginger supposed only a child of Jesse

146

Martin's could quote *Henry V* with any accuracy. At that thought Ginger gazed down to Oliver.

"You know anything from *Henry V*, Oliver?" she asked.

Oliver shrugged.

Henry snickered and prompted his brother. "The dolphin king."

"Yeah, yeah." Oliver grinned. He stopped and lifted his right fist to the sky. " 'But tell the Dolphin I will keep my state, be like a king and show my sail of greatness when I do rouse me in my throne of France.' "

Oliver beamed up at her as he took his mother's hand once more. Bea skipped by, giggling. Watching it all in wonder, Ginger smiled as her daughter went past them, for she hadn't heard a giggle from Bea in over a year. Now Oliver could quote Shakespeare at five if prompted by his older brother. Perhaps things were settling back to an odd shape of normal. There was a hope.

"The bus!" Bea yelled and took off running. Henry was right on her heels and Oliver, shaking free of his mother's hand, brought up the rear.

"Wait up!" he whined.

Ginger stopped where she was and watched them board the bus. Henry stopped at the door, letting Bea go in before him. That was just as Jesse had taught him to do. Then up came Oliver, and Henry helped his little brother reach the bottom step of the bus. That was just as she had taught him to do. Henry smiled broadly and waved at her as he climbed aboard. She waved back. The bus doors closed behind him and she thought to herself how lucky she was to have them all.

Ginger didn't move as the bus pulled away. It headed down the road and when it had nearly disappeared over the rise, she waited for the heaviness to return as it had done for a year and nine months. Today, it did not. All that filled her mind now was Oliver and his Shakespearean quote. She chuckled. She lifted her right fist to heaven.

" 'But tell the Dolphin I will keep my state, be like a king and show my sail of greatness when I do rouse me in my throne of France,' " she said. A crow cawed in reply from a tree far off in a field on the Creeds' farm.

"The word is not 'Dolphin.' It is 'Dauphin,' " a voice said behind her.

Spinning on her heel, Ginger turned and at the sight of him stumbled back, tripping in the ditch and hitting her head against the Creeds' fence. Her heart came to a full and complete stop.

"Good morning, Virginia Moon," Samuel said softly.

CHAPTER 8

HEAVEN AND EARTH

Samuel stood still, cap in hand, his uniform, hair, and bedroll exactly as it had been the last time she had seen him. Her mind floated inside her skull, having no direction or anchor, completely disconnected from the cold and morning light as she looked at him. Confused electrical signals flashed across her gray cells, trying to make sense of him. Why had he come back? How? Was he a crazy man? A weirdo? She tried to believe something of him. But there was neither belief nor sense. There was only the fear of a strange man returning to her family.

"Virginia Moon?" His eyes grew narrow with a look of sincere concern.

Without a thought, she slid toward Smoot's farm, her back firmly planted on the Creeds' fence.

"What is it?" he asked.

Ginger shook her head, moving sideways up the fence as if climbing a horizontal ladder. She needed to get away from him, unsure what he wanted or why he was back.

"Are you well, Virginia Moon?" Samuel was

sidestepping, his face never turning to look where he was going, his eyes fixed upon her. They were soft and brown just as they had been when he stood upon the fallen tree.

A scream wound its way up her trachea, climbing into her throat. She shook her head again.

"You've hit your head. Let me help." He reached out his hand.

"No!" Ginger screamed, and in that second her floating mind found anchor in her feet, which then realized it was time to move, and fast. Cold from standing in the water of the ditch, they jumped from the sinking mud, racing next to the fence toward the house.

The house. So far in the distance. So white. So warm. Was she coming any closer to it? She could hear her own scream as if it were someone else's terror far away. Running now, she was slow, the weight of her own muddy feet hindering her speed. She wasn't sure she was even moving.

Suddenly, Samuel was at her side and his nearness caused her to trip over her own heavy feet and fall down into the muddy snow.

"Virginia, you are afraid." His voice was gentle, nearly a whisper.

"Going home." She breathed, struggling forward on her hands and knees, the snow and mud seeping into her jeans and jacket. Her eyes gazed desperately at her white house on the little rise ahead.

"I have been trying. There is a bridge now across Laurel Creek and I have endeavored to cross it twice. I enter but find myself exiting through your bridge in the orchard."

Ginger didn't look at him. She tried not to see him, tried to focus only on her white home up ahead. But inexorably her eyes were drawn to his feet, which were planted right next to her; they were not sinking, but simply standing upon the snowy mud. She froze, staring at his tattered leather boots. Glancing back over his path, she found not one of his footprints anywhere in the mud and snow.

"How?" she whispered.

"I want to go home, but something draws me back here. Are you calling me, Virginia Moon?"

"Ginger!" A hand touched her shoulder.

"No!" she screamed and, flipping over in the ditch, found Eloise Schaaf standing over her. Ginger blinked, closing her eyes tightly and opening them again. The silhouette of Eloise Schaaf bent toward her. Shuddering, Ginger leaned forward, away from the fence, looking up and down the road. Samuel was nowhere to be seen. There was only Eloise Schaaf's pale yellow Ford truck stopped next to the ditch and Eloise herself hovering overhead.

"Ginger. Are you okay?"

"I—I—"

"Come here." Taking Ginger by the hand, Eloise

lifted her from the snowy mud and together they walked up onto the asphalt. Reticently, Ginger looked over the truck. Samuel wasn't there, either.

"Wh-what happened?"

"You hit your head?" Eloise asked.

"My head?"

"You were facedown in the mud. Come on. I'll take you home."

Ginger turned around and found she stood exactly where she had been when she waved good-bye to Henry.

"I ran." She coughed, holding her right temple as Eloise led her around the bed of the truck to the passenger side. Opening the door, she helped her in. The car was very warm, as the heater was on full.

"I'm muddy," Ginger said, trying to climb back out.

"It's all right. We'll clean it up when we get you home." Eloise shut the door and trotted around the front of the truck. Though of the same age as Osbee, Mrs. Schaaf appeared to be older. Her hair was short and gray-white in color and she had it neatly set by a beautician every two weeks. Eloise looked like a grandma. That was very comforting at the moment.

"I saw you slide in the mud," Eloise said as she climbed into the cab of her truck. "You hit your head? It looked like it but I couldn't tell. I was still coming around the corner."

Ginger held her temple. Engaging the engine, they drove toward Smoot's farm.

"You saw me fall?"

"Don't you remember?"

"Did you see anyone else, Eloise?" She scanned the Creeds' field and their dark gray house to the left and then the Schaafs' trees to the right, looking for Samuel.

"No. Just you. You okay?"

Ginger shook her head. "I don't know."

Pulling up the gravel drive, Ginger saw Osbee standing on the porch. Eloise stopped the truck and opened her door.

"Osbee, help me with Ginger."

"I think I'm all right," Ginger said quietly, opening her own door and sliding out.

"What happened?" Osbee exclaimed. "You're muddy."

"I fell."

"She hit her head on the fence," Eloise added. Carefully, Ginger climbed the steps of the porch as she held on to Osbee's hand. Once inside the house, they headed up to the second floor.

"Can you make it?" Osbee asked, following her.

"Yeah. I need to get out of these muddy things." Stepping into the bathroom, she flicked on the light and looked in the mirror. She pulled her muddy brown hair up, and just where her ginger-colored roots were growing back in over her right eye, she found a small gash and a growing knot.

"Here," Osbee said, leaning into the small bathroom with a fresh pair of jeans, a clean sweat-shirt, and neatly folded underwear.

"I'm okay. Just a lump. I think I'll take a shower."

"Eloise and I will wait."

Letting go of her hair, Ginger gazed over to Osbee. There was a red ribbon on the end of her braid.

"Wait? Wait for what?"

"We have an appointment in Winchester. But we'll wait to see how you are coming out of the shower. Eloise said you took quite a spill."

"*We* as in you and Eloise or *we* as in *you* have an appointment and Eloise is driving you to it?" Ginger's stomach turned. She felt sick.

"Take your shower." Osbee smiled brightly and shut the door.

Ginger stood motionless for a minute, wondering if her nausea was from the bump on her head or from Osbee's appointment. She shivered a little, which brought her mind back to her muddy state. Stripping out of her clothes, she climbed into the heat of the shower. It burned her extremities as warm water always does on cold skin and as she washed she thought of Samuel on the road. Perhaps he wasn't really there. Perhaps she had slid, hit her head, and then passed out. He could merely have been a dream or something in her unconscious state. Did she not run? She remembered running, but when Eloise pulled her from the ditch, it was quite clear she hadn't moved an inch closer to the house than where she had been when she waved good-bye to Henry.

By the time she opened the bathroom door, freeing the steam to float away like a warm, friendly spirit, she was absolutely convinced Samuel was just a dream—a thought from Bea's conversation left unprocessed by her sleep the night before.

"How you feeling?" Osbee asked, standing at the top of the stairs to the right.

Ginger rubbed her head. "Okay."

"Good. Go back to bed." Osbee pointed to the bedroom. "You were up all day yesterday and you probably tripped because you're still tired."

"I think I sh—"

"Bed." Osbee pointed again.

"What's your appointment?" Ginger asked as she obediently made her way to her bedroom.

"Nothing for you to concern yourself with. There are biscuits in foil on the stove. Coffee's all set to brew. Just press the button when you get up."

Ginger climbed into bed and as soon as she lay down Osbee drew the covers up under her chin.

"Tucking me in?" Ginger smiled.

"Someone needs to take care of you. You don't do it yourself, you know."

"You always say that."

"It's always true." Osbee kissed the bump on

Ginger's forehead. "All better?" she asked, smiling.

Ginger nodded.

"Good. Sleep well." With that, Osbee left the room, pulling the door behind her so that it was just slightly ajar.

Ginger closed her eyes, listening to the two women talk quietly as they moved around the house. The front door opened.

"No!" Osbee yelled. "Out!"

"Come here, Beau!" Ginger called.

"He's an outside dog," Osbee yelled up the stairs. The door burst open and in came Beau.

"Have a good appointment," Ginger said, taking her hand from beneath her covers and scratching the dog's head.

"Lie down," she whispered, and as Beau slid to the ground next to the bed the front door closed. Ginger could hear more muffled conversation and laughter. The car doors shut and the engine turned on. The wheels crunched as they backed down the drive. All was quiet.

Her eyes closed, her breath even, Ginger moved Osbee's red ribbon across her mind.

Something draws me back here.

Ginger's eyes popped open.

There is a bridge now across Laurel Creek and I have endeavored to cross it twice. I enter but find myself exiting through your bridge in the orchard.

She sat up. He was a dream. She was certain of

it. Gazing out her window, she looked over in the direction of her orchard. There was the covered bridge—a covered bridge over a dried-up stream in the middle of a hairpin curve of the Shenandoah.

"What use was that?" she whispered, and then shuddered.

Picking up the phone next to her bed, she dialed home. Her clock read eight thirty a.m. It was five thirty a.m. on the West Coast. The line picked up.

"Hello?"

"Mom?"

"Ginger?"

"Hey, sorry for calling so early."

"Tim! It's Ginger!"

"No. Don't wake Dad."

"We're up, honey. We're taking inventory."

Another line picked up. "Ginny Moon," her dad said, his voice quiet as it always was. "It's early there. You just get off work?"

"No. Day off."

"Good, good. What's up?"

"Um . . . I have a question."

"You need something?" her mother asked.

"It's kind of a crazy question."

"Oh, our favorite kind." Her parents laughed together.

"Hypothetically speaking. *Hypothetically.*" Ginger rubbed the knot on her forehead. Just a dream. She looked out at the bridge.

"Hypo-theti-cally," her father repeated.

"How would you get rid of a ghost?" She shut her eyes tightly, cringing at her own words. Ridiculous. The line was silent. Eight thirty-one a.m. Eight thirty-two a.m.

"Monica, baby?" Her father's quiet voice sounded like he was speaking through a megaphone after such silence.

"Yes, Tim?" her mother replied.

"Did our most practical, pragmatic, no-nonsense daughter just ask us how to get rid of a ghost? Did I hear that right?"

"I think so. Did we hear you right?"

Ginger grimaced at her bedcovers. She offered no answer.

"Ginny?"

"Yes." A one-word reply was all she'd give them. Somehow, this felt as if she were back in dance class, submitting to their view of the world.

Her father chuckled.

"You have a ghost, Ginger?" her mother asked.

"Hypo-theti-cally," her father whispered through his gentle laughter.

"I don't know."

"Tim, shh. What makes you think you do?"

Ginger thought of what made her think she did. If she said any of it, she'd feel like an idiot. "Do either of you know how to get rid of a ghost? Surely you have an answer amidst all that spiritual stuff in your store."

"The answer depends on the ghost," her father said. "Hypothetically speaking, is it a nice ghost or a mean ghost?"

"Nice." The answer popped out of her mouth so fast, she tripped over her own tongue. That's all she was going to say. One word.

"Didn't need to think about that answer, Monica, baby," Tim said.

"Well, that's a relief, Ginger."

"The simple answer, the one that might be most helpful, is simply to tell the ghost to step into the light," her father said.

The light. How many times had she heard that statement? Not only from her parents, but in many a bad movie.

"What light?" she asked.

"The light of eternity, Ginny. The Universal Mother. The Creatrix. The Alpha and Omega."

"The ghost sees it," her mother said, interrupting her father. "You can't see it and neither can I, so I can't explain it to you. Just tell the ghost to look for the light and then head into it."

"That's all?"

"Well, it should be all. How are the kids?"

Ginger gazed up at the ceiling. Ghosts to children. Her parents' way of looking at things could move fast like that. Their stream of consciousness ran ethereal and ephemeral at the same time. There was no separation. Heaven wasn't elsewhere. God wasn't elsewhere. To them, they were walking inside of God and God was walking inside of them.

"Good. They were quoting Shakespeare on the way to the bus stop this morning. Even Oliver. I didn't really know how much he had learned before Jesse . . ." Ginger trailed off.

She hadn't really talked to her parents about Jesse since the funeral. The memory of the funeral simply made her homesick. She'd rather speak of anything but that cold gray day. Cold and gray just as it was this day.

Ginger stood, the triangle of the American flag held tightly to her chest with her right arm and little Oliver, just three and a half years old, sleeping on her left shoulder. The flowers on all the arrangements fluttered in bright colors like butterflies suspended in a wire mesh, unable to light and fly away. Osbee held Henry, who still sniffled, in her right hand and Bea, utterly quiet, in her left. The Martins walked away in the distance, speaking with the army chaplain who had given the service. The grave was covered. The sky was gray. Seagulls cried overhead.

Ginger looked over at Osbee, who met her eyes. She gazed back to the Martins, wearing black like crows waiting to swoop down and steal the last of the provender from the starving.

"Ginny Moon." Ginger's father was at her side on the left. Crushing pain seized her body at the sound of his voice.

"We have to let him go now," he said. "We have to go now."

Ginger nodded. Gazing down, she found her father's hand out and in it were two small abalone shells.

"Great men are remembered," her father said, walking over to Henry and Bea. "Next time you come to Seattle, we'll take you to a great Native American chief's grave. A great leader. His name is Chief Sealth or, as the white people call him, Chief Seattle."

"Like the city?" Henry asked.

"They named the city after him. I brought this picture of his grave. Look."

Ginger gazed down at the picture that her father held out to Henry and Bea. A medium-sized white stone obelisk stood in the middle of a cemetery next to a small white church. It was an unassuming headstone and could be missed. It could have been anyone's grave but for the huge wooden catamaran suspended over it. Colorful paintings adorned its sides and all about the headstone were seashells and candles and other mementos left by various pilgrims. Ginger shut her eyes, remembering the peaceful quiet of Seattle's grave and the misty Puget Sound all around. Where she stood now, she could hear traffic and planes. She could hear the Martins talking. There was no lapping water. There was no peaceful silence.

"What are those?" Henry asked.

"Those are canoes his people put over him. It was how his people marked where he was buried. Maybe where Seattle is, he needs the canoes."

"He needs canoes in heaven?" Henry asked.

"Never know. See all those seashells?"

Ginger felt her mother's arm wrapping around her waist. She opened her eyes.

"Yeah."

"People leave those for him. They put things inside for him. See. I've brought some so we can leave these for your daddy."

"I don't have anything to put in it," Henry said, his voice tight with sudden worry. Bea hadn't moved. She didn't say a word.

"It's okay. I brought water from the place where Chief Seattle is buried. From right there." Her father pointed to the picture.

"We'll put this water in the shells for your daddy, okay? So he can know we remember him as a great man."

Henry nodded and took a shell. Her father offered a shell to Bea but she didn't take it. She didn't move. Glancing over, Ginger found her dad was offering her the shell. She took it from her father as she handed her mother the flag and stepped to Jesse's grave. She started to cry, tilting her head on Oliver's little back as she bent down. Together, she and Henry knelt on the grass, setting the shells next to the place where Jesse's headstone would be. Her father came over, opened a small glass bottle, and handed it to Henry.

"Just half, so your mother can fill the other shell for Bea."

Ginger felt as if she could die. Just lie down right there next to him and die. There was nothing left inside and nothing hurt so entirely. She knelt, watching her son pour water into the seashell.

Lie right here. She touched the edge of the dirt her husband was buried under and as she reached for the glass bottle from Henry she felt a tap on her shoulder. Holding her breath, Ginger looked up and found Bea standing next to her, just as she hoped she would be.

"That's my shell," Bea said. Ginger nodded and scooted over as she offered the bottle of water to Bea. Her daughter didn't take it.

"Daddy might mistake that for Lethe river water."

Cocking her head, Ginger glanced up at her daughter.

"What's that mean, Bea?" Ginger's mother asked.

Bea didn't answer. Instead, she knelt down and looked into the empty shell. "Looks like rainbows in there," Bea said.

"It does," Ginger's father replied.

Ginger said nothing. She wept softly.

Bea looked up at her mother and back to the shell. Then she reached up with her index finger, took a tear from Ginger's cheek, and dropped it in the shell.

"That belongs to Daddy," she whispered.

"Ginny Moon, where did you go?" her father called.

"Sorry. Sorry. I'm here."

"Not to worry," her mother said. "I'm glad the kids are remembering their father. What a thing to have Shakespeare given to you for memory."

"Yes," Ginger agreed. She watched Oliver standing with his hand raised to heaven and smiled.

"How's inventory going?" she asked, changing the subject.

"Good, we think. We'll be done soon anyway. Then it's just balancing it against the books."

"Wish I was there to help. I love inventory." She did, too. Inventory meant finding all the little things hidden, buried, and forgotten in the crevices of the shop.

"You always did. Maybe next year you'll be here and the kids can help."

Ginger rubbed the knot on her head, feeling happy at the thought of having Henry, Oliver, and Bea help take inventory and then incredibly sad at not having Osbee around.

"Maybe," she said. "Better let you get back to it."

"Okay," her mother said. "If you're sure."

"I'm good."

"Okay, then," her mother said.

"And, Ginny Moon?"

"Yeah, Pop?"

" 'There are more things in heaven and earth, Horatio, than are dreamt of in your philosophy.' "

"Thanks for that, Father." She shook her head as her father laughed his quiet laugh.

"Tell the ghost to step into the light."

"Yes, Father."

"I think our daughter is done with us again, Monica, baby. I love you, Ginny Moon."

"Love you guys, too."

"You will always be our Ginger Moon," her mother said.

"Bye, Mom."

"Bye, honey."

Ginger hung up and looked at the phone. "Step into the light," she said. "Pu-*lease*."

She chuckled at the statement. What was she living—a B-rated movie?

Movement outside her window caught the edge of her eye and when she turned to look at it a horrendous tingle seized her spine and shook her bones loose. Samuel stood on this side of the covered bridge, gazing about from left to right, from front to back, as if he had lost something. Then he stopped and lifted his head. He looked straight at her.

"Shit."

November 21, 1861
Shenandoah

Dear Juliette,
Jackson is now in command of the Shenandoah Valley and we have been marching for months. Several of us have decided the Union Army is composed not of men but of inanimate objects. We seem, as a unit, to be preoccupied with them. Or shall I say, Jackson is preoccupied with them. His aim is our aim.

In October, we headed out of Winchester to Canal Number 5 on the Potomac. Our aim was to destroy it or at least cause a bit of havoc in the area. Our purpose is not clear exactly, but it seems we are to endeavor to disrupt transportation lines and thus supply lines. So we waged war on Canal Number 5 of the C&O. It had been very warm for October, but the water was beyond cold and as the Union regiment on the other side of the river shot haphazardly at us, we worked on dismantling the dam. Only one of us was hit the first day. The second day brought another Union detail to the opposite bank. They had better aim and so we returned to Winchester, having achieved what we had set out to do.

As we marched, I saw farm after farm with none but women and children bringing in the harvest. The large plantations away to the east have slaves. Their masters are yet at home. No slaves have the small farms here in the west and the men are on the march with us or in other divisions. If the field was being worked close to the road, I would help set a shock of corn or toss a bale of hay into a cart as I passed. I sincerely feel winter will take not a few from these poor farmers' wives. When her man returns, he will find less waiting for him in children as well as crop.

Now I sit here, the chill on my spine not of excitement at movement, but rather at the cold of November creeping through my coat. There is little wind and a clear sky and the fire in front of me is bright though its warmth seems far away. I have not written you, for which I humbly beg your pardon. Since Manassas, I have had little clarity on what to write. I no longer wish to give to you so I may be empty. Your letters are sweet and I know you wish me to share, as a burden shared is less weight. So you have said. But, Juliette, I am hesitant to lean on you; it seems unjust. You are all brightness and possibility. You are what can be. You are the world that was for me before I crossed Laurel Creek, before the bird whistled to me, before the voice called to me. I wish you to remain as such, so that I may return to you, to the place I left before war when my heart and soul were free of a deathly weight. I was clean, never having watched the possibility of what can be for another man blown away from him in the flash of a musket. Never having taken from another the fullness of time.

Can you see? My weight. How can I write to you without it pouring from my hand into the pen and scratching scars into the peace of you. I remember what it was to ponder our life together—our farm, our children, our future. I shall write again, but not until I can hold my weight myself. I love you, Juliette. I hold you here with me, close my eyes, and flow in your peace. One day, I shall be with you, falling like the jar of clay that I am, letting you wash over me and be filled.

Your devoted,
Samuel

CHAPTER 9

WINTER'S LIGHT

Ginger quickly lay down in bed, squeezing her eyes shut as she pulled the covers under her chin. He was out there, having followed her back to the house. He was a stranger—a weird man who had come across the water and was somehow now obsessed with the farm or the bridge or—or— She dared not think it. She was hurting and lonely and the last thing she needed was a crazy man obsessed with her. Kindness was what was called for in the South, but her Seattle sensibilities had warned her time and time again that not everyone deserved kindness. The world was full of creeps.

"Virginia Moon?"

Ginger shuddered. He was outside on the porch. That was the direction from which his voice had come.

Her eyes popped open. Had Osbee locked all the doors? Where was Beau? Why wasn't he barking? She looked down and the dog was gone. When had he left?

"Virginia, I need to speak with you."

Ginger stared at her bedroom door. It was open.

If he gained access to the house, he could easily enter her room. She should call the police. Sitting up, she searched the covers for the phone. She needed to call, but she needed to shut and lock her door. Unable to decide which need was greater, Ginger flung her covers off and jumped out of bed. The telephone, which had been buried in the bedspread, flew across the room. As it hit her dresser, the back of it popped open and the batteries tumbled out. Two of them rolled under her dresser.

"Shit," she hissed, racing across the floor. She slammed the door and turned the lock. Her heart pounded in her chest. Her palms and feet were sweaty as she knelt down on the wooden floor, peering beneath her dresser. She found one battery had rolled all the way to the wall. Where was Beau? What if Samuel had killed him? Reaching her hand underneath the dresser, Ginger grappled with the battery. Her fingertips touched it slightly and it rolled right.

"Crap." She reached again but it was now in the center and beyond her grasp. She knelt back onto her knees and stood up to move the dresser.

"Apologies, Virginia."

Ginger spun around and found Samuel standing right in front of her. His cap, coat, and bedroll were gone. His white shirt was soiled at the neck and his eyes were gentle, softly gazing into her just like the day she had first seen him. She shook her head, staring from him to the door, which was yet fast locked.

"I normally would not come into a lady's room."

"Get out!" Ginger yelled, leaning back on her dresser and sliding across it toward the door.

"Please, do not be frightened. I need to speak with you and you will not come to me."

"I don't want to talk to you! Get out!"

"I do not think it is a choice at this time whether or not to speak with me, Virginia. You draw me here."

With her back to the wall, she reached for the door. She unlocked it. "I—I don't draw you here," she whispered.

"You do. I cannot cross Laurel Creek but through the bridge and when I enter—"

Ginger flung open the door and bolted out into the hall.

"I keep returning to your orchard."

"Leave me alone!" Ginger yelled over her shoulder as she stumbled down the stairs.

"I do not mean to frighten." He was at her heels, just behind. Where the steps creaked beneath her feet, his made no sound. "Please stop and listen."

Ginger reached the bottom and held her hand out to the front door. She found it locked. Just as quickly Samuel was in front of her, between the staircase and freedom.

"Beau!" Ginger screamed, backing toward the kitchen, her eyes fixed upon Samuel's. A tiny jingle behind her brought her gaze over her shoulder. There the dog stood at attention, his head cocked and ears pulled forward. Ginger stopped and stared at him. He neither barked nor growled nor came barreling toward Samuel as he would have done with any other stranger. He simply stood there, his eyes shifting between her face and the man at her back.

"Do not be frightened, Virginia Moon," Samuel said softly in her ear.

Beau wagged his tail.

"Please leave." Ginger breathed, her head light as her heartbeat surged in her ears. "Please leave me be."

"Why do I return here?" he asked. "I cannot leave until you tell me why you are calling me here."

What was it her father had said? What had her mother told her? It was not possible.

Beau yawned and trotted back into the kitchen.

"Step into the light," Ginger whispered, shutting her eyes as she said it. This was not real.

"What light?"

What light was it? What did her father say?

"I can't see it, Samuel. But you can. You know —the light. Step into the light."

"What are you talking about?"

"The Alpha and Omega."

"Virginia Moon, open your eyes, please."

"The Creatrix."

"Please look at me."

Ginger took a deep breath and opened her eyes.

Samuel stood in front of her with his arms crossed before his chest and his brows drawn together. Leaning as he did slightly toward her, he looked like any other living man. He must be a living man.

"What are you talking about?" he asked quietly.

"The Universal Mother?"

He shook his head, curling his lip. "What does that mean?"

"I don't know." She shrugged and tottered a little to the left. She needed air. This was not happening.

"Maybe you should sit down." He motioned her to the couch.

Ginger let go of her breath and backed toward the sofa. Slowly she seated herself as Samuel lowered himself to the chair next to her. Sitting on the edge of the couch, Ginger kept her back straight and her hands clasped tightly together upon her lap, just in case she needed to make a run for Beau and the kitchen. She watched the entwined fingers of her right hand turn a curious shade of purple.

"Breathe," Samuel said.

Ginger was breathing. Her rib cage ached from the speedy cadence of her shallow breath.

"Now. Let's start again."

"Step into the light," Ginger repeated.

"Virginia, the only light I see is the one outside and I was in it until you made me come in here to speak with you. If you wish me outside, then please join me. We need to speak together."

"You cannot see the light?" Ginger glanced sideways at him.

He leaned back in the chair and shook his head helplessly. "Why do you keep saying that?"

"My father said that is what I should tell you."

"You spoke with your father concerning me?" Samuel rested his head on his fist as he looked at her.

"Well, not about you."

"Not about me," he repeated.

"Not exactly."

"What exactly was the conversation, then?"

"You—you're—" Ginger couldn't say it. She couldn't breathe. She couldn't swallow.

"I am what?" Samuel prompted.

"I—I think you're—" She gulped for air.

"Yes? You think I am what?"

"Dead." She coughed.

"I am dead?"

Ginger nodded quickly and just as quickly she added, "You need to step into the light."

"I am hardly dead, Virginia."

"I think you are."

"Why?"

Ginger gazed at him. Why did she think so? "My doors are locked and you're inside the house."

"Yes."

Ginger frowned. "You didn't come through a window, did you?" Maybe he had. This was a hopeful thought.

"No. I came through the house into your room."

"H-how did you come into the house if not through a door or window?"

Samuel thought a moment and then smiled at her. "I willed myself through the house to your room. No, wait. That is not quite right. I think I did not so much will myself as follow your will. You are calling me."

Ginger rubbed her forehead and looked at the kitchen door. She needed help. "Beau?"

The dog's collar jingled as he came into the room.

"I have no body, so I can will myself places. Often, I get lost in time, but mostly I can get to where I wish to be."

"Come here, boy." The dog walked over, eyed the ghost sideways as he passed, and then seated himself next to Ginger's leg. She looked at Samuel. "You have no body?"

"No. I have been willing myself across Laurel Creek, as I have mentioned, but alas keep ending up back here. I think your call to me is stronger than my will."

"Samuel, why don't you have a body?"

"Because I left it long ago."

"That means you're dead," Ginger said, patting

Beau on the head. The dog at least was real.

"I am right here speaking with you, Virginia. Unless you have gone mad, I am yet here. Not dead."

"But you're not alive."

"I am here."

"You're a ghost."

Samuel closed his eyes and leaned his head back in the chair. The house was quiet with nothing but Beau's calm breath and Ginger's racing heart sounding in her ears. She gazed at Samuel, wondering if she should say something more. He opened his eyes as she was about to open her mouth.

"I would say I am spirit. Ghosts are those things that live in stories told over fires to frighten children. I do not wish to be frightening."

"You cannot see the light?" Ginger asked.

"Where does your father live?" he inquired, his voice clearly exasperated.

"Why?"

"So I can ask him why his advice to his daughter was such that she would say a thing over and over again and not know truly what it was she was meaning." Samuel chuckled and sat forward.

Ginger didn't. She cringed and leaned back and wished her father was sitting next to her right now.

"Where does your father live?"

"I'm not telling you."

"If I knew where your father was and what he

looked like, it would take me time, but I could get there. I am almost tempted just so he can explain to me the advice he gives his daughter. I would not give such to mine."

Ginger thought for a moment. Jesse's death had left her feeling as if she were spirit—as if she had died. Much of the time, she moved through the world performing the tasks of her life in an automatic way. She wasn't living anymore. She was existing. Now she sat across from a ghost—a soldier like her husband, but dead over a hundred years. Perhaps she was crazy. Maybe she had lost her mind. If she was in a clinical situation and told herself as a nurse what she was experiencing at this very moment, she would surely think she needed a little psychological help. That thought brought on another. Perhaps this was more of a nurse kind of moment and less of a spiritual one. Nurses ask questions.

"I see. So, what exact advice would you give your daughter if she was confronted with a gho— a spirit?"

Samuel smiled softly. "I would tell her to ask why he was there with her."

"What would be his reply, do you think?"

"That he did not know, but he cannot make his way home because she draws him to her."

"What does that mean exactly?"

"That he was finally free to cross the Shenandoah and found her weeping in the snow.

That he made his way down the road and found her listening to her child by a barn. That he almost found the way to Laurel Creek and she stopped on the icy road to help a boy."

"You stopped me. Not the boy."

"I was stopped from my path at the moment you were there and in that moment I found the boy. Had you not been there, I would have made it home."

"And the boy?"

"Did not notice him on my path. And every time I cross Laurel Creek—"

"You end up back here." She finished his sentence.

Samuel nodded and sat back in the chair. Ginger scratched Beau's head, thinking. There was no light. So now what?

"Maybe I should call my dad again."

"Why?"

"Well, if it isn't the light you need to see, maybe it's something else."

"Can we just endeavor to understand what it is first together without him? He seems not to truly know what it is we are addressing here."

"He's very knowledgeable in spiritual matters."

Samuel shrugged and shook his head. "I am not convinced of that."

Ginger smirked. Neither was she. "Okay, I won't call my father. So . . . now what?" she asked.

Samuel slumped in the chair and rested his head

again upon his fist, gazing out the window to the day. A crow sounded in the distance.

"You have a very nice farm," he said.

Ginger nodded. "Thanks, but it's not mine."

"Who does it belong to?"

"Osbee."

"Who?"

"My husband's grandmother."

"Ah, yes. I remember. And you live here with her and with your daughter."

"And my two sons."

"Three children you have."

Ginger nodded again.

"Where are they?"

"School." She played with Beau's ear, thinking she must have lost her mind. Samuel's knee was right next to her and she could reach out and touch it. Feeling the wool of his pants would at least make him real. But somehow, the thought that her hand would pass through his leg turned her stomach. Better to leave his knee alone.

Samuel cocked his head. "They leave home to go to school?"

"Uh, yeah. Most kids go to school at a school. You didn't go to school?"

"Not until VMI. I was taught at home by my mother and then with the reverend."

"Y-you went to VMI?" Ginger gazed over at him, her brows knitting together at the thought.

"I did. Why do you look at me so?"

"My husband went to VMI."

Samuel sat up straight. Ginger scooted away a little.

"His last name?"

"Martin."

Samuel thought. "Martin. I know no Martins."

"This is Smoot's farm. He's a Smoot on his mother's side."

Samuel shook his head. "Has this always been Smoot's farm?"

"Since 1799. Grandma's family has owned it until now."

"You said it was her farm. What do you mean, until now?"

"She's getting too old to farm it. It was going to be left to my husband. His dream was to raise his children here but he—he—"

"Was lost in a war."

Ginger nodded, brushing off the small pile of Beau's hair that had collected on her knee. The gesture also allowed her to gaze away from Samuel. His eyes had become so intense, she thought it better to look somewhere else.

"The farm will not pass to you?"

Ginger shook her head. "I think Osbee's selling it. I'm not a farmer and my family is . . . far from here."

Far from here. Not Seattle. Ginger didn't want to send Samuel in her father's direction. What if she just touched his knee? Just to check.

181

"So you will take your husband's children away from their father's land and his dream for them?"

Ginger shot her eyes back to Samuel's face. "Osbee's selling the land. Not me."

"She wants to sell the land?"

Her mouth opened but nothing came out. Osbee had been saying it was time to sell—that she couldn't farm, that Ginger needed to go back home.

"She does not want to sell the land," Samuel stated.

"I—I don't know. She says she's too old to farm it."

"Virginia, why cannot you farm it?" he pressed.

"I told you. I don't know how. And I work all the time."

"I do not understand. You work on the farm. What do you mean, you cannot farm?"

Beau gazed over his shoulder at her as if posing the question also.

"I'm a nurse, not a farmer. I go to work in a hospital and I'm gone most of the time. I need to work just to pay the taxes on this farm, which I do to keep my kids on it because it's what their father wanted. My children are growing up without me because I'm trying to hold on to this land—to his dream. But there is no one actually farming it and Osbee is too old and it's about time to plant."

"You do it."

Ginger stared at Samuel, who sat in the winter light, which had brightened as it poured in the window.

"I can't."

"Why?"

"I have to work." Ginger wondered if he was listening to anything she was saying.

"You say you are a nurse. What use is nursing when planting needs to happen? Why help in a hospital if there is no food? Stay home. Plant."

"By myself?"

"You have children."

"They are ten and eight and five."

"So?"

"They can't work."

"Why?"

"They have to go to school."

"Why?"

"Samuel, all children go to school."

"No."

"Yes."

"I was schooled at home until I went to VMI. My father had a farm. I worked as soon as I stood up."

Ginger dropped her hands to her lap and gazed at the man sitting in front of her in a soiled cotton shirt, fraying woolen pants, and tattered shoes. Home school. And who would school? She had to work. Plant. With what?

"The tractor's broken."

"Tractor?" Samuel asked, his eyes unblinking. "It plows?"

Ginger cocked her head. Wasn't that obvious? "Yes," she replied.

Samuel sat still, staring at his feet, thinking. "You have a barn. You have horses?" Samuel finally asked.

"Two," Ginger replied. "But they're just for play."

"No, Virginia. Horses can pull a plow."

Ginger scoffed. "They are not for plowing."

"What are they for?"

"For—for the kids to ride. Not for working." Ginger buried her head in her hands. They smelled like dog and this entire conversation was insane.

"Why do you look away from me, Virginia Moon?"

Wasn't that obvious, too? Pulling her fingers just off her eyes, Ginger glared in his direction. Samuel's soft brown gaze was as intense as the white light of the winter day outside.

"I cannot stay. I have to get home."

"Okay," she said, breathing a silent sigh of relief.

"Before I go, listen to me tell you what you are saying. Just so I understand. You have a farm but you cannot work it because you leave it to work. You have to work all the time to keep the farm and in doing so you leave it and your children, unable to see any of them grow. Your children go away from home to school, presumably to learn and grow. They cannot work the farm and grow. And you have what are obviously workhorses that do not work for things to grow. No one is home, growing. No one is working on home and everyone is everywhere but here, home— working but not working. Except the horses, which are here but not working. Is that correct?"

Ginger thought for a moment, completely perplexed. Was that right?

"Do I have it correct?" he repeated.

"I—I'm not sure. I think so."

"I can see why Osbee is selling the farm," he replied, standing up.

"It does sound—crazy, doesn't it?"

"Well," he replied, with a small shrug.

"I'm not a farmer, Samuel."

"Yes, you have said that. It seems to me that your husband is gone and, with him, any kind of anchor. Everyone is floating down the river, Virginia Moon, and someone has to grab ground before you all drown. Someone needs to hold on."

"It hurts to be here," Ginger whispered.

"Someone needs to hold on," Samuel repeated. "I suppose when a seed opens to put down a root, it must hurt. Growing hurts sometimes."

Ginger remembered Henry and his aching legs. She always knew when he was about to sprout taller because he always complained his legs hurt before he did so. Thinking on it, she hadn't heard Henry tell her his legs hurt in over a year.

Surely he was growing. Perhaps she wasn't around to hear him.

"Growing hurts sometimes," she repeated.

Samuel nodded. "And besides, what would Virginia be without its moon?" he asked with a half smile.

"Dark," she replied with a nervous laugh.

"I should think so. Now I am off to Laurel Creek again. Maybe we are finished here."

"Maybe you're not supposed to return to Laurel Creek," Ginger offered as she stood.

"And where should I go if not there? I have been trying to get there for many, many years."

"Maybe it is the light you—"

Samuel held up his hand to stop her. "If I cannot get across Laurel Creek, I am going to find your father and help him step into the light."

Ginger chuckled as Samuel headed for the door.

"Good day to you. Remember, a man is not dead if his dream yet lives. If his love lives. Think on that."

As was proper manners, Ginger followed him. She reached for the knob.

"And think of your dream, Virginia Moon, and the dreams of your children."

Before she could turn the knob, Samuel stepped through the door and was gone. Ginger gasped and then gasped again and the bright winter light beyond the front door windowpanes went gray as she slumped to the floor. Then there was blackness.

CHAPTER 10

THE VIOLET HOUR

A nudge on her right hip brought Ginger back from the warm dream of floating on an inner tube down the drifting slumber of summer's Shenandoah, a slow, green, spiraling journey shifting between dappled shade and a pale blue heaven. Walking on the right bank, Jesse followed her progress.

"Have I found your dream?" she asked.

"My dream is Ginger Moon."

"That's in Seattle."

"No. She's right here floating down a river."

"It's warm."

"Need to grab the bank before you end up at Harpers Ferry."

"I love Harpers Ferry."

"Yes, you always did. But you won't like those rapids in that inner tube. You need to take hold now."

"I'll be right over."

"No. Not my side. Take hold on your side."

"My side is your side," Ginger whispered.

She willed herself back to sleep—back to the river, back to the ebbing life of a Jesse dream.

But Beau nudged at her hip again with a loud yawn, and when Ginger opened her eyes, she found Regard's furry spine curled up on the crook of her neck with the afternoon light pouring down upon them from the staircase window above. Beau shifted his weight once more, gently shaking her at the hip. Ginger reached down, scratching his ear as she pondered how it was she had come to be lying on the entryway floor with the animals sleeping around her. Then it came back, bursting through her peaceful Jesse dream. When it did, she jolted up. Regard, startled, jumped away, hissing as he gazed around looking for what had interrupted his warm slumber.

Ginger stared at the front door, which was still locked.

"Shit." She placed her hand on her forehead. What to do? What to say? What to think? "Shit," she said again.

There was nothing now except the vision of Samuel passing through the door. Her very scientific, practical mind—the mind that saw what was there, that searched for connections between various unrelated events and could culminate all into a diagnosis, that could always identify a course of action—failed. Nothing allowed her to ignore this event. Nothing enabled her to make it something other than what it was. A ghost had been in her house, had spoken with her, had left through an unopened door. Samuel was a ghost.

"Holy crap," she whispered.

There were tires coming up the drive now, the crunching of their progress growing louder and louder until Beau could no longer ignore them. He stood, gazing over at Ginger as if to indicate that she should do the same. She obeyed, grabbing the banister for support. Regard, unhappy that Ginger was finished napping, hissed grumpily, then headed upstairs to find a pillow upon which to curl. As he skipped up the stairs, an engine disengaged. There were murmured voices. Wagging his tail at the closed door, Beau peered over to Ginger, who stood as still as the banister on which her left hand rested. He barked softly, mumbling, reminding her that she should unlock the door. As commanded, Ginger reached out with her right hand and turned the knob. She opened the door, blinking in the pale gray light.

"Ginger," Osbee declared with a bright smile. "You look like you just woke up."

The light and her voice were both very loud in the shifting reality that was scouring her mind.

"I did," she replied quietly.

"Hey, you all right?" Eloise asked as she came through the door with two grocery bags. "You look like you've seen a ghost."

Bea, who had been on Eloise's heels, stopped abruptly, causing a two-boy pileup behind her.

"Hey, Bea!" Oliver snapped. "Move!"

Bea stared up at her mother, her eyes seeking

an answer to the question Ginger knew was still on her daughter's mind.

"No ghost. Just woke up," she replied with a forced smile.

Oliver and Henry pushed past Bea, who was yet frozen at the door.

Samuel? Bea mouthed.

Ginger shook her head.

Bea frowned, nodding. "Samuel," she whispered.

"Bea, drop your bag and come help me get the laundry from upstairs," Ginger said.

The little girl shed her backpack and they both headed up the staircase.

"I saw him, Mama," Bea whispered as they climbed. "I saw him from the bus this morning. He was standing behind you as we drove away."

"Wait," Ginger said, shuddering as she followed her daughter into her bedroom. Bea bent down and picked the phone up from the floor as Ginger shut the door.

"You see him, Mama?" Bea asked, gazing up to her mother for reassurance.

For several minutes, Ginger stared into her daughter's eyes, unsure how to answer. Did her daughter need to know that she had spoken with Samuel? Would that scare her even more? Or maybe she should say she hadn't seen the ghost, helping her daughter to forget he had been wandering around the farm. He was gone now anyway.

With a deep sigh, Ginger sat on the bed, holding her hand out for the phone. Honesty was always best. Children could tell when adults were being less than truthful, and for her children as with most, that caused a certain level of distrust. They didn't know precisely what was being withheld, but were quite clear when something was. Best to either openly discuss the issue or to affirm that something was not going to be talked about because they were children.

Ginger sighed again as her daughter placed the phone into her hand. "Yes, I saw him, too."

A little furrow appeared on Bea's forehead. "He didn't go away like you said?" she asked.

"He has now, Bea. As far as I can tell."

"How do you know?"

" 'Cause I talked with Grandma and Grandpa and they told me what to say to him."

"Oh. What'd they say to say?" Bea's eyebrows perked up. Ginger paused before answering, wondering why what her parents had to say on the subject would be of interest. They were strangers who came bearing gifts a couple of times a year.

"To tell Samuel to step into the light," she replied.

Bea's lip curled. Ginger's smile widened. Samuel had had the same reaction.

"What light?"

"Not sure. I think Grandpa means heaven. I told Samuel and then he left. He thinks he can find his way across the—" Ginger stopped. The gaping mouth of the bridge in her orchard even now was breathing through the window on her back. Her smile disappeared.

"The what?"

"To heaven."

"What does he have to cross?" Bea pressed.

"You know, Bea, I'm not sure. He says he's trying to cross a . . . creek."

"River," Bea corrected.

"Uh, he said a creek."

"He said Laurel Creek. We found it in my atlas. But he needs to cross the river Lethe."

"What's that?" Ginger glanced sideways, the hollow wind passing through the bridge causing a shiver to roll down her spine.

"Dad used to say it's the river of forgetfulness. Samuel needs to cross it to get to Elysium."

"Elysium?" Ginger asked, sitting up straight. "Wh-when did Dad say this?"

"Dad was telling it to Henry and me while we were bivouacking last summer by the bridge." Bea turned her head and looked out the window. Ginger didn't. "Not last summer," Bea corrected. "The summer before that. Uh, before that."

"I don't remember that."

"You were at work. Oliver fell asleep and Dad began to recite *Hamlet* 'cause Henry wanted a ghost story."

A ghost story. Leave it to Jesse to recite *Hamlet*

and make sloosh when all his kids wanted was a simple ghost story and s'mores.

"Dad says the dead cross this river to forget the suffering of their life."

"Oh." Ginger had nothing else to say. She was off in her mind beneath a summer moon she had missed because she was working. She could just see Jesse act out *Hamlet* amidst the lightning bugs.

"He'll be back," Bea said.

Shaking her head free of fireflies, Ginger gazed down at her daughter. "Wh-who?"

"Samuel. Grandpa told him to go to the light, but that's not what he's looking for. He's looking for a way across the river Lethe. He'll be back, I think."

Bea stood up from the bed and looked down at the phone in her mother's hand.

"Where's the batteries?"

Ginger pointed to the floor beneath. Lowering to her knees, Bea moved her hand under the dresser as Ginger turned her head to the window. The light was fading as the sun crawled through the white mist of winter toward the west.

"I was afraid," Bea said with a grunt.

Ginger looked down and found her daughter splayed out on the floor, her left shoulder and arm missing beneath the dresser.

"You're not anymore?"

"Nope." Bea giggled as she drew her knees

beneath her. With a triumphant smile, she held her hand up and offered the batteries to her mother.

Ginger took them and snapped them back into place. "Why not?" Ginger was. She hoped Bea was wrong.

"Because Samuel wants to get across the river. He doesn't want to stay here." The little girl turned and headed to her own room.

Frozen on the bed, Ginger watched Bea pass the door with an armful of dirty clothes. She stood up and moved toward the bathroom. Though she knew she was walking, she felt as if she were floating. She was disconnected—in motion, sliding around in her head like a deckhand on a heaving ship caught in a maelstrom. Her arms grabbed the bathroom laundry basket; her legs carried her downstairs. Her lips smiled weakly at Osbee, who glanced questioningly over at her as she came through the kitchen door.

Laundry folded on the table gave way to homework, which then was cleared for dinner—pinto beans, collards, and corn bread. This was a standard dinner in the Smoot-Martin household. Not only was it nutritious and cheap, but it was Jesse's favorite and was served at least three times a week.

On her way out to check the horses, Bea asked if anyone wanted to come with her. Osbee gazed over to Ginger with raised eyebrows. Ginger shrugged, hearing herself offer to go, but Oliver jumped at the chance. With a grin, Bea took Oliver's hand and shut the door behind them.

Stepping over to the sink, Ginger poured herself a cup of coffee and took a sip. She watched Bea and Oliver cross the yard to the barn. Oliver had not complained about beans and collards. The more she thought on this, the more she realized he never complained about beans and collards. She had never been aware of his notable good humor at that meal. But then, maybe that was just another thing she missed, occupied as she was with her work.

"Henry?" Her voice was distant as she set her cup down. Rolling up her sleeves, Ginger dipped her hands into the soapy water of the sink.

"Yeah?" He didn't look up from his book.

"Your legs hurt anymore when you grow?"

"Yes. I take Motrin like you said."

"Oh." At least he was taking care of it. Yet a small churn of guilt rolled over in her stomach. She hadn't known and wasn't there to care for him.

He stood. "I'm going out to check the horses with Oliver and Bea," he said, shutting his book with finality.

He stood and slid into his coat. The door banged shut and there was silence in the house. As Ginger washed the plate, she noticed the white sky was now dimmed and the snow was lit purple. Henry ran to the barn, his dark body but a racing shadow.

Henry stood by his mother as they gazed down upon the infamous bridge over Antietam Creek. He took her hand in the silence that followed their father's dissertation on Burnside's efforts to cross it with the Confederate cannon raging iron and fury at them from the other side. In that quiet, Oliver, who was just three and situated upon his father's shoulders, continued to whistle the strange birdcall he had been whistling ever since they crossed the cornfield where Jackson had fought near the Dunker Church.

"Why is it sometimes called Antietam and sometimes Sharpsburg?" eight-year-old Henry asked his father.

"The North often called the battles the names of the rivers nearby, whereas the South called them by their towns. So Manassas to the South is the Battle of Bull Run to the North, as Bull Run Creek flowed through the field of combat. Antietam—North. Sharpsburg —South."

"Yeah, but why?" Henry pressed.

"I'm not really sure," Jesse replied, staring down at the bridge. His eyes were unfocused, gazing away to a far and distant place where he soon was to be deployed. Ginger wished they had not come here. It was too close to his leaving and he was always dark at these times. Battlefields were dark places—not good when one's mood was dark.

Oliver stopped whistling and sat up straight, jerking his head around in his mother's direction.

"I heard it again!" he said excitedly. "The bird answered!"

"Shh, so we can hear," Ginger said with a shiver, and they all stood still waiting for the bird. It had answered eerily in the Dunker Church. The chapel was small and white and the interior was almost a perfect square. Around its periphery, two rows of wooden pews encircled the center where the preacher would stand, relaying God's message or marking the time for the hymns. There was no organ, no piano. There would have been just voices singing in multiple and complex harmonies as a sacred harp.

But there was no singing this day, just the bird whistling a question over and over. Oliver answered as Ginger and her family searched the pews and the cast-iron stove for the bird that surely must have been caught somewhere inside. But they didn't find it, and as they moved on, walking together hand in hand or upon shoulders, the bird whistled after them. Ginger fought the urge to look back, feeling greatly like the outcome of doing so would be the same sentence passed on to Lot's wife but uncontrollably she gazed over her shoulder. A thin shimmering dust cloud wavered in the apricot-colored light and then the bird went silent. Since that moment, there had been no birdsong, though Oliver whistled and whistled.

Now dusk hung around them in a purplish hue, the air misty from a gentle spring thunderstorm that had passed over as they pulled into the battlefield parking lot. The bird called in reply far afield.

"There it is!" Oliver smiled brightly. His face was all life and light, contrasting his father's dark eyes as they gazed over to Ginger.

"It is the violet hour," he said, wearing an apologetic smile.

"Can we stay?" Bea asked excitedly. "A Smoot can see the spirits in the violet hour. That's what Grandpa Henry always said."

"Well, spirits need rest and we need to eat," Ginger replied, shaking her head. "Smoot or no Smoot, the violet hour is best passed indoors and with food."

Bea slumped and she turned from the bridge, skulking back in the direction of the car.

Henry let go of his mother's hand, trotted after his sister, and cried out, " 'In the world's broad field of battle, in the great barnyard of life.' "

He nudged Bea as he passed her and she quickly gave chase, yelling, " 'Be not like those lazy cattle; be the rooster through the strife.'"

They laughed as they raced up the hill.

"Who's that they're reciting?" Ginger asked.

"Oliver Wendell Holmes, the senior," Jesse replied.

"That's my name!" Oliver declared, riding upon his father's shoulders toward her.

"You hear my bird, Mama?"

"I did." She forced a smile as she tiptoed up to Jesse, kissed his cheek, and then took his hand.

"Shall we tell a story from Beatrix Potter tonight?" she asked her son.

"Yeah, yeah. The tale of Jeremy Fisher?" Oliver offered.

"The life of a frog does have a lot to teach," she agreed. "And is a far lighter tale than that of battlefields."

"Sorry," Jesse whispered. "Frog it is." He pulled her to him and kissed her and arm in arm they followed Henry and Bea through the growing darkness.

The heavens had turned a fluorescent purple; the entire farmyard looked like a snow globe made of amethyst waiting to be tilted into motion.

"The violet hour," Ginger whispered.

"That it is," Osbee agreed as she wrapped her right arm around the younger woman's waist. "The hour for ghosts to walk free."

Ginger turned and looked into Osbee's face. The purple light poured in the window, softening the old woman's wrinkles. She was a beauty in her day, Ginger had no doubt.

"I hope not," Ginger replied.

February 19, 1862
Winchester

My love, Juliette,
We have returned to Winchester, from where
we left in January. It was strangely springtime
weather the day we left; the day after it turned
with a winter storm, blowing in, and has
seemingly ne'er a thought of retreating since.
We marched as one body through the weather
to Bath. Again, we engaged the Baltimore and
Ohio Railroad. We have good reason to disturb
that line as it replenishes our enemies, but
many of us have sat around fires in quiet
laughter. We are not in battle with men; we
fight fire and metal.

With several skirmishes behind us, we came
to the Potomac River on the Virginia side,
where we found the town of Hancock,
Maryland, garrisoned. We shot artillery into the
town for two days without much effect but did,
yet again, win against the railroad. We
destroyed a part of the line. Having victory
over boxcars, we, with low humor, cheered our
success and withdrew, as we could not find a
way over the river.

Next, we headed to Romney. There was a

small defeat of some of our forward lines at Hanging Rock Pass, but we entered Romney nonetheless on the 10th. Winter had set up camp with us and there were many in our company who had never experienced such. I had great sympathy for them. As we had no ability to move forward into Maryland as planned, hindered as we were by snow, Jackson left part of our company in Romney and we followed him back down to Winchester.

We arrived on the 24th, at which point we heard that the commander of the regiment we left in Romney complained to Richmond. I am unclear what exactly transpired, but that division was removed from the Valley District under Jackson, leaving us with only our 4,000 men. Hence, we are left securing the lower Shenandoah with half the strength. There is now movement north of here and I feel we might be obliged to leave the poor townsfolk of Winchester yet again. How they continue I cannot say. First they are under Confederate control. Then Union. Then Confederate. Winchester seems to be the fulcrum around which this tedious affair is balancing.

We skirt Maryland, my Juliette, and if I may— is there anywhere else you can stay? I cannot say where the war will move but I am afraid for you in Sharpsburg. Please, if possible, take your aging father from there. What we shall find on the other side of winter is anyone's guess. Please, dearest.

I shall say my humor has returned as Avery falls back in my mind as memory. I know, though, there will be more fighting to come. I purposefully think of this day, this moment, as all there is. I try not to think too much of what is to come. But night returns and now and then I hear that bird and I think of you. Is it you, my love? Do you whistle to me from a far, distant place, calling me to you? What was last fall a dark portending call is now this spring a song of hope. Please keep yourself safe.

Your devoted,
Samuel

CHAPTER 11

THE CALF HAS INSURANCE

Ginger trotted to her truck, hot coffee in hand and the kitchen light flowing from the open door where Osbee stood. It was cold and still and the night sky was so clear, Ginger could see the Milky Way churning slowly above her. She climbed into her wretched truck, the smell of vomit hiding just under the veil of cold air, waiting to be found by the warmth of the heater—*olly, olly oxen free.* Ginger really had no wish to seek the vomit but it came free without asking, so as she turned onto 81 she dug through her bag and found her perfume. She sprayed it around liberally.

There was no new snow and the roads were clear. As she approached Oak Flat, she held her breath, tiptoeing past Samuel and Jacob Esch and any further weirdness that might pop out of the dark trees on this winding road in West Virginia. Grace had it that she pulled into the empty parking lot of Franklin District Community Hospital with no unexpected passengers, so she parked her car in the employee parking lot and hiked over the snow to the emergency room.

Reality still had not found its anchor and

Ginger's mind was still sloshing around like sloosh in a hot pan, but somehow the familiar face of Margery T., RN, unlocking the glass door was settling. There was work to be done, people to help and heal, and nothing can keep one in the reality of the moment greater than an emergency. To Ginger's disappointment, though, the ER was empty. The acute care was empty and as Margery T., RN, shuffled out the glass door on her trek to her vehicle, Ginger looked longingly at the silent ambulance resting in the driveway across the street.

"Work, work," she mumbled to herself and headed to the medicine cabinet to take inventory. Margery had already finished that. She walked into the kitchen; Margery had restocked the cupboards and had obviously scrubbed the counters. If she had actually scrubbed the kitchen counters, then it followed that everything else was complete. Kitchen counters usually were cleaned in rural hospitals even after wiping down the waiting room. Good thing there was no cleaning staff at night, for they would have found themselves with nothing do except keep Ginger company at the triage station. So odd. It was Friday. Something always happened on Fridays.

There Ginger sat, arranging and rearranging the thermometers, the sphygmomanometer, the files in the drawers. Leaning forward, she put her head on the desk, gazing at the clock, which read three thirty-two a.m.

"Ginger?"

She looked around, the mist hanging heavy before her. It was soft purple and at her feet the river lapped the edge of its muddy bed. The water was inky and thick—liquid obsidian.

"Ginger, can you hear me?" It was Jesse. His voice called through the mist over the water.

"I hear you. Where are we?"

"It's the violet hour."

"I can't see you, Jesse."

"I'm here, across the river."

"In Elysium?"

"I am home." He laughed deeply. She loved that laugh. It was earthy and always came easily to him when he was up to something. Usually what he was up to was something mischievous—something for her to discover.

"What are you up to?" She folded her arms over her chest.

He laughed again as if she'd caught him in his mischief and, in his laugh, the mist cleared a little. She found him resting his back on his ash tree, a twig fishing rod in hand with the line bobbing in the black water. He was dressed in a soiled shirt and butternut wool pants and his tattered shoes sat next to his thigh. His legs were long in front of him, his right one lying on top of his left. A small smile grew on his face when he saw her and, in response, a small smile grew on hers.

Ginger gazed around, looking up the steep hill of the state park behind her and down the river's edge. Surely she must have crossed in the boat, but she could not find it anywhere.

"How can I get across?" she asked.

"You have work to do over there to come over here."

"But that's home," Ginger said.

"Is it?"

His smile faded and he looked at her with shadow eyes—with eyes like Samuel's. She caught her breath. "Is—is this the river Lethe?" she whispered.

He rolled his shadowed eyes. "This is the Shenandoah, Ginger. How many years have you lived here?"

"It doesn't exactly look like the Shenandoah. The water is black."

"That's because you're on that side."

Her throat grew thick as her chest tightened. "I want to be by your side," she said.

"I am always at your side."

Ginger began to weep, her tears reflecting the violet sky above as they fell into the inky water of the Shenandoah below. "This is a dream," she whispered.

"It is. It is your dream and I am yet in it. See? Now you must build the bridge to your home, Ginger, my love. There shall I always be."

There was a rapping above and when she gazed up she saw a crow tapping the branch above her head. She looked across the river and found the fog falling again.

Jesse smiled a small smile at her as he disappeared behind the violet veil of mist.

"Wait!" she yelled.

Ginger started, blinking in the light of the emergency room, watching the clock on the desk roll from three thirty-three a.m. to three thirty-four a.m. She lifted her hand to her face and found her cheeks damp with tears.

A gentle rap at the glass door brought her fully to her feet. Quickly coming around the triage desk, she found a disheveled man standing at the door. He had a long, graying brown beard and held a knit hat in his hands. His red-and-black-checkered wool coat hung loosely over his thin frame and his jeans were tucked into his untied leather work boots. He smiled, his hazel eyes bright. Ginger walked to the door, thinking he looked exactly like any picture of an Appalachian mountaineer that had ever been taken or drawn.

"Sorry," he said, his words muffled by the glass door.

"This is what we're here for," Ginger said to reassure him as she turned the lock. She swung the door open and his face grimaced as he walked in.

"Ah din't come in earlier," he explained, "because ah din't feel lahke anything happened. But as ah was laying in bed, mah lower back just began pitchin' a fit."

Ginger took the man by the elbow and led him to triage. "You're here for your back, then," Ginger said, as she began to take his vitals.

"Ah had a car accidint this morning."

"Oh?"

"Ah hit a calf."

Ginger stopped squeezing the sphygmomanometer and pulled the stethoscope from her ears.

"Beg pardon?"

"Ah hit Jack Wolfe's calf."

"Jack Wolfe." Ginger smiled, remembering the old man who had wanted a candy bar.

"Yuh." The mountaineer grinned. "Ah see you know 'im."

"I met him once," she said. "So you hit his calf."

"Jack's not all he once was, yah know, and ah think he's let the place go some. Not 'cause he's lazy."

Ginger shook her head and decided to wait on the blood pressure. She grabbed the mountaineer's wrist to take his pulse.

"Anyways. Ah was a-comin' down Old Moss Road, slow and the lahke, and ah came 'round the corner and there the calf was before ah even seen it. Hit it straight on. Kilt it."

"I see. What is your name, please?"

"Joshua. Joshua Wheldon."

"And what's your date of birth?"

"March 9, 1952."

Ginger typed the information into the computer and, as was typical, Mr. Wheldon's medical history popped on the screen. Seemed everybody hereabouts had visited the ER at some point and been entered into its computer system. As expected, he had no insurance. ERs in rural areas were pretty much used for general medicine by the surrounding communities. Payments were usually made in cash or over time or never, depending. She entered Mr. Wheldon's vitals and complaint into the screen and printed it. Then she had him sign the permission for treatment and payment forms.

"Ah might could've been kilt."

"Calves are big creatures." Ginger stood and took Mr. Wheldon by his arm, helping him toward a bed.

"Jack was so upset. But he said for me not to worry about the car or anythin' 'cause the calf had insurance."

"What's that?" Ginger asked, stopping their progress toward the bed.

"Jack said the calf had insurance so y'all be paid and sich."

"The calf had insurance," Ginger repeated, nodding as she helped Mr. Wheldon to the bed.

"Yup."

"Well, Mr. Wheldon, why don't you take off your coat and let me get the doctor."

"Yes, ma'am."

Ginger stepped back into triage, grinning at the irony. The calf had insurance. What kind of world was it when livestock had insurance and people went bankrupt paying for their medical care? As she picked up the phone, there was a rap at the glass door again. Coming around the triage desk, she found the doctor already standing out in the snow. It was not Anna Maria D., MD. It was a very clean-cut young man with dark hair and dark eyes. When Ginger opened the door, he hurried in.

"Damn, it's cold out there," he said, his accent clearly Northern. His name tag read, "Ernest P., MD."

"Doctor?" Ginger prompted as they walked to triage.

"Patterson. Dr. Patterson. The patient's car backfired so loud, I thought it was a gun going off."

"You're not from around here, are you?"

"No. Albuquerque. What do we have?"

"A car accident."

"Ah, a FIRT—Failed Impact Resistance Test. He's driving a GTO, so I'll guess he hit a . . . 1972 Ford pickup."

"No," Ginger said, hiding her frown.

"A pole?"

"No," she said, her hidden frown deepening. She didn't want to tell him. He sounded condescending and she liked Mr. Wheldon.

"What, then, Nurse, ah—" He read her name badge. "Virginia." He chuckled.

"A calf."

"What say?"

"He hit a calf."

The doctor's eyes brightened enormously and he smiled quite broadly. Was he going to laugh?

"It's very quiet tonight, Doctor," Ginger said with a chill to match the night outside. She led Dr. Patterson to Joshua's room. Entering, the doctor's demeanor changed to a very professional one, so Ginger saw that at least he had clearly been trained. He took the chart Ginger offered to him.

"Good evening, Mr. Wheldon. Seems you've had a car accident."

"Yessir. Ah have. Mah back is just a-achin'."

"Hmm. Let's take off those shoes and your shirt and have a look."

Ernest P., MD, walked to the sink and washed his hands. With a snap, he put on latex gloves. As Ginger washed her hands, she caught, out of the corner of her eye, Joshua Wheldon pulling a large hunting knife out of his boot. Ernest P., MD, backed up toward the wall, his eyes wide on the knife and his hand reaching for the telephone.

"Uh, Mr. Wheldon," Ginger said calmly. "Go ahead and just drop the knife on your coat."

"Ah-rahght," he said and, as directed, he dropped the knife.

Ginger chuckled inwardly to herself. Such things used to surprise her, too, but out here in the rural areas, whether Washington, Virginia, West Virginia, or anywhere else, people generally carried hunting knives or guns on their person. It was not for show. It was for survival—literally. She smiled kindly at the doctor and nodded reassuringly.

Composing himself once again, Ernest P., MD, began his assessment. It took about half an hour, after which time he indicated to Mr. Wheldon that he thought the man had pulled muscles in his lumbar region. He prescribed muscle relaxers and painkillers and instructed the patient to return if he wasn't feeling better in a week. Then Ernest P., MD, left the patient with Ginger.

To avoid Mr. Wheldon bending, Ginger helped him on with his boots.

"Ma'am?" he said.

"Yes, Mr. Wheldon?"

"Did ah do somethin' wrong?"

She stood and looked into the man's hazel eyes. "What do you mean?"

"Well, mah knife."

"Oh. No, Mr. Wheldon. Dr. Patterson isn't from around here."

"Ah kinda noticed. You're not, neither."

She smiled. "No. I'm not, and you're fine. Now, here is your prescription to fill and a couple of pills to take when you get home. See you through the night." She helped the man to his feet. "You understand the instructions?"

"Yes, ma'am."

Ginger motioned him to the door. "If you see Jack Wolfe," she said, "tell him to keep the chocolate bars down to one a day."

Joshua Wheldon turned around, grinning ear to ear. "You do know Jack!" he declared.

"Oh, yes. I do. And only after one meeting." They laughed together.

"Ya know anyone what needs a cow?" Mr. Wheldon asked.

Ginger shook her head, confused.

"The calf a-dyin' just made ole Jack realize he cain't keep his farm goin'. Cain't keep the fences up and sich. He's kinda afraid for his cow. If yah meet anyone that needs a good milker, let me know. I'll tell Jack."

Ginger nodded, and as they turned to the glass door, they watched a thin shadow of a person slip and slide across the parking lot.

"He don't look lahk he's a-walkin' too good."

Ginger squinted into the darkness as she turned the lock on the door. The thin shadow stopped and threw up.

"Ya need help with 'im?"

The shadowy figure stepped closer to the light and then sat down in the snow.

"No, thank you, Mr. Wheldon. That's very kind."

"He's mighty sick," the mountaineer said.

"He's mighty drunk," Ginger corrected and, securing the door open, she walked out into the clear, cold night to retrieve Jacob Esch.

"You be careful, Mr. Wheldon, crossing the parking lot," she said as she approached the boy.

"Ah will. Good night, ma'am."

"Jacob Esch?" she said, bending down. He smelled of whiskey.

"My side hurts," he gurgled, holding his right abdomen.

"How much alcohol have you had?" she asked, helping him up. Even in this light, she could see his face was pale and pressed in pain.

"Just a couple. I started throwing up. I hurt something awful." He grunted.

"Let's get you inside." With his left arm swung across her shoulders, Ginger walked Jacob toward the glass door of the ER. Before they arrived, Ernest P., MD, came trotting across the icy parking lot.

"I'll take him," Dr. Patterson said, relieving Ginger of her burden.

"He has pain in his lower right abdomen," she said, walking briskly but carefully ahead.

"Yup," the doctor replied. "You been throwing up, uh—"

"Jacob," Ginger prompted, stepping through the door. She waited for the doctor and his patient to pass and then shut and locked winter outside.

"Jacob?" Ernest P., MD, finished.

"Yeah."

"You been drinking?" he asked.

"I think I threw it all up," Jacob replied with a moan as he was lowered onto the bed.

"Let's get this shirt off."

Dr. Patterson helped Jacob off with his shirt and then laid the boy down as Ginger washed her hands. When the doctor turned to wash his, Ginger stuck a thermometer in Jacob's mouth. It beeped as the doctor's gloves snapped into place.

"A hundred degrees, Doctor," Ginger said.

"Yup." He nodded as he helped Jacob lie back.

"How long have you had the pain?" the doctor inquired.

"Since last night."

"Last night early?" The doctor pushed across Jacob's abdomen, left to right.

"After dinner. I threw uh—ahh!" The doctor pressed the abdomen right where the appendix was and, as expected, Jacob went off like an alarm does when the right button is pushed.

"I'll get the on-call surgical team," Ginger said, turning to leave.

"Yup," the doctor replied.

First she phoned the hospital exchange to call in

the surgical team and then she rang Yvette in acute care to prep surgery. When she returned, she found the doctor helping Jacob off with his clothes. She started Jacob's IV.

At five a.m., Jacob was rolled into surgery. At six a.m., Dr. Patterson's relief showed up.

"We got that in time," Dr. Patterson replied as he walked into triage. Aside from Jacob, there had been no other patient.

"Yes, we did," Ginger replied.

"You working tonight?"

"I am."

"I'm here for a week," Ernest P., MD, replied. "I suppose this was a quiet night."

"Yes," Ginger said. "We're used as general medicine as well as emergency care."

Dr. Patterson nodded. "Not enough money out here to keep a GP, I suppose."

"And very little insurance," Ginger affirmed.

Dr. Patterson nodded again.

"The calf had insurance, though," she added.

"What say?" Ernest P., MD, tilted his head.

"The calf Mr. Wheldon hit. It had insurance, so we'll be paid. So Mr. Wheldon says." Ginger waited and watched Dr. Patterson process her words.

"Mr. Wheldon has no insurance?"

"Yup." She said it exactly as the doctor always did. A wry smile grew on his face.

"That's just wrong," he said.

"Welcome to American medicine."

"Something's wrong with us."

"We're independent. Don't like anyone telling us what to do. Need to turn a profit on everything, including illness and death, you know." Ginger smiled.

"The calf has insurance!" Ernest P., MD, announced. "I gotta call my dad with that one. All that money to put me through college and a dead cow pays my fee."

They looked at each other and laughed.

"Holy cow," Ginger added.

They laughed louder.

"I work the six p.m. to six a.m. shift," Dr. Patterson said. "What do you work?"

"The two a.m. to two p.m. shift," Ginger replied. "Nurses and doctors have different shifts here."

"Okay. See you tonight," Dr. Patterson said, shaking his head and chuckling as he walked toward the glass door. Morning was waking outside; it stretched its long rays into the clear sky as it yawned.

"Sleep well," Ginger said, deciding she might like Dr. Patterson after all.

The door shut. She looked at it. No need to lock it. She turned and walked down the hall past the doors into acute care, where Jacob had been taken. She found him lying quietly, the IV dripping slowly in the dim light of his room. She stepped over to check it.

"You're not from around here, are you?"

She gazed down and found the young man peering up at her with a pop eye.

"No. Neither are you."

"I'm here by mistake. By many mistakes." He closed his eyes and faded back into a drug-induced rest.

CHAPTER 12

CUTTIN' A SHINE

When Ginger stepped out at two thirty p.m. Saturday afternoon, the world was less white. She blinked as if waking from a short nap, listening to the dripping tears of snow melting as winter realized it was losing its grip. The sun was a warm fifty-two degrees, according to the large, round temperature gauge on the hospital's brick wall. She shuddered. Not from cold, but from the anticipation of the smell in her truck and the fact that the world was telling her as clearly as it could that it was now time to plow.

"Maybe it's colder in the valley," she said to the slush that gave way under her feet.

She knew, though, there was little time now to put off the inevitable. The world was waking up, ready to grow again, and she and Osbee could not plant on their own. Osbee was also clear on this point, for she was selling the farm. On the other hand, Ginger was not clear at all. She didn't want to be clear because it meant the time was approaching to leave Virginia—time to say good-bye to Osbee. It was time to let go of Jesse.

When she opened the truck, she didn't even

220

wince at the odor. She was aching, her body spent and weak from the growing pain of loss. She climbed in, feeling as if she would never stop losing—losing Jesse, losing his dream, losing Osbee, losing her children's childhood.

"I'm so tired of losing," she whispered as she engaged her engine. The roads were shiny and wet as if it had rained. The snow was a patchwork of white and brown and as she drove down the hill to Harrisonburg the valley spread below her, a mist-covered quilt of green and white rolling hills glowing brightly beneath a golden peach sun. She opened her window, finding birds chirping louder than the caw of the crows. The sun was warm but the wind was cold. She did not roll up her window. Instead, she turned the heater on. It seemed to Ginger that winter hadn't even put up a fight last night. What had been the dead of winter yesterday was the sheer rise of spring in glory today, having won the battle with not one little skirmish.

She drove on, gazing around at the trees whose branches were covered with tiny bright green buds that sparkled like so many small green Christmas lights in the sun. The valley was clear and fresh, cleaned by some mysterious house-keeper the night before and ready for all that was new.

Yet as she turned onto her lane and looked in wonder at the miracle of Virginia's waking spring, winter was still upon Ginger. Solomon Schaaf sat his tractor, feeling the earth call to him. He waved as she passed, his face as bright as the sun above. He was in his element—an earth sprite sewing a field of dirt to make a cloth of wheat to adorn his land in a golden dress some months from now.

The Creed farm had long, winding furrows set as if by magic overnight. Grasses budded green through the unplowed patches of snow in the far field. Finally, if there had been any question in Ginger's mind as to the state of the seasons before, the two cars that made their way slowly toward her as she headed home on the road punctuated the fact that it was spring. She smiled through the windshield at both drivers.

Though they were strangers, she knew them. They were going for a Saturday drive and had seen the sign on Highway 81 pointing to the covered bridge. As so many people had done over the years, they exited and followed the road this way and that to the end of the lane where the covered bridge stood in the open field near a fruit orchard and small family cemetery. They had stopped, finding nothing really to look at but the bridge spanning a small, dried-up stream. Perhaps they took a picture, perhaps not. Either way, with nothing much else to do, they turned around and made their way back to the highway.

Ginger's stomach hurt. Up ahead was the rise of

Smoot's farm. There in the driveway was Ester and Hugh Martin's black Mercedes, sitting like a vulture waiting for a death. As she bumped off the asphalt, she found her three children slumped over the railing near the front steps. There, right behind them, leaning on the post of the porch with his arms crossed, was Samuel Annanais. Ginger slammed on her brakes.

No one moved. They stared at her as she stared at them. Slowly, she disengaged the engine, not daring to make more of a ripple in the heavy stillness that enveloped her. It was Samuel who left the porch first, followed as if obediently by her children—Bea, then Oliver, then Henry. Ginger sat motionless, her eyes tracking their progress from the house to her truck door. Bending down a little to peer at her through the glass, Samuel smiled a reticent smile as he reached the front end. Henry trotted from behind, reaching the door first, and, as his father taught him to do, he opened it for his mother.

"Good afternoon, Virginia Moon," Samuel quietly greeted.

Ginger said nothing.

"We all see him, Mama," Henry whispered.

The ghost, Oliver mouthed, his eyes wide, his body shaking. Ginger gazed sideways in his direction and he smiled secretly at her. He wasn't afraid. He was wound with excitement.

"Your youngest was cuttin' a shine in the house

when I came across the bridge. Could hear him all the way in your orchard."

Ginger made no response.

"Grandma and Grandpa Martin are here with Mr. Glenmore, a lawyer," Henry said.

"They talk and talk and talk," Oliver breathed, slumping his shoulders and rolling his eyes back into his sockets.

"When I reached the porch, your children were pushed out the door." Samuel shrugged apologetically.

Ginger sat, having no idea what to do. It would be a mistake to say her mind raced. It didn't. It had seized. It had come to a complete and utter stop. She had nothing to say—nothing to offer. She had nothing. The birds somewhere in the eves sang a little *do-re-me* to fill the void.

"Virginia Moon, I cannot go home."

"He can't cross the river, Mama," Bea added. "He keeps coming back here."

River . . . that was a body of water.

"I can hear them talking to Grandma Osbee, Virginia, through the window. They seek to sell the farm."

"What will happen to Penny and Christian?" Oliver whined.

Ginger winced. She had reached the day she didn't ever want to live—the day her children would know they were leaving Osbee. They would be removed from the grace of Mr. Mitchell and all the others on this hairpin curve of the Shenandoah. But she wasn't choosing to do such a thing. It was happening without her consent. It was an inevitable wall of reality bearing down on them—a flood of change in their small world. A disaster.

"I can help," Samuel said.

Ginger peered up into his soft brown eyes. They looked at her just as they had done when he stood on the fallen tree. Her seizure made no answer.

"I am supposed to help," he added.

The birds stopped singing. Silence. Stillness. A picture formed clearly in her mind: Samuel on the tree. She was on her knees in the snow by the fallen ash near the river, asking Jesse for something—anything. Ginger felt a trickle of movement in her synapses. It was small. It was flowing from the center of her body through the middle of her mind and found its way to her mouth.

How? No sound came out. Just movement.

"I am a farmer."

The trickle became a steady stream and the sound of the flood rushing down the dry and cracking riverbanks of her nervous system shook her body. She began literally to shake with the oncoming wash.

"Mama?" Oliver whispered, touching her knee.

Great fields of grass grow from a flood. Thousands of seedlings get a chance when the wash subsides, and without flood or fire or volcanic eruption, the earth withers. Destruction, from which is born creation, isn't Providence causing tragedy. Providence uses tragedy for good. It isn't always clear how and in the middle of the loss it isn't clear anything good will ever come. But it does. Always. What is shed in death feeds life. That is the nature of things. Life rises from disasters.

"We rise," Ginger announced and she leapt from the car. She grabbed Oliver's hand and headed for the porch.

"Mama?" Bea called.

"Henry, shut the door and grab your sister," she said over her shoulder. Her eyes were fixed upon the front doorknob.

"What are we doing, Mama?" Henry asked.

"Cuttin' a shine," his mother replied, reaching for the doorknob slowly as if it would run away if she made any sudden moves. She held on to it as she heard Bea and Henry come up the stairs behind her. Then she turned it and opened the door as if it were any other day she was coming home. She stepped inside with her children as if it were any other day they were walking into their house. Hand in hand, Ginger and her children stood next to the staircase in front of the open door.

"Ginger," Ester declared, smiling politely as she rose from her seat at the dining room table.

There Osbee sat with a pen poised over a stack

of papers; a man with salt-and-pepper hair leaned over her. Hugh sat in the chair next to Osbee. All four pairs of eyes stared in the direction of Ginger and the open door.

"That's Mr. Glenmore. He's a lawyer," Bea whispered so quietly Ginger almost missed the statement in the flood of nervous noise in her ears. Gazing at Osbee, she spotted the tattered red ribbon at the end of the old woman's braid. Ginger smiled brightly.

"Upstairs," she commanded.

"Ginger?" Osbee inquired.

A great bustling and banging of feet up the stairs drowned out any further calls from the dining room table—and there were others.

"Henry, go into your room and find any shirt for you and Oliver with red on it. Hurry."

Grabbing Bea's hand, Ginger headed into the bathroom and flipped on the light.

"What are we doing?" Bea asked as her mother faced her toward the mirror.

"Remembering the lessons of history. Brush your hair, please, Little Bea."

Rooting around in the cabinet, Ginger pulled out two small red plastic barrettes. One was shaped like strawberries and the other cherries.

"Those are from when I was a baby."

"We need the color, Bea. No argument."

Bea nodded solemnly as her mother clipped them into place. Then she hissed as she rummaged under the sink looking for one other red hair accessory.

"This good?" Henry asked.

Ginger popped her head from beneath the cabinet and looked at her boys. One had a Spider-Man T-shirt on and the other a Dale Earnhardt "No. 18" sweatshirt.

"Perfect. Comb your hair, please."

As Ginger bent her head to go under the sink again, she found Bea's hand held out, offering a red plastic hair clip with two of the five teeth broken off.

"Red like Grandma Osbee," Bea said, smiling triumphantly as if she had figured out a perplexing puzzle.

"Exactly. And the first thing I do when we go to the store next time is buy new hair ties," Ginger said, returning the smile. "All red. Remind me."

Taking the hair clip, Ginger stood, and as her two boys finished combing their hair, she swirled her brown curls up into a bun on the back of her head and secured it with the hair clip. Her strawberry blond roots had grown out just enough to encircle her face, giving her, in the light of the bathroom vanity, a halo effect.

"Ain't no saint," she said to her reflection.

She then gazed at her children, who were looking up at her for instructions. They were truly their father's offspring. They were children as all other children, arguing and poking at one another. But in moments like this, they were a unit. They worked together as a unit. She looked from one to the next. Each different, but altogether they were a whole and they were hers and she loved them. She also realized how much she had missed them over the last year.

"We rise," she said.

Bea looked at Oliver, who looked at Henry.

"We rise?" Henry repeated.

"We rise," Oliver and Bea said. Oliver shrugged at his mother.

She kissed each of their heads and, taking Oliver's hand, she led them to the staircase, where she stopped abruptly. Beyond the staircase window, Ginger spotted Samuel standing on the front grass, his back toward her with his hands clasped behind him. The wet asphalt road below the rise of the Smoots' farm ran straight off into the distance, glistening like a river of water in the afternoon sun.

"We rise together," she whispered.

He turned halfway and looked directly at her through the glass. He smiled. She smiled in return and, taking a deep breath, descended the stairs.

They plunged together down to the first floor, and when they all stood by the open front door again, Ginger pulled her children in front of her, bringing up the rear. She turned and found Osbee still seated, but now Hugh and Ester were standing in front of the dining room table between Ginger and the old woman.

"H-how are you, Ginger?" Ester asked, still holding that polite smile. Ginger looked at Ester's smile. It was a smile, all right, but it was also a baring of teeth.

Ginger held her breath, forcing a tight lifting of her lips in return, and then looked over to Osbee. The old woman hadn't moved an inch and gazed at Ginger quizzically. Ginger turned her head slightly, motioning to her red hair clip. Then she rested her arms on Henry and Oliver's shoulders and, bending down, kissed Bea on one of her red barrettes.

"Ginger?" Hugh inquired, taking a step in her direction.

Ginger didn't look at him. She didn't answer. Her ribs ached with the strain of holding her breath as she waited for Osbee. The old woman looked away, her focus now on the papers in front of her. A lump formed in Ginger's throat. Her heart pounded in her ears.

"We rise together," Oliver said softly.

Osbee spun her head and stared deeply at him. Then she smiled like the spring day outside, her eyes swimming as she looked from Oliver to Bea to Henry. She put the pen down and rose.

"Mother?" Ester said, turning toward Osbee.

"Coffee?" The force of Ginger's held breath was uncontrollable and the word came out like a shout of victory more than a spoken courtesy. Ginger cringed as it echoed through the quiet of the house.

"This isn't your land, Ginger," Ester said.

Ginger closed the open door.

"I think I'll wait a while, Mr. Glenmore," Osbee said.

Ginger turned back toward the dining room. She stepped amid her children and found Bea taking her hand. Henry and Oliver followed and, as they advanced, Hugh and Ester retreated toward the table.

"This farm belongs to my family," Ester said as Ginger passed by.

"Are there any cookies left?" Ginger asked, grinning at Osbee, who was still smiling, her eyes moist.

"Cookies!" Oliver yelled and, pushing by Mr. Glenmore, scrambled toward the kitchen.

"This is my inheritance, Ginger. The land belongs to my family."

Ginger stopped, touching Osbee's braid, thinking how beautifully Jesse's grandmother wore her age.

"Mrs. Martin? I'm not sure why you are saying that to me. The land is Osbee's," Ginger said, pushing Bea and Henry toward the kitchen. As directed, they followed Oliver.

"Mother was signing papers before you arrived," Hugh said. "You obviously have counseled her on something other than selling."

"I haven't said a word to Osbee," Ginger pointed out.

"Hugh," Osbee said. "I'm old but not befuddled. I can think for myself."

"You were ready to sign," Mr. Glenmore said.

"I do beg your pardon, Mr. Glenmore, but this is not your business," Osbee replied.

Mr. Glenmore stepped back, narrowing his eyes. He turned smartly on his heel and headed to the front door.

"Mother! That was rude."

"Ester, that was a fact," Osbee said. "I was ready to sign because I was thinking only of myself. Oliver reminded me that there are others here to think about."

"The land doesn't belong to—" Ester began.

"The land belongs to whomever I say it does. Right now, it is mine to do with as I please."

"You can't farm it."

"We can," Henry said from the kitchen door, cookie in hand. Startled by his tone, Ginger stared at her ten-year-old.

"Henry, leave this to the adults, son," Hugh said. "Why don't you go get some milk."

"I'm the man of this house now," he said, stepping into the dining room.

Osbee gazed from Henry over to Ginger. She raised her eyebrows in question. Ginger shrugged and shook her head.

"Son," Hugh said.

"I am not your son," Henry said.

"Henry!" Ester declared.

"My daddy is dead. He's not coming back. This is Grandma Osbee's land, where my daddy wanted us to live. This is our home. We're gonna do what my daddy wanted us to do. We're gonna live here. We're gonna plant. And we're all going to VMI."

Ginger stood as dumbfounded as the rest of the adults in the room. This was entirely unexpected and entirely out of character for Henry.

"You are a very strong young man, Henry," Hugh said earnestly. "Your daddy would be proud. So, man to man. Your mama and grandma can't manage this farm alone."

"We can manage," Ginger said.

"We're not alone," Henry added.

Ginger's heart stopped. She shook her head at her son as he stepped toward Hugh. Bea and Oliver peered around the kitchen door.

"I mean, you and your brother and sister, too, of course. You'll help, but that isn't enough to farm."

"It's not just us," Henry said.

Ginger slid behind Osbee, hoping to reach Henry before he said anything else.

"No? Then who? The other farmers? They've been helping for two years now. Hard to—"

"Not them," Henry replied.

"Uh, Henry," Ginger said.

"Then who?"

Ginger breathed in. Henry stared squarely at his grandfather. There was a pause, a moment. It was the space between the notes of a song. It was the emptiness between the spokes of a wheel. There was a purpose to this pause; Ginger knew it as surely as she was standing there, but it was beyond her grasp. Instead, she felt the need to help her child. She needed to fill the space. She struggled to find something—anything—to say to break the silence, but nothing came to her mind.

Finally, Henry offered, "Help always comes when you need it. Have to sit still for it to find you."

He was quoting his father. Ginger held still in wonder. Eight years old when the man died, but Henry could quote him to the word.

"Well, that is true. But it's time to plant now."

"If you go and it comes, it won't find you."

Ginger's mouth dropped open. That's what Jesse had said that day at Manassas, when Ginger was pregnant with Bea—exactly what he had said, exactly how he had said it. Yet Henry had been but a baby then. How could he remember?

"What does that mean?" Hugh asked, looking toward Ginger for help.

"We've been sitting still since Daddy died and help has finally come."

Henry nodded to Osbee, then brushed past his mother and headed for the front door. As he opened it, Bea and Oliver rushed from the kitchen to follow. Oliver dropped one of his many cookies as he shut the door behind them.

The house was still. No one moved. They just stared at the front door.

"I'll get coffee," Osbee finally said.

"I'll help," Ginger breathed.

"Help always comes when you need it," Osbee added and then chuckled.

....

March 24, 1862
Somewhere other than Kernstown

My love, Juliette,
Your star has shone upon me all winter as the cold gnawed my bones. Your eye fixed in my direction, watching me walk the long miles I have walked. I sought it each night, willing the sky to be clear. Many nights heaven was thickly covered, warm in her clouds as she snowed and rained down upon us. We—the thinly covered. We—the frozen-footed, unfed sorry souls of the South.

So many miles we have marched as if seeking no other object than spring. Surely if we kept walking we'd run into her eventually. But she was always just over the next rise, rolling through Winchester and out again. Finally, we found her, green buds peeking out from the end of limbs. Leaves unfurling from their long sleep—yawning, stretching, waving happily as if it was she who had sought us those long, dark months. And we could almost see the days becoming longer. We could almost feel the wind becoming warmer. We could almost hope home was just over the next day, found at the end of the next week.

One month of spring—one month of hope. Then, yesterday's loss at Kernstown. Even Jackson couldn't stop the men running away, grabbing the poor drummer boy and forcing him to beat the rally. We beat, all right—but not to rally.

The only work I do now which seems to be of any use at all is the short stops I make on the march to help a farmer's wife turn a horse or release a plow or child from the mud. Others have begun to follow me in these brief moments, each of us living the memory or perhaps the dream of home. The click of a hoof as the horse moves through the field. The smell of weeds and dirt as the furrow is rolled. The bell ringing to call all home for a supper of beans and collards. I hadn't truly noticed the absence of that bell until yesterday. It sounded across a rolling field and it seemed the entire column stopped, hearkening to the call. I held my breath, thinking we were all going to make a break for it. I imagined her response as the entire army rose out of that woman's field, cap in hand, seeking a place at her table. I laughed out loud as we started to march once more. The imagined surprise on her face is all that has lifted my spirits since.

I am bitter at our loss and with the cold, my love. Apologies. But often I imagine you are somewhere close to the road as I walk. I was relieved to hear you moved with your father from Sharpsburg to your cousin's in Strasburg. I hope to find you in a field or beneath a tree or by a river. I shall meet you again at last, cap in hand, and there I hope to find a place at your table.

Your devoted,
Samuel

CHAPTER 13

MOONSHINE

The house had been full of words and shuffling feet as Ginger tried to serve coffee to the Martins. They, however, would not settle; instead they followed Osbee from one room to another, trying to beat sense into her with argument and tenacious pursuit. But everyone was talking and no one was listening any longer, so the words just floated about the kitchen, dining room, and family room like a bunch of notes played absently by a small child on a piano. None of it made sense and it wasn't a pretty tune, to be sure. Eventually, the long drone of discord found its way to the door, down the steps of the porch, and was silenced by the slamming of the Mercedes's doors. At the exact moment the car rolled onto the asphalt, Beau came slinking out of the barn. Coward.

Ginger kissed Osbee on the cheek and, without any words, they made dinner. All was quiet as they ate, after which there was just a soft murmuring as baths were taken. Osbee mentioned something about exhaustion when she passed by the door to the bathroom. Ginger was towel-drying Oliver when a mumbled "Good night" was followed by the gentle closing of Osbee's bedroom door. That was soon followed by Bea's door shutting and Oliver climbing into bed next to his brother.

By nine p.m., silence fell through the house and Ginger slowly walked around it, room to room, turning off the lights, locking the doors. As she did so, for the first time she pondered how many people had done these things in the 144 years the Smoots' farm had stood. Then she wondered why she hadn't thought about it before this night. When Samuel and ghosts rolled across her mind, she shivered and went upstairs quickly to bed.

There she lay down, covers tucked beneath her chin, listening to the wind and watching herself kneel in the snow near Jesse's tree. She had asked for anything and so here she was, in an old house, on ancient land, waiting for a ghost to help her—farm.

"Be careful what you ask for," she whispered, breathing in the scent of coffee that was now brewing in the kitchen. She hadn't slept a wink, and when her cell phone alarm sounded at eleven thirty p.m., she turned it off. It was time to get up—time to go to work. As she rolled out of her covers, a large shadow moved in the far corner of the room. An electric zap of terror seized her spine and instantly she reached for the lamp next to her bed.

"Don't!" Samuel said, but it was too late. It

240

was reflex; she turned the knob. *"Ahhh!"* he yelled. In the flash of light, in the second the bulb came to life, Ginger saw Samuel in the corner of the room with both of his arms flung across his face as if recoiling from a large flame. Then he was gone.

"Samuel?" Ginger called.

The door burst open and Osbee rushed in. "What?" the old woman asked, her eyes wide as she stood barefoot in her white nightdress.

In the light, Ginger could just make out a shadow of red undergarments through the cotton. She grinned a little. "Uh, bad dream," Ginger said with a shrug as she endeavored to recover from her own start. "So sorry."

"Holy Moses!" Osbee said, grabbing her heart. "That didn't even sound like you."

"It was a really bad dream," Ginger added, climbing out of bed. "Sorry to wake you. Go on back to bed."

Osbee shot her a sideways glance, shaking a little as she turned to go. Before she left, she paused to offer, "We'll talk tomorrow when you get home."

"Yeah. Oh—and Ed Rogers is coming to fix Henry's Child."

Osbee stopped, gazing over her shoulder. "Who?"

"Ed Rogers. Jesse bought parts for Henry's Child before he, uh—"

"Yeah, okay." Osbee waved to stop the rest of the sentence. "Good thing, 'cause we'll need that tractor now."

"Time to plow," Ginger said as she followed the old woman into the hall.

"That's for sure. Drive safe, daughter."

"Always," Ginger replied. "Love you, Osbee."

"Love you, too."

Ginger shut the bathroom door, stood still for just a second, and then, faster than Oliver could grab a free cookie, she was dressed and tiptoeing down the stairs. She found Beau sleeping on the couch with Regard resting just above him on the windowsill. Both raised their heads as Ginger entered the living room.

"Samuel?" she whispered. She stopped to listen. Nothing.

"Samuel?" Stepping into the kitchen, she turned on the light. There was no sound except the popping of the coffeepot as it finished brewing.

"Uh, sorry," she whispered to the empty kitchen. "I didn't realize it was you."

Ginger poured coffee into her traveler's mug, grabbed her lunch from the refrigerator, slipped into her coat and boots, and quietly stepped out of the house. The yard was darker than the night before even though a sliver of moon hung above. Snow reflects light and as most of it had melted away during the day, the moon had no help brightening the night. Coming around the back of the house, she found a shadow sitting on the front fender of her truck. She halted.

"Samuel?" she whispered.

"I did not mean to startle you, Virginia. I was hoping to speak with you and could not determine how best to wake you."

"I was awake," she replied, walking toward the truck.

"Oh," Samuel said, standing free of the fender.

"Why did you yell?" she asked.

"I cannot be in light."

Ginger thought for a moment. She had seen him in the day and opened her mouth to say such.

"Electric light," Samuel interrupted. "Electricity hurts me."

Ginger shut her mouth, not sure she wanted any further explanation.

"To be in your house . . . itches a little."

"Itches," she repeated.

"Yes. I can will myself through your doors and windows, but not through the walls, as there is electricity there."

She nodded as if to indicate she understood. She had, of course, no true comprehension of what he was talking about but it seemed the polite thing to do. What were manners when dealing with a ghost?

"Um, is that what you wanted to tell me?"

"No. But it is why I could not help you with the sick boy on the road."

"Ah." Ginger smiled. "You couldn't get in my truck."

"It is full of electricity. And light hurts. Bright light hurts greatly."

"But not the sun," Ginger stated.

"No. Nor moonshine." Samuel pointed up at the moon, which smiled down at them like the Cheshire cat.

She nodded again and lightly danced from one foot to the other. It was cold. "I, uh, have to go to work."

"I know. I— Would you mind if I rode with you?"

Ginger cocked her head. "I thought yo—"

"I can sit back here," Samuel said, walking back to the bed of the truck. "And this window opens, yes?"

He pointed to the little sliding window in the back of the cab. Oliver called it "Beau's window."

"It won't hurt?"

"It'll itch a little, I think. But we can talk. Would you mind, Virginia?"

"Not at all. Mmm. There'll be headlights on the freeway."

"I think I can duck. If I dissipate, though, I'll only end up back in your orchard."

Reticently, Ginger shuffled to the driver's side. "You dissipated when I turned on my light," she said.

"Yes."

As she opened the door, Samuel, who was climbing into the bed, coughed loudly and held his hand over his nose. "What is that smell?" he asked, shaking his head.

"Jacob Esch hurled in my truck," Ginger replied, turning on the truck. She then reached back and opened Beau's window.

"Who is Jacob Esch and what is 'hurled'?" Samuel said as he lifted himself into the truck bed.

"The Amish kid you found in the ditch. And 'hurled' means he threw up."

Ginger shut her door, turned her lights on, and began to back down the drive. There was Samuel, a ghost, sitting with his head in Beau's window. She shivered a little and so turned instead to her side windows to back down the gravel drive.

"Amish. So they yet live?"

"Yep. You had Amish back the—" Her sentence stopped with the truck. What were ghostly manners?

"Back then," Samuel finished her sentence. "We did."

Ginger put the truck in drive and slowly made her way down the road.

"Where are you from?" Ginger asked.

"I have said, Virginia Moon. Laurel Creek."

"There were Amish in Laurel Creek?"

"No. My best friends had a friend who was from Pennsylvania. An Amish on rumspringa."

"I see."

Ginger came to the spot where she'd fallen near the fence—where Bea saw Samuel standing as she rode away in the bus. Samuel had not said anything and she looked in her rearview mirror to see if he was still there. He was, his eyes lifted to the sky.

"Light hurts, Virginia Moon. I can smell and see and hear. But I cannot touch or taste. I am left here in the world, but am not of it. That is how the Amish say they live."

"How's that?" Ginger turned right.

"They are in the world, not of it. But truly, they are of it. They can feel the sun and the wind. They can feel the warmth of soup on a cold night and taste the salt of its broth. They can work all day beneath heaven and feel the aches of their muscles. They can touch hair, feel breath, taste lips."

How long had it been since she'd tasted Jesse's lips? She felt an ache in the center of her body as a car came toward the truck and she could see Samuel disappear from her rearview mirror.

The car passed. Darkness grew. Had he dissipated? "Samuel?" she called quietly.

"I am here, looking up at a Virginia moon."

She smiled and leaned forward to see it, too.

"To farm beneath a Virginia moon," he said.

"Hard to farm in the dark, I reckon, Samuel," she said with a giggle.

"The orange one that rises on the harvest. Huge and round on the horizon. No sound but insects, the click of horse hooves, and the scour of the plow."

Ginger imagined the quiet of plowing so. "I love that moon," she said. "I like it when it's warm on those evenings."

"Mmm. A ginger moon," he whispered.

Ginger giggled.

"What's funny?" Samuel asked.

"I was thinking about my name."

He popped up in her rearview mirror. "I love your name," he said.

She smiled to his reflection. "My mother always wanted to name her daughter Virginia after her grandmother. My father wanted to name his child 'Moon.' You know my dad? The one you want to meet?"

Samuel nodded, staring at her intently.

Ginger sighed, thinking about her father. *Step into the light.* What if it hurts? "Yeah—Virginia Moon. My hair is strawberry blond, so my parents call me Ginger Moon."

They had reached Highway 81 and Samuel lay down, saying, "But your hair is dark."

"Mood hair," she replied, accelerating.

"What?"

"My hair changes with my mood. Like a mood ring." She laughed.

"What's a mood ring?"

247

Ginger stopped laughing with a little cough. That joke didn't translate. There must not have been mood rings back *then*. "It's a little ring with something inside the glass stone that changes color with the heat of your body. Supposedly, different colors mean you're feeling this way or that. Doesn't really work or anything. It's just a— thing. It was popular a while ago."

"You change your hair with your mood?" Samuel asked.

Ginger shook her head. This wasn't working. "Just a joke, Samuel."

"Your hair changes as a joke?"

"No. The mood thing—that's a joke. The hair color—the mood ring." For the love of Pete.

"Why do you change your hair?"

She rolled her eyes. Could she switch subjects politely? "I don't know. To change something. To see something new."

"Is that why you drive so far to work?"

Ginger thought. "I don't think I do those two things for the same reason."

"We passed a hospital on our way, Virginia. It is closer to home."

"I know."

The cab of the truck fell silent. Cars passed on the left and Ginger wondered if ever anyone would believe she had a ghost riding with her. Until this morning, Samuel could be explained away logically. Now he was her companion on her travels. Was she calling him, keeping him with her? He had said as much.

"When my husband was alive, I was more. I was greater than I am now."

"You are the same person."

"No—not the same. I never used to question if I was pretty because he thought me so. And smart —he thought me so. It's like I am myself and I have respect for myself, but with him I was more myself. And he was more himself with me. Now I am just myself. I was more because he thought me so."

Ginger switched into the left lane. A BMW had been going too slow for her. This made no sense.

"Look—I was born a traveler. I had a wanderlust to see the world. To be of it and in it. To walk on as it rolls endlessly beneath my feet and be dusty and sore from the road. But with him, I didn't need to go anywhere to do that. Every day was something new. Another day to figure stuff out with him. We weren't done with anything. We weren't even sure we were done having kids."

She returned to the right lane.

"But now, here I am. No more kids. I didn't even get a choice in that. I don't even know who I am anymore or what I want or what I like. How can I raise children and do them any justice? This wasn't our plan. We were together in this. We were greater. I want him back. I want to see him and tell him he is more—more than anything else in the world."

Ginger broke off, her voice cracking. Flipping on her blinker, she turned the endless loop off 81 and onto the road that climbed into the Blue Ridge. She wept as the truck wound through Harrisonburg and crawled up the hill. The sky was clear, the air cold. She said nothing for miles as she struggled to stop crying. She came to the spot where Jacob Esch had lain drunk in the ditch and she wiped her stinging eyes.

"Are you still there?" she asked as her voice steadied.

Samuel slid up into Beau's window.

"I called to him, Samuel. That day in the snow. And you came. An answer to my prayer."

"I . . . am an answer to your prayer, Virginia Moon?"

"As sure as I'm sitting in this smelly truck." She sniffled, taking a sip of her coffee.

"I have never been an answer to a prayer. I have been prayed over. I must confess, I was hardly an obedient son. I perpetually spilled things I shouldn't have touched or broke things I shouldn't have played with or rode away to a far, distant place on a horse that was not our own. Many a time have I heard the prayer 'Lord, give me patience with this boy' as the switch hit my backside. Never would my father believe I would be the answer to anyone's prayer."

Ginger looked up at the rearview mirror. Samuel's face was shadowed by the light of her dashboard and he was smiling in the darkness of the empty road.

"Well, maybe, Samuel, one day I'll meet your father and set him straight."

"Will you?" He chuckled.

"Yes."

"And what will you say to him?"

"I will say that in the darkest day I have ever lived, your son came as an answer to my prayer. And I know now—I know, Samuel—my husband rode the Elysian Fields home and is watching over me. Watching over our children."

She put on her blinker and pulled into the hospital parking lot, which held more than ten vehicles. In her three shifts at Franklin, the parking lot had never had so many cars when she arrived. It was a busy night at the hospital. The truck crawled closer to the lights.

"Better go now, Samuel. This is no moonshine and I would never wish you to hurt on account of me."

"Very well. I will be home when you return," he said quietly, and as Ginger turned into a parking space far from the emergency room door, she gazed over her shoulder to find Samuel gone.

CHAPTER 14

PEAS IN A POD

Ginger walked into a full ER.

There were six people seated in the waiting area. A man of indeterminate age leaned forward, holding his stomach as a woman about Ginger's age rubbed his back. There was a young girl around fifteen years old with hives sitting with a woman who looked to be her mother. Both the girl and her mother were texting and didn't look up. Seated very near the door was a middle-aged man staring at the TV on the far wall. Finally, Ginger spotted the young man who had come in with the two-year-old bronchitis two nights before. He coughed miserably, forcing a smile as Ginger stepped around the triage desk.

There she found Margery T., RN, pulling a cuff from the arm of an old woman who was seated in one of the hospital's wheelchairs with a rag held to her eye by her frail, shaking hand. The old woman grinned up at Ginger. Nurse Margery did not. Peering toward the back rooms, Ginger could see both Janet and Debbie, the acute care LVNs, buzzing around the hall.

"Okay, Mrs. Kimber," Nurse Margery said. "All done. Janet?"

Janet walked briskly to triage.

"Please take Mrs. Kimber into room two."

"Yes, ma'am," Janet replied and grabbed the handles of the wheelchair.

"AGA," Margery said. "Acute Gravity Attack."

"Ah."

"Her Yorkie got under her feet," Nurse Margery added. "Her son out there brought the dog in against his will because his mother was quite agitated. She was more worried about it than herself."

"The dog okay?"

"Don't know. Looked chipper so I touched its paws and ribs and nodded to Mrs. Kimber. She seemed satisfied." Margery stood. "The choly is next," she said.

Dropping her purse in the drawer, Ginger looked at the list of names on the entrance sheet. Mr. Russell, cholecystitis, an inflamed gall-bladder, was next. Ginger poked her head around the wall of the triage desk.

"Mr. Russell?"

The man holding his gut lifted his bottom from the seat but could not straighten up beyond ninety degrees. As he shuffled slowly over, he was held across the back by the woman who was with him.

"He's in terrible pain," she said. "It happens every time he eats pizza."

"Yes. Have a seat, Mr. Russell."

For two hours, Ginger sat at triage as Nurse Margery aided Dr. Patterson in the back. Mrs. Kimber was sent home with her son, who turned the TV off as he left. Lauren O'Brian, who had the hives, was given a shot of prednisone and released with a prescription for the same. Todd Parker had bronchitis. After receiving antibiotics, he walked out as a twenty-five-year-old expectant mother, Ruth Agee, and her husband walked in with breakthrough bleeding.

So it went, one after another—a true full-moon night in Franklin District Community Hospital. At six thirty-two a.m., an hour after Nurse Margery finally left, Ginger stood at triage completing the discharge of Mr. Russell and his wife.

"No more pizza," she said.

Mrs. Russell shook her head and as Mr. Russell signed the release Ginger heard the ER doors open. They closed as she checked to make sure there were, in Mr. Russell's instructions, clear directions to go see the nearest GI physician. It was there in black and white, just as it had been for three months' worth of prior ER visits. As she handed Mrs. Russell the papers, she heard breathing on the opposite side of the triage wall. It was loud and heavy and scary, as if Darth Vader had entered the emergency room. The Russells looked at Ginger with concern. She looked at them, listening intently. Finally, she smiled a half smile and then asked, "Mr. Wolfe?"

A throaty guffaw was the only response.

"Good night, Mr. Russell," Ginger said as she helped the man to his feet. He no longer stood at a right angle to the floor. He could lift himself to forty-five degrees. Following the Russells around the triage desk, she found the waiting room empty except for Jack Wolfe, who stood as pale as the fluorescent lights above him.

"Been eating chocolate bars, I reckon," she said.

He didn't answer, for his breath was too labored. Instead, he smiled weakly as Ginger took him by his arm.

"You're lucky Margery is gone," she said.

He coughed a laugh.

As she helped Jack Wolfe by room one, she found Dr. Patterson washing his hands in the sink while Janet ripped the paper sheet off the bed and wadded it up.

"Janet, we will have another guest coming into acute care."

"Would you like your usual bed, Mr. Wolfe, or a room by yourself?" Janet asked with a broad smile. "You have a choice tonight."

"Mr. Wolfe?" Dr. Patterson inquired as he gazed from Jack to Janet to Ginger.

"Dr. Patterson," Ginger said. "This is Jack Wolfe —sixty-six-year-old white male. He's COPD, CHP, diabetic, noncompliant. Mr. Wolfe, this is your doctor for about fifteen more minutes."

Jack harrumphed.

"He's laughing at us," Ginger said and continued to room two of the ER.

Dr. Patterson furrowed his brow, and after pulling out a paper towel to dry his hands, he followed Ginger and her patient down the short hall.

"We need blood work," the doctor said.

"I'll order the usual," Janet replied as she headed toward acute care.

"Mr. Wolfe!" a voice loudly declared from behind.

Startled, Ginger stepped on Jack's left foot as she was about to lower him onto the bed. "Sorry," she whispered and gazed over her shoulder.

There she found a short, dark woman with salt-and-pepper, long braids, maroon lipstick, a white coat, and a stethoscope. Her badge read, "Dr. Demazilliere." Her smile was so bright, the night shift squinted as they looked at her.

Jack Wolfe moaned.

"Come to spend some quality time with us, have you, Jack?" she inquired, reaching her hand out to Dr. Patterson. "Sorry I'm late, Doctor. Problems with the grandbaby. I'm Mavis Demazilliere."

"Ernest Patterson." They shook hands.

"You must be Nurse Martin."

Ginger looked over her shoulder quizzically. "I am."

"Call me Dr. D. Name's hard for some people to say," the doctor said. "Jack here talked about you when I saw him in town yesterday."

"He did?" Ginger asked, helping Mr. Wolfe off with his coat.

"Yup. Said you wouldn't give him a candy bar or a dollar."

Jack winked at Ginger as she laid him back on the bed.

"But he did take your advice and looked at the contents of the candy bars he was purchasing. Three Musketeers bars have less salt."

Jack smiled and broke into a deep, throaty cough, closing his eyes with a wince.

"Oh." Ginger shrugged and found Dr. Patterson looking at her with a smirk.

"Best advice he's gotten in a long while. He's gonna eat 'em anyway. Try to find the least worse one. Good. Good. Well, let's have a look at this gold-star body of yours, Mr. Wolfe. It just keeps a-goin' no matter what you do to it."

Dr. Patterson chose to stay, helping to stabilize Jack Wolfe as a seventy-two-year-old man with gout came in complaining of chest pain. Ginger and Dr. D. dealt with the newcomer, Barry Bartholomew, who was followed shortly by a screaming ambulance flying out of the driveway across from the ER. The waiting room filled up again and there was no downtime from seven a.m. until Ginger's shift ended at two p.m. At that time, she handed off her patient load to her relief, grabbed her handbag, and headed for the door.

Just as she was about to walk out, she stopped. She had meant to discuss chocolate bars and her private medical advice about choosing which ones to eat against doctor's orders with Mr. Wolfe but had found no time to do so. With a scowl on her face, she about-faced on her heel and headed to acute care. There was no need to ask where he was; she could hear his breathing before she got to his door. Very gently, she opened it and found Jack Wolfe lying in bed with his eyes closed.

But she was surprised to see in the second bed Jacob Esch, flipping through channels on a silent TV. His eyes met hers and then went wide.

"Sorry," she said softly. "I was going to talk with Mr. Wolfe." She stepped back out.

"Virginia Moon, RN?" Jack rasped.

"Yes, Mr. Wolfe."

"Nurse Virginia?" Jacob asked, scooting himself up in the bed. He winced.

Ginger cocked her head. "Yes?"

"Come in, come in," Mr. Wolfe said. "Didn't get you in trouble, did I?" He breathed in heavily and smiled through weepy eyes.

"Not at all, Mr. Wolfe," Ginger replied. "But I did want to talk to you about doing things that are not good for you."

"I'm sorry I threw up in your car," Jacob blurted out.

She gazed at him and then Jack. "You were sick," Ginger said.

"Nurse Margery says it was a real mess. Were you able to clean it up?"

Jack watched her with a pop eye.

"I'm nearly there," was all she could reply. The boy looked stricken.

"As soon as I am out of here, I'll clean it," he said.

"Thanks, Jacob. But I live far away and I'm not sure I'll be back."

"You'll be back," Jack said.

"Really? And how do you know that?"

"Because something's happening." He closed his pop eye and breathed in as if the sheets weighed two hundred pounds.

"What's happening?" The question came out of her mouth before she could stop it. She bit her lip, not sure she wanted to hear the answer.

"I am an expert on ERs. I've been in them for years—especially this one." Jack breathed. "I have found that those who choose to administer medical care in an ER do it because we are just a bunch of illnesses walking through a door. If we have vital signs, we're either admitted or released. If we don't have vitals, y'all try to get us to have 'em. If you can, we're admitted. If you can't, we're off to the soil to rest. No name. No

259

connection. No nothin'. That's ER, isn't it? The ER cares but don't really care."

His eye popped open and his gaze hit her so hard, she leaned back against the door. She had no answer—no answer because it had always been true of her.

"Now, you know me and Jacob here, and look, you have your purse and you're off and where are you? Here." He muffled a laugh as he closed his eyes.

Ginger gazed at the man, who was so pale and weak. As she rested against the door, she thought how odd it was that she should be there. Mr. Wolfe was very sick—on his way out, really. But he was going on his own terms. It was why she had made the chocolate bar comment in the first place. What did she mean coming in here?

"When you come back, I'll clean your car," Jacob repeated.

"I most likely won't be back, Mr. Esch. I'm not going to practice nursing much longer."

"Why?" Jack Wolfe inquired.

"Because I'm going to far—" Ginger broke off. She stared at Jack and then peered over to Jacob Esch.

"Did you say farm?" Jacob asked.

"Mr. Wolfe. Joshua Wheldon came in here and said you had a cow for sale."

"Not for sale."

Ginger paused. She was sure Mr. Wheldon had said the cow was for sale.

"Josh Wheldon said he met you. Said you were right nice to him."

"You don't have a cow?" Ginger queried.

"I have a cow. A Guernsey."

"Best milkers, Guernseys," Jacob said. "Great cream."

"You're not selling it?" Ginger pressed.

"Beautiful ginger-colored girl," Mr. Wolfe said.

Ginger stood straight up from the door. "Beg pardon?"

"My cow. Named her Ginger. She's a beautiful ginger color."

Ginger's mouth dropped open.

"You got a farm, Nurse Virginia?" Jacob asked.

She shook her head. "I'm making one," she whispered.

Jack tilted his head and stared at her with his pop eye. "Need a cow?"

She nodded slowly.

"I've got a cow that needs a good home. But not for sale."

"What you need?" Jacob asked, shimmying up straighter in the bed.

"Need to take the goat with her," Jack replied.

"Goat milk is good on a farm, too," Jacob said with a bright smile.

"Billy goat," Jack whispered.

"Ach." Jacob's nose screwed up as if he'd smelled something awful.

"Ginger needs the goat. They're family."

Ginger shook her head. Which Ginger needed a goat?

Jacob stared slack-jawed at Jack. "Billy goats are smelly and nasty," he said. "Not useful at all unless you're looking to breed goats."

"Ginger's free with the goat."

"How much without the goat?" Jacob asked.

"Not for sale," Jack said.

Jacob sat on the bed looking at his hands for a minute.

Ginger just stood there, watching the entire conversation with not a word to say. She was still processing the fact that the cow's name was Ginger.

"Good milkers are thousands of dollars, Mrs. Martin," Jacob said at last. "Guernseys have really good milk."

"Ginger has the best and a lot of it," Jack rasped.

"You getting a lot of cows for a dairy farm or what?" Jacob asked.

Ginger shrugged.

"What kind of farm you got?" Jacob asked.

"I—I don't know."

Jacob's jaw went slack again. "You don't know what kind of farm you have?" His lip curled slightly.

"It was a corn farm but I have to make it keep

me and my kids and Grandma Osbee . . . together."

"Mrs. Martin lost her husband in the war," Jack Wolfe explained through a cough.

Jacob stared at her for a long while.

She shifted from her right foot to her left.

"You have a family farm, you need a milker. Cows are never free, and though I think the goat is a waste, if it comes with the cow, you should take it."

"I should take it," Ginger repeated.

"Done!" Jack Wolfe announced and held out his hand.

Ginger walked over and took it.

"Best decision you've ever made, Virginia Moon."

She shook his hand and gazed up at his drip. It was going too slow. She reached up and adjusted the flow.

"Mr. Wolfe. Since you and Mr. Esch here are roommates for a bit, maybe you can tell him all about your wild life."

"I drank too much. I smoked too much. I had a great time doing both," he said hoarsely.

She released his hand.

"I'd do both now if I could," he added.

"I know. Mr. Esch is thinking he might want to do so also." Ginger flicked her eyes to Jacob, who slid down deeper into his covers. She smiled wryly.

"I don't regret any of it," Mr. Wolfe said.

"I know," she replied as she walked to the door. "Thank you, Mr. Esch, for advising me about the cow."

He shrugged as he tucked the covers beneath his chin.

"You two stay out of trouble."

"I'll call Josh Wheldon," Jack said. "He'll help with the cow. Where you live?"

"Far from here, in Virginia."

"You said that. Where?"

"A place called Smoot's farm. Off of 81, north of Woodstock." She opened the door.

"Near the covered bridge?" Jacob asked, scooting up a little.

Ginger spun around to look at him. "Y-yes. H-how do you know that?"

"I love covered bridges," Jacob said, grinning. "That's a pretty one."

She nodded slowly.

"I can tell Mr. Wheldon how to get there," he added and rolled over.

"Thank you," Ginger replied, dumbfounded.

She stepped out of the room and as the door closed behind her she heard Jack Wolfe say, "Something's happening, Jacob Esch." And then he laughed.

May 22, 1862
Near Front Royal

Dear Juliette,
We've been marching, if marching is what you could call it. For nine days now, our commander has us marching and then, after a time, we stop and are ordered to lie down. Not sit. Not stand. Lie down. Rest completely. Then, after a time, we stand again and march on. So it has been and though Jackson's order is strange, we obey. I will say that after marching long and in this fashion, we have become as one body, fast moving and silent when ordered. Some say we are like wolves. We are not a pack of wolves. We are a pack of cats—silent when ordered and fast. As we move, chills race my spine, for we have become a truly dangerous thing to behold.

Alas, there has been no place where we can demonstrate our nature, exactly. We are simply waiting. The sea of blue before us grows and grows and the great battles are now in the west and on the Atlantic. If those efforts push the battle in our direction before we find a place to pounce, I'm afraid we shall be no more than a tick on the back of the

Union, squeezed from both sides until we let go.

I know this valley, and as we march I watch our progress etched on the horizon by the passing mountains. Winchester is again in Yankee hands, and if I know anything, we will take it back. Jackson has sent men out this day—scattered them to tear at railroad tracks and cut telegraph lines. But the rest of us will not war on machines this time. Tonight is rest for us and will be much needed for what must be ahead of us on the morrow. But we are tense like a great cat with eyes closed, body tight, poised and camouflaged, waiting to show off our nature.

And we shall—tomorrow, if I am not much mistaken. I am not mistaken. I hear the bird and as I lie here, stealing a secret letter to you by firelight, I answer the call. I whistle just as it does. Uncertain am I to its purpose, but I know it is a friendly spirit. It sings in me courage and will. I want to fight now. I want to fight so the war will end. There will be nothing of my future with you until it does. Your peace fills me so completely now and I know I cannot find you until the war is done.

So I say, let it come. Let screams and smoke and keening beasts fill my ears and eyes. Let my hands grow black and burnt from musket fire as blood pours upon the Earth. The Valley of Death must be crossed to reach the other side, where now I know you wait. Only in its crossing shall spring weep its gentle tears and wash all away.

I sing the bird. I am crossing now to you. And I shall see you on the other side. Pray for me, Juliette.

Your devoted,
Samuel

CHAPTER 15

MR. ROGERS
TO THE RESCUE

The wind was cuttin' a shine in a clear blue sky when Ginger left work and her drive home seemed to take thirty minutes less time than usual. She wasn't sure if it was a tailwind pushing her truck or if the mountains had blown Smoot's farm closer to Highway 81, but as she drove down the lane on this blustery Sunday afternoon, she found people and cars blocking her drive. They were seeking the bridge and in so doing they filled her drive like so many leaves swept by the wind into a pile, impeded from further progress by a great mound of dirt. She slid by a station wagon that was leaving, as it had found nothing much to look at, which was always the case when coming to Smoot's farm. Then she pulled up into her drive behind a red Dodge pickup and disengaged the engine.

As she opened her door a large bang sounded from the direction of the barn and quickly she hopped from her truck, slammed the door, and trotted up the gravel incline. A rolling crash from the direction of the bridge made her jump and she froze in place, unsure which direction she should go.

"Good afternoon, Virginia Moon." Samuel was at her back. She didn't even need to turn around.

"What's going on?" she asked.

"Well, Mr. Rogers is here with his wife fixing the tractor. Grandma has taken Henry and Oliver to ride the horses in the corral to keep them from getting underfoot in the barn. The horses seemed relieved also. Bea is watching Mr. Rogers fight with Henry's Child with great concern, but she will not talk about it and I did try to talk with her. And five men with a strange vehicle have maneuvered around your orchard and bridge toward where I came across the river."

"Holy cow!" Ginger declared and, dropping her purse and lunch bag on the gravel drive, took off at a run toward Jesse's tree. She had forgotten about the park ranger and she seethed with anger at herself because she hadn't discussed it further with Osbee.

Deep ruts in the streambed next to the bridge made her hiss and her feet beat like a drum across its wooden floor. Loud sounds of a chain saw poured through the walnut and ash and she flew like the crows above her head in that direction. She skidded to a halt as she emerged from the trees and screamed, *"Stop!"*

Three men worked the trees. One was atop the pine with a chain saw rattling away at branches while two others were securing a heavy chain to Jesse's fallen ash. A large ATV was attached to a winch, around which the other end of the chain was secured. Two men stood next to the winch supervising the entire operation and none of them made any indication that they had heard her.

"*Stop! Stop! Stop!*" she yelled, waving her arms as she trotted over to the ATV.

The man with the chain saw was the only person facing in her direction, and when he saw her he cut the machine off.

"Stop," she said, holding her chest from her run. Silence echoed and in the sudden quiet the trees creaked above her head as if irritated by the windy gusts that blew down the Shenandoah.

"Ma'am?" the man nearest her inquired. His green uniform made it clear that he was a park official from the other side of the river.

"Wait," she said.

"Uh, wind's expected to pick up and we're already working in unsafe conditions," he said, walking closer to her.

She nodded as a small branch from a walnut tree to the right tumbled from above, punctuating the man's sentence.

"What's the plan?" she asked.

"Beg pardon?"

"What are you doing?"

"We need to detach the trees to clear the river." He gazed at her with an isn't-that-obvious look.

"River needs to be clear," Samuel said from behind.

"I want that tree left whole," she said, pointing to Jesse's ash.

"I don't think that's possible. The top branches are tangled in the pine," the ranger said.

"As whole as possible. C-can you, like, swing it around so it lays flush to the river's edge that way?" She pointed up the river to the left.

"I can, but if the water rises with the spring flow, it might be picked up anyway."

Ginger bit her lip. Her throat tightened as tears threatened. How to tell this man who stood with a perplexed look on his face what the tree meant? How to explain without going into anything too deeply? This was something she didn't want to share with anyone. It was hers alone to bear.

"Sometimes it is best to open a wound to help it heal," Samuel said.

Ginger gazed over her shoulder.

He stood with his hands behind his back, looking into her gently. "But you know that, being, as you are, a nurse."

She nodded and, turning back to the ranger, said, "Losing it in a wash is a risk, I know. But I need to keep it. It belonged to my husband. He's, um—" She peered up to the crackling branches above her head. A tear rolled down her cheek as she returned her eyes to those of the ranger. "He died in Iraq and that tree was his favorite place.

He taught his kids to swim here. I just need . . . *to keep it if I can*." The last words she didn't say but shrugged as she mouthed them.

As Ginger gazed from one man to the next, they all nodded and, without another word, the two men who had been attaching the chain began to detach it.

"If we move the winch over there," the man on the pine said, pointing to his right, "we can pull it around and lay it behind that boulder there. I think it can reach."

"We'll make it work," the ranger said. "Sorry for your loss."

Ginger shrugged again and smiled a little as she took a deep breath. "I'll make some coffee for you guys. It's cold out here," she said and, turning around, gazed into Samuel's soft brown eyes. As if she had taken his hand, he turned and together they walked back toward the house.

"That was hard," she whispered to him.

"It's private," he replied.

Ginger looked over to him and he to her.

"Never heard a tear shed that wasn't personal," she offered.

"Never shed one myself that wasn't personal," he added.

A great gust roared through the bridge. Like a flood of water, the wind rushed at them. Ginger put her head down, pulling Jesse's coat tighter around her body, and as she looked at Samuel she found that he, too, slumped forward as if in effort against it.

"Can you feel the wind?" she called.

He grinned and stood up straight, his hair and clothing perfectly still, as if it were a heavy summer's day with hardly a breeze to mention. He said, "I was commiserating."

They laughed together as the trees shook and moaned behind them, seeming both angry and sad at being left alone with five strangers in their midst.

Squinting in the small, flying debris, Ginger approached the bridge, saying, "Need to fix that streambed. Look at those ruts. What a mess."

"Let the water heal it," Samuel replied as they entered the covered bridge.

"There is no water," she said.

They were quiet as they cleared the bridge and walked past the orchard. Apple and pear trees rustled and danced, their limbs whispering that the little white buds were ready to bloom.

"Why is there a bridge if there is no water?" Samuel asked.

Startled, Ginger turned her head and found his look of puzzlement laughable. He had pondered the bridge over a dried-up stream in the quiet between them. "So people will drive down Highway 81 and see a historical marker indicating that it is out here and they'll get off and drive five miles of back roads to see it."

His face reflected his mind; it mulled over this information as they passed the walnut tree. "Why?"

"So there will be something to talk about down here where nothing happens." She burst out laughing again, remembering Jesse and once having this exact conversation with him.

Samuel let out a chuckle and shook his head, just as she had done all those years ago. She was now Jesse, living with that bridge, watching the cars come down the lane, one after another after another. They'd stop, look, look harder, sure there was something to see, shrug at the fact that there was a whole lot of nothing, take a picture maybe, turn around, and go back to the highway. There was no purpose to any of it, no purpose at all. And that was funny.

"Ginger?"

She nearly jumped backward, surprised to see Ed's wife, Lorena, standing in front of her.

"Uh, hi," she said awkwardly, gazing back to Samuel. He had stopped and stood a polite distance off to the right.

Lorena smiled, following Ginger's gaze. "What was so funny?"

"Oh, I was just remembering a conversation from long ago. Some wind we're having." She changed the subject.

"Not a thing can rest in it," Lorena replied. "Ed is nearly finished with Henry's Child."

"Excellent." Ginger's smile widened. "Can I see?"

"Of course. We brought dinner also."

"Ah, you didn't need to."

"I know, but we did. That way we can stay." Lorena let out a small laugh.

"You'd be invited anyway."

"I know," she said, entwining her elbow with Ginger's.

There was a loud pop and then a hesitant cough of an engine. The tractor sputtered and spat as Ginger entered the barn. Henry's Child seemed none too thrilled at being awakened from its long sleep, but Ed Rogers had nudged it fully to life and it chugged along in idle, the exhaust filling the barn with smoke.

"These things are sensitive," he said to Bea, who stood next to Penny's empty stall, her face impassive. She didn't nod, didn't smile. Nothing moved on her but her eyes, which flicked between Henry's Child and the man bent over its engine. Finally, they turned at last in her mother's direction. A crease deepened in her stony brow.

"Mama?" Bea walked over, full of purpose. Henry's Child warmed to the idea of moving as Bea's gaze fell between Lorena and her mother. She was looking at Samuel.

"Yes, Bea?"

"I'm thinking about something. Something's happening."

That was what Jack Wolfe had told Jacob Esch. She could have said something, could have prompted her daughter with a question. But in this quiet moment, filled only with the sound of Henry's Child stretching to move at last, it was as if she was in a breath between notes again. She waited. Ed Rogers cut the engine off and Ginger hung in the silence of that space like valley air between two mountains, waiting to be moved by wind.

"Mr. Rogers gave us Penny and Christian."

Ginger said nothing.

"He really loves Henry's Child like Grandpa Henry loved it."

"I don't exactly love it," Ed Rogers corrected.

"So Mr. Rogers has Christian and Penny's bridles and yokes and such."

Ginger said not—a—thing.

"I'm thinking . . . Henry and Oliver and I . . . Well, Henry's Child is mine. That's kinda how it's been and—and I'm thinking we give it to Mr. Rogers because he will care for it like Grandpa did. And he can give us Penny and Christian's stuff and we farm like—like the help that's come used to do. Back then."

Bea motioned her head toward Samuel.

"What help?" Lorena asked, confusion furrowing deeply between her eyes.

A huge gust blew through the yard, shook the walnut tree, and bound into the barn, sending the exhaust from Henry's Child scattering like unwanted rain clouds in a bright blue sky.

"Farm with horses," Ginger repeated her daughter's idea.

"Um, you can't do that, Ginger," Lorena said.

"I agree," Mr. Rogers said. "There's a lot to learn in farming and that just adds to the complication."

Ginger turned around, looked at Samuel, and then gazed past him toward the covered bridge.

"There's no purpose to that bridge . . ." She breathed. "Except to bring people down here."

"Where they find nothing happening," Samuel said, chuckling.

Ginger spun on her heel and looked intently at her daughter. "Little Bea. That there is your daddy's tractor."

"I know," Bea said, her eyes moistening as she straightened her shoulders.

"I can't ask you to give it up."

"I know," she said, her face twitching in hidden hurt. The little girl swallowed.

Birds chirped as they flew by. The wind blew through the barn, rustling and whistling as it did so. No one moved. No one spoke. Finally, Bea turned with square shoulders, raising her chin bravely to look upon Mr. Rogers.

"We need Penny and Christian's stuff, please. I'll trade you Henry's Child for it."

"I think your daddy would rather you keep this," the man answered.

"I think this is exactly what my daddy would want if he was here. We really need this stuff, Mr. Rogers."

Ginger gazed at the man, who met her with steady eyes. His look appeared as if he was going to question this decision of Bea's, but Ginger shook her head at him. He breathed in, picked up a white rag, leaned back against Henry's Child, and began wiping his oily black hands.

"Well, this tractor is worth quite a pretty penny, Bea," Mr. Rogers said. "I'm not sure that the horses' yokes and such are of equal value. What else you think you'll need?"

Bea looked over at her mother, who shrugged. She knew nothing of farming.

"Tell him you need plows, tillers, harrows, rollers, planters, mowers, and rakes," Samuel said.

Ginger smiled.

So did Bea. "I need plows, tillers, harrows, rollers, planters, mowers, and rakes," she said.

Mr. Rogers stopped cleaning his hands and stared at the little girl.

"You have those, Mr. Rogers?" Bea asked.

Samuel snickered.

"Maybe a tedder, too?" Mr. Rogers asked with eyebrows raised.

"I do not know what that is," Samuel said.

"Um, sure," Bea replied.

Samuel laughed. Bea looked over at him, grinning. Ginger watched Ed follow the little girl's gaze. He saw nothing and shook his head.

"Not a thing," Ginger whispered.

"All right, Miss Bea," he said, standing up. "I'll estimate the cost of this tractor and bring the requested equipment plus anything else I think you'll need. Does that work?"

"I think that'll do," Bea said, offering her hand to Mr. Rogers.

"To self-sufficiency," he said, smiling for the first time as he took her palm in his.

Bea's eyes opened in surprise at the friendliness of it. She smiled back as he shook her hand. "What's self-sufficiency?" she asked.

"Farming to live," he replied.

Bea nodded, letting go of his hand. She wiped her palms on her pants, staring long at Henry's Child. Her eyes moistened again as she turned to her mother but, without looking up at Ginger, Bea squared her shoulders again, breathed in deeply, and left the barn slowly. They all watched her go, and when she reached the walnut tree she broke into a run, racing for the sunroom door. It banged closed behind her.

"That's a courageous little girl you've got there," Mr. Rogers said.

"Amen," replied Samuel.

CHAPTER 16

THE GOOD, THE BAD, AND THE GOAT

It was Monday when Ginger opened her eyes. Her alarm had not gone off at eleven thirty p.m., as she had the day to herself and she had slept deeply the entire night. It was the first true rest she had had in a long while and she rolled over to see exactly what time it was.

The clock read five thirty a.m. and the smell of coffee wandered into her room to confirm that it was time to ready the kids for school. With a lightness she hadn't felt for nearly two years, Ginger lifted herself from the bed. She looked out of her window and there, staring at the ruts in the streambed, was Samuel. As soon as she saw him, he raised his eyes to the window. He waved. Ginger smiled and waved back.

Beau's tags jingled as she grabbed her bathrobe.

"Morning, Beau. You don't have to get up unless you want to."

The dog thought about it a minute and fell back onto his side, letting out a great rush of air— a sigh of relief.

"Yeah, I thought as much."

She left her room and walked to Bea's. Opening the door quietly, she looked in. There she found Henry and Oliver sleeping on the floor in a bivouac they had made of their blankets. Bea was snoring with a little whistle from the bed. It was time to wake up—time to go to school. But she had no desire to wake them. In fact, she wanted to stay right there and watch them until their eyes opened of their own accord.

As she watched, she felt Samuel climb the stairs.

"Good morning," she whispered to him.

"Time to get the children up," he said. "Time to milk the cow and feed the chickens and collect the eggs and ready the horses for the day."

She turned her head and found him leaning next to her on the door's post, gazing into Bea's room. "There is no cow and the horses have nothing to do just yet."

"There are still things that need to be made ready. Work starts at sunrise."

"It's a school day."

"School is at home," he said.

"No, it's not."

"Why not?" he asked.

Ginger thought for a moment. Why not? "I think I have to sign up for that. I don't know."

"Well, maybe you will work on that today and we will all stay home for once and make a life here."

"I guess I can call them out sick, but just for today."

"Just for a day? That makes no sense to me whatsoever. A farm is not just for a day and school is at home. Where else would it be?"

"Nowadays school is at a schoolhouse. But if you insist, you can wake them up and get them ready for work that needs to be done, though I have no idea what that would be because we've got nothing to farm yet. And just to let you in on the ways of this family, you will find Oliver whining when he opens his eyes. It's best to tell him you can't hear him when he whines. That way, you will not cause the rest of us to have to listen to him get his way when he whines at you."

Samuel leaned forward and stared into her eyes. She saw the shadow of his brown irises and shivered a little, but refused to look away.

"There was no whining in my family," he said.

She shook her head. "Good luck with that." She bit her lip, holding back a laugh as she headed to the stairs. Little did he know Oliver.

"Virginia Moon?"

She turned on the first stair and gazed back at him.

"What are the children's names, please?"

She curled her lip in confusion and said, "You don't remember?"

"We've not been introduced. Their full names, please."

"Ah. Yes. Well, they are named after writers. So they are Henry Adams Martin, Beatrix Potter Martin, and Oliver Wendell Holmes Martin."

"Thank you."

"No, really. Thank you."

He made a little bow then and they looked at each other, the small smile on her face matching the one on his.

Ginger returned her attention to the stairs she was descending and heard Samuel above announcing, "Time to get up! There is work to do! Up!"

"Morning." It was Henry's voice first.

"Get your brother up, Henry Adams Martin."

"Coward," Ginger breathed.

"We have got work, Beatrix Potter Martin. Time for breakfast."

"It's Monday," she heard Bea say. "We have to go to school."

"Today home is school. Oliver Wendell Holmes Martin!"

She stepped down into the family room just in time to catch the beginning of Oliver's morning whine. Beau came racing down the stairs.

"Smart dog," Ginger said with a yawn. "Morning, Osbee."

"Samuel get the kids up?" the old woman asked.

Ginger's jaw shut so fast, she couldn't get her tongue out of the way. "Ahh!" Her hand reached for her mouth as if to stop what had already occurred.

"Coffee?"

"You thee him?"

"Yes, I see him. I met him yesterday."

Ginger moved her jaw up and down as if practicing how to do so without biting her tongue. Osbee held out a steaming cup.

"Are—aren't you thocked?"

"Shocked? Yesterday, yes. I had to leave the barn. Thought I was like to faint. Henry was standing there smiling like anything as I grabbed a broom. I had no idea who the stranger was but Oliver stood next to him like he'd known him forever. They just kept saying he was, well, you know. Then Samuel disappeared. Then he came back through Christian's stall. Henry and Oliver had to steady me and at that moment Bea brought in the Rogerses. They took me out, saying we were gonna ride the horses. Had to sit down a long while with Samuel next to me, I'll tell you. Watched the boys go round and round for hours."

"Where is breakfast?" Samuel asked, entering the kitchen.

"Cereal's on the table," Osbee replied, pointing.

Samuel stepped to the open box of Cheerios and pursed his lips.

"We have real work today. We need a real breakfast. Eggs and meat and bread. Hot, hot, hot."

Ginger and Osbee looked at him and then at each other.

"That kind of breakfasththt ithn't tho good for you," Ginger said.

"Why is your speech strange?" he asked.

"She bit her tongue."

"Ah. That was not very smart of you."

Ginger frowned at Samuel and he smiled broadly.

"Hot breakfast, please," he said, pointing to the stove. "I have to leave. I am itchy. I will await the children in the barn." He walked by Osbee. "The coffee smells wonderful," he added. Then he disappeared through the sunroom door, whistling a tune as he did so.

They both just stood there, still as stones.

"Itchy?" Osbee asked.

"Electrithity maketh him itch. We got bacon?" Ginger asked, opening the refrigerator.

"I don't think I can get used to that," Osbee said, nodding to the door.

"That maketh two of uth," Ginger replied.

They made breakfast as ordered and after bundling the three children in winter clothes Osbee led them out the back door to the barn. Ginger wandered around the house with only one direction: the avoidance of calling her children out for the day. She was entirely uncomfortable pulling her kids out when they were not sick and she worked feverishly to justify their absence in her own mind. Finally, she called the school and mumbled something about a family matter. The school secretary's voice was more than concerned, asking if there was anything anyone at the school could do. Somehow, being a war widow brought out a certain giving gentleness in some people and Ginger knew the secretary's offer was rising out of that kind caring. Quickly, she thanked the woman and hung up the phone, a feeling of deep guilt lingering inside her as she showered.

Once washed and dressed, she sat down at her desk, gazing out her bedroom window to the covered bridge. The deep guilt of calling her children out for the day sank to an even deeper sense of internal betrayal. She was about to research homeschooling, but as she made ready to flip on her computer, she stopped. As a matter of choice, homeschooling was more than a betrayal to herself; it was a betrayal to Jesse.

Ginger had grown up in a place where the world, with all of its complexities, wandered in continuously. She attended public school, the education of which was far more than learning to read and write. It was how to get along with others of differing beliefs and ways. Her childhood was a kaleidoscope, giving her a certain adaptability of vision. She learned to accept others as they presented themselves, search for what was common, tolerate that which differed from her.

She could approach anyone on the grounds of who they were, not who she needed them to be. She didn't need to like them; she learned she just had to try to understand them. It made her sensitive and watchful and formed her into the excellent nurse she was.

On the other hand, Jesse had been raised in a private school where everyone held thoughts and beliefs similar to his own. The world was presented how it should be, not as it was. Differing ideas were filtered through teachers and his parents. But the older he grew, the more his nature could not fit the small world of his childhood. He likened it to confining a great rainstorm into the flow of a spigot. Such a thing was impossible and, true to that statement, he didn't fit into his parents' world.

When he went to VMI, it was less a spigot but still a confining flow. It wasn't until he joined the army that he came face-to-face with the kaleidoscope of Ginger's world. He stumbled often, trying to understand what it was he believed and what he did not, measuring his own sense of self against the whirling chaos of possibility. It took him a good ten years to come to himself.

From these differences, it was always understood that the Martin children would attend public school. The chaos of the world never unsettled Ginger, and Jesse wanted that for his children. So here Ginger was about to betray herself and Jesse, and the longer she sat there, the more her loss and the pain of it engulfed her. This was a decision regarding their children. This was something they needed to do together. Who was she to take Henry and Bea and Oliver away from their friends—away from the new kids they had yet to meet, away from this year's teachers and next year's teachers and those memories every child has of their school days?

"I can't," she whispered. "It's not fair."

She poked at the scratches on the desk and wiped the dust off the top of her laptop. She leaned forward, then back in her chair. She opened the right drawer, riffling around the bottom of it; she retrieved a pencil and the empty envelope of an old bill. The pencil was obviously Oliver's because it had been chewed up and the eraser was gone. Turning the envelope over to doodle, she caught her breath. There, in Jesse's own handwriting, was a quote:

"Americans like to think of themselves as uncompromising. In fact, our true genius is that we compromise. Our entire government is based on it."—Shelby Foote

Ginger stared at the writing—the tight, precise curvature of the letters, the tiny spots of ink where the pen halted before it was moved in another direction. When did he write this? What was he thinking about before he wrote it? What did he do after? But she knew what Jesse did. Maybe not right after, but sometime after. He answered a call to duty. And she? She waited for him to return. Their common ground, soldier and nurse, was to care for others—to put the greater good before their own. They understood each other through the need to serve. Their service was different and, in that difference, they had to compromise.

"Our entire marriage is based on it." She touched his letters, running her finger around their curves, retracing Jesse's tracks.

"Okay," she said to the air. "But before I take them out of school, I'm going to ask them about it. It's only fair."

She waited for an answer—another message. Maybe another envelope would show up. Maybe the lock to the little gold key. Maybe another—

Quickly, she stood. "Not another ghost," she said, sternly pointing up to Elysium.

She hurt but laughed a little to herself, leaving the computer and homeschooling at the desk. As she stepped to the stairs, she gazed out the staircase window. There, heading directly for her gravel drive, was an old International pickup truck hauling a livestock trailer.

"I know who that is," she said excitedly and raced down the stairs. She swung the front door open and the cold air floated in to greet Beau, who trotted from the kitchen through the dining room, into the family room, and wound up standing next to Ginger. The trailer drifted slightly to the right of her driveway and stopped. The passenger door opened and out stepped Jacob Esch. He was dressed in jeans and a flannel coat and held his stomach tenderly.

"What are you doing here?" Ginger called down the hill.

"I brought the cow with Mr. Wheldon."

"No . . . you should be in bed," she said.

"I was released."

"Yes. To go home to bed." She frowned. This boy had no idea what was good for him.

The driver's-side door opened and Joshua Wheldon stuck his head out. "Mrs. Martin, can yah please move yur truck?"

Beau glanced up at her as if waiting for the answer. "Just a minute." As she went to shut the door, she saw Henry heading down the hill. Beau launched out the door and down the porch. "Henry?"

Her oldest stopped dead in his tracks.

"Can you help Jacob there inside and have him sit down, please?"

"I'm fine, Mrs. Martin."

"Henry, please. Thank you." Ginger shut the door with finality.

Rushing through the house, she slid into her rubber boots and Jesse's coat, grabbed her car keys from her purse, and headed out the screen door. She found Samuel leaning against the walnut tree.

"Where is everybody?" she asked him.

"Working in the barn and the summer kitchen."

"I have to move the truck. The cow's here. What's in the summer kitchen?"

"A kitchen. It is used in the summertime to keep the heat out of the house. Hence its name."

She stopped and looked at him. He breathed into his hands as if they were cold.

"Thanks. That clears everything up," she said, heading to her truck. She giggled when she heard Samuel laugh quietly as she passed. Coming around the corner of the house, she found Jacob leaning on Henry as he walked up the gravel drive.

"Thank you, Henry."

"I'm fine," Jacob said.

She opened the door and repeated, "Thank you, Henry."

Joshua Wheldon maneuvered the trailer around and backed it up the hill. After parking some twenty yards down the road, Ginger walked back home and climbed her drive, and when she reached the top of the hill, Mr. Wheldon opened the door of the trailer.

"Mornin', ma'am," he said.

"Good morning, Mr. Wheldon. I very much appreciate you bringing the cow."

"That fence sure needs mending. Almost run over it." He pulled the ramp down from the trailer.

She nodded, saying, "It's never been built."

"Posts are up." He walked up the ramp. "Come 'ere, Ginger, my beauty."

As the cow cleared the trailer door, a great rush of joy caught hold of Ginger. The cow was truly ginger-colored with soft, sensitive brown eyes that gazed around as she walked gently down the ramp.

"Ah, she's beautiful," Ginger said, a lump growing in her throat.

"She's one in a million."

Osbee, Jacob, and the children came out of the summer kitchen, smiling, mesmerized, as the cow sauntered toward them.

Bea put her left hand over her mouth and stepped forward, petting the cow's nose with her right. "What's her name?" she asked.

"Ginger," Mr. Wheldon said.

Bea's eyes popped wide and she flicked them over to her mother. There was a split second of silence and then Osbee and Oliver and Henry and Bea burst out laughing. Joshua Wheldon looked over to Jacob, who shrugged.

"My name is Ginger," she said sullenly.

Then they laughed, too. Still snickering, all followed Mr. Wheldon with Ginger-cow toward the barn, every hand in the yard touching the soft, warm sides of her as if carrying a magical beast to its sacred home.

Suddenly, there was a sound. *"Neaaaaaaaaah."*

Everyone turned around, and as Ginger's eyes fell upon the open end of the trailer, the magic moment screeched to a sudden halt. Her smile disappeared. So did everyone else's.

There, at the top of the ramp, was a three-and-a-half-foot dark gray billy goat with a little black beard and two nine-inch pointy horns. One eye had lashes of white, making it appear like it wore a monocle. It gazed slowly at the group with its copper caprine eyes as if devising some horrible end for each and every one of them.

Joshua Wheldon handed Oliver the cow's tether and stepped forward. "Ya gotta take the good with the bad," he said. "Unfortunately, ya got really bad here." He untied the goat's lead from the side of the trailer. "Ginger Martin, may I introduce you to Beelzebub the goat."

It looked at her sideways with those copper caprine eyes, raising its lip in what appeared to be a wicked, wicked grin.

"Bubba for short," he added.

July 2, 1862
Malvern Hill

Juliette, my love,
It is raining. The water stings my wounds. My body aches and my stomach hurts. Do not worry. I am but scraped—a tattering of flesh and fabric by ball and bayonet. I am hungry and tired. No deep wounds here and many of them on the mend.

I have been in the fight. As we made our way moving the length of the Shenandoah Valley in May, we marched in the shape of the letter "H"—two parallel lines with a transverse of the third, which is the road between Luray and New Market. Is it not true that opposite angles are equal? We marched and marched through mud and mountain, hill and haven. The more I marched, the more I fought and the more I fought, the more I could see as Jackson sees—precise, methodical, mathematical, cold. The arc of an angle, the ticking of time, and the opportune moment to move—victory assured.

We are not a cat. We are merely its paw, moving silently from one place to another and from nowhere, the claw unsheathes and we flail any before us. Then we recede and move again. Four hundred miles in a month we have marched and fought in this manner and for what? Always our paw is held hidden in the Shenandoah. The arm of the cat if but out-stretched a little farther can scratch at Washington. In May, we were the cat to the Union's mouse.

As I fought, all the while, I heard the bird and instead of the yell, I whistled back. I am the butt of many a joke, but then so is our commander. So I whistle and in that Valley of Death, I have come to know this bird. It is the Child's Eye. Remember your child's eye? There was a time when every day was new—the first time the scent of honeysuckle hung upon a heavy summer mist. The wonder of a chicken squawking as it fled your child's hand. The caprine gaze of a goaty eye as it chased you to the kitchen door. A great black sky sounding a thunderous clap as it tossed giant balls of water onto far fields of wheat and then broke open like darkened glass, shedding golden light across the horizon. The drops of water shone like millions of tiny diamonds in that light upon the golden sheaths. The Child's Eye wakes up in this world that God made, knows as a child knows that we are part of God, explores and learns and helps and then falls soundly to sleep within the love of God.

So when walking the Valley of Death, I hear this bird and hear life exquisitely. I can see as Jackson sees, with a man's eye. The precise movements of the muskets, the feinting of bayonets are but gears in the machine of war. But all the while I whistle and see so clearly with my Child's Eye the sky as blue and the tiny grass under my feet. I see a man at the end of my bayonet, but cannot meet him Child Eye to Child Eye. His eyes are on mine and as I take his life from the beautiful world that God created in love, I know I have closed forever the possibility of seeing through his eyes. And as I battle, I pray those eyes open to a honeysuckle summer day with a black sky shuddering as it opens and sends a single finger of light dancing over great golden fields of wheat that shine like a million tiny diamonds. I pray he settles peace-fully in the love of Elysium.

So I sit here in the rain, scratching this letter, aching from the battle and the day of digging graves upon Malvern Hill. I love my aches because I can see with my Child's Eye. I am yet walking within the love of God even as I hunger. And just moments ago, someone said they heard Jackson, as he sat his horse above Port Republic, watching two lines converge to an acute angle, the arc of which exploded in war, saying, "He who cannot see the hand of

God in this is blind, sir, blind." It caused me to burst out laughing, the howl of which echoed across the fresh graves of the dead. The others looked at me with a sideways glance and so I have settled into this letter. My love, I see with Jackson's eyes the cold, mathematical precision of war. But this is the Eye of Man and it is the Hand of Man. It is what I hear that gives me pause. The bird sings, bringing me back to the joy of my Child's Eye and I know, as this Hand of Man falls where it will, God sorrows. Utterly.

Your devoted,
Captain Samuel E. Annanais

CHAPTER 17

HOMESCHOOLING

Joshua Wheldon brought the goat off the trailer. Everyone backed away except Beau. He stood about as tall as Bubba and they eyed each other, taking full measure of size and strength. It was the goat that looked away first, at which point Beau's tail, having frozen in place at the sight of Bubba, wagged slowly. Ginger wasn't sure if they were friends, but she was quite sure Beau had made more peace with the goat than anyone else in the yard.

As Bubba and the cow were taken into the barn, Ginger did not follow. She stood separate and alone, watching the procession. Jacob Esch, who yet leaned upon Henry's shoulder, began to speak to Bea and Oliver regarding the care and keeping of a cow. His voice was soft and sure, with a slight accent that betrayed his upbringing. He was not English. He was not a Yankee. He was Amish, no matter how lost Ginger knew him to be, and in that moment she realized that he would be staying. She gazed over as if waking from a warm dream and met Osbee's eyes.

"Bea and I have cleared the room on top of the

summer kitchen. Mostly it was the old lamps from the house. Their glass chimneys are now in the kitchen sink, soaking."

"Probably need to go get fuel for them."

"I think so. New wicks, also."

"Osbee?"

"Yes, daughter?"

"Osbee, isn't this . . . weird? People just showing up with what we need?"

The old woman chuckled. "No. It's unbelievable."

Ginger nodded, looking around in search of Samuel. He wasn't there.

"I've got to clean the room over the summer kitchen. It's dusty and the mattress up there needs to be unwrapped. Hasn't been slept in since Jesse was a teenager." Osbee grinned as she pulled her braid forward. There was no red ribbon any longer. "Should have sheets for it some-where," she continued as she walked to the sun-room stairs.

"We need anything else from the store?" Ginger inquired, following the old woman to the house.

"Not that I can think of," Osbee replied, holding the door.

Ginger leaned into the sunroom, picked up her purse, and headed down the gravel drive toward her truck. As she walked, she took out her phone. Regard, who was lying on the fence rail at the end of the drive, yeowed as she passed. "Be right back," she replied absently as she dialed her parents.

The line picked up. "The Ginger Moon," her mother said in greeting.

"Yes, it is," Ginger answered.

"Tim! It's our daughter," she yelled.

Another line clicked. "Ginny Moon! What's up? The ghost settled now?"

Ginger opened her truck door. "Yes, I believe he is." She smiled up at herself in the rearview mirror. Her eyes smiled back.

"Excellent!" her father replied brightly. "Any other spiritual matters we can help with?"

Ginger laughed a little, which was instantly returned with a louder laugh from both her parents on the other end of the line. It continued for a while and then faded softly into silence. Waiting.

"No, no. I just called to say—" She broke off unexpectedly. Why had she called? Her chest seized, tightening with longing and sadness. She let out a small cry as she comprehended her own purpose.

"To say you are staying there," her mother finished.

Ginger didn't answer. She closed her eyes in the rushing realization that she was not going home.

"You don't have to come back here, Ginny, if your life is there," her father said.

"I miss you," Ginger whispered. "I miss your world."

"Our world is everywhere. It's your world. It's right there to find. You just need to open your eyes and reach out your hand and invite it in."

Her father was speaking again in his spiritual way but today his words made perfect sense. "I don't know how."

"Oh, I suspect you've already done it, Ginger. It's why you are staying."

"I'm staying for Osbee."

"And Henry and Bea and Oliver. Yes?"

Ginger opened her eyes and looked down the road to its end.

"Sometimes, Ginger," her mother said, "we look at the horizon and see the end. But you have to remember that's only the end as far as we can see. If you move a little farther, closer to the horizon, it moves and there is more to see between you and the end. Good and bad things between you and the end. But you gotta keep moving."

"Gotta take the good with the bad," Ginger said quietly.

"Yes, Ginger," her mother replied.

"Why?"

"See, Monica, this call is spiritual."

They all laughed. Ginger started the truck and put it in gear as she wiped her eyes.

"Remember, Ginger, bad happens. It's the way

of things. But always something good is made from the bad. It's hard to see in the bad. But good will be made of all things. And you only know it's good because there was bad."

"Yin and yang, man," her dad said. "That's the whole point of that spiraling circle of black and white."

Ginger drove slowly, watching Mr. Schaaf circle his field of winter wheat. He was not cutting it. He was not weeding it. What was he doing? Looking forward, she saw the road's end. It did not back up. It ended.

"The road ends," Ginger said.

"The road is made by humans, Ginny, my dear," her dad replied. "The horizon is not."

She sighed and came to a stop at the crossroad. Gazing up in the mirror, Ginger half expected to see Samuel there. He was notably missing. What was there was the thin line of asphalt she had come down with the Smoots' farm at its terminus. Moments before, it had been where she began. Now it was at the end.

"I suppose," she said, "it's all about perspective."

"Whose daughter is this?" her father exclaimed. "Monica? This strange young woman talking about perspective is calling us, imitating our sensible, practical daughter."

Ginger didn't need to see. She could hear her mother roll her eyes. In the stillness on the line,

Ginger thought that the phone was like the road. It began where she was and ended with her parents. To them, the phone line began where they were and ended with her.

"It's me, Dad. I'm just starting to think about what you have been thinking about for a long while."

"We ponder," her dad said. "We don't think."

She rolled her eyes just like her mother.

"I wish I could see you guys," Ginger whispered.

"Well, we could come out. You want us to come out?" her mother asked.

It was a lot of money to cross the country. Money they really didn't have.

"She's not answering," her father said. "Does that mean no, Monica?"

"No, Tim. She's thinking about money."

She was about to ask how her mother knew such a thing, but felt as though she was floating on the line with her parents, on the road with the farm. She was a feather drifting and the wind that held her aloft enveloped her. It was a moment to do nothing. She held silent and still.

"She didn't say no," Tim said.

"No, she didn't," her mother affirmed.

"That must mean yes!"

"Sounds good to me," her mother agreed. "We'll call you with our flight info."

"And remember, Ginny," her father began.

"Hang up, Tim, before she says no."

"Oh, good-bye, Ginny Moon." There was a click.

"You'll always be our Ginger Moon," added her mother and without another word the line went dead.

The feather she was hit the ground as the line died and, startled, Ginger gazed at the phone. As she flicked on her blinker, there was a loud honk. She jumped in her seat and looked up. To her right, old Mr. Schaaf sat upon his tractor just opposite her. His face was still, frozen in a small frown of concern. She smiled and rolled down the window.

"You all right there, Ginger?" he asked, yelling over his engine.

"I'm fine. What are you doing?" she inquired, circling with her finger, motioning to his field.

"Planting alfalfa over the winter wheat. Time to plant."

Ginger nodded. She thought a moment and added, "Do I have winter wheat?"

"Yes, we planted it. We'll get to your fields—"

Ginger shook her head. "We'll take care of it this year, Mr. Schaaf. Thanks!"

His face darkened again.

"We've fixed Henry's Child and have a new plan," she said, smiling as brightly as possible to allay Mr. Schaaf's look of deep concern.

He nodded, his face barely shifting from his frown.

"Gotta get to the store," she added and waved as she turned the corner.

She drove out of the fields and farms, beyond the hairpin curve of the Shenandoah. Pulling up to the hardware store, she parked and walked in. The benefit of not working on a weekday is that there are very few people out and about and help is readily at hand. She realized she had no idea what fuel to get and so she called Osbee and handed the phone to Dave, the hardware guy. She was then directed to purchase several bottles of Coleman lamp fuel and the new wicks, with which she left the store and headed back to the truck.

She approached her car door and as she was about to open it she peered at her ethereal reflection floating in the window. Her hair had grown out about an inch and a half since she'd last colored it, and the ginger color at the roots looked confused and a little frightened by the brassy, washed-out, dark brown tint of her curled ends. The longer she stared at herself, the clearer a view she had of how she had been walking around the world. She looked overworked. She looked overwhelmed. She looked tired. She looked as if she didn't care how she looked. Inasmuch as Mr. Schaaf's horn had caused her to jump, so did her next thought: her parents were coming.

"Mood hair?" she said to her curls. "Time for a cut."

Quickly, she hopped in the truck and drove into downtown Woodstock. The main street in town was small, with period buildings from the 1910s through the 1950s lining the sidewalks. Woodstock had a long history, like many small Virginia towns, part of which was the sprawling growth of suburbs and houses covering farm fields and flowing streams on its outskirts. That sprawl was imposing its shoulder on the loop of the Shenandoah wherein Smoot's farm still stood and threatened to push the five farmers there into the river with its weight. But they were stubborn people, the Smoots and their neighbors, and no one had sold. Not yet anyway.

After pulling into the back parking lot of the beauty salon, Ginger made her way through the cold, shady alley back onto Main Street. As expected, there was no one in the waiting area, so Ginger was immediately asked to sit in a chair and was thus forced to look at herself in the floor-to-ceiling mirror in front of her.

"So, what do we want?" the young woman with a beautiful blond French bun asked as she touched Ginger's brown curls, pulling them this way and that.

Ginger wondered if the girl was as confused and frightened of what she was touching as her roots seemed to be. "Cut it off, please."

"Beg pardon?" The girl held two handfuls of Ginger's dark brown curls and stared at her in the reflection.

"I think I'd like to start fresh. So please just cut it all off."

"You mean, cut off all the brown? Uh . . . it will be short."

"That's okay," Ginger replied. Her eyes widened at her reflection. There she saw herself with a smile upon her face that she had not seen in so long. She took in a deep breath, the upturn of her lips retreating just a little. Smiling at Jesse had always been returned with such brightness. She had loved his face but truly had been enamored of it when she watched him look at her smiling. "Starting fresh, but keeping the root," she said, winking at her own reflection as if it were Jesse who had done so.

A small crease between the young woman's immaculately trimmed eyebrows belied a small concern with her customer's decision. But the customer was always right, so shortly thereafter Ginger watched the brown curls fall to the floor and drift across the white tile on the gentle breeze that blew in under the beauty shop's door. Slowly, methodically, the strawberry blond curls of Ginger's birth sprung to life, relieved as they were from their dark burden. The hairstylist's face brightened as she came to realize the nature of Ginger's hair, and when she had finished, the young woman smiled greatly at her own master-piece.

"Would you mind?" the stylist asked, holding out a thin red cloth headband.

Ginger laughed a little and nodded. Carefully, the headband was wrapped around Ginger's short curls, pulling them gently back from her face.

Together, customer and stylist grinned at who they found in the mirror. Ginger saw her natural self, her pale skin and soft freckles. Her long neck held her heart-shaped face. There was one longer curl remaining on the left side in the back, which the stylist wrapped around her finger and pulled forward.

"I love that curl," the young woman said. "I think you luckily missed it in your last hair color."

"You are leaving it?" Ginger asked.

"Yes! You look like a painting on the front of a Jane Austen book."

They laughed.

The hairstylist pulled off the smock with a soft shake and took Ginger's offered credit card.

"Maybe next time you feel like coloring your hair," the young woman said, "you can come in."

"So you can talk me out of it?"

The hairstylist blinked innocently, saying, "Not at all. Customer's always right. Maybe we can just talk it over."

Ginger signed the receipt, leaving more of a tip than she knew she could really afford.

"Will do," Ginger said. "Thank you."

The young woman opened the door. "You're welcome."

As Ginger stepped back into the world, it seemed to have become a warm spring day. She twirled her long curl as she turned left and then left again into the shadowed alley. She thought about Jesse's eyes as they looked at her, wishing she could feel his gaze upon her again. Walking from the alley, she stopped. Behind her truck, across the parking lot and on the other side of the street, was a small field of grass that had obviously been some building at some time. Off center in the field, she saw a man in a butternut uniform seated on a chair. Leaning forward and squinting, she began to walk toward him.

"Samuel?" she whispered.

The closer she came, the more she could see. He was seated with his right shoulder toward her. He was smiling and laughed a little as he stared ahead. In his profile, she could see a knick on his right ear.

"Samuel?" Ginger called, trotting past her truck and across the parking lot.

He didn't look in her direction. Instead, he picked a rifle up from the field and put it across his lap. Then he shook his head and said something. He put the rifle back into the grass.

"Samuel?" Ginger called louder as she crossed the street.

As he straightened in his seat, the smile on his face faltered. He sat still even as Ginger entered the field.

"Samuel," Ginger said as she approached his chair. "Samuel, it's me." Stepping up to him, she reached out to touch. Her hand stopped before reaching his shoulder. "It's me."

He continued staring ahead with a fixed gaze. Stepping behind his chair, Ginger followed his eyes, trying to find what was keeping his attention.

Standing still just behind him, she reached out with her left hand and placed it upon his right shoulder. There was a blinding flash and Ginger froze where she was, blinking to gain her sight. When her vision returned, she found herself standing alone in the field. She turned around and then around again.

"Where did you go?" she asked.

There was no reply—just the sound of the breeze rustling the overgrown grass at her knees.

CHAPTER 18

SOME CHRISTIAN

Confused and unsettled, Ginger stumbled back to the truck and was now driving through Woodstock toward home. She blinked over and over again, her eyes continuing to recover full vision. If she hadn't been thrown off-balance by the weird goings-on in her world recently, the episode in the field had knocked her to the ground. She was sick, nausea rushing like the waves of a spring run on the Shenandoah. The flash was an omen. It had to be. She never was one to believe in anything like omens, but the last six days had completely changed her outlook on everything.

"Samuel!" she yelled up at the blue sky above. "Samuel, what the hell is going on?"

She reached the hardware store at the edge of town and pushed on the accelerator. Something bad was happening at home, she was certain. There was a brewing somewhere, somehow. What it was was not clear, but it was whirling like a great black summer thunderhead and it was bearing straight down her little lane and was going to land on her gravel drive.

Her tires screeched as she rounded the corner of

her road. Mr. Schaaf's tractor sat exactly where she had last seen it but its seat was empty of its former occupant.

"Oh, God!" she breathed and then, gazing ahead, she slammed on her brakes.

A traffic jam on her lane? It was. Trucks and trailers and cars that were parked or trying to park lined the narrow shoulders of both sides of the road. There were people walking in the direction of her house. Young people. They were jostling one another, and if she peered up the part of the road that was clear, she could just make out about five or so standing in her front yard.

"What the hell?" Ginger pulled to the right and parked in the ditch directly in front of Mr. Schaaf's tractor. She climbed out, grabbed her purse and the fuel, and slammed the truck door. With a quicker gait than anyone in front of her, Ginger walked up the lane, overtaking a young woman and two young men. They had to be no more than twenty, if that.

"Excuse me," she said.

They stopped and turned around.

"Um. What is going on?"

"Colonel Rogers asked for some volunteers to come help him."

"Rogers," Ginger repeated. "Ed Rogers?"

"Yes, ma'am. Can I carry something for you?"

Ginger gazed at the young man and, very slowly, her gait lessened until she had come to a complete stop. He was six foot at least and dark with dark hair and matching eyes. It was his hair and its tidy cut that gave him away.

"You from VMI?" she asked, unloading her Coleman fuel into his offered arms.

"Yes, ma'am," he said. "I'm Dijan Little."

"Dijan Little," she repeated.

"He ain't so little." The other young man snickered. The young woman laughed.

"I—I'm Virginia Martin," Ginger said. Together, they continued their walk toward the house.

"Martin? Like Captain Jesse Martin?" Dijan asked.

"Yes! He was my husband. You knew him?"

"Nah. My dad's a professor at Washington and Lee and a friend of the colonel's. They talk about him."

"Your dad knew Jesse?"

"Mmm. My dad teaches philosophy. Captain Martin and the colonel and my dad had great conversations in Latin."

"Ah." Ginger nodded.

As her right foot hit gravel, she found that the five people standing in front of her house were actually a group of students pulling up the posts of her snake-rail fence. The rest of it had already gone missing. Following the drive, she came to an abrupt halt and her eyes widened.

"What are those?" she yelled up the hill. From

nowhere, Ed Rogers appeared and was now marching toward her.

"There you are!" he said, his face stern as he trotted down the drive. "We've got a lot of work to do."

"What are those?" she repeated, pointing to the large back ends of two cream-colored horses.

"Mules," Ed Rogers said. "You'll need them because Christian hates to work and Penny can't keep him straight."

"I—I don't think I—"

Ed Rogers took her purse and indicated that she should follow him up the hill.

"This is Augustus and this is Agrippa," he said in introduction. "You'll like the mules better than the horses. Get your boots on."

With no more said, Ed led Ginger by the hand into the house. There in the kitchen she found Lorena, Eloise Schaaf, Merry Whitaker, Genore Mitchell, Marilou Creed, and Osbee. Each was in some stage of cooking something and the house was thick with moisture and scent from their efforts. Mr. Rogers dropped her purse on the stair step without so much as a pause and headed straight into the kitchen.

"I tried to call you," Osbee said, a wide smile growing across her face as she reached up and touched Ginger's hair. "Love the headband."

"Your hair is beautiful!" Lorena said.

"Thanks. Sorry I didn't call. I wasn't thinking."

She smiled at her neighbors, who smiled reticently back. She could tell they were concerned and wanted to say something to her but Ginger wasn't allowed to stop. Ed pulled her into the sunroom and only then let go of her hand. He pointed to her boots.

"What are we doing?" Ginger asked, obediently slipping out of her shoes.

"We've got people finishing the fence around where your garden beds will go. I've got people clearing out the barn, several others tidying up in the summer house, and a couple more building a chicken coop."

"Chickens?" Ginger declared, sliding into her left boot.

"One of our neighbors donated his flock," Lorena explained through the sunroom door. "It was causing trouble with the neighbors."

"Not yet." Mr. Rogers motioned his wife to silence.

Ginger stood straight up. "Why? What's wrong with the chickens?" she asked, her eyes narrowing.

"Nothing. You'll need eggs," he replied. "Come on. I need you to harness the horses."

"The horses?"

"We've got a lot of help today, so time to learn to plant while everyone's doing everything else."

There was a loud scream from the direction of the barn.

Ginger tripped forward in the sunroom, her right boot barely on. As Mr. Rogers opened the door, four people raced with terrified eyes in his direction. On the heels of the last person was Bubba, head down and at a run.

"Look out!" the woman in the front yelled as she flew up the stairs.

She nearly knocked Ginger over as she cleared the door. Balancing herself on the windowsill, Ginger watched the three young men behind her skip the bottom three steps of the sunroom stairs and achieve the slate floor in one great leap. The last one grabbed Mr. Rogers by the arm, pulled him inside, and slammed the door. There was a clickety-clickety clicketing up the stairs outside and then *BAM!* The door shuddered, squeaking a little in pain. So did everyone in the sunroom—everyone, that is, but Mr. Rogers.

"What are y'all doing?" he inquired, his voice steady and stone like his face. Instinctively, everyone straightened to attention, more or less—even Ginger.

"That goat's possessed!" The man talking was of Asian descent with short black hair and a square jaw. His wild and wide eyes looked past the colonel. Ginger swallowed at the thought that the goat had scared even him. He didn't look like he could be scared.

"It is a goat," Mr. Rogers said, and quick as the flash in the field he opened the door.

Ginger saw the goat reel and jump back, landing effortlessly on its feet a yard to the right of the stair steps. *"Neeeeeahhhh,"* it said, looking for all as if it were laughing. With a little clickety jump, it turned, let out a small bluster from its nose, and sauntered away in the direction of the covered bridge.

Ginger shivered as she watched it go and then her eyes caught a gleam of red paint peeking from around the corner of the house.

"Is that Henry's Child?" Ginger asked, bobbing her head up and down like a hungry chicken as she tried to see more of it. Ed's rough hand slipped into her palm.

"Had to move it to make room in the barn," he said.

"Room?" Ginger was pulled reluctantly out of the sunroom and down the steps. She couldn't see where Bubba had gone.

"We've got equipment. Let's move."

There was a *pop* somewhere behind the barn and an engine engaged.

"Wh-what's that?"

"I brought a small tractor an—"

"I don't need a tract—"

"It's not for fieldwork. It's for power. They're getting hay up into the top level of the barn."

"I—I have no ha . . . Who?" Ginger and Mr. Rogers entered the barn.

"We've got help, like I said. And I brought

hay. You'll need it until you get your crop in."

"Ah!" Ginger brightened. "Solomon Schaaf says I have winter wheat in the field. Time to plant the alfalfa." She filled with a little bubble of pride for knowing something that was going on and needed to be done.

"That's just the beginning."

Her bubble popped. She frowned a bit, thinking Mr. Rogers had taken some pride himself at poking her and listening to her deflate.

"Mrs. Martin?" She found Jacob standing next to Christian's stall door. Henry was yet at his side.

"I told him to go in," her son said quickly.

"Why aren't you in bed? You're still recovering." Ginger scowled.

"You can't horse farm your acreage," Jacob said, ignoring her. "This is very hard and you've only got yourself and three kids."

"It is what she wants to do," Mr. Rogers said.

"She's never done it, though," Jacob replied, his eyes firm as he gazed at Ed Rogers's stone face.

Ginger looked between the men. A standoff. Jacob was young and lean with a kind face and a gentle manner. Ed Rogers was older. No less kind but he was a forceful presence. It was like looking at the two sides of humanity. There were similarities here—discipline, neatness, order, duty. But when push came to shove, Ed's side of humanity would push and shove and Jacob's would yield and yield and yield again.

She placed her hand upon her heart, for before her stood the two sides of her own marriage, with its conflicts and comforts. What was true above all else, to Ginger's mind but not to Jesse's, was that Jacob's way was the correct one. There could be no contention between two people if one side would not contend. Most of their marital arguments arose from this simple point and it was from this point love had to overrule reason in order for there to be any peace. That overriding love had killed her husband in a far and distant land not so long ago.

"Help comes," Henry said, breaking the silence.

Both men started.

"It does come, Henry," Ginger agreed. "Have to hold still and wait."

Henry grinned. "And we rise together," he added.

Mother and son beamed at each other. Then Ginger took a deep breath and turned to Jacob. "You know about all this stuff?" She motioned to all the yokes and harnesses that now hung neatly on fresh pegs in the back of the barn where Henry's Child used to sit.

"I do."

"So I have two teachers," Ginger said, smiling.

Jacob pinched his lips together and gazed down to Henry.

"And we have two students," Jacob said quietly.

"Nah," Henry said. "Bea and I made a deal. I first learn how to take care of the cow. She's in the field. Wait here."

Henry trotted toward his mother. She grabbed his hand as he passed and gave it a little squeeze. He smiled and then headed out of the barn with a yell. "Bea!"

"You get the horses out," Ed instructed. "I'll get the mules."

"Let me get the yokes," Jacob said.

"No," Ginger replied adamantly. "Is Mr. Wheldon still here?"

"Yeah," Jacob said, cocking his head. "If he wasn't, neither would I be."

Ginger shrugged and opened Penny's stall door. She found Beau seated toward the far right corner with Regard curled up anxiously behind him.

"Can you go ask him to help with the yokes, please? I won't have you lifting heavy things and ripping your stitches out," she said over her shoulder. "Hello, Penny."

The horse came forward and placed its muzzle on Ginger's shoulder. Penny nickered softly and Ginger closed her eyes, breathing in. Horses smelled of earth, and Ginger brushed Penny's cheek gently, a slow peace filling her in the midst of the chaos she had found greeting her upon her return from town.

A loud whinny startled her from her moment. "For the love of Pete, Christian, I'm coming," she said as she grabbed Penny's leader rope. "Too many weird people doing too many weird things. Huh, guys?"

Beau lowered himself to the ground as Regard cowered behind him.

"You're a good friend, Beau. Don't know what you see in that goat, though." She attached the leader rope to Penny's bridle. Opening the back door of the stall, Ginger led the horse out toward the corral.

To her right, she found a small tractor puttering away at the end of the barn. Where rubber wheels should have been, it had instead metal ones, which at the moment were lifted from the ground. Around the left wheel, the one that faced Ginger, a large belt was wound and as the wheel turned the belt moved. Following its trajectory, Ginger found its other end wound around a wheel that was attached to what looked to be a luggage ramp—the kind that moved suitcases onto an airplane. But instead of suitcases, rectangular cubes of hay were being tossed from within a large trailer by a couple of strangers. At the top of the ramp, a young man stood in the upper barn door, grabbing the hay and then disappearing inside. At that moment, Dijan Little's head poked out of the door and grabbed the next oncoming bale.

"Elevator." Ginger gazed down and found Bea standing next to her.

"Doesn't look like an elevator," Ginger said.

"For hay," Bea continued. "We'll need to take it into the back door of the barn and through the upper floor with the next delivery. Don't need to move the bales so far across the upper floor that way."

Ginger stared at her daughter. "Really," was her only reply.

"That's what Samuel said. He really liked it."

"Ah! You've seen him!" Ginger declared.

"He's around."

Christian screamed and kicked his stall door.

"I'm coming!" Ginger yelled back. She handed the rope to Bea.

"Take Penny—" She stopped. Where was she supposed to take Penny?

"I'll follow Mr. Rogers and the mules," Bea said and veered left out the stall door.

Christian kicked the door again.

"Hang on! Pushy, Christian. You just wait to see what's in store for you now," Ginger said as she lifted the stall's handle. Opening the door, she found the horse's head on top of hers, pushing his way out of his stall. "You just wait!" she said through gritted teeth as she grabbed his halter with her left hand. With her right, she lifted his leader rope from its hook by the door. Forcefully, Ginger pushed Christian's chin down into his chest and with a stubborn reluctance he backed up into his stall. "Some Christian you are," she hissed, attaching the lead to his harness.

"Virginia Moon?"

Ginger turned around and found Samuel leaning against the wall. When he saw her, he jumped to attention.

"There you are!" she declared. "I saw you today in town."

He stared at her, his eyes wide and turning moist.

"What's wrong?"

Slowly he stepped forward, motioning with his hand around his own head.

"Oh." She giggled. "Yeah, I cut my mood hair. Hey, I saw you in Woodstock today. Couldn't you see me? I was right there. I called your name."

He stopped in place, his jaw moving, mouthing her name over and over. Ginger thought if a ghost could grow pale, Samuel had done so.

"What's wrong?" she repeated. The hay elevator's noise grew distant, as did the rustling above her head from Dijan Little and his buddy's efforts. The blue skylight beyond the door dissipated into white as if a great fog had spread like a blanket over heaven. Even Christian's earthy scent faded away.

"Ginger moon," he whispered. A tear ran down his cheek.

"Yes?" Ginger shrugged, shaking her head. What had gotten into the man?

Stepping forward, he reached for her face, passing his hand an inch over her right cheek and following his index finger over the single curl that rested upon her neck. *Ginger Moon,* he mouthed, his eyes moving around her face as if he were memorizing every small wrinkle, every tiny curve.

"Samuel?" Ginger whispered.

He recoiled, pulling back suddenly.

"Oh," he said and then he disappeared.

July 11, 1862
Upon the Shenandoah

My love, Juliette,
I cannot write. I cannot think. I can only look in wonder at my photograph. My entire understanding of God's creation has slipped beneath me like—like mercury beneath my finger. I cannot breathe.

I was granted a short leave and a horse last Friday. Peter, my sister Ann's husband, has been always of weak constitution. I received a pressing letter from Ann that he is bedridden with a fever. Their baby, Ezra, is but a month old and has been sent to the Reverend's house for care lest he contract his father's illness. My father endeavors to keep the crops and cows and Ann reports he, too, is coughing even as he works. She worries for him, for Peter, for herself.

So I rode hard and entered Woodstock on Saturday, hoping to reach home and see my father, leaving time enough reserved for a visit with you in Strasburg. I stopped and thought to have my photograph taken—a gift to you upon my arrival and a remembrance when I leave again from your side. I sat for the photographer and what emerged has sent me lost, uprooted from my purpose and duty and blowing around the valley like a wind with no direction.

The photographer was in awe, seeking to explain the picture away with reason. He thought perhaps the plate had been used before. But he admitted he never before photographed the like and he knew his plate was clear prior to my sitting.

Juliette, I sat, deciding whether to hold my musket or not, when I heard the call of my name—Samuel? It was a question—like the question in the fog. I held still—Samuel? The question once more, yet louder, imperative. I whispered, Yes? And again. Samuel? Yes, said I. And then, Samuel, it is me.

The flash, smoke, and silence. But as the photograph was given to me the next morning, there, standing behind me, was a woman—a spectral being with her left hand resting upon my right shoulder. She is a spirit seen through the lens of a machine, caught by the eye of man. It is no less an omen and I have been unable to continue home, lest she follow me there.

I send the picture to you, Juliette. See you her dress? It is loose with arms bare. The hair, held by a ribbon, has let loose a single curl upon her neck. She appears to me from another time, as if from my grandmother's days. I have seen the like of ladies painted in the days of Edwardian England or even those of Napoleon's court, with ancient Greece as the measure of fashion and beauty. But how is she in my photograph—now?

So here I sit, dangling my feet in the tiny creek which trickles into the slow flowing Shenandoah on this hot summer's eve. I rest my back upon this large, misplaced boulder and the moon rises before me, orange and full and round; I see it as the moon of October—the moon of harvest. The moon, the boulder, and I are out of place and I have now come to believe, as I scratch this letter, there is a purpose unknown to me here and I cannot understand what it portends. I shall not be returning to Laurel Creek. Ann and my father shall do as they can. I must return to the Valley of Death, to war, for only at its end will we have our future. The ghost calls my name, whistles to me as I fight but I seek not to understand her. My farm, my children, my love—this is my future.

I see thee, my love, with my Child's Eye. In the ginger light of this full moon, your eyes seek for me even now. They pour a warm glow into my heart, my soul, and rest as full and soft upon me even as the ginger moon rests upon the horizon. You are here with me, Juliette. You await me just over the horizon. You are my love, my Ginger Moon, and I shall meet you over the river. Please keep this photograph and let me ride— ride to release this spirit from me.

Your devoted,
Samuel

CHAPTER 19

THE CHICKENS COME HOME TO ROOSTER

Christian threw his head, lifting Ginger off her feet. If her attention had been distracted before, it was now fully present in the stall with Christian. She jerked the lead, growling as she shoved his chin into his breast. The horse whinnied in protest, his eyes wide and focused on the open stall door. If given half a chance, Christian would force his will upon whoever held his tether or rode his back if an open gate or door was within sight. At this moment, the door was more than within sight. It was within six inches.

"There are no bloody apples, you nasty horse," Ginger yelled. "It's March!"

"Problems?"

Christian stopped all movement and in his sudden stillness Ginger was tossed forward by the motion of her own effort. She hit the doorpost with her shoulder. Looking at Ed Rogers standing just beyond the stall, she winced as she gained her balance and realized the man had the same effect on beasts as he did on people.

"Now you know why you need the mules," he stated.

"He just wants the apples."

"There are no apples. It's March."

Just for a second, she saw the fixed demeanor of his eyes change. They narrowed a little and brightened a lot. Then they were fixed again and focused on Christian's large, round eyeballs above her head.

"Yes, thank you for that," Ginger replied with a harrumph and dragged Christian reluctantly out of his stall and toward Ed Rogers.

"The harnesses and collars are set up out in the corral."

"Are they?"

"They are and Bea is already finished brushing down Penny and is working on Agrippa. You need to move. We don't have all day."

She could see only his profile, but his left eye was bright again.

"All day is exactly what we have," she replied.

A crack of a smile rose on his lips and then disappeared.

Looking ahead to the corral, Ginger spotted several farming implements. "We working on those?" she asked. "They look like great instruments of torture."

They did for sure. There was a jumble of accoutrements that looked like metal disks and poles and rakes that would be pulled by a tractor. Beside these were two flatbed wagons that rested near a little red two-wheeled cart with a bench on top of it.

"Not today. We're finishing the storage barn today and those—"

"A storage barn? Where?"

"Behind the big barn there." Mr. Rogers pointed. A group was clearing and leveling a large square of ground fifty yards from the back of the barn.

"Is anyone in class today at VMI?" Ginger asked.

"If they all could have come, I believe they would have done."

Ginger stopped before the corral gate. "Ed, this is way too mu—"

"Henry's Child is worth a lot more, Ginger."

"Hay and horses and mules and storage barns and equipment and—"

"It's a fair trade," he interrupted, gazing into her eyes. "I mean to make it fair."

"And help," Ginger finished.

"Henry had more than one child, Ginger. And he was as dear a friend to me as any. I am tied to VMI through the blood of generations and he is tied to me and so . . . we are come here to stand for Henry's child."

Tears threatened as she watched Ed Rogers swallow hard.

"We've got work," he said and opened the gate.

As Ginger pulled Christian into the corral, she

watched Bea, who was standing on a large wooden crate, settle the large collar on Agrippa's neck with Jacob's help.

"Jacob, did you lift that?" she asked, pointing to Agrippa's collar.

Jacob gazed at her with the same round, wide-eyed look Christian had given Ed Rogers in the barn.

"You are not to lift anything. That must have been the doctor's orders—am I right?" she added.

Jacob nodded.

"He didn't lift it," Bea replied. "Mr. Wheldon did before he had to go help Henry and Oliver with the cow. The goat won't go away and it's scaring Oliver. Mr. Wheldon also brushed Augustus for you, Mom. You need to brush Christian so his tethers and collar won't rub the dirt against his skin and make scratches."

Her daughter must have received that piece of information from Ed Rogers because her tone was exactly like his. Ginger chuckled as she obediently reached into the bucket and pulled out the rubber brush.

As she cleaned up Christian, Mr. Rogers, Bea, and Jacob completed collaring and tethering Agrippa, Penny, and Augustus. Then slowly and methodically, they all taught Ginger how to collar Christian and set him in team with Augustus. It was slow going, as there were so many lines of leather and chain, each with a different name and each with a specific way of sitting on the horse so as not to unduly rub the skin and cause injury. Ginger was more than happy that Bea seemed to be picking it all up so quickly, as she felt certain she wouldn't remember ninety percent of what was being told to her by tomorrow morning.

Having the two teams now standing side by side, Bea held the four leads for Penny and Agrippa and Ginger held on to Christian and Augustus.

"Okay," Ed Rogers said. "We're simply going to practice starting and stopping."

"Shouldn't we be attached to a plow or something?" Ginger asked.

Jacob shook his head with great concern. "Mrs. Martin, first you need to figure out how to get the horses going. Then how to get them to pull. Then how to get them to plow. And you've never plowed. I'm not sure this is all going to work."

"I know how to plow," Bea said and shook her reins. She made no sound whatsoever, and with just that little shake Penny and Agrippa moved forward. Bea walked behind, pulling away from her mother, Ed Rogers, and Jacob. Christian whinnied loudly and pulled. Ginger lurched forward, losing Augustus's left rein.

"Whoa!" Jacob said, but he didn't have the reins and so the horse felt no obligation to listen. As Ginger bent to pick up the rogue rein, Christian leaned into his collar hard, pulling Ginger to the ground.

"Holy shi—" she yelled but the last word was cut short by a mouthful of dirt. She rolled over as she was dragged forward, twisting the reins and gazing up to the blue sky.

"You better get up, Mrs. Martin," Jacob said. "I'd help but you told me not to lift anything." He laughed and walked forward, following Bea.

"Christian!" Ginger spat as she rolled over on her stomach. Augustus, who had walked just one foot, now leaned back against Christian's pull, allowing Ginger to get to her knees. The horse was still leaning into his collar and as Ginger peered up the reins, trying to figure out how to untwist them and rise to her feet at the same time, she watched the mule turn its head to the left and nip Christian on the shoulder. Startled, the horse backed up, rearing a little as it did so. The reins loosened and Ginger took the opportunity to scramble to her feet. She yanked on the knotted reins and yelled, *"Whoa!"*

Through the small dust cloud she had created by rolling around in the dirt, she could just make out Augustus's right eye looking back at her. He seemed to have a look of pity and as he turned his head forward Ginger could swear he shook it just as Jacob had done moments before. Ginger spat again.

"That's why you have Augustus always with Christian," Ed said as he leaned against the snake-rail fence. "Look at Bea."

Wiping her mouth on her sleeve, Ginger gazed over and saw her daughter trotting behind the horse team. She looked so small compared to the beasts in the lead but a soft *"Whoa"* floated across the corral and there was no question who was in control when obediently they stopped. Jacob slowly caught up to the little girl and said something to her.

"I'm thinking that Bea takes Christian and Augustus," Ed Rogers said.

"I don't think that's a good idea."

"I didn't think so, either, but she knows what she's doing."

Bea came around and headed straight and then turned and stopped right next to her mother. She squished her nose in disgust.

"Your mouth is muddy, Mom."

"I think Bea should take Mrs. Martin's team," Jacob said as he hobbled up.

"Amish kids do a lot of the plowing," Bea said, handing her reins to Jacob. Gently, she took the twisted mess from her mother's hands, whirled the reins around, and having straightened everything out, shook the leads gently. Augustus pulled, with Christian following and clearly not in charge. As Jacob moved to follow, he handed over Penny's and Agrippa's reins to Ginger.

"I think maybe you'll be able to do this, after all," he said, pointing to Bea and smiling as he followed the little girl.

Bea made another loop around the corral, and when she finished, Ed Rogers combined all four beasts into one team, handed the reins to Bea, and off she went, circling the corral without one hiccup.

Taking Ginger by the elbow, Mr. Rogers led her to the little red two-wheel cart with a bench on it. Together, they pulled the cart into the corral, and when Bea stopped, they attached it to the horses.

Bea jumped on the cart and took the reins.

"Come on, Mom!" Bea called excitedly.

Ginger climbed up and sat down next to her daughter.

"Come up," Bea said and the animals pulled forward.

"It's not 'giddyup'?"

"Mr. Rogers said not for these guys."

"Ah." They veered right as they circled the corral.

"It's quiet, huh, Mom."

"It is," Ginger agreed.

"I like the clicking sound of the horse hooves. You can hear the dirt, too, as you ride around on it. Much better than the tractor." She turned and smiled at her mother. Bea actually looked happy.

"So, Bea. Umm . . . You are okay letting go of Henry's Child?"

"I already did, Mom. That's why everyone's here." Bea swallowed her last word.

"We could change our minds if you want to."

"Nope. We're going this way. It's why Samuel's here."

Ginger nodded. "You seem to have this horse thing pretty much down."

"Can't wait to go to the field," she said. "I plowed a lot with Daddy. I miss that."

"Yeah. Uh, what da ya think about staying home and working and schooling here?"

"We all know that's what we're doing. Samuel kinda told us we needed to."

"He did?" Ginger frowned. It wasn't for Samuel to say anything.

"Need to stay home to make home if you've lost your home," Bea said. She looked over at her mother.

"Have we lost our home?" Ginger stared into her daughter's eyes.

"I thought we did. But it's been here all the time. I couldn't see it because we kept doing things like we did when Daddy was around—like nothing changed. It was like we kept waiting for him to come back." Bea looked ahead and added, "But he isn't coming back."

Ginger sat still, the click of the horse's hooves beating like the small, gentle heart of her daughter, distant and silent for so long. "No, he isn't, Bea."

"I'll miss school. So will Henry. But Oliver won't." Bea gave her mother a half smile. "Maybe our friends can come over and help. It's not like we're moving to Seattle or anything."

"That's true."

"Whoa." The horse stopped and Bea grinned. "I like it when the sun's about to come up and the birds have just finished their morning song and there's nothing but the smell of dirt and the sound of wind in the grass and trees. That's how it was starting the day with Daddy."

"Was it?"

"Then the tractor started and ruined everything." Bea burst out laughing.

Ginger brightened and said, "That's what your daddy said, isn't it?"

Bea nodded, still laughing, and managed to say, "He loved Henry's Child but he hated Henry's Child."

"I didn't know that," Ginger replied.

"You never plowed with him." Bea stood and stretched a little. "Here, Mama. You try." Bea handed the reins to her mother and with quiet instruction from her daughter Ginger circled the corral again.

"Mrs. Martin?"

It was so difficult to answer whoever was calling her, for she had just had more with her daughter than she'd had in the last year and a half and she didn't want to be anywhere else. Shaking her head, she looked over and found Mr. Schaaf leaning against the corral with Mr. Whitaker, James Creed, and John Mitchell.

"Ah," she said, climbing off the bench. "Sorry for the traffic."

"You really gonna farm with horses?" Mr. Schaaf asked.

"Yes, sir. We really are," Ginger replied, nodding in her daughter's direction.

"Oh," the man replied. None of them said anything, but by their stance she could tell they thought this was a daft idea. She couldn't blame them. What was she? An emergency room nurse. They had been farming all of their lives and this—this was a bit nuts.

"I know it sounds crazy but we have help here." She motioned to Mr. Rogers and Jacob. "We're starting on a new road."

"Let's hook Bea up to the drill and have her start," Ed Rogers said.

"What's a drill?" Ginger asked.

"A grain drill," John Mitchell replied. "For planting."

"Ginger, open the gate all the way. Bea, take yourself out to the northwestern end of the field. I put the drill out there."

As Ginger pulled wide the gate, she found Samuel standing to its left. When Mr. Whitaker came to help, he nearly stepped on the ghost's feet.

"Watch out!" Ginger declared, looking at Samuel.

"What?" John Whitaker asked, gazing around.

"I'll go with Bea," Jacob said, hopping onto the cart.

"No lifting," Ginger replied.

Bea smiled at Samuel as she passed him on the cart, so small behind the horses and mules. He bowed as Bea passed.

"Let's go to the garden. We need to talk about what plants now," Mr. Rogers said.

"You're not from around here, are you?" It was James Creed directing the question to Ed.

"Uh . . . no."

"We'll tell her what she needs to plant in them beds," the old farmer announced.

"That'll do. Well, then," Mr. Rogers said with a shrug. "I guess I'll see how the equipment barn is coming along."

After shutting the gate, Ginger followed the four old farmers. Mr. Schaaf seemed smaller than the rest of them though he was two inches taller. He had a limp in his right leg and Ginger touched his arm and was about to mention she should take a look at him, but the old man shook his head, brushing her away.

When they rounded the corner of the barn, Ginger found two large squares of property to the far right of her gravel drive, each enclosed by a beautiful snake-rail fence.

"Oh." She breathed.

"Better use for that wood than lining this here drive," John Mitchell said.

"Wheldon said the goat would eat everything unless there was a fence," Mr. Schaaf said. "The rail fence on the drive would have been pretty, though."

Ginger silently agreed but the need to keep the goat away from the garden seemed the more pressing matter.

"Sometimes the best use for a thing is to add beauty. Like flowers," he added.

"I agree," Ginger replied out loud.

"Mama!" Oliver said. "Come look!"

With John Whitaker at her side and the other three farmers following behind, Ginger made her way past the gardens, across the front yard, and to the orchard.

"What is that?" she asked.

"It's a chicken coop that can move," Henry said proudly. "Me and Oliver made it with Emma and Sarah, here. They go to VMI."

"Thanks for helping," Ginger said to the two young women who were standing with Henry and Oliver. They nodded.

"Emma says the chickens can take care of the soil," Oliver explained. "We just move it around the gardens."

"I see. What is that?" Ginger asked again.

Henry and Oliver looked back at the coop, confused.

"That?" Ginger pointed.

"That is a turkey, Mrs. Martin," Sarah answered.

"I know it's a turkey. What's it doing with the chickens?"

"It's Rooster," Oliver replied.

"No, it's a turkey," Ginger said.

The large black-and-white bird bobbed its head several times, turned, and wobbled its wrinkly chin. Its beard had a yellow tinge, as did its breast feathers. Two white streaks ran from its nostrils down its snood, looking for all the world like a long, thin mustache.

"No, Mama. His name is Rooster."

"Gotta take the good with the bad," Henry said.

Around its left eye was a circular patch of white skin, giving the turkey the singular presence of an old man wearing a monocle, reminding her of Colonel Mustard from the game Clue. The turkey not only looked like a cousin of the goat; it also looked like it was planning everyone's demise.

"Rooster," she said.

Upon hearing its name, the bird cocked its head and fixed her with its black beady eye.

"Colonel Mustard in the drawing room with the candlestick," Ginger breathed.

CHAPTER 20

THE MORNING CHORUS

Ginger lay in bed listening to the silence of the night, which was rolling over in bed just as she did now—a last cozy snooze before dawn. But she wasn't sure she had even slept. Her mind had been busy running over the day from beginning to end as a sequential set of events like a movie that perpetually restarted. Rooster and Bubba. Christian and Augustus. Little Bea planting the alfalfa with Jacob as Mr. Mitchell and Mr. Schaaf looked on in amazement. The evening coming far too soon for amateur horse farmers with Jacob Esch climbing into Mr. Wheldon's truck. He hadn't stayed as expected.

That was one of two points that had bothered her most of the night. She hadn't realized how she had placed the boy in her farming plan in so short a time and now he wasn't there. The other point that kept her from sleeping was Samuel— or more precisely, the absence thereof.

Samuel had been around the entire day. He had disappeared on her in Christian's stall but reappeared here and there in the field with Bea. Yet even as the military academy left with Mr. and

Mrs. Rogers late in the evening after dinner and Mr. Mitchell took a few cookies and headed home with his aging friends, Samuel hadn't appeared. They lit up the house with kerosene lamps and beeswax candles rescued from the attic of the summer house as a warm welcome to him, and all were disappointed when he didn't show.

Pulling her arms from her blankets, Ginger rolled over again, gazing up at the window, which was lit lavender-gray in the darkness of the room. Her left hand found its way to the curls upon her head and she smiled, remembering her reflection in the window of her truck. Closing her eyes, she heard a single bird sing. It whistled high and then cut off sharply. It was followed by another bird and another. A crow cawed in the distance and somewhere the gentle, soft gobble of a turkey answered the horizon.

"Better than a rooster," she whispered.

"Why do you suppose they do that?" The question came from the corner above Ginger's head. She opened her eyes and glanced toward the window again.

"The sun's coming up," she replied.

"I know. But what purpose does singing before dawn serve the birds? The cows don't sing. The horses don't. Neither does the dog at the foot of your bed or the cat in the crook of your knees. Why do the birds sing?"

Ginger had never really thought about that. She

just loved them singing if she had slept well and wished they would shut up if she hadn't. Why do birds sing the sun up?

"Maybe—maybe they're calling to each other making sure they all survived the night."

"Maybe."

"Maybe one starts and it's the only time they can really hear their song in the chaos of a noisy day."

"Hmm. They like the sound of their own voices? I can say that about many a man." Samuel chuckled quietly.

"That's not what I mean." Ginger sat up and looked at him, a standing shadow in the corner. "A morning chorus. A choir is only as good as its members listening to the voices of the others around them."

"The morning chorus." She couldn't see it, but she knew he was smiling.

"We lit the house without electricity last night."

"I know. I was here."

"You were?"

"Yes." His voice was just a shadow.

"Why didn't you say something?"

"I was . . . thinking."

"About what?" Ginger tossed off the covers and sat on the edge of the bed. Regard lay as if nothing had happened—a lump underneath a mound of blankets.

"About being here. About a picture I once held

in my hand. About a bird's call in the cannon roar. About a friend long gone."

Ginger had no reply. She had no idea what any of that meant and to ask would be to know something of Samuel's past. This conversation she felt sure would be better held in the light of day when only his eyes went to shadow.

"About you," he finished.

"What about me?" Ginger whispered.

Samuel said nothing, nor did he move. He was a frozen shadow growing longer as the sky brightened outside the window. Suddenly, she felt a great wash of sadness pour over her. She wasn't ready for this. He was in her plan just like Jacob.

"Are—are you leaving me?"

Samuel let out an audible breath. "No."

For herself, Ginger brightened, but at the same moment she felt Samuel's weight. Carrying the dead. Her husband. Samuel. But he wasn't really hers to carry. She looked at the floor.

"If what you needed to do is done," she heard herself say, "then you should go . . . home. The kids and I will be fine." She was lying. Well, not exactly a lie. But not a truth, either. She had no idea what she was doing with this farm and to say it would all be fine was ridiculous.

"This is home, Virginia Moon. We have to make it so."

She nodded, relieved, but not so relieved, either. The same unsteady sense of the world that had come to her on the road when she first realized Samuel was spirit crept from her toes, which rested on the cold wood floor, up her legs, into her stomach, over her shoulders, into her mind.

"I'm unsettled," she said softly.

"I know. I, too, feel without ease. There is something here, Virginia Moon. Something has been flowing as a wash of water for over one hundred and fifty years and I feel it creeping closer than ever I have."

"What is it?"

Samuel shook his head. "I do not know. I see only pieces of it but no clear connection between any of them."

"Pieces of it? Like you being here. A picture you once held in your hand. A bird's call in the cannon roar. A friend long gone?" Ginger asked.

Samuel nodded and in the first ray of light his shadow was illuminated. First she saw his tattered shoes, then his woolen pants, then his disheveled shirt. The light stopped on his lips and there Ginger could see him mouth, *You.* She swallowed hard.

"I saw you yesterday, Samuel. In Woodstock."

"Yes. I, too, saw you."

"Why didn't you answer me when I called your name?"

"Because you called me from here, Virginia. Now. I only saw you—heard my name called there—then."

Ginger thought for a moment. "Then. You mean back then? In the war?"

Samuel nodded.

Closing her eyes, Ginger listened to the morning chorus, trying to steady herself in the shifting of reality.

"I saw you in Manassas," she said without opening her eyes.

"I did not see you. But I moved my head to find your voice in the cannon smoke, and in that moment a minié ball missed me and hit Avery."

"Is—is that the friend you are thinking of? The one long gone?"

Samuel shook his head and replied, "No. His name was Jeb. We both deserted after the battle at Cedar Creek—"

"Ah! That's just up the road here!" Ginger declared.

"It seemed far from here back then."

There was a quiet rap on the door.

"Mama?"

Ginger stared at Samuel's lips, waiting for the light to reach his eyes.

"Yes, Bea."

"Time to get up. We have work to do."

Her eyes sought Samuel's, which remained in shadow as if the sun had stopped its motion.

"Yes, we do."

Bea opened the door a crack and looked in. "We

need to get up earlier, Mama. I should be finishing breakfast and heading to the fields."

"Really?" Ginger gazed over at her daughter. The sun was cool gray upon Bea's face.

"Daddy and I were always out in the barn when the birds started to sing."

"Okay, Bea," Ginger said. "Then we should set our clocks tomorrow. I don't smell coffee."

"Grandma went out with Henry and Oliver," Bea replied. "She says you have kitchen duty."

"I see." Ginger chuckled, searching the floor for her slippers.

"Oliver will bring in eggs. Ah! Samuel! Good morning!" Bea shone like the sun.

"Good morning, Bea."

The little girl yawned and, leaving the door open, headed for the stairs.

"She's not used to fieldwork like me," Bea said.

"You are used to it?" Samuel inquired as he left the shadow of the corner and walked out the bedroom door.

Ginger followed both down the stairs, thinking of the chorus and the shadow that was Samuel. He had deserted his regiment. Maybe he couldn't cross over because he was being punished for something.

"My daddy and I used to work the fields from when I was just a baby in a carrier on his chest."

"What does that mean? 'A carrier on his chest.'"

348

Ginger reached for the light switch at the bottom of the stairs and stopped herself just in time.

"Like a backpack, only it goes on the front and holds babies."

Walking into the kitchen, Ginger turned the knob on the side of the kerosene lamp and lifted the plunger. She pumped it several times to pressurize the fuel in its base, spun the plunger back in place, and turned the lever. A gentle hiss whispered to the mantles and she struck a match, setting the lamp aglow. She blew out the match and lifted the lantern to its hook above the table. The day before, an electric light held that spot. But today was like when Osbee was a child. The same old lantern now hung on its same old hook, happy to be serving again in light from the buried darkness of the attic.

"You went out on your father's chest into the fields? Virginia Moon, you agreed to that?"

"I wasn't here often," Ginger replied, scanning the counter for the coffeemaker. It was not in its proper spot next to the sink.

"Where were you?"

"Working. Look, the way Jesse saw it, babies go out in the fields on the backs of their parents everywhere else in the world. What's the difference? Where's the coffeepot?" Ginger opened the cupboard below the counter whereon used to sit the coffeemaker.

"Jesse," Samuel said softly.

"Where's the coffeepot?"

"On the stove," Samuel replied. "Jesse is your husband's name?"

On the stove was a steel pot. On the counter next to it was an old hand-operated coffee grinder, a glass jar of coffee beans, and a piece of paper.

"Yes," Ginger answered, lifting the paper and reading. "Holy cow! I'm supposed to make coffee in this?"

"You cannot make a pot of coffee?" Samuel asked.

"Well." Ginger looked over at him. "Not this way. I just use the coffeemaker that plugs into the wall. But you are here and electricity makes you itch, so . . . percolated coffee on the gas stove. And kerosene lamps." Ginger pointed to the kitchen light above the table. "Changing out of deference to you."

"Here. Let me show you," Samuel said.

"And farming with horses like you used to do," she added.

"It is easier to teach what you know," he replied, motioning for her to fill the coffeepot with water. "I know nothing of tractors."

"But you know farming. So we'll learn what you know."

As Ginger put the pot under the faucet and was about to turn on the water, a shrill scream filled the kitchen and without another breath Ginger was out the kitchen door, through the sunroom, and onto the stairs in the cold March morning. There she saw Oliver running toward the summer kitchen with his small basket of eggs held tightly to his chest. His eyes were white and wide as a full moon and when he reached the door he banged it madly with his right fist.

"Help!" he screamed.

The goat rounded the corner at full speed. Grabbing the broom that hung on the sunroom wall, Ginger leapt from the stairs and stormed toward Bubba. Just then, the door of the kitchen opened. However, the summer kitchen had a farmer's wife door and Henry had only opened the top.

"What's wrong?" Henry asked.

Without so much as an inhale to answer, Oliver dropped the basket and, as any great Olympic gymnast might do, flew over the door as if it were a vault, tucking his short legs beneath him. He then disappeared in a tackle with his brother into the kitchen. At that moment, the goat hit the bottom part of the door at full speed, setting it to shudder with the impact.

"Neaaaahhh," it said as Ginger, stalking silently like Regard, stepped closer. Bubba didn't have a chance, for by the time it turned its wicked caprine gaze in her direction, the broom came down on the top of its head. The goat didn't even wince but did jump a little in surprise, at which point Ginger swung and batted its rear legs out

from under it. The force of her swing sent Bubba flying to the left, rolling backward, its feet flailing in the air as it tried to right itself.

"What's it like, Bubba?" Ginger hissed as she came on. "Minding your own business and out of nowhere something nasty comes at you, scaring you to death."

The goat pulled its feet under its body and stood, lowering its head for a run. Before it could start, Ginger whacked it on the left shoulder and the goat stumbled to the right, skidding in the dust to a stop. It hunkered down and leapt forward, coming straight at her. Before she could make another swing, it hit and the force of the impact did—nothing. Dazed, Ginger stood still for a moment, waiting to hurt or fall down or something. Nothing. Then she tossed her broom down.

"Come on, you little shit!" she yelled, and as commanded Bubba turned and came back at her, hitting her thigh.

"Is that all you can do?" she asked. Hands on hips, she turned to the summer kitchen and found Henry, Osbee, and the wide eyes of little Oliver peeping over the door at her.

"Oliver," Ginger said as she turned her back to Bubba. "Come here." The goat butted her in the rear end. She didn't even flinch. "Whatever, Bubba. Oliver?" Ginger reached the door and held out her hands.

"No!" Oliver screamed.

"Look at him, Oliver! He can't even bruise me. Come here!" Grabbing Oliver's hand, she pulled him from the kitchen.

"No!" His voice was high and terrified. He writhed in her arms.

"Mama!" Bea called.

"Oliver!" Ginger commanded. "Look at me!"

Whimpering, Oliver looked with red, tearful eyes at his mother.

"I would never put you in danger—do you know that?"

Oliver nodded a little.

"Do you know that I will never put you in danger?"

"Yes," he whispered.

"Look down."

Reticently, Oliver looked down and the goat, at that moment, rammed Ginger's hip.

"Whatever, Bubba," Ginger said, smiling.

Oliver kicked a little, hitting the goat's horn.

"Neeaahhh," it said.

"Whatever," Ginger said with a little laugh.

Oliver smiled as Bubba butted his mother again. "Whatever, Bubba," Oliver said.

"Bubba is a goat. We don't want to be mean to him but we don't want to be afraid, either. His pointy horns and weird eyes made me scared. But when he hit me, I realized there's nothing to him. He's just doing goaty things and it's me being afraid—afraid of what I thought he was and what he can do. And he seems to like making me afraid but right now he's learning I'm not moving."

"He's bigger than me," Oliver whined.

"Yep, and he'll use that. But he can't really hurt you. He's a goat. If he pushes, push back. Okay?"

Oliver wasn't sure. The frown on his face told the story.

"You need to get down and face him, Oliver."

"I don't want to." He clung tighter, burying his face in her neck.

"I might be out in the field or in the barn and he might hit me and knock me over, but he can't hurt me. You see? Because I'm not afraid anymore."

Ginger rubbed Oliver's back, rocking him gently in her arms. He smelled like hers. He was her baby. He was Jesse's baby. He was their last baby and when that thought crossed her mind she held him tighter, hanging on to the little boy who would one day be too big to hold this way.

Oliver squirmed in the tightness of her embrace and, slowly, crawled down her body to the ground. He held her leg, looking sideways at Bubba.

"All the eggs are broken," Ginger said.

"Not all," Oliver replied. "I didn't get them all."

"Too many to carry?"

"No. Rooster chased me."

"Really?" Ginger said, and at that moment Bubba charged, aiming for Oliver.

"Mama!" Oliver yelled, trying to climb back up.

Ginger left him on the ground, petting his head in reassurance, and when the goat hit him, his eyes popped open in surprise.

"That feels like Henry or Bea pushing me."

"That's all it is."

Oliver let go of her leg and looked at Bubba. "Whatever, Bubba!" he yelled.

"Why don't you get the basket and we'll go get the rest of the eggs."

Oliver stood up and walked to the door.

"Oliver! Look out!" Henry yelled.

"Whatever, Henry," Oliver said and faced the oncoming goat. It hit him and the impact caused him to stumble backward into the door. "Go away!" Oliver yelled and pushed Bubba hard. The goat backed up and blinked in its goaty way.

When he picked up his basket, egg ooze dripped from its bottom.

"Osbee, you got another basket?" Ginger asked.

The old woman nodded and walked away from the door.

"What are you doing in there?" she asked Henry.

"We're straining the milk and cleaning our buckets."

"Ah."

"Then we're gonna clean the stove in here."

"I'm gonna help with that," Oliver added.

Osbee handed her the basket and a long stick, saying, "You'll need this."

"Why?"

"Turkeys have beaks, feet, and feathers that are all pointy."

Ginger took the stick and handed it to Oliver. She gazed over to the sunroom and found Bea, Beau, and Samuel standing on the steps. She eyed the dog.

"Where were you when I was being attacked by your new friend?"

The dog yawned.

"Come, Beau. Let's go talk to Rooster."

Taking Oliver's hand, she turned around and headed toward the orchard. She didn't need to look; she knew not only Beau but everyone else was following. As they walked down the hill, there were a couple of shrieks as Bubba surprised somebody in the group, but eventually Ginger would hear *"Whatever, Bubba"* and then nothing. She supposed Bubba had grown weary and had slithered away, waiting to come upon them unawares at a later time.

When they came to the trees, they found the chickens up and pecking the ground. Rooster stood large in their center, casting his beady eye in Ginger's direction. Her spine tingled.

"I just can't see how this is a coop," she said. "It's supposed to be my orchard."

The fifteen chickens and Rooster chattered behind a metal grid fence that formed a large square around a quarter of her orchard. Inside was a rather large henhouse on wheels with a rather large ramp leading up to a rather large door. The size was to accommodate Rooster, who had walked toward Ginger and Oliver and was even now puffing up his feathers.

"We move it, Mama. It'll be here for ten days; then we'll move it to another section of the orchard. It'll feed the chickens and fertilize the ground."

Henry, who was doing the talking, had obviously spent quality time with Ed Rogers the day before.

"What need is there for this?" Samuel exclaimed.

"You didn't do this on your farm?" Ginger asked.

"No. We let the chickens run about." He waved his arms around the yard. "They'd roost in the henhouse at night."

"We can't do that," Henry replied.

"Why not?" Samuel inquired.

"Sarah and Emma from VMI said that the chickens will make a mess with their poop everywhere and ruin the farm equipment by nesting and such. There's also foxes and raccoons and stuff that'll eat them."

"Not with that monster among them," Samuel said, pointing to Rooster.

"I suppose, Samuel," Ginger said, "things have changed a bit since you were . . . around."

"I cannot see how farming could change. It is growing things."

"Maybe it hasn't changed in purpose," Osbee replied. "Just method. We had chickens when I was a girl and they ran around the yard between the front and the back and the barn. Pooped all over the porch. Went missing. I think this is wonderful! More . . . hygienic."

"Hygienic," Samuel repeated.

"Clean," Ginger said.

"Thank you for defining the word, Virginia," Samuel said.

She smiled and added, "I suppose you know the word. But I don't suppose you washed your hands all the time like we do today, either."

"We washed our hands."

"At every meal?"

Samuel tilted his head. "There wasn't water at every meal. Especially while marching."

"Bingo!" Ginger replied. "Things have changed for the better."

"Let me have the basket, please, Mama," Oliver interrupted, stick in hand.

"You ready?" Ginger asked with surprise.

He nodded and, taking the offered basket, loosened the wire fence from the post. Slowly he climbed in, squaring his shoulders as he stood opposite Rooster. Not a breath was taken in the entire group until, unexpectedly, Samuel entered the arena.

"I—I'm not scared, Samuel," Oliver whispered.

"I know," the ghost replied, walking up behind the little boy. "Sometimes, though, it is better to not face a danger alone when what an opponent can do is not fully understood."

Oliver nodded. The turkey scratched a little at the ground, straightened its neck, and with a loud gobble rushed at Oliver.

"Oliver!" Bea cried.

"Drop the basket and move forward," Samuel said with a steady voice.

As Ginger leaned over the fence to grab her boy, Oliver dropped the basket, lunged forward holding the stick like a bat, and whacked the turkey across its breast. In the dawn sun, feathers and dust flew. Rooster let out a wail and rolled over to Oliver's left.

"Now," Samuel said. "Time to take measure."

The turkey shook itself as if clearing its head from the wallop and straightened its neck as if it was going to try again. Ginger leaned away from the fence, smiling proudly at her very small boy.

"What's he gonna do?" Oliver whispered, not taking his eyes off the bird.

"Not sure yet. Stand your ground."

Rooster looked at Oliver. Oliver looked right back at Rooster. Having thought about it, the turkey backed away.

"Pick up your basket and go about your business," Samuel instructed.

The little boy bent down and lifted his basket from the dirt. Crossing the chicken paddock, he moved his stool next to the hen coop, lifted the lid on the roosting boxes, and removed seven eggs. The chickens chattered and clucked around his stool, and when he stepped down, they followed him back to the fence where he had entered.

"Goats come in different shapes and sizes," he said to Samuel as he climbed through the fence.

Samuel nodded, smiling at Ginger, who was just elated.

"They do?" Henry asked, attaching the wire fence back to the post and looking at his little brother in awe.

"Rooster's just another goat," Oliver said.

September 23, 1862
Winchester

My dear Juliette,
I thank you for your letter and your prayers and the prayers of your pastor. I know he meant well by instructing you to burn the photograph, but I thank you for not so doing. I feel as do you. It would be turning me to ashes. The bird sings, the muskets pop, and somehow night descends with me yet standing. I am sure it is your prayers that keep me safe and I sit here next to a stream to converse across the autumn wind with you.

We waged war again on metal and steam, coming to Bristoe August 26th. Our humor grows black and deep and we did have quite a time in this battle. The trains would come down and we, having barricaded a bridge, watched them fly from the tracks, one after the other. A great hail of triumph rose from us as each one tumbled into the ravine. Alas, all good things come to an end and the last train stopped short of our trap. It backed up and disappointed us entirely. Our only consolation was that a Northern Senator came to us within the train before and he lay near a fire, regaining his composure from the fall. I stood just beyond the fire and watched him come around. Upon discovering he was the guest of our leader, Jackson, and with eyes full of absolute awe, he asked to be lifted to see this great man that had so discombobulated the Union army. So he was lifted and eyes of awe turned to a look of utter disappointment. His look matched our mood what with the lack of trains to route. He saw, of course, Jackson, who stood as familiar to us as any. We have stopped noticing him really. But the eyes of the Senator forced us to see anew a dirty, bearded man in a disheveled, tattered butternut uniform, wearing a private's cap drawn forward on his head so his eyes are barely visible, sucking on a lemon. He simply looked like one of us. This filthy example of manhood was taking down the great blue wave? "Oh, my God!" the Senator declared. "Lay me down."

So we move on and when Jackson passes not a few call out, "Oh, my God! Lay me down." Jackson hears this without remark. We are sure he has no idea to what the men refer. We chuckle at his passing, especially if the remark is made in response to one of Jackson's nearly impossible requests for action by us men.

August 29th we came again to Manassas, and

as if that place hadn't seen enough, we fought once more. Of course, we were after the metal beasts again, but the men in blue came on and we, together with Longstreet's division, fought. As is always with Jackson, we won the battle, sending the Union's Pope and what was left of his troops falling back toward Washington.

We marched and fought and then we, with great trepidation, crossed the Potomac into Maryland, as ordered by General Lee, to invade Northern lands. Juliette, such peace I had, knowing you had gone south. With the breath of autumn, we came to Sharpsburg upon the quarter moon, and as it waned crescent, the bird sounded across the great rolling fields near Antietam Creek. The farmers scurried to town, leaving the fields ripe and ready for harvest. We came for harvest, too, but not to draw corn or wheat. We came for man.

I cannot tell you how surely I knew this to be my end. I, in the quickening of battle, entered the little church there. White and square, its pews set to encompass the edges of the walls, surrounding the empty space in which the minister would stand and measure out the beats of a song sung in praise. I stood in the empty center, thinking to sing, but the bird sounded next to me. I spun around, seeking for it. It was there and then it left the church. I followed it outside and as I walked out the church door, I spotted a little boy upon his father's shoulders. A child he held by his left hand and a woman in his right. Upon her right trotted a third. I whistled to the bird, and when I did, the woman stopped and looked back. And it was she—in the photo-graph, Juliette. She holds children and a man. She looked into my eyes, a spirit set against the growing wave of blue on the far horizon.

Who is she, my love? I waved to her but she turned. And as she walked away, she seemed as you, walking away from me. I watched her, seeing your arms. Your hair. Your hips moving the fabric of your dress. And I burned. I am yet here, surviving even our loss at Sharpsburg, standing tall though the harvest lay beaten and bloody in the fields near Antietam and I burn for you.

Your devoted,
Samuel

CHAPTER 21

ACOUSTIC SHADOW

The interstate was busy, even in the rural Shenandoah at eight thirty in the morning. It was as if winter, having retreated so entirely from the valley in the last few days, had set the cars and semis free of ice, rushing like a swollen river about to overflow its banks. Not once since she entered the freeway in Woodstock did Ginger feel she had control of the truck. She seemed to be endlessly pushed toward every exit by the sheer volume of vehicles flying north on their spring run.

As she tried to maneuver herself into the middle lane, she gazed up into the rearview mirror, wishing upon hopeless wish to see Samuel there. After Oliver conquered Rooster, or at least gained the turkey's respect (maybe), Samuel, without a word, walked away toward the bridge. Bea had run after him before they went in for breakfast to ask if he'd come to the field, but she returned, reporting upon entry to the sunroom, that he was gone.

They'd cooked and eaten breakfast, which consisted of fresh eggs and fresh milk and toast and coffee brewed in the percolator. Ginger had to admit that the entire event, the food and the company and the expectation of the day, made her feel as if things were actually changing for the better. With a lighter spirit, she climbed the stairs to change from her pajamas and, having dressed, pulled her hair back into the red headband given to her at the salon the day before. She even smiled at the pretty young woman who gazed back at her from the mirror.

"Eggs taste better when chickens eat bugs," Oliver said as he stretched his neck and body to peer over the dashboard. Even in the booster seat, he barely could see.

"They eat bugs?" Ginger asked, finally able to slide to the left and settle into the rushing middle lane.

"Chickens eat grasses and bugs and stuff. That's why we have to move them around. They'll pick an area clean in less than a day."

"Why do all the egg cartons in the best stores say 'Hundred Percent Vegetarian Diet' then?" Ginger mused.

"Henry asked that same thing. Jacob says it's to make you feel better. He says animals have their own ways and we try to make them people."

"Ah. Beau and Regard are people, though, aren't they?" Ginger inquired. Oliver always had said they were, anyway.

"They're mooore like us," Oliver replied,

rolling his eyes. "That's because they live with us. But Jacob says they're animals with their ways, too."

"I see."

"Is Jacob coming back?"

"Not sure. I guess he has his own ways," Ginger replied, grinning over at Oliver.

He rolled his eyes and flopped back in the seat, returning once again to the video game in his hands.

Though breakfast had created a lightness of spirit, Ginger had been weighed down by the knowledge that she had to go to the school and withdraw her kids. It was on her mind when she, with the rest of her brood, headed for the barn after breakfast to harness the horses and mules. There was no procrastinating anymore. She couldn't call them out again. She couldn't lie. She didn't want anyone's sympathy for a feeling of loss she wasn't having this day. So, once Bea was in the fields, escorted by Osbee and Henry, Ginger headed for her truck with Oliver following on her heels. She thought she should leave him and then the next thought was that it was better he come. He'd be backup. As they drove away, the sun had just peeped over the mountain on the other side of the river and in her rearview mirror she saw Samuel standing on the edge of her drive, casting no shadow in the morning light. There was comfort seeing him, for she knew he'd watch over things while she was gone.

So she headed to the school and it really had not gone well at all. She grimaced just thinking about it. Mrs. Castro, the principal, had taken Ginger into her office, leaving Oliver with Mrs. Perry, the school secretary. Mr. Taylor, the school counselor, *happened* to walk in and it was two against one. They both were so certain that things should stay as they were with Henry, Bea, and Oliver. School should continue. It was a safe and stable environment, with extra support for them in this difficult time. Truly, Ginger couldn't argue, because she believed everything they were saying was right.

But she also knew that there was no choice to stay in school. To stay in school was now impossible because, stable, safe, and the same though school was, things had changed. Her children wanted to change. Bea had said it best: her father wasn't returning and to deny the fact was simply to make pretend. It wasn't real. Her kids wanted real.

"Sometimes it's harder to fight what's happening," Mr. Taylor said, leaning forward and looking sincerely into Ginger's eyes. "Sometimes we just have to go with the flow."

"Exactly," she replied, and with an apologetic smile, she stood. It was too hard to continue as they were, so why fight? Ginger was going with the flow and, difficult as it was, she opened the door, flowed out into the office, signed her children out of school, took the homeschooling information from Mrs. Perry, and after a tortuous round of hugs, she left with Oliver in tow.

"Sorry," she mumbled to the memory. The hugs were meant sincerely and had great care in them. She just was unable to accept them with a grateful heart this day.

"Sorry about what?"

"Just talking to myself."

"You ever hear of acoustic shadow, Mama?"

"No."

"Sometimes, people really close to the war couldn't hear the guns and stuff but people farther away could. The people close in who heard nothin' were in acoustic shadow."

"Where'd you learn that?"

"Samuel told us about it when he got us up this morning. He says he's in the acoustic shadow. What does that mean, Mama?"

Ginger gazed toward the river on her right and replied, "I don't know."

She didn't know. Samuel had said he was yet in the world but not of it. There were senses he could still feel and others he couldn't. Was that a ghost? To neither be the beginning of something nor to feel the end but to float aimlessly within the emptiness between the two? Ginger had known this as well. She had waited in the silence;

she sensed it as the space between notes. Without that silence, there was no rhythm, but a note must follow for a song to live. She, too, had been surviving in acoustic shadow, waiting for more than a year with no end and no beginning—just existence day to day. Perhaps she was a ghost. Or had been until the day Samuel arrived.

"Where we going?" Oliver asked, stretching forward. He put his video game down and picked up one of the papers from the school that sat on the seat between them.

"It's a surprise," Ginger replied, her stomach rolling over as she thought of her destination.

A large red fire truck passed. Its lights were off and its siren silent and Oliver leaned against the window watching it creep by. Had it been sounding the alarm, he would have been crunched up in his seat with his hands covering his ears.

Traffic slowed and slowed and finally Ginger crept back into the right lane and was pushed off the next exit by the volume of vehicles. Ahead was Route 11 and she took a left onto the old Valley Turnpike.

The wonderful thing about Virginia was that there were beautiful country roads that went anywhere you needed to go as an alternate to the highways. The state was old. Paths were many. Even the Native American trails were still around. So north they went on the turnpike through little towns and farms as the sun pulled clean away from Massanutten Mountain. The road was green and clear with a gentle layer of mist floating to the right, hovering over the Shenandoah, which snaked in and out as if following toes at the mountain's foot.

They didn't talk; instead they rolled down their windows and turned the heater on. Ginger didn't know what was in Oliver's mind, but what she cogitated on was the turnpike's age coupled with the perpetual thought that anywhere along here Samuel may have roamed back then. Oliver popped up straight in his seat and turned his head from the left to the right, scanning the area as if looking for something.

"You okay there, Oliver?" Ginger asked.

"Are we near Cedar Creek?"

"Yes," Ginger replied. Cedar Creek was the battlefield their family visited most often. Ginger never really understood why, but then she realized she had never asked Jesse. Time with him was all there was back then. What they did was not relevant; it was that they were together. "Why" never came into consideration and thus, like so much else about him these days, it would remain a mystery.

"Are we going to Cedar Creek?"

Ginger gazed over at her son. Since Jesse died, they had not gone to any battlefield as a family.

"Yes."

"Henry and Bea aren't here," he said.

"I know." Technically, she wasn't going to bring Oliver, either, but she'd needed backup at the school.

Oliver looked down at his feet and then back up to the road.

"Will they be sad?" Her little boy looked as if he was going to cry.

"Maybe. But maybe I can bring them back another day—one at a time. Just to feel Daddy again."

Her son nodded, his face turning down. He was a bright person, Oliver. His sadness was always worn so clearly.

"We don't have to go," she offered, holding her own disappointment inside in case he decided he wanted to return home.

Oliver looked over to her. In his hazel eyes reflected the morning sun. Henry and Bea were all their father's—dark with gray eyes. But Oliver was all hers—strawberry blond hair, freckles, and hazel eyes. Who would the next Thee-Me have looked like? She would never know.

"You want to go to Belle Grove Mansion?" she asked.

"Nah. The drive toward the creek."

They entered the battleground and at Water Plant Road Ginger took a left, following the street to Bowman's Mill Road, which wound through the southern part of the battlefield.

"Can we stop here?" Oliver asked.

Ginger stopped. "We're not at the creek," she said.

"Can we get out and walk?"

Pulling over, Ginger turned the car off and they climbed out. Taking his mother's hand, Oliver headed out into the field. Ginger didn't need to say anything, for Oliver was leading this expedition, and without a word they walked in the damp morning grass. The birds chirped and crows cawed as they made their way south and east. Small hills of woods rose in front of them, behind which rose Massanutten Mountain. It was quiet as only the country can be quiet and Oliver let go of Ginger's hand, trotting ahead. He whistled and Ginger came to a sudden halt.

She hadn't heard that sound since they'd last been at a battlefield as a family. Oliver whistled his birdsong only then. It had been missing, and as it sounded in front of her, a little spot was filled in the great chasm of loss that was her husband.

"Oliver." She breathed as he trotted farther away. "Oliver, wait."

Then Ginger felt the ground tremble beneath her feet and she gazed down at the grass there. It turned a purple color as if the sun were just rising or just setting—as if she were standing in the violet hour. Oliver's bird sounded in the distance and when she gazed up to call her son once more, she saw men—thousands of them swarming around her and to the horizon. They raced the edge of the field, the hill with mountain trees behind them aflame in the red-gold and orange leaves of autumn. Smoke and dust and pops of fire broke through the violet light. The ground shuddered again as man and horse, wide-eyed and openmouthed in the exploding earth, spun around her from southeast to northwest in a great torrent of blue and butternut and blood.

She covered her mouth, horrified, as an eruption of ground not one hundred yards away caught a large group of men by surprise. Bedrolls, caps, muskets, belts, heads, hands, feet, and unidentifiable body parts burst in all directions. She shook as the ground shook, wanting to run, to turn her gaze away, to close her eyes.

"Oliver," she called, and when she flipped her head in the direction of the bird, she found she stood in the center of the spinning whirlwind of war. If she moved ten feet in any direction, it would drag her away. Standing with her, in the eye of this storm, were two men. One was a black man with skin so dark his blue uniform looked light. His cap was at his feet and his musket at his eye. It was his eye that drew Ginger in, for it was hazel, but not any hazel she had ever seen. It was mutable, changing as she watched from gold to green to gold. He pulled the musket from his eye, which grew wide; his brow furrowed in great pain. Following his gaze, she found another man, younger, who was white with sandy blond hair in a Confederate officer's uniform. His gun was drawn down to the ground and from his very hazel green eyes tears fell.

Trembling beneath Ginger's feet caused her to totter, and as she steadied herself she found three Union rifles pointed directly at her held by one Union officer and two privates. The officer had the same look in his wide brown eyes as the black man had in his. Ginger took a step back, spinning to the right, opposite the direction of the turbulence around her. Then into her right ear the bird whistled softly and when she came around she froze, her eyes growing wide and in as painful a wonder as everyone else in the center of that battle.

For there before her, not nine inches from her nose, was Samuel. He looked right at her and she at him. He passed his right hand across her left cheek to brush her hair away, following her chin as if to circle the single curl at her neck within his fingers.

"Samuel?" she whispered, reaching for the light brown hair, which blew softly across his forehead by some wind she could not feel.

A small smile grew on his face as she watched his mouth say, *Ginger Moon.*

She nodded, touching his ethereal lips. When she peered back to his eyes, she found no shadow. Instead they looked so familiar to her. He gazed at her, making her more than she could ever be—stronger, kinder, steadier, more beautiful. This was Jesse's gaze in Samuel's eyes. It was love.

His eyes grew moist just as tears fell from hers and he mouthed, *I see you.*

"And I, you," she said.

Something moved over his right shoulder, drawing her attention. A Union cavalry rider was flying past in the great whirlwind around them and his rifle was pointed directly at Samuel's back.

"Samuel!" Ginger yelled, pointing. But as she did so, he moved his hand back to her face, drawing her gaze back to him.

I'm ready, he mouthed. In her peripheral vision, she caught the flare and smoke of the rifle fire behind him.

"No!" she screamed.

A great cloud of dirt and smoke rose suddenly around her and she couldn't see anymore.

"Samuel!" she yelled. "Samuel!"

Suddenly, a small hand slid into hers. She grabbed it.

"Mama?"

Blinking in the early spring sun, Ginger shook her head, looking at the little hill and the mountain, bare yet of leaves. She felt her pant legs heavy with morning dew and a whippoorwill sang as it flew overhead, a singular sound in the silence of the country.

"Mama, Samuel's at home," Oliver said.

She looked down at her son and nodded, unsteady and weary. "I think we should head home now," she whispered hoarsely.

"Did you hear my bird?" Oliver asked.

"I heard you whistling," she said, leading him back to the truck.

"I heard a reply," he said.

Ginger tried to smile, to endeavor not to feel the great pain of war that freshly wounded her mind, her heart. It was Samuel there, but Jesse, too, dying in war and the silent screaming and terror of the men she had just seen was no less than that of her husband and his troops in a land far away. She could imagine him so, courageous always but also utterly frightened.

When they reached the truck, she secured Oliver in his booster seat. Shutting the door, she came around the bed of the truck. She stopped to gaze once more over the grassy field of Cedar Creek, which moved so peacefully as if it had no memory of the bloody scars that once tore through its soil.

CHAPTER 22

A PLACE AT THE TABLE

They turned left, making their way down the small Virginia highway that led to their little road at the end of which was Smoot's farm. Mother and son said nothing on the short drive home from Cedar Creek and it was a short drive—shorter than Ginger had remembered. Now realizing how close it was, she wished for it to be a little longer, as she hadn't yet regained reality. Jesse's gaze in Samuel's eyes as the bullet fired ran through her mind over and over and small, short, uncontrollable whimpers escaped her lips as she drove. Oliver had even taken her hand without a word on the last outcry and had not let go.

She turned left onto their road. Mr. Schaaf was out on his tractor and he waved as they passed. Ginger didn't because one hand was held by Oliver and the other was on the steering wheel. Oliver waved and said, "Grandma and Grandpa are here."

His voice carried a slight sadness to it, which caused Ginger to slow down. Her head began to pound.

The Martins of Richmond—indeed they were

here. The black Mercedes was pulled right up to the top of the drive as if taking over, and Ginger, weary and hurting, wanted to simply stop, reverse, and go somewhere else. She even contemplated doing so, but what would she tell Oliver? She braked a little more, trying to come up with some story for Oliver when Samuel appeared on the porch and motioned earnestly for her to come. Drained as she was, she parked at the bottom of the hill so as not to obstruct the Mercedes from leaving. She hoped it would do so soon and take its occupants with it.

Hand in hand, mother and son climbed the drive. Samuel was gone as they came to the front porch and so they headed to the back, looking to see who was about. Henry opened the door to the summer kitchen.

"Who's with Bea?" Ginger inquired.

"Samuel. Grandma and Grandpa are here again with that man."

Ginger nodded, putting her left hand to her left temple. "Come help me with the stove, Oliver."

"Mama's hurt," he said.

Henry looked up at Ginger.

"I'm all right. I have a headache, that's all."

"I'm hungry," Oliver said.

"I've milk in here but we're gonna need to wait for lunch," Henry replied, opening the bottom door to the kitchen. "Grandma and Grandpa wanted to talk to Grandma Osbee alone."

"With Mr. Glenmore," Ginger added.

Henry nodded solemnly as Oliver stepped into the summer kitchen. A squeak on the right brought Ginger's attention there, and standing in the sunroom door was Ester Martin. Ginger managed a tight smile. Ester wasn't smiling.

"Hi, Mrs. Martin. It's good to see you again so soon."

"What do you mean, Virginia, by selling Henry's Child?"

"I didn't sell it," Ginger replied, confused by her mother-in-law's lack of civility. She was always civil.

"Where is it?"

"Ed Rogers traded it for all the farm equipment and the hay and the new bar—"

"Legally, that's selling it." She stepped out of the door and stood at the top of the steps. Her navy woolen pants and red silk blouse looked cold and wintery as she stood in the fresh spring sun.

"Oh. Well, then legally Bea sold it. She made the agreement."

"Blaming a child, Virginia? She's eight years old. You are legally responsible for her actions."

"Mrs. Martin, I'm not blaming anyone. I'm simply saying if that tractor was anyone's, it was Bea's and—"

"It was mine, as is this land."

Ginger continued. "And as she was ready to let

it go and we needed to plant, it was better to trade it. Legally or no, Bea made that decision and I had to support it."

"We're taking the land," Ester said, smiling a little.

Ginger squinted with a small shake of her head.

"Mom is signing papers as we speak."

"Signing papers?" Why would Osbee do that?

"Yes."

As she took a step forward, Ester crossed her arms in front of her and set her feet, in their shiny spectator shoes, apart. She was placed solidly across the backdoor stairs. Samuel's presence moved in behind Ginger.

"Is Osbee signing papers?" she asked, gazing down at the ground.

"I told you she was," Ester said. "Why would I lie?"

"She hasn't yet, but she is afraid," Samuel replied.

"About what?" Ginger asked.

"About anything," Ester said. "Do you really think I'd lie? You owe us money, Virginia, and quite a pretty penny at that. Henry's Child is worth more than what it was traded for."

"They are suggesting that in her age she has lost her wits and is being taken advantage of by you," Samuel explained. "That they will sue you for the cost of Henry's Child and anything else they can come up with, putting the money left to you by your husband for the children at risk. Osbee cannot have you take that risk."

"Lost her wits?" Ginger blurted out.

"I beg your pardon?" Ester quipped.

Ginger looked up and found a deepening frown on her mother-in-law's face. Her in-laws were suggesting Osbee had lost her wits? How would they prove the old woman was crazy? Perhaps Osbee had been talking to Samuel in front of the Martins. That would indeed look crazy.

"Has Osbee talked to you while this was going on?" Ginger asked of Samuel.

"Of course," Ester replied, her hands now on her hips.

"No," Samuel said. "That surely would have given them reason. But I felt obliged to stay with her while you were away. I have been most occupied since you left, going between the house and Bea."

Ginger chuckled and gazed up to the sunny Virginia sky.

"I cannot see that there is anything funny about any of this," Ester said.

"Well, Mrs. Martin, I can." Smiling happily through her pounding skull, Ginger was in motion, veering right, heading back down the gravel drive and around front. "You go take care of Bea. I've got this," Ginger said to Samuel.

"Virginia!" Ester trotted down the stairs, her

shiny spectator shoes sounding like tiny hooves as she did so.

"I'd go back through the house if I were you, Ester," Ginger called over her shoulder.

"I think I should like to see this," Samuel said.

"Well, go check on Bea and come back," she replied. As Ginger rounded the front of the house, Samuel disappeared. She made her way to the front porch steps, and before she could land a foot upon them Osbee burst out the door, her face stricken as Hugh held her back by the arm.

"Hugh, let go of her," Ginger said, her face, she was sure, now reflecting the drumming pain in her head.

"Gi-Ginger, daughter. I thi—"

"You sign those papers?"

Osbee shook her head, her eyes round and watery.

"We'll sue," Ester said as she rounded the corner of the house.

"Let go of her, Hugh," Ginger repeated.

"We have legal grounds," Mr. Glenmore said, stepping from behind Hugh.

"You've got nothing." Ginger guffawed. "You're trying to scare Osbee with the threat of having her declared incompetent and I am telling you, as a nurse, she's not. Now let her go."

Hugh and Mr. Glenmore stared with slack jaws at Ginger.

"We have not said anything of the sort," Hugh objected.

"Have her tested. It won't show a damn thing."

"Anyone in their late eighties shows something," Mr. Glenmore offered. "Not that we're going to do anything."

Ginger's eyes popped open. "Not that you're doing anything," she repeated. "Threatening like this can be considered blackmail, you know. That's illegal, too. Go ahead. Call any doctor or psychiatrist or whoever. For any one you call, I know ten who'll come and honestly check her out and will find that there is nothing incompetent about her. And if I wasn't certain she had her wits, I'd be afraid. But I'm not afraid and neither should you be, Osbee. Now, Hugh, you let her go or I'm going to call the police right now. You're not from around here but we are and the police won't take kindly to you laying a hand on Osbee."

Reluctantly, Hugh released Osbee, who shakily walked toward Ginger. When she reached the stairs, she missed the first step and Ginger lunged forward to catch her.

"We need that root of yours, Osbee," Ginger whispered in her ear, pulling the old woman into her arms. "It can shake but don't you let them pull you up."

Together they descended the last couple of stairs, and once Osbee had her footing on the firm ground, Ginger let go.

"Hugh!" Ester screamed.

Ginger jumped at the desperate sound of the voice and looked over to the edge of the porch. Her mother-in-law launched into a sprint, her shiny spectator shoes gleaming in the late-morning sun with Bubba right behind her.

"Oh, my God!" Osbee exclaimed and Ginger, without another thought, leapt toward the Mercedes.

"Bubba!" she yelled. "Stop!"

As she cleared the corner of the house, she found Henry, Bea, and Oliver racing toward her.

"Ester!" Hugh cried from behind.

"Get the broom!" Ginger shouted to Henry.

"Open the car!" Ester shrieked, coming around the back of the Mercedes at a run. Ginger could make out only the tips of Bubba's horns on the other side of the vehicle as he chased her, his speed increasing as he passed the trunk. The goat must have seen her father-in-law, for Bubba stopped short and changed direction, now racing toward Hugh.

The man skidded to a halt and turned on his heel, his red tie flying around on his white shirt like a ribbon on a May pole as he took off toward the orchard.

"Bubba!" Ginger yelled. "You little shit! Stop!" She ran after Hugh and the goat, her feet pounding the dirt in time with the pounding in her head. She cleared the little ravine between her yard and her orchard.

"Stop running and face him, Hugh!" Ginger shouted.

Hugh was nearly to the trees.

"Turn around and stop!"

Hugh turned around but didn't stop. He backed right into the chicken paddock, losing his balance as he hit it. The thin fence crumpled under the man's weight and he went down hard on the ground. Bubba cleared the fence with a little jump, coming up short, then hovered over Ginger's father-in-law. Highly agitated by the ruckus, Rooster puffed up his feathers and veered left, flanking the goat and Hugh to attack from the side.

"Rooster!" Ginger screamed, as if that were going to do any good at all. Out of the corner of her left eye, she saw a flash of a small body. Oliver raced by her with his stick. He hurled himself over the fence and the flock of chickens, squawking in terror, flapped madly through the broken gate, and headed toward the cemetery. Rooster fixed one beady eye on the stick and skidded to the right. Oliver adjusted his trajectory to match, and the turkey, with a screeching gobble, raced after the chickens.

When Ginger landed from her own leap over the fence, she grabbed Bubba by the right horn and tossed him toward the chicken coop.

"Hugh!" she said. "Hugh, are you all right?"

The man rolled over in the chicken dirt and with help from Ginger and Oliver got to his feet. Henry arrived with the broom just in time to whack Bubba's horns with it as the goat turned for a counterattack.

"Whatever, Bubba," Henry said.

"You okay?" Ginger asked, brushing Hugh's dirty white shirt. "You went down pretty hard. Let me look at your arm."

He brushed her away.

"No need," he said, holding his left arm with his right hand. Stumbling a bit as he walked over the broken fence, Hugh, with all the dignity he could muster, made his way back to the car, gazing reticently now and then over his shoulder. Ginger followed him.

"I think I should look at the arm," she repeated.

"I'm sure it's fine," he said.

"I'm not."

When they came to the ravine, Ginger trotted forward and moved to support his weight by wrapping her arm around his waist.

"I do not need your help, Virginia."

He began to limp toward the car. Ester and Mr. Glenmore were already safely inside. He opened the driver's-side door and moaned as he climbed in. Ester rolled down her window when the car started.

"You'll be hearing from our lawyer," she said,

her gray eyes icy spots below her disheveled frosted hair.

"He's in the back there." Osbee nodded toward the backseat. "What's he going to say?"

"Remember, Mother, this was your choice," Ester said, and the car rolled down the drive. Osbee, Samuel, Henry, Oliver, Bea, and Ginger stood in the front yard and watched the Mercedes back up. It turned around when it reached the bottom of the drive.

"What did she mean by that?" Samuel asked. "It is she who was coercing her own mother."

"She means to scare us," Ginger replied, watching the Martins head down the lane. "To make us afraid of what she's going to do."

"What's she going to do?" mumbled Bea.

"I don't know," Osbee answered. "But whatever it is, it won't be good."

"I think . . ." Oliver said carefully, holding his stick between his hands like a maestro who has just finished conducting a masterpiece and is listening to the applause. "I think . . . Grandma and Grandpa are just goats."

There was a moment of utter silence and then everyone burst out laughing. Oliver gazed around, confused by the reaction.

Ginger bent down and kissed him on his head. "I think, Oliver, you are exactly right," she said.

"We're hungry," Henry announced. "Come on, Oliver."

"We went to Cedar Creek today," Oliver said to his older brother as they headed around the side of the house.

"You did?" Bea asked, following them.

"Yep. We walked around for a couple minutes in a field but then Mama got hurt."

Osbee took Ginger's elbow, inquiring, "Hurt?"

"I have a headache," she replied with a shrug. Together, they climbed the steps. She opened the door for the old woman, and before she followed Osbee in, she paused. At the end of the porch Samuel stood. Without looking at him directly, she whispered, "I saw you today."

"I know," he replied. "I see you today."

The body parts, the Union rider, the spark and smoke of his gun were now part of her memory. She stepped into the house, closing the door behind her.

Ginger found Osbee in the kitchen making egg salad sandwiches. She took two aspirin and they made lunch in silence. They both started when the phone rang.

"I hope that's not Ester," Osbee breathed.

Ginger picked up the phone before it could finish its second ring. "Hello?"

"Hello? Virginia? It's Deanna."

Who is it? Osbee mouthed.

The nurse registry, Ginger replied in kind.

"Virginia?"

"Sorry. Yes, Deanna. It's me."

"Franklin is asking for you tonight."

"Uh, Deanna. I was needing to talk with you. I need to remove my name from the registry."

"Really? Is everything all right?" Deanna's voice held the same concern as had Mrs. Castro's and Mr. Taylor's at the school.

"Yes, yes. We just need to plant now and all hands are required."

"Plant?" Deanna repeated.

"Yeah. I live on a farm."

"Ah, that's right. Well, do you think you could give us one more night?"

"I do—"

"They specifically requested you because there's a Mr. Wolfe in acute who is asking for you."

Ginger pulled air between her teeth and thought for a minute. This man had given her Ginger-cow, in the bartering of which he had said something was moving. Whatever it was that Samuel had so keenly sensed moving for 150 years was felt also by Jack, and when last she saw the man he was quite ill. In a very deep way, Ginger felt she owed him, because he was connected to her—and to what was moving. All she had to give in return were the tasks she'd been educated to perform.

"What's the shift?"

Osbee looked over at her. A small crease passed quickly across the old woman's brow.

"Same as the last one."

"I'll be there."

"Thanks, Virginia. And then I'll take you off the roll. Let us know, though, if you want to pick up some shifts now and then."

"Will do. Thanks, Deanna." She hung up.

Osbee didn't look at her; rather the old woman continued to cut celery sticks.

"Jack Wolfe, the man who gave us the cow, is in the hospital and is asking for me. I have to go."

Osbee nodded.

"This is my last time."

Osbee looked over at her and said, "You know what is best, daughter."

She placed the celery sticks in a glass of ice water and headed to the sunroom door to call everyone in for lunch.

As they ate, Henry quietly delegated the work that had to be done. The tasks given to Ginger were cleaning the lunch dishes and planting the garden. Thus she found herself wandering out to the barn, picking up a hoe and a rake, and exiting through Christian's stall. The cow was nowhere to be seen in the barn. She wasn't worried, though, as she was quite sure Henry knew where everyone and everything was. He was so like his father—an organizer, a planner, a leader.

The tidy planting boxes were lined up next to the snake-rail fence that encircled the first garden patch. They were wooden rectangles five feet long and three feet wide and in each of them the students from VMI had dumped beautiful black dirt, not Virginia clay. With her headache numbed by the aspirin, she began to rake. For a good while she worked, breaking up the soil and smoothing it out. After that, she hoed small furrows in the dirt. The work with hoe and rake and dirt and sun rolled the war to the back of her mind.

When the soil was set, she planted the seeds that Ed Rogers had left. There were tomatoes and lettuce and peppers, as well as broccoli, cabbage, and cauliflower. According to Mr. Rogers, they were a little late to plant for transplants, but this would have to do. Once complete, Ginger watered everything. The sun reflected gold as she closed the glass lids of the planter boxes.

Alone and unoccupied, she wandered back to Cedar Creek in her mind. It was Samuel there but it was Jesse's eyes and the vision changed as if she were seeing her husband shot in a war so far away. She held her throbbing head, walking out behind the barn, past all the farm implements, which sat in their new home without purpose at the moment. She felt their pain.

Gazing toward the covered bridge, she spotted Ginger-cow and the goat far afield and, with them, Rooster and the chickens. She walked toward them and as she cleared the back of the barn she found Oliver, Osbee, and Henry fixing the chicken paddock. In need of an occupation to silence the battle in her mind, she headed out to round up the chickens and Rooster.

It was slow going for sure. It took the better part of the day to get them across the field and into the orchard. Oliver came to help with Rooster, holding his stick like a baton and motioning Rooster in the right direction. After all the fowl were back safely in their pen, Henry and Ginger went to fetch Bubba and Ginger-cow.

The cow came easily. The goat . . . Well, Ginger decided he needed a tether with a chain to keep his whereabouts known and to prevent him from causing further mischief with visitors. When they came into the barn, it was four in the afternoon and, according to Henry, time for milking. Planting a stool next to Ginger-cow for his mother, Henry began to teach her how to milk. She wasn't very good at it and after about fifteen minutes his patience ran out. Nudging his mother from the stool, he took over and Ginger headed to the house.

Osbee was in the kitchen lighting lamps. They started supper, saying very little to each other as was their usual, comfortable way when working. Chicken and biscuits with mixed vegetables was the bill of fare and shortly after six all the children trudged in—filthy, smelly, and tired. Henry handed a bucket of milk to his mother and, following Samuel, he and his siblings went up for a bath. The look of confusion on Ginger's face regarding the bucket of milk and its disposition caused Osbee to remove it from her hands, with a low mumbled direction to set the dining room table for dinner.

Gathering the plates and utensils, Ginger headed into the dining room. How long had it been since they had eaten together there instead of the kitchen? Was it Thanksgiving? Christmas? No— she had worked Christmas Eve. It was Thanksgiving. She set the table for six, as was always the way—for they left a plate still for Jesse—and wondered why exactly they were eating in the dining room. When Bea and her brothers came down, the look on their faces showed they were just as perplexed.

Shortly Osbee entered with a pitcher of milk and one of water.

"Ginger, my dear, we need one more service."

They did? Counting six place settings, Ginger shook her head and was about to say the number was correct when Osbee added, "And if you'll take a seat at the head of the table, please."

"That's Daddy's spot," Oliver said.

Osbee nodded and repeated, "Ginger, please."

After pulling the extra plate, fork, knife, and spoon from the cupboard, Ginger slid her own plate down the table and placed the extra one next to it. She moved a side chair into place and then reluctantly she sat down, the view from Jesse's chair awkward and uncomfortable.

"Now I will sit in Ginger's spot to the right and leave the new chair empty. Oliver, you will sit in Bea's spot on your mother's left. Henry, you sit in Oliver's spot next to me, just to mix it up, and, Bea, you'll sit in Henry's spot, next to Oliver. And, Samuel, will you please sit at dinner with us? You will sit at the end."

Startled, Samuel stood at attention, looking from one chair to another, his eyes wider than Ginger had ever seen them. Then he looked down at his disheveled, dirty clothes and shuffled uncomfortably from one tattered shoe to the other. Ginger smiled, leaning forward, placing her elbows on the table and resting her cheek on her right hand. He was so Southern. Could he sit at the table in his state of appearance?

Henry and Bea giggled at his awkwardness and quickly sat down in their new seats.

"Oliver," Bea whispered and brushed her hand at him as if it would put him in his seat. He seemed confused, so Bea patted the chair next to her. With a shrug, Oliver sat down in his new spot on his mother's left.

"Please sit, Samuel," Osbee said as she went back into the kitchen.

He met Ginger's eyes and was gone. All at the table let out a soft moan of disappointment.

"Wh-where'd he go?" Oliver asked.

"Maybe he's changing," Osbee said, returning

with glasses and placing one at every plate, including Samuel's.

"Can he change?" Henry wondered.

"I don't know," the old woman replied and stepped back into the kitchen.

As she came in with the chicken and biscuits, Samuel reappeared. He was now wearing his jacket, buttoned up neatly. The rest of his appearance was the same.

With both hands, he brushed the front of his coat to smooth it and then he sat down slowly as if the chair was going to up and run away from under him.

"You look fine, Samuel," Osbee said reassuringly as she sat down next to Ginger.

He gave a nod as he looked around the table, adjusting himself in his seat. She watched his eyes move from person to person and when he finally rested his gaze upon her she peered back into the shadow of his soft brown irises. They had been so clear this day at Cedar Creek and though they were but shadows holding her within them, she felt she could still see Jesse there. She smiled a small smile and, in return, a matching smile appeared on his lips.

"Your elbows are on the table, Virginia Moon," he said quietly. She popped up in her seat and quickly she put her hands in her lap.

"Their good manners are from their father?" Samuel inquired.

Henry, Bea, and Oliver snickered.

"I did say that," Ginger noted.

"We'll give thanks tonight," Osbee said, folding her hands before her and bowing her head. Everyone followed. "Thank you for the food and for each other," Osbee began. "Thank you for the love and peace we have in this house. And thank you . . . thank you for Samuel, who stood with me today when I thought I was alone, standing with me like family. We are grateful he finds a place at our table. Amen."

"Amen," was the response.

"Samuel?" Bea lifted her glass and handed it toward her mother for milk.

"Yes, Bea?"

"Why are your buttons all different?"

He thought a minute and laughed softly. "That, Bea, is a story. It starts when I was heading to war."

"Please pass your glass, Henry," Ginger said.

December 14, 1862
Fredericksburg

My love, Juliette,
We sit in ranks upon Prospect Hill, the dawn seen through thick fog as a drop of blood falling into water—a diffuse pink glow on the horizon. It will rise into the heavens as it did yesterday, taking with it the mist and leaving a harrowing view of what the day will bring on the field below. If this battle follows the many others before, the Union defeat will now proceed with a careful withdrawal. Cowardly is my only word for it. Why fight and withdraw? We are armies; our purpose is to fight, but with each withdrawal, we simply prolong this war, with mounting dead and the people, over whose fields we battle, reduced to eating what we leave behind under our feet. I'm afraid there will be no one left to celebrate or mourn the conclusion of this war on either side. It worries me deeply. So we wait as messengers ride up and down these hills and order us to hold position.

The battle yesterday was horrendous. Here on Prospect Hill, the Union broke through our line after achieving the top, but we countered and drove them back. By the end, we figure the losses nearly equal on both sides—4,000 to 5,000 each. I moved with the bird's call, causing my own Lieutenant, Fletcher Hallings, to be hit in the arm. He rests next to me even now, the deep wound in his upper arm bandaged tightly. How he is going to fire his musket with the rising dawn is a quandary, but he will not leave my side.

The fight on the hill next to us, Marye's Heights, was a one-sided victory. Seven assaults were pushed back with 9,000 Union soldiers dying afield as the sun set. We sat in the darkness, death sounding around us as if the earth itself hurt from holding the weight of such agony and let forth the deep, soulful moan of a mother's loss all night. In answer, the sky came to life, a gentle stream of spectral color flowed across heaven. Never have I seen such and those around me whispered in wonder that it was God celebrating our victory.

But they do not see with their Child's Eye. I do. The earth keened for her lost children as heaven above opened, showing us the fires and candles of Kronos's Hall reflected in his raised glass as he greeted the victorious dead into Elysium. I have been convinced I alone see with my Child's Eye and so did not share my view, as surely a war of words would break out in the dying night between my men and me.

Hope came, though, in the likes of a messenger

from Marye's Heights. It seems a man, a solitary South Carolinian, sat behind the stone wall at the base of the Heights. He was as close as any who were there from 9,000 dying men crying for help, for water, for death, separated by nothing more than a pile of stone. My love, this singular man crested the wall as the Northern Lights streamed above, risking his own life to bring water to the dying—to answer the call for help.

As the messenger relayed the story, many men cursed him for helping the enemy. I held my tongue, for I now know another in this war sees with their Child's Eye and there is no explaining such to those who do not. I gazed over to Fletcher and found his face bright and full of hope at the news from Marye's Heights. He met my eye and darkened quickly, but I winked and smiled. In response, he smiled, chuckling a little even as he was in pain from his wound. With Fletcher, we count three who see with the Child's Eye.

There is no evidence this war shall ever end yet I have found hope, for I know now of others who seek to right all of this wrong. I know one who will, against orders, act to make right. My journey has become less lonely, for I have found comfort and companionship in others here. I have found a moment of joy as I travel to you.

Your devoted,
Samuel

CHAPTER 23

JAR OF CLAY

The moon was out. Its cool glow lifts the world from the deep, sorrowful shadows of the new moon. Dark and despairing in its separation from the warm light of its mother, the sun, the new moon drifts in darkness, gravity causing it to endlessly fall toward earth as if seeking comfort in the blinding black void in which it moves. Earth forever pushes the moon back the way an elder sibling pushes away a pestering younger one when the mother is gone. But the moon by its nature can only be selfless and small and as its mother, the sun, touches it once more, it exhales softly in gray and white over the earth, eternally sharing with its elder sibling the joy felt in their mother's glow.

Lying on her side, Ginger found the world beyond her window bright against the darkness of her room. The window should have been shielded from her eyes by the shoulder of her husband, but he was not there. Instead, her view was inside her mind, held back then with Samuel on an autumn field in the violet hour of Virginia with tumultuous war raging around them. She couldn't shake the vision and her head throbbed as it rested upon her pillow. Weary though she was, no sleep had come nor would it. The alarm on her cell phone was going to sound shortly and she was going to get up for work. She couldn't wait. Work would close her mind's eye.

She reached across the bed to the empty space where Jesse had once lain. It was cold and smooth, untouched for so long. Brushing it as if it were his back, she felt Samuel enter. Without a warning, she began to sob quietly, uncontrollably until the soft gray-white light beyond the window was but a blur.

"I see you," he said.

"I saw you die," she whispered, her chest heaving the emptiness beneath her hand.

"No," he replied adamantly as he sat behind her on the bed. "No, you did not, Virginia. You did not."

"The gun fired behind you."

"It did not hit me."

"I was there." She gasped.

"You were there, Virginia Moon, but you were not then. As I am here but am not now. I did not die upon the field of Cedar Creek."

She inhaled as if to catch her breath from a long run.

"I moved to hold you, thinking you had come from beyond to fetch me and I was ready to die. So close you were to me. And the bloody bullet missed." He chuckled dryly, a small hint of anger rising in his voice. "It hit another."

"Another?" she whispered.

"Yes. I was yet living after Cedar Creek."

Ginger reflected upon the eyes staring at her in the violet hour so long ago—one hundred and fifty years ago. A bullet fired but Jesse had not died. Samuel yet lived.

"I saw my husband there," she said.

"Where?"

"In the violet hour of Cedar Creek."

A hush fell over Samuel. Ginger felt it as palpable—as if Samuel were physical.

"He was in your eyes," she added. "He died."

The hush grew in weight, pushing against Ginger's body, putting pressure on her chest. She inhaled against it.

"Tell me, Virginia Moon. How did your husband die?"

Ginger exhaled, inhaling just at its end, for she knew to exhale completely would crush her beneath the ethereal weight in the room. Back then—back then—doors of the car in the drive shut with finality. Gazing out the window, two men had walked up to the porch and she quickly stepped outside, refusing them the courtesy of a knock.

"He fought across someone else's land far away."

"Where?"

"It doesn't matter really, does it? He always said once war starts, it's always wrong because there are always innocents everywhere in the cross fire. Any soldier that has been in the fight knows this. It's why so many of them have trouble when they return. But if a war is started by another, someone must fight. Jesse felt that to serve one's country was the highest duty—to protect family and country. Most people who become soldiers feel the same. Sometimes the president, the commander-in-chief, asks soldiers to do things they do not agree with. But they are people of duty and follow the command without question. They have taken an oath to do so. It is what they are trained to do. In times like these, Jesse said one cannot fight against the wrongness of war. One can only resist it by doing one's duty—by finding the right where it can be found among all the wrongness." She softly guffawed. "That convolution never really made sense to me until two men walked up to the porch here a year and a half ago."

"How did Jesse Day Martin die, Virginia?" Samuel whispered.

"He and his men were fighting in an area of small streets and two-story buildings. The battle was hot and they were in a tight place and so were ordered back. As they made their way under fire, they came to an intersection. To the left was a man crouched flush with a wall, holding two little boys and a little girl. His neck was bleeding.

"Jesse motioned his men on and he himself disobeyed orders, turning down the street to help the man. His soldiers were . . . well, his men, and three of them disobeyed his orders and followed."

Smiling at the night, she added, "He always said you get what you teach, don't you? Anyway, two of them cleared the corner before snipers began to fire overhead. The third held the corner, offering cover fire. One of his men was shot in the head before he got twenty feet. The other reached Jesse, who handed him the girl and a boy. Jesse grabbed the other boy and tried to lift the man. He pushed him away, motioning down the street. Thirty yards on the other side was a door that was cracked open and a woman desperately waved them to come. So my husband and his soldier ran down the open street toward the door and just as they let go of the kids, a bomb exploded."

Ginger watched heads and arms and body parts fly in the violet light of Cedar Creek. Her breath grew heavy, full of hurt.

"Did the children live?"

"I don't know. The soldier covering them ran into the street and was shot. The rest of his troop returned and came on. None would ever agree to leave anyone behind. Jesse was unconscious when they got to him and he died on the way out."

"I am sorry, Virginia Moon."

"I'd be mad, you know. Really pissed off at him for not looking after his own, but I know what he saw." She rolled over and looked up into the shadows of Samuel's eyes. "He saw himself—just a man trying to get his babies home. There but for the grace of God go I, so to speak. We all judge a situation that someone is in with how we think we'd react. Truth to say, very few of us are willing to lay down our lives for another, no matter how we think we would. A soldier, though? That is exactly what they choose to do when they sign up. They leave their spouses and children and try to stay alive though their lives aren't theirs to keep or throw away any longer. Their lives belong to their service. So Jesse saw a father with children struggling on a street beneath a rain of bullets. There was no other choice really but to help because it is wrong for children to be subjected to gunfire. That is the wrongness of war. Jesse had to make a decision to make this right somehow because he cared—cared for the man and his children as he cared for his own. Bullets don't care. People do."

"He is a great man, Virginia."

"No. No, he was not. He was a just man, Samuel. Every man isn't great. Every soldier isn't a hero. But sometimes in your life, you're faced with a choice and it makes you. That choice made him. Jesse was a good, honorable man. But he was a great father."

The hush in the room lifted a little as Samuel reached out his hand and brushed a tear from her cheek. His touch was not upon her skin, but she did feel it.

"I can feel you, Samuel." Her voice was shaky as she reached for his hand in disbelief. "Your touch."

"And I feel you, Virginia Moon. Your loss."

"Y-you called my name, there on Cedar Creek. You knew it then."

Samuel shook his head. "No. I saw upon a summer's night, as I wrote to my love, a ginger moon. Autumn's moon rising in July as I held a picture of you standing next to me in my hand."

"I was there," Ginger replied. "In Woodstock. What happened to our picture?"

Samuel nodded and said, "I sent it away, not sure of what—who you were. Not sure what you meant. You were there but not then. And the moon and our photograph left me out of place. Ginger moon was simply a name I gave for that feeling—being out of place."

"But I *am* Ginger Moon."

"I know that now." Samuel chuckled.

"I've been without a root, Samuel. Out of place. I'm not so out of place now."

"No?" Samuel dropped his hand and gazed out the window.

"And neither are you."

"But I am. Perpetually between my beginning and my end."

"Samuel," she said, "I've been empty since Jesse died. I have lived in the acoustic shadow for over a year."

He looked back at her and, though his eyes were shadow, she knew he wept.

"Now I'm with you, Samuel. And I will be right here until you find your end—until you can go home."

"Home to my love, Juliette Marie. She was beautiful beyond words. Kind and sweet."

"And you love her still."

"Beyond words. But she was then. And I am now."

"You'll find your way back to her, Samuel. I know it. I believe you're halfway home."

"Am I, Virginia Moon?"

"Yes. I'm sure of it."

The alarm on her phone sounded quietly and Ginger reached over to the bed stand to turn it off.

"I do hope so," Samuel said, standing. Without another word, he exited through the bedroom door.

"But when you go," Ginger whispered, "I think I will hurt."

"So will I," his voice softly replied.

Ginger climbed out of bed and slid into her slippers as she opened the door.

"I know how to make coffee, Samuel. Just not without electricity, which, I may add, we are now not using out of deference to you."

He laughed softly somewhere unseen as she passed Bea's door.

"Because you are here, but are not now," she added, stopping at the top of the stairs and gazing out to the road washed in moonlight, glistening like a river.

"I am here, not now," he agreed.

"As I was there, but not then." She didn't really understand that. It was like Jesse's rightness in the wrongness of war statement and she thought she'd need to wait until something happened to make it clear. She shivered.

"We are together, Virginia Moon, somewhere without form, like the emptiness within a jar of clay. The jar is missing, but the purpose remains."

Ginger looked through the crack in the door and saw Bea on the bed and the boys bivouacked on the floor.

"They worked hard yesterday," she noted.

There was no answer.

She made her coffee, packed her lunch, and by the time she was dressed and out the door her headache had dissipated into a muted pain. She didn't see Samuel again until she drove down the lane and looked back in her mirror. There he stood, at the end of her driveway, motionless in the moonlight. There he would stay to watch over things until her return.

Before she entered the freeway, she stopped for gas and, while there, entered the little convenience store. She picked up a Three Musketeers bar and with her gift tucked away from the heater she drove down Highway 81, through Harrisonburg, and headed west. The moon drew black lines across the gray asphalt as she climbed through the trees to Franklin. There was no snow, not even a hint in the shallow trenches at the road's edge, and Ginger tried to remember a time when the winter had gone so completely in so short a time. She wondered if it would return, one last blast of snow on its way out.

As she rounded the next bend, her headlights flashed on the sign that read "Oak Flat" and she shook her head remembering Samuel and Jacob and the scent of vomit in her truck. The smell was there still, though just a hint now, a secret that the backseat kept from the front. She laughed a little to herself, recalling how she'd yelled at Samuel to get in the truck. That was less than two weeks ago. There was no way she would have guessed then that she'd be here now, farming with her children. Life just changed for her with the turning of the season.

Her headlights flashed again on something up ahead and Ginger slowed down. She stopped abruptly.

"I cannot believe it." She breathed, her lips pulled tight across her teeth. She put the truck into park without turning it off, opened her door, and stepped out.

"Is that Jacob Esch?" she asked, pointing to . . . well, Jacob Esch. His left arm was flung over another boy's shoulder and together they were stumbling in the ditch next to the road.

"Yea-ha," the other boy replied, clearly intoxicated.

"Who are you?"

"Eli—Eli Beiler."

"You and Jacob have been drinking?"

The boy giggled. "A little."

"Well, Eli-Eli Beiler. Did you know Jacob just had his appendix out and is on pain medication?"

"No, he's not."

"He's not?" Ginger cocked her head.

"Makes him feel funny."

Closing her eyes, Ginger shook her head, hoping that when she opened them somehow the two boys would be gone. She put both her hands on her hips and opened her right eye. Nope—the boys were still there.

"Where are you two going now?" she asked.

"Back to Mr. McLaughlin's farm up there in Oak Flat."

"What's there?"

"Our beds." Eli laughed.

She sighed, saying, "Get in. I'll drive you."

411

"Ah! Thank you, ma'am." As Eli struggled out of the ditch, carrying the deadweight of Jacob Esch in his arms, Ginger opened the back door.

"It's not as cold as it's been," he said as he dumped Jacob into the backseat.

"How much have you guys had?" She twisted her nose at the thick smell of alcohol that rolled off them.

"Not too much." He giggled again as he shut the door.

"Has Jacob thrown up?" Ginger opened the door to the front passenger seat and then walked around the front of her truck.

"Uh, yea-ha. He didn't have hardly anything and he threw up."

She smiled brightly. "There's a blessing." Backing up, she turned the truck around and headed back to Oak Flat.

"May I ask your name, ma'am?"

"I am Mrs. Martin."

"Oh! Jacob talks about you! You farming and never have done before."

"That's right. I've got a few things to say to him, so maybe he'll have more to talk about with you than farming."

Eli hiccupped and pointed left at the Oak Flat sign. She turned, driving about a mile down the road and then veering off to the right down a steep gravel lane that wound through dense forest.

About one half of a mile in, the trees opened up to a white house with a red barn.

"Can you turn your lights off, please?" Eli asked in a whisper.

Ginger looked over at him, finding the boy crouched forward as if sneaking by some sleeping predator. She half smiled, imagining Farmer McLaughlin would be about as happy as she if awakened by two drunk Amish boys.

"We have the little shed to the right," he continued, motioning to the side of the barn. Flipping her lights off, Ginger crawled across the drive in the moonlight and put the truck in park. Ever so quietly, Eli opened his door and hopped out.

"I'll open our house," he said as Ginger climbed out of the driver's seat. She came around the bed of the truck and opened the back door. Pulling Jacob by the arms, she raised him until he was seated, at which point Eli returned and together they carried the boy into the shed.

It was less of a shed and more of a bedroom, with bunk beds, a little bathroom on the left, and a space heater glowing warmly. It was carpeted and clean and it seemed that Farmer McLaughlin had taken care to provide a home for these two boys.

"Nice place," Ginger noted as they dropped Jacob on the lower bunk.

"Yea-ha," Eli said and with a small gag stumbled into the bathroom and shut the door.

"At least it wasn't in the car." She looked around the room for a paper and something to write with and, finding none, stepped out of the shed and back to the truck. She flipped on the inside light and rummaged through the cab and her handbag, finding only an old eyeliner pencil.

"Why is it when you need to write something, there's nothing to write on?" She gazed up into her rearview mirror and a thought passed across her mind. She giggled wholeheartedly as she turned off the light. Back in the shed, she heard Eli still vomiting in the bathroom.

Lowering herself onto the bed next to Jacob, she pulled the cap off her eyeliner.

"Tell me, Jacob, my dear. After a night like this, do you walk into the bathroom and face yourself in the mirror?"

She chuckled softly as she wrote, *Call Mrs. Martin,* and then her cell phone number backward across his forehead. Once that was accomplished, she popped the lid on the pencil smartly and stood. She crossed the doorstep and as she shut the door, she said, "Good night, Jacob Esch. Sleep well."

Still snickering from her great idea, she wished she could see Jacob's face in the mirror the next morning. Then she gazed up and stopped short. There was an older African-American man standing by her driver's-side door in the moonlight.

"You are not Miriam Schrock," he stated.

"N-no. I'm Virginia Martin. A nurse at the hospital where Jacob had his appendix out. I— uh, I found the boys walking on the road and gave them a lift home."

"They been drinking again?"

Ginger shuffled from one foot to another. She knew the answer but thought it not her place to say so.

"No need to tell me, Mrs. Martin. I know they have. And I'm sick of it. One day I'm gonna wake up and one of 'em will be dead from it."

"It's a nice home you've made for them here."

He nodded. "And they've been good workers. They're real good boys. I been waiting for them to come to their senses and go back to their parents, but I just can't have this anymore. Worries me sick."

Ginger nodded, supposing she, too, would worry about them.

"Maybe, Mr. McLaughlin, they need to be men now. Maybe to be responsible to somebody besides themselves."

"That's what's been on my mind of late. Wish they'd go home."

"We'll see. Maybe before they go home, they have to grow up."

Mr. McLaughlin shrugged and opened her car door.

"Thank you," she said. The man gave a nod and

backed away as Ginger started the truck. She put it in reverse, gazing back in the mirror. Before she took her foot off the brake, she rolled down the window.

"I don't suppose you have children."

"A boy and a girl," he said. "They're both marines in Afghanistan."

Ginger smiled. Of course they were. "I don't suppose they went to VMI?"

The farmer cocked his head and replied, "Yes. They did. How'd you know?"

"Just a lucky guess. You must be proud of them."

"I am."

She leaned out the window and looked at Mr. McLaughlin steady in the eyes.

"And they have a great father."

The man shrugged and as she backed up he stood still in the moonlight, watching her go.

CHAPTER 24

THE THREE MUSKETEERS

When Ginger arrived at Franklin District Community Hospital, she found the front door wide-open with an ambulance backed in, its red and white flashing lights sending secret semaphore messages to the quarter moon. No one was in the waiting room and there was a great deal of mumbled conversation floating down the hall. As Ginger came around the wall of the triage desk to drop her handbag into the drawer, Nurse Margery entered and picked up the phone.

"Ah! Virginia! It's a full moon for sure. We've got Hamburger in here. Mr. Wolfe has been asking for you. He's in room two."

Hamburger—someone was hit by a train.

"Acute two," Ginger repeated.

"No, no. Room two here." Margery motioned to the ER. "He's PBOO and the only patient in acute. I needed the LVNs and the nurses' aides. We've got an anaphylactic reaction, a severe asthmatic with bronchitis, and the Hamburger just came in. You take Mr. Wolfe. We've got the rest."

PBOO—"Pine Box On Order." Ginger reached down into her purse before shutting the drawer, pulled out the Three Musketeers, and walked it into the waiting room. She set it on the chair nearest the triage desk and, heading back into the ER, passed the Hamburger with Nurse Margery, Dr. Patterson, and one of the LVNs in attendance. She found Janet, the other LVN, in the hall tending to the asthmatic. With Jack Wolfe in room two and the anaphylactic reaction in room three, there was no more room at the inn.

"Janet, let me take a look at Mr. Wolfe, and if I can, I'll move him back to acute. It'll free up room two."

Janet nodded and peered into the open door of room three.

Reaching for the handle, Ginger closed her eyes and took a deep breath. Death was a given in ERs, but personal involvement rarely was. The cow had changed that, as had whatever was moving Samuel and Ginger and, well, everybody around them. Ginger warmed a little as she remembered the calf had insurance and, opening the door, she found Joshua Wheldon sitting at Jack's side. When he saw her, he smiled a great, sad smile and stood.

"Ah am so glad you've come," he said softly.

Ginger took his offered hand and then gazed over to Jack. He was gray, his chest heaving in shallow breaths as he struggled to get the oxygen that was fed to him through the tubes at his nose.

"Me, too," Ginger said.

"Virginia Moon?" Jack whispered hoarsely.

"Yes, Mr. Wolfe. I am here."

"How's my cow?"

"Fine. Fine. She's a good milker."

"Said she was. And the goat?" He laughed and then went into a severe coughing fit, his body convulsing with the effort. Calmly, Ginger stepped to his bedside and lifted him up a bit to take the pressure off the back of his ribs.

"Now, Mr. Wolfe. We can't have you laughing anymore. This is very serious."

His eye popped open above the deep circles beneath and he managed a small grin.

"The goat is a menace but I feel that Bubba has learned a certain level of respect for the rest of us."

Jack eyed her quizzically.

"Respect came in the manner of a large wooden broom on his backside."

If Mr. Wolfe could brighten, he did.

"No laughing." She laid him back down in bed slowly.

I want a candy bar, he mouthed.

Mr. Wheldon replied, "Ain't no candy bar for you, Jack. Nurse Margery says it's against orders."

Ginger winked and Mr. Wolfe smiled a little more.

"That's right, Mr. Wheldon. He can't have candy because he's really sick." She looked over her shoulder at the man, meeting his eyes with great seriousness. "However, sometimes sickness is helped by candy bars, wouldn't you say? A little happiness brings health in other ways than physical ones, if you catch my meaning."

His eyes widened. He nodded.

She smiled like sunshine and turned, unlocking the brakes on Mr. Wolfe's bed as she disconnected his oxygen tube from the wall. "Now, I'm gonna wheel Jack back down to his usual room in acute. If you can open the door for me, that would be great. And I think I saw a candy bar in the waiting room, but I can't be certain because Mr. Wolfe isn't allowed to have them."

Jack chuckled.

"No more laughter, Mr. Wolfe." Stepping down to the end of the bed, Ginger gave it a great pull, which moved it away from the wall, and set it in motion toward the door. "If you please," she said to Mr. Wheldon.

He opened the door, setting it ajar, and through it Ginger pulled Jack into the hall.

"Room two is free, Janet," she called as she turned the bed and pushed it toward acute care.

"I am glad to see you, Virginia Moon," Jack mumbled. His eyes looked down at her as she pushed him forward from the foot of his bed. The automatic doors between the ER and acute opened as she came to them.

"I'm glad to see you, too."

"I've written a letter to Jacob Esch," he said. "A story of my life."

"Really? Is it a good story?"

"I don't regret any of it."

"I know you don't." Ginger came to a stop and opened the door to acute two.

"But I was thinking he wasn't raised like me. He's dutiful and responsible." Mr. Wolfe smiled again and took a deep breath.

"Don't you laugh until I get you to the oxygen again," Ginger said with a scowl. She pushed him into the room, slowly setting the bed flush with the wall. Reaching for his oxygen tube, she attached it to its spigot and turned it on. Then she checked his IV, making sure it was feeding properly after the move.

"Okay. You can laugh."

He didn't, but looked at her deeply. "Stay with me," he whispered. "Hold my wrist like you did."

"I will," she said and took his wrist gently. She counted—one, two, three. The pulse was there but shallow like his breath and she felt no need to look at her watch. Instead she stared back into Jack's weakening eyes and watched a single tear roll down his temple to the pillow.

"No need to cry. I still feel your pulse."

He gurgled a chuckle. Joshua Wheldon entered and, with him, he brought the weighted presence that was always around near death. Often, Ginger would hear nurses talk to the presence as if it were sentient, chatting to it quietly as they hovered around the dying, and she found them odd for doing so. But now knowing Samuel, she wondered at it.

"You know? I think dinner is in order, Mr. Wolfe. I bet you'd like some watery, salt-free chicken stock with a dry, tasteless cracker. Let me go get that." She turned and, in her sunniest fashion, grinned at Mr. Wheldon. "I'll be right back," she said to him, nodding a little.

Softening the room's light, Ginger stopped at the door and thought. She shrugged. Why not? "Wait till I'm back," she whispered to the heaviness in the room.

Heading to the kitchen, Ginger pulled out a packet of soup stock, poured it into a bowl, filled it with water, and stuck it into the microwave for one minute. Then she grabbed a tray, tossed onto it a napkin, a spoon, and a cracker, and leaned against the counter waiting for the microwave to finish and for whatever was happening with the chocolate bar to happen. With the microwave's beep, she lifted the soup, set it on the tray, stirred it a little with the spoon, and walked back down the hall. Slowly she opened the door, stepping back into the room.

"Mr. Wolfe, are you chewing on something?" she asked with a sideways glance.

He shook his head and swallowed. Placing the tray on the counter near the door, she lifted the napkin and slid past Mr. Wheldon. He shrugged nervously at her with three-quarters of the candy bar yet in his hand.

"What's that on your lips?" she inquired, squinting at the chocolate edges of his mouth.

"Nothin'," he whispered, a chocolate cough following the word.

She wiped his mouth with the napkin and as she did his lips rose a little at the edges. He closed his eyes.

"Rest now," Ginger murmured. "All is well."

Taking his wrist, Ginger counted—one, two, three. The room grew still and quiet. One, two, three. Joshua Wheldon stood for a while behind her and then, slowly, as time passed and Jack's breath grew impossibly labored, he made his way around the end of the bed.

"I need a candy bar," Jack announced clearly through closed eyes. He lifted his left hand, reaching into the air, moving his body back and forth in agitation.

Ginger looked up at Mr. Wheldon, who pulled from his pocket the rest of the Three Musketeers and placed it into Jack's waving hand. His fist closed around the chocolate bar and he quieted, lowering his hand to his stomach.

One, two, three. One, two, three.

"We should sing somethin'," Mr. Wheldon said, his shaky voice breaking the stillness. "Shouldn't we?"

How hard it was for most to stand in the room with death, for always a certain silence came with it, partners arriving together to bring the inevitable gift. It was familiar to Ginger because she was an ER nurse. Yet as she held Jack's wrist, she realized her comfort with it had become more than that. Ginger had lived in this silence for a year and a half—the emptiness of the acoustic shadow. She had learned that even in that emptiness there was purpose, like the space within the jar of clay. Now she heard so clearly, pouring across the acoustic shadow, the sound she had been missing. And that sound came from Joshua. He felt the loss coming and was even now standing between notes. But the next note must be sung for there to be a song. He was yet living even as death came on.

"Please," Ginger whispered, swallowing hard. "Sing."

In a hushed voice, he began singing of Jacob's Ladder, but his words were mumbled in the weighty presence of the room and Ginger couldn't make them out exactly. His tune, however, flowed in time with her count—one, two, three.

As the song ended, Mr. Wolfe's pulse slowed and his breath crackled. Ginger lowered her head to look at her watch and then she snuck a peek at Mr. Wheldon. His eyes flicked between the candy bar in Jack's hand and the foot of the bed and the ceiling above. If he were not a man of duty and a true friend, she felt he'd make a run for it. But he stayed and she, reaching across the bed, took his hand in her free one. Startled from his solitary and undesired visit with death, he met her eyes.

"Sing again," she said, her hand holding his steady.

He squeezed firmly, grateful for the company on this road, and he sang, this time a little louder.

One, two, three. One, two, three.

"Ginger, my love," Jack whispered.

Joshua stopped his song.

One, two.

"Beautiful."

One.

"The gate is open."

There was a release of breath and then—it passed.

"All is well," Ginger repeated.

They stood, the four of them—she, Mr. Wheldon, death, and silence—hands held for a while as pictures floated by: a car wreck, a cow, a candy bar. There were so few memories with this man and surely there would have been many had their acquaintance been conjured earlier. Mr. Wheldon was ready; he let go of Ginger's hand, setting himself free. In doing so, the circle was released and death and silence drifted quietly apart and away from the room, returning once more into the ebbing flow beyond death's door.

The rest of Ginger's shift that night was truly

like a full moon. Three car wrecks, one of which involved a Two Beers, as well as two broken arms, a twisted ankle, and a stroke arrived to join the party with the asthmatic, the anaphylactic reaction, and the Hamburger. The Hamburger miraculously survived long enough to be medevaced to Winchester with the stroke.

At eight thirty-two a.m. the coroner came for Jack Wolfe and at two thirty-two p.m. Ginger walked out of Franklin District Community Hospital into a sunny, rather warm West Virginia afternoon. Huge, puffy clouds floated by, sending shadows drifting across the large, round thermometer on the wall of the hospital, which read sixty-eight degrees.

"Balmy," Ginger mumbled as she dug in her handbag for her keys. She crossed the football field of a parking lot to her truck and as she climbed in she felt the buzzing of her cell phone. She pulled it from her purse and read the number. She didn't recognize it. To answer or not to answer, that was the question? She decided.

"Hello?"

"Mrs. Martin?"

Grinning like the wild, wonderful West Virginia afternoon, she replied, "Why, Jacob Esch. How do you feel?"

"Terrible."

"Good, good," she replied.

"Eli says your truck smells like vomit."

"How kind of him."

"No—I mean, did I throw up?"

"Not last night."

"Before."

"Yes. It still smells like your throw-up."

"I'm sorry. I should clean it up."

"Not to worry."

There was no reply on the line and Ginger sat, staring down at the keys in her hand, thinking how different this quiet was from the silence of death.

"Mrs. Martin. Jack Wolfe died last night."

"Yes, he did."

"He wrote me a letter."

Ginger moved her keys a little, which sent several reflections of light dancing around the cab of her truck.

"Mr. Wheldon dropped it off early this morning," he added.

"Mr. Wolfe thought kindly of you, Jacob. I'm sure he wasn't one to write letters to just any boy he met."

"He said I was a man of duty and responsibility—not like him at all."

Ginger looked out the window of the truck. The evergreens beyond the edge of the parking lot swayed in the spring breeze, pushing the clouds above on their way.

"I'd like to clean your truck, Mrs. Martin."

"Thank you, Jacob."

"And h-help you. With your farm, I mean. I'm from a farm."

"I'd be most grateful."

"Um . . . you leaving work soon?"

"Now."

"Okay. We'll meet you at the road to Oak Flat."

"We?" Ginger tilted her head as if the wind moved her.

"Eli Beiler is coming, too. Is that all right?"

Ginger thought. "Is he a man like you?"

"I think so."

"Fine."

"Okay. Bye."

"Bye."

The line went dead and Ginger started her truck. As she pulled out of the parking lot, she wondered if it was such a good idea to bring Jacob and Eli to Smoot's farm. She had three little kids; if the two of those boys got into trouble as a pair, splitting them up would probably be the best idea for her own family. The more she thought, the more she realized that a couple of days earlier Jacob had been part of her farm plan, but he left. Now, he was asking to return and with him, he was bringing Eli. He was bringing another pair of hands to help. Perhaps this was how it was supposed to happen. "Supposed to"—she was starting to sound more and more like her parents.

She drove down the winding road and when

she came to the last curve beyond which was the intersection to Oak Flat, she slowed down and flipped on her hazards. Rounding the turn, she rolled forward and then stopped abruptly. There were Jacob and Eli and next to them stood a pretty girl in overalls with sandy brown hair pulled back in a red handkerchief. She smiled shyly at Ginger as she lifted her massive backpack to her shoulder. Before she could get it securely situated, Jacob took it from her and handed it to Eli. Giving a nod and a great white smile to Ginger, Eli crossed the road without looking either way and tossed three large backpacks into the bed of her truck. Jacob hobbled over, held steady by the girl, and opened the front passenger-side door.

"Uh, this is Miriam Schrock. Miriam, this is Mrs. Martin."

"Nice to meet you," the girl whispered uncomfortably.

Ginger half smiled at the girl and asked, "You raised on a farm, too?"

"Oh, yes, ma'am. All three of us were. We're from the same church district."

"Ah, well. Hop in."

The relieved smile on Miriam's face required no explanation. She was out in this crazy world with these two guys and there was no way either of them was going to leave her behind. It was time to move on from Mr. McLaughlin's farm and she didn't want to be the one who prevented it.

"The Three Musketeers," Ginger said as Jacob climbed in next to her. Eli and Miriam slid across the backseat.

"The candy bar?" Eli asked, confused.

"The book, if you'd like to read it," Ginger replied.

"Sorry about the smell in your truck, Mrs. Martin."

"We've already had forgiveness on that subject," Ginger replied. "And just look at the help I get because I met you! Small price to pay."

She looked over at Jacob, whose face brightened as if he'd known her his whole life, and then she gazed into the rearview mirror. Two young lives sat in her backseat. Behind them, the road to Franklin District Community Hospital and last night's death rolled away.

"Don't forget to close the gate, Jack," Ginger whispered.

April 14, 1863
Falmouth

My love, Juliette,
We have spent the winter here, just outside of Fredericksburg—we on one side of the Rappahannock, those people on the other. Through cold and snow and rain and mud, we have called to each other, mocked each other, stood silent as droves of us died of sickness and were buried. We've spent Christmas together. I now firmly believe we have more in common with each other than anyone else back home.

The snow is gone, the river flows, and life has returned but we are yet here in camp. Will we be always across the river from each other, waiting for the other to make the first move? It is as if no one wants to start the killing again. Jackson himself went to the river's edge with several ladies. The other side tipped their hats as good manners dictate and the ladies waved back. They could have killed him easily, but now I think they feel as I do. He is family. You do not kill a strange but brilliant uncle, do you?

Lieutenant Fletcher Hallings has healed up

nicely. He took to a lung infection shortly after we retired from Fredericksburg and I had great concern that he was not going to live. Never have I seen a face so pale. Had he gone, I think the weight of the war would be heavy upon me once more. I worry now at losing him. However, after careful thought, I believe he will not die in this war and neither will I. The war will go on perpetually and I will die of old age, my hair thin, my teeth gone, and my coat with its mismatched buttons hanging too large upon my fragile frame. What a sight I will be then when finally I return to you!

The dream of you I have held in my mind changes with each night. It has been one of our wedding, another of our life together, building a home, yet another with our children. As time moves and now a picture of myself as old and in your arms flows across my mind, I realize the dream is ever changing. What is needed to see me through this moment will give way to another to help me through the next. A dream can change and as it does, the one before dies. I mourn the loss of each dream like the passing of an old friend. Sometimes—sometimes I cannot clearly see what shall come next. I sit then, in that moment, silent as if in an acoustic shadow waiting to hear what is next but hollow with loss.

The wheel turns and spring will give way to summer. Perhaps we shall still be here, watching the river flow as the cicadas sing a lullaby. Perhaps we shall be elsewhere, fighting. I am not sure what the year will bring but I am quite certain it will not bring an end to the war. It will continue and I will march the length of Virginia following it.

I must close now. Oddly, we are called to the general's command. Perhaps we move, after all. I do hope so, though I think I now shall miss my brothers across the river—another loss left to mourn.

Your devoted,
Samuel

CHAPTER 25

SHENANDOAH BURNING

By the time her truck reached Harrisonburg, the evergreens had brushed all the white, puffy clouds away, bringing on their tail a huge black sky, which crawled inexorably north as if night itself had forgotten directions and rolled in from the south. There was, however, neither quarter moon nor stars in this night sky. There was rain—rain like a summer rain running the edge of a hurricane, whose eye glared down on Williamsburg and Richmond, but whose sweeping arms flattened and spread west like a scythe.

Ginger didn't like the sky and the Three Musketeers in her truck disliked it even more. Dodging through traffic in Harrisonburg, she rolled onto 81 with a great confluence of cars, whose drivers all obviously had the same notion: to outrun the storm. Whenever any one person has a bright idea, inevitably many, many others have the same; the general outcome usually is a mess of some sort, in this case a traffic jam. Several times she had thought to get off and take the old turnpike, but others would have thought of that also and instead of crawling on the highway she'd be stopped dead on the turnpike, for certainly the turnpike had seized up when the rain came on.

There were no drops of water in this storm. It started as a dusting mist falling on the windshield like a whispered secret of some great event that would shortly ensue. Cars behind her disappeared, taken into some other world beyond a veil of black. Jumping from the cab when traffic stopped momentarily, Eli rescued the three backpacks from the truck bed. He shut his door just in time; the rain hit not in drops but as one great, heavy mass. It smashed into the back of the truck as if someone, trying to carefully lower a great load of dirt, had inadvertently dropped the entirety of it, sending the shocks on the rear wheels bouncing. The pounding on the roof was so horrendous they all crouched lower in their seats lest it blow off and take their heads with it. Inch by inch, the traffic crept north. Not a word was spoken and all attention was drawn forward through wide eyes straining to see the road ahead, praying for the exit sign to Woodstock.

It came and Ginger slid off the highway, her truck rushed down the ramp by a flood of water. As they drove through the town, the traffic signals were out and the shops were dark. She turned left and the truck, finding a familiar road, followed it home. The Mitchell house was dark, as was the Whitakers'. Mr. Schaaf and his tractor were nowhere to be seen. The Creed house was but a vague shape beyond the wall of water, and up ahead the soft yellow-orange windows of Smoot's farm winked through the rain, the only sign of warmth and life in the great blackness. Ginger was glad all over again that they had started using the kerosene lamps.

Pulling up the drive, Ginger stopped when the passenger-side door was just next to the porch. She threw the truck in park and got out. Dragging the backpacks from the cab, Eli and Miriam made their way to the porch. The front door opened as Ginger helped Jacob from the cab and, together, she and the Three Musketeers, drenched by the storm, stepped into the house at five o'clock p.m.

As Ginger stood dripping in the entryway, she found a scent in the house that was very familiar but she wasn't quite able to place it. Osbee had made ginger cookies and coffee and the moist heat from both hung heavily in the glow of the many lamps that were lit throughout the family room. But something else filled the air—a cinnamon-orange fragrance as if Christmas had returned but forgot to bring the snow.

"Jacob!" Bea called as she shut the door and wrapped her arms around his waist.

"Hey, Bea," he greeted, letting go of Ginger to return the hug.

"You're wet," she stated.

"You stayin'?" Oliver asked from the dining room, one ginger cookie held in each hand.

"Who are they?" Bea asked, gazing over to Miriam and Eli.

"The Three Musketeers," Ginger said, grinning. "Come to rescue us from our farming ignorance."

"I'm not ignorant," Osbee called from the kitchen.

Bea looked sideways at her mother.

"Eli and Miriam, this is my daughter, Bea. And that cookie monster over there is Oliver, my youngest."

"You guys going to live with us?" Oliver asked.

"Yes, they are," Ginger replied. She kicked off her boots.

"Where are they sleeping?"

"I'm still working that out."

As Ginger headed through the dining room, she saw her mother and Beau walking behind Henry, who was coming through the back door with a bucket of milk. She started.

"Mom," Ginger said.

Her dad popped out from behind the kitchen wall. "Ginny Moon!" he announced, flinging his arms wide-open. He was tall and thin with round spectacles, thinning hair, and a square jaw. He never changed.

"Dad!" She ran forward and he took her in his arms. Burying her head in his chest, she felt the embrace of home as if she'd never left. She counted his heartbeat—one, two, three. "Dad," she whispered, her eyes welling up at the strength of his wiry arms and his very loud heart. She felt her mother encircle her from the back and she rested now just as she used to when she was little, having crawled between them in bed after a bad dream.

"You have made a great deal of progress since we talked last," her mother said.

Ginger released her father to look at her mother. She was a foot shorter than her dad and her strawberry blond braid swung forward over her right shoulder. Just a few gray hairs had come in at the temples since last they were together and her brown eyes moistened as she held Ginger's face in her hands.

"Why didn't you tell me you were coming?"

"We did," her dad replied.

"I mean coming now. You must have packed immediately after hanging up the phone."

They all three laughed. Wrapping her arms around her daughter's waist, Monica turned to Jacob and his friends. "And who do we have here?" she asked.

"The Three Musketeers," Tim replied, kissing Ginger's head. "Gonna show us how to farm."

"I know how to farm," Osbee said, stepping in from the kitchen.

"Jacob's Amish," Bea explained.

"Really?" Tim replied. "Cool."

"Uh, Mom, Dad, Osbee. This is Jacob Esch, Miriam Schrock, and Eli Beiler. These are my parents, Mr. and Mrs. Barnes."

"Tim and Monica," her dad corrected.

"Call them what you're comfortable with," Ginger said. "And this is Grandma Osbee, or Mrs. Smoot if you want."

"Nice to meet you," Osbee said.

"Nice to meet you," Miriam replied.

"Come in, come in," Tim said, motioning to the kitchen. "We've brought Market Spice tea from Seattle."

"Ah! That's the cinnamon smell," Ginger declared, walking arm in arm with her mother.

"You forgot what it was?" Tim asked, incredulous.

Ginger laughed and as she stepped into the kitchen she froze. Samuel was there, leaning next to the stove, his arms folded before his chest.

"Welcome home, Virginia Moon," he greeted.

Everyone was in the kitchen now. Ginger did not reply. Instead she looked at Osbee, who was peering behind Ginger's father to the Three Musketeers. Henry washed his hands in the sink next to Samuel and looked over his shoulder at his mother, a smile growing across his face. She opened her eyes wider at him to ask the question without asking the question. He shrugged a little. Oliver giggled.

Slowly, Ginger turned her head to the left and

up, gazing into her father's eyes. He was smiling so big, Ginger raised her hand to her mouth to stop the laugh. That answered that question.

"I don't see," her mother whispered in her ear, the sheer disappointment silencing the joy she felt for her father.

"Oh, Mom, I'm sorry," Ginger replied.

"Me, too."

There was now no movement, no sound—just an awkward silence.

"Miriam," Ginger finally said, turning to the girl. "Would you like to get out of your wet things?"

"Yes, ma'am."

"Eli?"

"Sure," he replied in his easy way.

Ginger stepped forward and when she gazed over to Jacob, he met her eyes with a deep crease growing between his eyebrows.

"Henry, Bea? Can you please take them upstairs to change?"

Henry wiped his hands on a towel and motioned to Eli.

"You raised Amish, too?" Bea asked, taking Miriam's hand.

"I was," the girl replied, following Bea into the dining room.

"You learn to plow?"

"I did."

The conversation continued and when it was but a murmur from upstairs, Ginger said, "I see why you left last time you were here, Jacob."

"I—I think Miriam, Eli, and I can't stay," he replied, quietly. "I thought maybe—maybe it was just my medicine that made me see him last time."

"You're supposed to stay," Ginger said.

"Monica! Is this our daughter?"

"Please, Dad."

Jacob glanced over to Ginger's father, asking, "You see him?"

"We all see him," Oliver replied.

"I don't," Monica added.

"I found you in the ditch, inebriated," Samuel said to Jacob.

"Y-you did?"

"Yes. I stopped Virginia on the road so she would find you."

Jacob hobbled over to the kitchen table and lowered himself slowly into a chair as he turned his gaze to Ginger. "He shouldn't be here," the boy said.

"He can't get home, for one reason or another," Osbee explained.

"Why can't you go home?" Jacob asked Samuel.

"I don't know."

"He doesn't see the light," Tim offered.

Ginger's eyes popped open as she flicked them in Samuel's direction. He glowered.

"He's come to help us make the farm home," Osbee said. "Just like you, Jacob. And now your friends are here with you. You can tell them about Samuel or not. Choice is yours, but we have a place here for Samuel in our home and at our table, just as we have a place for all of you. Who knows who else will show up and for what reason. All we know is we are all here now and we have a place and a home and a lot of work, so our home will be here for us. Do you have a home right now?"

Jacob gazed around the kitchen, looking at everyone but Samuel.

"I know where it is. I'm just not sure how to get to it anymore," he replied.

"I am the same," Samuel said.

They looked at each other, each taking measure.

"I think it best, if possible, not to tell Eli and Miriam. It's not—with us," Jacob requested.

"As you think best," Ginger said. "Now, if y'all don't mind, I need a shower and we need to get dinner going and sleeping arrangements made."

As Monica and Osbee made dinner, Eli, Tim, and Ginger made their way out to the summer kitchen through the fury of rain to light the stove for heat and make the bed. Oliver, seeing the transformation of the attic over the summer kitchen change from a storage space into a bedroom, wanted desperately to sleep with the big boys and began a perpetual request of Jacob and Eli that lasted from the striking of the first match that lit the stove, through dinner, and past the dishes.

Eli acquiesced and, without being asked, he made the offer to Henry, too. Thus, as all four boys and Bea headed out to care for the horses and mules, Ginger and her parents pulled two cots and two sleeping bags down from the attic of the house. Henry and Oliver were tucked into the double bed and Eli and Jacob made their way to the cots. Monica and Tim took the twin beds in the boys' room, while Miriam and Bea slept in Bea's queen bed. At ten p.m., Ginger climbed the stairs with her lantern, entered her room, and shut the door. Beau, who had followed her, collapsed on the floor.

"That's exactly how I feel," she said as she placed the lantern on her desk and sat down. The rain hitting her window sounded like tiny metal beads tapping the glass. She closed her eyes and listened to the wind coming in waves at the house like an ocean tide, quiet as it flowed out and then roaring in. The light of the quarter moon was blanketed by the black clouds above and there was an uneasy emptiness in the house, even though it was full of people.

"Samuel?" she called.

"Yes, Virginia Moon."

"Thank you for watching over things."

"I would be nowhere else."

She opened her eyes and gazed at her reflection on the black glass before her. She didn't see where he was, but she knew he was there. And now was the time to ask. "What happened to Juliette, Samuel?"

He didn't answer.

"Was she home over Laurel Creek when you were at war?"

"No. We were not yet married. She was from Sharpsburg and I had asked her to take her father south as we were going to come into Maryland."

"Antietam," Ginger breathed.

Samuel's head nodded in the reflection as he said, "Yes. But I did not know that at the time I asked her to move. She left before that battle."

"Where'd she go?"

"First to Strasburg and her cousin. As Sheridan came through the valley in September, I received a note that they were heading farther south to a cousin of her cousin. She didn't know where that would be as they were leaving in haste but would write as soon as she arrived. I never heard from her again."

"Did she die?"

Samuel gazed up in the reflection as he placed his left hand on his chest. "I found—" He broke off.

Ginger turned around to face him and asked, "Found what?"

"The farm near Strasburg was burned to the ground and we found four bodies. Nothing but bone among the ashes."

"You don't know if one of them was Juliette."

"I do."

"How?"

"Because one of them was her father, burned but recognizable by his clubfoot and his cane. She would never have left him."

Ginger listened to the wind scratch the roof.

"So we came to Cedar Creek, the rising blue tide amongst the flaming leaves of Virginia. And as I fought, I prayed for death to come and bear me to the arms of my love."

Samuel lowered his head and peered across the room from the shadow of his eyes.

"And I came," Ginger said.

He nodded, continuing. "You were there in answer to my prayer. I moved to hold you and you disappeared. The bullet that you saw hit Jeb."

"Wh-who's Jeb?" Ginger asked, confused.

"I didn't even see him, for I was filled with you. And then you were gone and the smoke cleared and Jeb, my best friend and son of the other man I called father, the Reverend Harker, whose buttons secured my own jacket, fell before mine own eyes, blood pouring from his gut onto his blue uniform. He served in the Northern army with his brother, Zach, and I for the South. War tearing us apart. Now here he was, a man I had known all my life, as close to me as if he were my own brother, bleeding by a bullet meant for me."

"I saw him," Ginger whispered.

"I knew then, it was over for me. We were lost

and duty called me elsewhere, for I held Jeb in my arms and he begged me to take him to Ruth. I knew his love. I knew that burning. So I picked him up and headed south, crossing the Shenandoah on a fallen tree to gain the other side of the river—the side that was not set ablaze by Sheridan.

"And we came to rest two days later at a place I had been before. I found myself across the Shenandoah from where I had sat several years before, looking at my picture with you as I rested on a large boulder. It was where I saw the ginger moon, an autumn moon in July, and began to feel out of place. How strange it was that I was there again. There but on the other side of the river."

Samuel's voice faltered. He shook his head, burying his face in his hands. He sat for a minute, trying to say something, but Ginger could only hear the cracking sound of words half spoken.

"Breathe, Samuel," she said.

Shaking his face free of his hands, Samuel whispered, "I tore Jeb's shirt apart for bandages. I laid him next to a tree as I crept down the steep embankment, thinking to fetch water. The farm on the other side was burning from Sheridan's march, and as I cleared the wood I saw across the river a little boy in a Confederate cap waving to me. Behind him, as near to him as I am to you, Virginia, were three Union soldiers."

His chest heaved as he gazed up to the ceiling,

his voice finding itself and growing stronger.

"I tossed my cap on the small sprout of a tree next to me, hoping to hide my allegiance, and called to the little boy, telling him to take off the cap—to run. Then I heard three pops and felt fire in my belly and my chest and my shoulder and I fell back into darkness, crying out for the boy, who now would die, and for Jeb, who would now die because I had failed to complete the duty to him."

Samuel's shoulders shook and, though there was no sound, Ginger knew there to be a keening somewhere in eternity from the sound of his cry.

She stood and reached out, placing her hand upon his tousled hair. She did not feel it on her skin, but felt it just the same. "Lie back, Samuel."

Obediently, he stretched his gaunt figure in the space once occupied by her husband.

"You are a good and honorable man, Samuel Ezra Annanais. Now rest. I'll watch over things tonight."

She returned to the desk, sat down, and as she went to put out the lantern she gazed once more at her reflection in the dark window. The lantern hissed a little as the mantles dimmed and then there was nothing but the sound of wind, the tapping of rain, and the creaking of a sleeping house.

CHAPTER 26

THROUGH THE GLASS DARKLY

Ginger drifted between dream and dawn. There was singing. Someone called her.

"Virginia Moon."

Samuel?

Ginger started, lifting her head from the desk. The light was gray-purple and the morning chorus had begun.

"Samuel."

Gazing out the window, Ginger found the world a shimmering of green seen though a thick, floating mist.

"I hear something I have not heard in a long while, Virginia Moon." She heard Samuel's voice but still did not see him.

"Mama! Mama!"

It was Henry on the stairs and Ginger flew from the desk, blowing past Samuel, who stood at the foot of her bed, and flung open the door. "Henry?"

"Oliver's gone."

Ginger looked down the hall as if she'd see him. Instead, she found Osbee in her bathrobe and her parents opening their bedroom door.

"What do you mean, gone?"

Jacob's head popped around the bottom of the stairs. "Mrs. Martin. A bird woke me up. It sang and sang and as I lay there listening, I could not remember ever hearing a bird with that song. So I sat up to look out the window and found Oliver gone."

"Bird?" Ginger's heart fluttered.

"We locked the door when we went to bed and it was open when we got up."

Ginger headed down the stairs.

"He took some cookies," Henry said. "We've been calling him."

"How do you know that?"

" 'Cause his dirty shoe prints are in the kitchen by the cookie jar."

"Maybe he's feeding the chickens," she muttered, reaching the bottom of the stairs and opening the front door. It was a cold spring morning. "Oliver!" she yelled.

"Eli went out to the chicken paddock."

Ginger stepped out on the porch. "Oliver Wendell Holmes Martin! You get back to this house!"

A shape came trotting through the fog from the direction of the orchard.

"Oliver!"

It was Eli, and he ran up, winded. "He's not with the chickens."

"Damn it, Oliver," she hissed, turning toward

the dining room. The entire household was now on the staircase.

"Get your clothes on," she ordered, irritated that Oliver had wandered off without telling anyone. "We've got to find Oliver."

As she made her way into the kitchen, she heard stomping and banging above her head.

"See there." Jacob pointed.

Following his finger, she spied on the floor near the counter by the cookie jar muddy, Oliver-sized shoe prints. She opened the door to the sunroom, following his tracks. Grabbing Jesse's coat, she slipped into her boots and headed down the back porch stairs. She found Eli at the bottom.

"Did you look in the barn?" she asked.

"Nah. The footprints go toward the chickens."

"Well, I'll head out that way. You go check the barn. Maybe he doubled back or something."

"They're pretty recent," Jacob said. "Not washed away by last night's rain."

"Oliver and those damn cookies. Should've locked the sunroom door," Ginger said, following her son's tracks toward the orchard. She wished there was less fog.

"We'd have nowhere to go to the bathroom if you did that," Jacob said.

"That is the first thing we're doing, Jacob. Putting a toilet in the summer kitchen." Ginger stopped. She had been heading to the orchard as a matter of habit, but when she looked down, she found only Eli Beiler's footprints.

"Wait," she said, holding her hand up. "He didn't come this way."

"Mama?" Bea called from somewhere in the fog.

"Bea. Take Mom and go out to the fields. Tell Henry to take Dad down the road toward the Creeds' farm."

"Will do," her dad's voice sounded in the mist.

Ginger was ten yards from the summer house and found Oliver's tracks had disappeared into a patch of grass.

"What about me?" Osbee asked.

"Go with Miriam onto the Schaafs' land."

She stepped onto the grass and walked through it.

"There's no tracks on the grass, see?"

"Neeeeaaahhhh," sounded from somewhere in the mist.

Ginger stopped. "Bubba? You better hope I don't find that you scared him again, or it's goat stew for supper. Oliver!"

"Virginia Moon." Samuel was a butternut shape in the gray morning light.

"What is i—?"

"Shh."

She looked back at Jacob, who shivered.

"Do you hear it?" Samuel asked.

"What?"

"The bird."

"There's a lot of birds, Samuel."

Then there was the distinct sound of Oliver's bird.

"Oliver!" Ginger yelled, stepping forward into the fog.

"Oliver?" Samuel asked, facing her.

"Yes." Ginger cocked her head. "Oliver's whistle."

She saw, then, Samuel pucker his lips and from his ethereal body came Oliver's bird.

"It's you," she whispered, reaching up to touch his mouth.

"It's Oliver?" he replied. "Oh, my God! Oh, my God! I know where he is. I hear him! To the bridge." Samuel disappeared.

"Samuel!" Ginger called, running through the grass. The bridge rose like a black, yawning mouth in the fog and she entered, her footsteps pounding its wooden planks. Her heart raced as she cleared it, now worried that Oliver had gone missing. Gazing down to where she had sunk ankle deep in snow nine days earlier, she found Oliver's tracks deep in the mud.

"Oliver!" Ginger screamed as she sped up, flying toward Jesse's tree. "Oliver!"

She tripped through the copse of woods and skidded to a halt in the mud. The Shenandoah was swollen; the little sandy spot where the creek met the river was submerged. Jesse's ash, which she had had the rangers move back to the bank after it had fallen, was now back in the river, having floated ten feet downstream. A single limb hooked around another ash root and was the only anchor the tree had holding it in place. Bobbing up and down in the water, its own roots were now center stream, jutting out of the river sharply.

"Oliver!" Ginger called, gazing up and down the riverbank.

"He's there."

Ginger looked up and found Samuel standing on the tree midway between the bank and the roots. His face was terrified as he pointed across the water.

"Hurry!" he yelled.

"*No!*" She flicked off her boots, ripped off her coat, and stepped onto the tree.

"Mrs. Martin! The water's too cold!" Jacob's voice was behind her but she didn't respond.

"This way," Samuel said.

The tree bobbed in the swollen river and so she got down on all fours to crawl its length. As she moved, she fixed upon Samuel's tattered boots ahead of her. Branches tugged at her feet and twigs scraped her stomach and ribs.

"There—" Samuel pointed straight across the water, but the tree ended in its tangle of roots.

"He's whistling. He's weak. Hurry!"

Ginger slid into the water, frozen fingers clutching her chest, seizing her breath. She picked her way around the prickling roots and when she got to the end she found a small evergreen had fallen into the river with five feet of water rushing between its top and the roots of the ash. She watched Samuel jump easily across the space.

"You'll have to swim it," he said.

The water was a spring run, cold and speeding downstream. Tucking her feet behind her, Ginger hung on to a tiny root and then let go as she pushed against the ash. She was free in the river, reaching for the evergreen. She missed.

Tumbling in the frigid water, Ginger was grabbed by the river and pushed downstream. She was under and then above, the sound of burbled splashing and the deafness inside the river's body silencing any call for help she might make. She was under again, kicking and rolling and in the confusion something hit her hand. Without a thought, her palm was filled with something and reflexively, as an infant wraps around an offered finger, she grabbed and pulled herself closer to it. Her face achieved the water's surface and she took a deep breath as she pulled on the bare limb of a willow that hung in the water. Quickly, she grabbed another and then another, moving like a monkey swinging on branches, half submerged in the river, until she reached the bank. There she pulled herself up the steep shore by the willow's roots and lay in the mud, gasping for air.

"Virginia! Hurry!"

Rolling over, she slid on the muddy bank as she crawled back toward the fallen evergreen. Gazing over the river, she now saw her entire family on the other side and she thought of her Jesse dream and Elysium.

"I'm on the wrong side," she whispered, following Samuel up the embankment.

They reached the spot where the large pine that had straddled the Shenandoah to bring Samuel to the Smoots' farm had once stood. The fallen tree left a gaping hole and, next to it, stood Samuel.

"He is in there."

She gazed down and, ever so softly, she heard Oliver's bird.

"Oliver!" she yelled and slid down into the hole. Loose soil gave way under her feet and she grabbed a root to stop herself from sliding uncontrollably down the steep incline. "Oliver?" she called, lowering herself carefully upon the ladder of roots. Her feet hit stone and, crouching down, she found that she had entered a small cavern. "Oliver?"

Sitting on her bottom, she scooted farther in. "It's Mama. I'm here. Where are you, Oliver?"

Above her head, a whistle sounded. Below her, a whistle replied. It was to her right. Carefully, she slid farther down, and when she ducked her head to peer into a particularly narrow break in the rock to her right, she found Oliver lying on his back, staring up at her from beneath a Confederate cap.

"Oliver," she whispered as she turned on her stomach and stretched her arms through the narrow space.

He whistled, his eyes tired and frightened and weeping. He was bleeding from his neck, a deep gash cutting his throat right across his larynx.

Ginger reached her hands underneath his shoulders. "I've gotcha now," Ginger said. "Mama's here."

She inched him out, sliding him toward her as she rested his head in the space between her arms so as not to move his neck too much. Her back and arms burned with the effort, but she knew she needed to move slowly in case his spine had been compromised. Clearly he had fallen.

"Mrs. Martin?" It was Eli Beiler above.

"I found him," she called. "We're going to need something to pull him out straight—need to make a stretcher."

"Got it covered, Ginny Moon," called her dad.

She pulled Oliver free and as she did he pointed back into the crevice. He whistled again. A whistle came in reply.

"Samuel heard you," Ginger said.

Oliver's pajamas were soaking and his left boot was missing. She pulled off his pants and ripped them apart, creating a bandage around his throat.

"Your bird is Samuel," she said as she felt around his chest and down his arms.

Nothing broken there.

He nodded slightly and whistled again, pointing back to the crevice.

"Don't move your neck, Oliver."

There was a sprinkling of soil from above and Ginger leaned over her son to cover him from the falling dirt.

"Ginny Moon?"

"Down here, Dad."

She scooted over and her father slid down with a small stretcher made from tree debris and tied together with willow branches.

"Good job," she said.

"Eli's pretty handy," he replied. "Hey, Oliver. We're gonna get you out."

The little boy pointed back to the hole as Ginger laid the small stretcher flat across the stone floor.

Tim asked, "That's where you fell in?"

"Let's slide him on," Ginger said.

Oliver shook his head and whistled, motioning to the crevice.

"No moving your head, Oliver," Ginger ordered. "Can you get your arms under his bottom, Dad?"

"Yup," Tim said, slipping his arms beneath Oliver's thighs.

"On count of three," she said, returning her own arms under Oliver's shoulders. "One, two, three." They lifted Oliver onto the stretcher. "Okay. We need to secure him to it."

"Ah! Need more willow branches!" Tim called back up the hole to Eli.

Oliver whistled again and pointed adamantly to the crevice, but Ginger and her father ignored him. Eli lowered a rope that Miriam had brought with her and, together, she and Eli lifted Oliver from the earth. Ginger climbed out next and then sat on the edge of the crevice, holding the rope for her father, who crawled out last. As she did so, she watched her mother and Osbee row across the river in a small inflatable boat.

"Where'd they get that?" Ginger mused as she knelt down beside Oliver. His pulse was strong and his pupils dilated and contracted as she shadowed them with her hand. Those were all good signs.

"From the springhouse," Miriam replied. "Osbee said it belonged to your husband."

Ginger reflected on this as she gazed down into her son's eyes. She hadn't ever been in the springhouse. The stream from the pond had stopped flowing and so its purpose ceased with the water. She had no idea it was used as storage.

Oliver shook his head and whistled a whisper of whistle.

"Please, Oliver, don't move your head." The

wound on his larynx was deep and was even now preventing him from speaking. Ginger was worried that his voice would not recover if he injured it any further. Tears started to pour from his eyes once more as he pointed to the hole. "You're okay now," Ginger said. "We're going to lift you down to the boat. Oliver, stop moving your head."

But he wouldn't. He just kept trying to whistle and continued pointing to the hole. Ginger looked back to the black crevice and then returned her gaze to her boy.

"Is there something down there?"

Oliver gave a thumbs-up.

She frowned. Oliver tried whistling again but it was now just air passing between his lips.

"You want me to go back down there and get it?"

Oliver gave another thumbs-up.

Her father said, "I don't think that's a good idea."

She turned her head, peering at once to her father, then to the hole, then to Osbee, who was nearly to the bank of the river, and finally back to Oliver. His neck was bleeding again as fresh blood shone crimson on his makeshift bandage.

"Dad, lower me down," she said, standing. "Miriam, if that boat gets to this side while I'm down there, you and Eli carry Oliver to it."

"I don't think this—"

"Oliver needs me to go back down there," Ginger said, holding the end of the rope out to her father.

Reluctantly, Tim grabbed it and, slowly this time, Ginger slid down the loose soil sides of the crevice and entered the shadowed darkness of the earth. Letting go of the rope, she crawled back across the rock, returning to Oliver's prison.

Across the bloody stone from which she had just extricated her son, Ginger spotted something white. Squinting, she leaned forward and, as she did so, something white slid down. It was the bone of an arm and it lay across a butternut uniform—a uniform secured with mismatching buttons.

"Oh, my God." She breathed. Samuel had said he had fallen after he was shot and so here he had died.

Samuel whistled a reply. The sound was now far and distant—floating away on the Shenandoah.

....

May 10, 1863
Guiney's Station, Virginia

Dear Juliette,

Alas—Jackson is gone. A great victory is made and, with it, a devastating loss. We, Stonewall's Brigade, must now follow another. Our com-mander, queersome yet brilliant, has died, shot by his own men as he audaciously sought to continue battle under a full moon. But even her light could not save him. All things shift to gray and white in her eye. What a man is and what he seems are one in the same in the full of her. But fear clouds a man's vision, casts shadows in his mind, and there is no fault to lay at her pale feet. There is only love for her light and forgiveness for those who set their muskets to fire in the shadows.

And what saw Jackson there in the shadows? He did not die of his wound. His left arm is lost—buried here in Chancellorsville. It was a heaviness in the lung that took him. We stood outside, ready to run messages or fetch water. Anything to help. We heard him call out orders from the window above, commanding men to move here, follow there. Then a quietness fell. The wind rustled the trees, which were fully leafed out in the deep green garments of spring. We heard, softly on a Sunday's gentle breeze—he said, "Let us cross over the river and rest under the shade of the trees." Those were his last words as he passed, and I sit here writing this letter beneath a waning Virginia moon, wondering what it was he saw. Did he hear my bird? Did he cross the river Lethe, taking up a bowl and drinking deeply from it, leaving the sorrows of this war forgotten?

So this day and this letter, I have come to my last brass button, Juliette. I hesitate to send it, as now I shall have none to see me home. Jeb's mother thought it superstitious and nonsense but these buttons hold my family's past; they secure me to my place in this world as surely as the Reverend's buttons secure the jacket on my back. Until this moment, I have not felt so bound to them. Today has made it difficult to let the last go. Yet, I must— I must trust Providence to be my guide, for to carry this one further is to risk its loss from the set. I should not create another orphan of this war. They have no home but with you and now you hold my future and my past. You hold the full of me.

My love, know an hour does not pass when you are not on my mind. Your dark hair and gray eyes look deeply into mine as we dance on a summer's night. I have no feeling but you in my arms, spinning around the floor as the moon dances with the earth. Days shall follow days. Months shall follow months. And all the while, I am returning to you, following the path that leads home across the river to dance once more beneath a Virginia moon.

Ever yours, devotedly,
Samuel

CHAPTER 27

THE CARETAKERS

Ginger sat next to her son, who slept in the hospital bed, resting as only a child can do.

She hadn't brought Samuel up from where he rested. On the contrary, she skittered away from his bones as quickly as possible, nearly jumping from the hole in three lunges up the rope. She said nothing to her father, and when meeting her son's wide, hopeful eyes, she simply mouthed, *Later,* as she lifted his makeshift stretcher into the boat.

They left Eli, Miriam, Osbee, and her mother on the other side of the Shenandoah and, together, Ginger and her father crossed the river. With the help of Henry and Bea, they carried Oliver across the covered bridge and through the orchard to the waiting ambulance that was surrounded by all of the neighbors. Into their care, she left her children and her family and climbed into the ambulance with her son. Sitting beside him, she let go, watching the EMT work on her boy. Now and then, she glanced up to the window to find her father following in the truck.

When they arrived, the emergency doors

swung open and Oliver was whisked away into Woodstock ER. Ginger followed where she could and was left to wait when she couldn't, just like any mother who brings her child to the ER. She knew everything in the place, yet all of it was unfamiliar, as she had never worked in Woodstock. And she had reasons not to.

She had always made it a point to work far from her home. Working locally meant knowing the people who entered your ER. They'd be on your children's soccer teams or would wave to you in restaurants or smile at you in the grocery stores. Private matters pass through the doors of an ER and, through her life, Ginger never wanted to know intimately the people she served. Her service was intimacy enough. She wanted the freedom of a separated life—of knowing her neighbors only with the information they were willing to share. Thus, her service called her from home and now that she sat next to her son, listening to the morning chorus rise again, as she and Oliver had now been in Woodstock Hospital for twenty-four hours, she was grateful she had always done so. No nurse knew her. No doctor was her familiar. For the first time in her life, she was simply a woman with CKS with GACP— "Cute Kid Syndrome" with "Gravity Assisted Concrete Poisoning" (falling/jumping down a far distance). She didn't have to take care. She was taken care of.

The door opened slowly and on the other side of it Ginger found her parents.

"Good morning, Mom. Dad was supposed to go home to sleep."

"I made him bring me back. I decided I'd sit with Oliver. You need to go home," her mother replied.

"I can't leave him."

"Why not?"

"I want to be here when he wakes up."

"I know, Ginny Moon," her father said. "But he's fine. His throat is stitched. Nothing's hurt in his neck and back. He only has scratches and a broken rib. They're just keeping him overnight to monitor him and, look, it's already day. Nothing to worry you and Mom will call us when he wakes and is ready to go."

"I can't leave him," Ginger repeated.

"I'll be here," Monica said, sitting on the arm of the chair where Ginger sat. She wrapped her arm around her daughter's shoulders. "Let someone else take over."

"What if he calls for me?" Ginger asked.

"I'll call you."

Ginger's father reached down and grabbed her hands, pulling her from the chair. "We'll eat and shower and if we feel okay, we'll just come back. It's not far. Come home with me, Ginny Moon."

Reluctantly, Ginger followed her father out the door, led by his steady hand holding hers.

"We'll take care of him," Nurse Mary Lou said as they passed the nurses' station. Ginger nodded and, without a word, climbed into the elevator, went down a floor, and came out into a beautiful spring day.

They said nothing as they drove. Ginger simply looked around the green, misty morning still in the fog of her son's injury. They passed the field where Samuel had once sat for a picture, down the road where Ginger had driven for lantern fuel, onto the lane where her husband last traveled away from his home, and as they pulled up the gravel drive, Ginger found Osbee standing in the cemetery.

Without another thought, she climbed out of the truck and walked through the orchard, the morning dew cold on the bottom of her jeans. Rooster gobbled to her as she passed the paddock. The chickens were up already, pecking the ground and chattering to one another of yesterday's events.

The wrought-iron gate creaked a little as Ginger entered. When it did, Osbee stood up, freshly pulled weeds in her hands. "You look tired, daughter. Go rest. Oliver is well."

Ginger nodded and looked around. "Should we have brought Jesse home here?" she asked, wishing she had his grave to care for. To stand alongside Osbee and work with love—Ginger could think of nothing more she'd ever want to do.

"He belongs where he is."

Ginger bent down and plucked at the skeletons of weeds, their lives long gone with last year's winter. As she worked around the bottom of a small stone cross, Osbee moved next to her and did the same on the headstone to her left.

"I didn't know there was stuff of Jesse's in the springhouse," Ginger said, her fingers turning muddier with each weed she pulled. Her back hurt as she thought of Oliver and Samuel lying in that narrow space within the mountain.

"There's a lot of stuff in there from times past. It was the only building to survive Sheridan's march."

The grass and weeds pulled from the small cross revealed an engraved name covered with mud. Squatting down, Ginger followed the letters with her dirty fingers, pulling the dirt from within them.

"Seen a small box that fits the gold key?"

Osbee stood up, snickering. "You still have that key?"

Ginger smiled up at her with a nod.

The name she'd uncovered was smeared still with mud but free to be touched by the light of the sun. When she sat back and read it, her heart rolled with a thundering sound in her ears as if a boulder had moved away from a far place.

"Juliette Marie Smoot," Ginger whispered.

"Mmm. My great-great-grandmother."

"She didn't die."

"What's that, daughter?"

Ginger jumped to her feet, startling Osbee, who fell in the wet grass on her bottom.

"Samuel!" Ginger yelled as she flew out the cemetery gate.

"No one has seen him," Osbee called after her but she didn't care. She knew exactly where he was and she raced through the grass, the thundering in her chest echoing in the bridge as she passed it.

"She didn't die in Strasburg!"

Crossing through the copse of trees, she stopped abruptly. Jesse's ash was gone.

She covered her mouth, gazing up and down the river, searching for her husband's tree.

"No," she breathed, and as she stepped to follow the river downstream to find it, Ginger spotted Samuel standing on the other side.

His eyes were as soft brown as the day they met. A wind picked up his hair. How was the wind touching his hair? Was he here now or was she looking there then?

She stood gazing down to the river's bend, which had taken Jesse's tree in its wash, and then across to Samuel. She had never wavered. She was her husband and he was she. They were one together and neither of them failed to serve. She closed her eyes, faltering in her own mind, not knowing what to do.

The Shenandoah babbled at her feet, its breath now cold, now warm, kissing her neck and caressing her hair. Then she heard its voice: duty. The voice of duty falls weighty on the soul; it is imperative. It must be followed. Anyone who hears the call of duty knows this. But in its carriage, duty lightens the path. In its weight, it gives purpose and meaning. In its lightness, it gives roots.

Ginger felt her root—not her husband's, not Osbee's. She knew her duty and, gazing around, she found Jesse's boat sitting next to the boulder with the rope and oars resting within. As she walked over to it, Osbee, Bea, Henry, and her dad barreled through the trees.

"What are you doing, daughter?"

"I'm bringing him home from war," she replied quietly.

Without a sound Ginger pushed the boat toward the river. As she did so, she found Osbee bending to help. "Please, Osbee. This is a duty for me and Henry and Bea. Can you take Dad, find a couple of shovels, and go dig a spot near Juliette."

Osbee stood up straight, shaking her head.

"It is a long, sad story, I think," Ginger added. "Come on, guys. Time to bring Samuel across the river."

With a frown of confusion, Henry and Bea hopped into the boat without a word. Ginger sat facing her father on the shore as she pulled on the oars. "It's a river, Dad. Not a light." She chuckled.

Her father smiled through serious eyes and shrugged.

The Shenandoah took hold of the boat, slowing now to let them cross without a battle. There was no need to talk—no need to ask directions. She simply looked into Bea's and Henry's eyes. They were fixed on a point on the opposite bank and she knew if she rowed in that direction, she would come to Samuel.

When the boat bumped the shore, her children climbed out, their demeanors as solemn as the day they stood on the hill in Arlington.

"Hi, Samuel," Bea said quietly.

"Good day, Bea," he replied.

As Ginger bent down to grab the rope, she closed her eyes, feeling the warm wind turn cold and warm again. She hurt, feeling the oncoming loss like the water of a growing flood.

"This isn't loss," she whispered to the river. "This is found."

Turning around, she found Samuel's eyes upon her. They were steady and moist at their edges. His hair was tousled by a wind.

"You are here," she stated.

"I am," he replied.

"The wind touches you now?" she asked.

"Not the wind you feel," he whispered.

She inhaled sharply, refusing the loss, and said, "C-can you see the other side?"

He nodded, his chest rising, deepening with breath.

Ginger said nothing as she passed him.

Together, Bea and Henry followed their mother up the steep embankment. The only sound was that of little pebbles rolling away underfoot, dislodged from their spot in the earth and heading down to the muddy bank. No bird sang. No wind breathed. No river flowed.

When they came to the crevice, Ginger tied the rope to a tree and with a firm nod to her children she lowered herself into the cavern. Her feet hit the floor and, squatting, she crawled down to the right. Her son's blood on the stone had dried and was deep brown. Stretching out on her stomach, Ginger slithered inside until her arms could just touch Samuel.

"It was Oliver, Virginia. Oliver was there and then, wearing my own cap on the opposite shore. I thought—"

"You thought him living then." Ginger lifted his skull from its place by his left hip and placed it in the crook of her arm so it didn't roll away in the deeper part of the crevice.

"The pine that fell that brought me across the river to you had grown old these one hundred and fifty years. Yet it still wore my hat that I placed on top of it when it was but a sprout."

"It was Oliver's bird that called to you."

"It was my bird that called to him."

"All of it to bring you here, now."

"And you. Can you reach me, Virginia Moon?"

"I can. And I know where Juliette is," she said

472

as she gently moved his bones around in his uniform so she could pull him from the hole.

"Where is she?"

"She's waiting for you." Ginger removed his feet from their tattered boots.

"A-are you taking me to her?"

"Yes." She rolled the boots up in the pants and tucked it all in a ball. "You will rest with her this night—where you belong."

Slowly, she pulled Samuel from the crevice and held him to her aching chest as she crawled back up the cavern. When she reached the rope, she wrapped it around him and Bea and Henry pulled him out. Ginger then climbed out after him, and as they walked down the hill Bea held Samuel's shoes, Henry held the rope, and Ginger held Samuel and her breath. They climbed in the boat and floated into the river.

Ginger rowed toward the opposite shore and when she was halfway across she gazed up and found Samuel sitting in the boat, his solemn face staring down at her children. Their shaking shoulders told of tears, though they made no sound. Instead she heard the Shenandoah singing, its voice rolling deep, quenching all who came to her shore. She thought of her Jesse dream, of floating weightless on the water. She wanted that; Ginger wanted her dream, so she pulled in her oars. Gently, the Shenandoah took hold of her children and slowly turned the boat north.

"Did you know," Samuel said, "that I met your father?"

Bea sniffled. "You did?"

"It took me a while to realize you belonged to him, but then, Bea, you did look so familiar when we first met by the barn. Do you remember?"

Bea nodded. So did Ginger. It seemed so long ago that Samuel had crossed on the fallen tree, but it was no more than two weeks. A lifetime had happened in two weeks.

"He crossed the river, thinking to run away. It was time to go home to his parents and he wanted to stay here, so up the mountain he climbed and as the violet hour came on he lost his way. I helped him bivouac and we spent the night, as the violet hour turned to rain, speaking of war and sloosh and VMI. Of honor, duty, service. To find what is right when in wrongness. To honor family though you disagree. Honoring does not mean to agree. It doesn't even mean you have to like your family. But you do need to acknowledge that your parents brought you into this world."

"That's what Daddy taught us!" Bea declared.

The Shenandoah shifted in her bed, bending as she flowed north. The boat eased with her and when Ginger looked over she saw the western shore and home drawing closer.

"And he taught you sloosh and bivouacking on rainy nights," Ginger added, thinking she should

474

grab the oars and row them farther out into the river.

Henry asked, "That was you?"

"That was me. I never knew I raised a boy."

The muddy bank crept closer.

"A man does not die if his dream yet lives, if his love lives."

Ginger gazed over to Samuel as the Shenandoah reached for the shore. Wanting her dream to continue a little longer, Ginger shook her head and as she reached for the oars she stopped. How long had Samuel waited? How long had he dreamed?

"My dream was to love—to raise children on a farm and find a place at the table."

"Wait a little more," Ginger whispered. As tears rose in her eyes, so they flowed from Samuel's.

"And I have done so. I have lived my dream." The wind flowed across Samuel's shirt, billowing and dissipating like a cloud.

"Don't go." Bea wept.

"I am with your daddy and we are just on the other side of the river. We'll always be there."

The bottom of the boat scratched the shallow bed of Shenandoah.

"I love you all," Samuel said softly. "Tell Oliver."

"We love you, too," Henry whispered.

The boat came ashore, and as Samuel disappeared, they heard his voice singing softly, "Let me cross over the river and I shall rest under the shade of the trees."

CHAPTER 28

Now We See Face-to-Face

Ginger's hands were filthy and the air flowed into her lungs like water. Summer was coming early and Virginia was full of herself, wearing a heavy gown of heat and humidity. As Ginger dug through the bricks in the floor by the back wall, she was convinced this springhouse had never really worked. The years of perfectly dry junk that had been piled in it gave testament to that fact. The pond should have released water, cooling the building so it would keep milk from spoiling. It also would run through it, down the creek bed, under the covered bridge, and flow to the Shenandoah. But clearing the years of furniture and farm equipment from the building had done nothing to release the water. Instead she found the floor of the building bricked over.

"I think, Dad"—she grunted as she hit a brick with her pick—"that this was just here to look like a springhouse. I don't think that pond ever flowed."

"Oh, yes, it did!" her dad replied as he tossed the growing pile of debris from his daughter's efforts out the door. "You can see right where you are working the edge of the older floor. These bricks are newer, which means they are not original to the building. They don't belong."

"That still doesn't mean the springhouse *was* a functioning springhouse."

"Well, why else would it have been built, Ginny?"

"Who knows? Why is the covered bridge here?"

"Ah! So people could read the signs on Highway 81 and follow—"

"Yes, thank you, Father," she said as her pick fell again, the brick breaking in half beneath its steel point. Sweat fell from Ginger's neck and hit the floor like rain. Her father chuckled, his feet shuffling softly as he cleared their work area. Bending down, Ginger lifted the two halves of the brick she had been working on. As she removed them, the older one next to it moved from its resting place.

"Shoot!" she breathed as she tossed the two halves of the broken brick over her shoulders.

"Hey! Watch it!" her dad yelled.

"Ah! Sorry," she replied. "I think I broke the original floor."

"Let me look."

Scooting over, Ginger let her father inspect what she had done. "Did I screw that up?" she asked.

"No," he mumbled as he squatted down. The back of his shirt was soaking wet. He was not from here and she was sure if the heat was bothering her, it must be torturing him.

"Maybe we should take a break, Dad."

"This brick was moved before, as was this one," he said.

"Hey! Look!" Her father leaned forward a little more and when he stood up he held within his hands a small, dusty box the size of a pound box of chocolates. The wood was scratched in places and as her father held it up for inspection, rotating it around in his hand to see all sides, Ginger spied a small brass lock with a tiny keyhole.

"I have that key!" she declared, leaning her pick against the wall.

"To this?"

"I think so." She smiled a great smile. "It belonged to Jesse."

"How'd he have the key if the box was buried under here?" Her father pointed to the old brick floor.

"Who knows! Let's go check to see if it fits."

Excited, Ginger stepped from the springhouse and found the air no less cool even though there was a breath of a breeze. The key? She thought for a moment; it was in her desk drawer. With her father following close behind, she made her way toward the house by way of the cemetery. As they passed it, they fell into their own thoughts as they gazed at the newest addition to the family plot. Samuel's grave was just like Juliette's, a simple stone cross standing above his resting brow with his name chiseled at the bottom. Juliette's cross was weathered and gray, old. Samuel's was white, sparkling in the late spring sun. Ginger thought one day, when she, too, lay beneath that soil, his would look just like any of the other headstones there. Nothing would set him apart as he stood apart now. Something in that thought saddened her and as she turned into the orchard she felt the emptiness of his loss. Two months he'd been gone, but it seemed like forever.

"Miss you," she whispered.

"Lots of people at the stand," her father noted.

Ginger gazed over to the vegetable stand that Eli and Jacob had made. The Smoots' crops weren't yet ready, but there were bushels of apples and pears from Ginger's orchard. There was a line at the stand and Miriam had Oliver scampering around like a mouse on a corn silo floor, putting fruit into bags and handing them to the paying customers. Then Ginger peered down the road and found cars parking one by one all the way down on the right side. People walked in the middle of the street, laughing and talking with one another. Children raced toward the covered bridge, where Henry stood watch.

Once upon a time, people would come down to Smoot's farm, stop, and turn around. Now they stopped and got out. They bought eggs, walnuts, apples, and pears and picked their own herbs from the garden near the barn. Fresh vegetables grown by all the other farmers on this little hairpin turn of the Shenandoah ended up at Ginger's vegetable stand, and after the visitors bought things, they'd wander over to the field to watch the land farmed with horses and mules. There was something to see, something to learn, something to eat, some-thing to do now at Smoot's farm.

The forty-two acres would now be given to Ginger, not born a Smoot but a Smoot all the same, trusted to her to be worked and then passed along as it had been since 1799. It was her home and her work. But she had yet to find her dream on it. She spent her days working the farm with her family and there was a great deal of work to be done. It was no longer solely a corn and hay farm. It was milk and eggs and vegetables. It was corn for animal feed and husks grown to be sold for the table. It was picking fruit and nuts and finding buyers in the local markets for the first time. Ginger worked the books, bought the seed, planted, plowed, and, like any farmer, prayed for good weather.

Through good weather and bad, the farm was now school, too. With the designated curriculum from the school district in hand, Ginger, her parents, and Osbee took up the responsibility of Henry, Bea, and Oliver's education. There was breakfast in the morning, class until noon held by one adult or another, while the rest went out and worked. Lunch would be eaten together and then all would head out to the fields and barns once more. The children had settled into the life of a farm family, their days filled with work and one another and friends coming to visit.

A screaming child brought Ginger's attention back to the orchard where she was walking. A father, mother, and unhappy toddler stood under a pear tree, the mother trying to give the child water.

"Cooler in the shade," Ginger said to them as she passed.

"So hot here," the woman replied.

"Where you from?" Tim asked.

"Seattle," the man said.

"Welcome to Virginia!" her father said, handing the dusty wooden box to Ginger. "Come. There're benches out behind the house under a grandfather of a walnut tree. Much cooler there."

"Oh, thanks!" the woman said, visibly relieved.

"Ever been to the Ginger Moon?" Tim asked as he walked away from his daughter with the Seattleites.

"I love that store!" The woman grunted as her screaming daughter tried to squirm from her arms.

Ginger shook her head. Her father was still out here but his heart was in Seattle. Her mother had returned to the shop the week before, as she and Tim had stayed in Virginia until Oliver was mostly healed, leaving the Ginger Moon in the capable hands of their employees. But it had been two months and someone had to go back home. Someone had to start wrapping things up on the West Coast. In the time Tim and Monica had lived on Smoot's farm, they had discovered that things had shifted—things had moved on. They had become part of the farm. They were part of Henry, Bea, and Oliver's daily lives. They were two more pairs of hands to serve the land and grow the family. The Ginger Moon and all they had built in Seattle was no longer their future. Their life was here and so Monica returned to Seattle to start settling their affairs there while Tim oversaw the construction of the doty.

After a month of Osbee's house being filled with people, Ginger asked Jacob and Eli if they would build a doty in the same manner as in an Amish home. In their world, grandparents live in the addition to the original house, or doty. It was natural for one to be made onto Osbee's house; it fit in easily just behind the porch on the north side. The dining room window became a door and the echoing sound of hammers falling meant a sitting room was being constructed just on the other side. A small set of stairs would open up onto a bathroom and bedroom. Tim himself wanted to stay and set the bathroom fixtures in place. Once finished, it would be time to leave for Seattle to aid his wife in the settlement of their affairs. Until then, he decided to clean out the springhouse and make the water flow, enlisting his daughter to help. Ginger wondered if he would stay and just leave Seattle to her mother.

"Dad," Ginger called after him. "Maybe you can go back with them. Ask them when their flight leaves."

Her father laughed and took the two-year-old from her mother. Instantly, there was silence except for the hammers banging away on the other side of the house.

"Keep it going there, Miriam," Ginger said when she passed the vegetable stand. As was always the case when day shifted toward the violet hour, Ginger spotted Solomon Schaaf wandering up the road. The day Ginger began to farm her own land with Eli and Jacob, the old farmer watched from a distance, sitting upon his tractor. As time went on, he could be found chatting with the boys and soon the boys would walk him home to take dinner with the old man and his wife. It was as if there were no fence now between their farms, and in the stillness of their return each night Ginger could hear Eli and Jacob speaking in whispers in their mother tongue. She didn't know the language but understood what was happening.

They were men. They were available for hire and slowly they spent less and less time with Ginger and more with Mr. Schaaf. They kept his farm pretty much going and the only thing that was left to him to do was tending his fields with his tractor. Ginger knew it wasn't because Jacob and Eli wouldn't use the machine. It was because plowing his fields was the one task Solomon Schaaf loved to do above all else. No one would take away the old man's love of work until he was ready to let it go.

So there Solomon was, walking toward Smoot's farm with a basket of eggs for the vegetable stand, and as she waved to him he smiled, handing the basket to Oliver and then heading to the bridge, where Henry stood guard. The task delegated to Ginger's eldest this day was the guarding of the bridge. People were allowed to walk through it and around it, but the path to where Jesse's tree once stood was strictly for family. She waved to her son, who gave a nod in return. As Ginger climbed the porch, she found the black Mercedes still in the drive.

"The battle continues," she breathed and, without hesitation, grabbed the doorknob, opened the door, and stepped into the house.

"What do you mean, Virginia, building onto this house?" Ester demanded from the dining room.

"Good day, Ester. Hugh. Mr. Glenmore. It's almost dinnertime. Will you be staying?" She smiled a great Southern greeting and then turned to the right to head up the stairs.

"We can sue," Hugh said, standing from his chair. "My arm was broken by your negligence with that goat."

"We're having a light dinner with salad and bread and apple tart. The kids made fresh ice cream," she added as she climbed the stairs.

"Did you hear me, Virginia?" Hugh called after her.

"Oh, sit down, Hugh." Osbee's voice was confident and unafraid. "If you're thinking about suing, I remind you to remember it's still my land."

"And the kids' home," Ginger hollered as she entered her room. Before there was another word, she shut her bedroom door. Dusty box in hand, Ginger stepped over to her desk and opened the top drawer. She shuffled through papers. A whippoorwill sounded far afield. She stopped and gazed out her window.

The bridge stood sturdy in the growing violet hour. Holding her breath, Ginger waited, hoping somehow Samuel, her friend, her supporter, would appear just once more.

"He won't show," she whispered. "He's been found."

Leaning into the window, she peered far to the right, past the orchard, past the chicken paddock. Samuel's cross was bright, reflecting now the purple glow of Virginia's sky. One day it would be just as all the others were—dull, aged, and forgotten by all except family. She thought then of her childhood trip through the mist to Chief Seattle's grave.

"All gifts left for the gentle, honorable man," Ginger whispered, her breath causing her bedroom window to fog.

Buried in Arlington, Jesse was one of many remembered for their service and duty because of where they rested. She wanted that for Samuel. But here he was next to Juliette, where he belonged, and no one would know his sacrifice—the years he spent between his beginning and his end. The last duty of pulling his friend from the battlefield and trying to bring him home. The love he gave up in service to that duty. That seemed so wrong.

She stood staring at Samuel's cross and felt the world shift—shift in the way it had done when Samuel was around. A familiar stillness surrounded her. She did not move. She waited in the space between—waited once again to be enveloped by acoustic shadow.

"Samuel?" she whispered. "Samuel? Is that you?"

But there was no acoustic shadow. Something inside her opened, as if eyes closed for years finally gazed out onto the world seeing all things as new—as if she was seeing with her Child's Eye. In that vision, rising from the mist of her breath upon the window in the light of the violet hour, she saw her dream. She'd build it, just like the giant structure that she remembered stood over the grave of Chief Sealth.

It would rise beyond the covered bridge in the shape of a bivouac sheltering two graves from the storm. She saw a small building just on the edge of Schaaf's farm, where people would come down the road and get out of their car just as they were doing now. But instead of just a farm to wander about in, they'd enter that building to see a butternut uniform with mismatched buttons. They would find—what would they find?

"Love," she said to the violet hour. "Love in the chaos of war."

The streambed was dry now, but she'd clear the springhouse and then it would flow under the bridge and return once more to the long-awaiting embrace of the Shenandoah. Ginger stood in awe, watching the sparkling little creek reflect the violet hour with her Child's Eye.

"A butternut uniform and what else, Samuel?" she asked.

Her hand moved and touched the dusty box, bringing her eyes and mind back to it. What had her husband left her? A message? A final note telling her—what? Or was it his childhood dreams of his own future? Jesse was gone but at least she'd finally have an answer to one of the mysteries he had left her: the key.

"The key," she said, shaking her head at herself. It wasn't in the dresser. It was still in her purse.

Reaching over to the foot of her bed, Ginger grabbed her handbag and rifled through it. She found the yellow envelope, and as she flipped it over to release the key she dropped her purse on the desk chair.

Her heart sped up as she lifted the key. It slid easily into the keyhole and, with a small turn, she heard the lock click. Slowly, she opened the box.

Inside she found one, two, three—she counted fourteen brass buttons scattered on top of folded papers, which were tied together neatly with a black ribbon. Ginger lifted the box at an angle and coaxed the buttons out onto her desk. Then she extricated the papers, and when she did so, her heart stopped.

There, at the bottom of the box, was a photograph of Samuel, his form seated in sepia exactly as she had seen him in Woodstock. And next to him, with her hand resting upon his shoulder, was the image of Ginger herself—an apparition, a ghost. A spirit standing by his side. There and then as here and now.

AUTHOR'S NOTE

I have studied the Civil War from the West Coast much of my life, never really believing I'd get to walk on the land where it was fought. I personally owe a deep debt to Shelby Foote for spending twenty years of his life living in the history of that time so I can come along many years later, pick up his narrative in a bookstore in Washington state, and listen to him as he walked me down that road. A map in a book was all I had for so long that when I actually stepped onto the grass and gravel of those places, I can only say it was spiritual. It would not have been so had it not been for the lifelong work of Mr. Foote.

With that said, I'd like to leave the reader with an opportunity. A shift in life can come from anything—a character in a book, a comment by a neighbor, a movie, or a three-thousand-page narrative. I have found if ever there was a path that needs walking, it is your history. Talk with your grandparents. Listen to your aunts and uncles, cousins and parents and siblings. Everyone comes from somewhere, so go, put on your shoes, and follow the map. When you walk through history, you become part of it. You find your place in it and it becomes your history. It becomes your story. I invite you to find your story. . . .

ABOUT THE AUTHOR

Nicole R. Dickson resides in North Carolina. For updates on Nicole R. Dickson, please visit her Web site at www.nicolerdickson.com.

QUESTIONS FOR DISCUSSION

This Conversation Guide is intended to enrich the individual reading experience, as well as encourage us to explore these topics together— because books, and life, are meant for sharing.

1. What is the purpose of the covered bridge?

2. What is the meaning of the Civil War to the Smoot family?

3. Jesse was good friends with Ed Rogers. Why did he not share that relationship with Ginger?

4. Why does Jesse have the key?

5. Who is sending Samuel to Ginger?

6. What is the significance of the Shenandoah Valley in the Civil War?

7. Ginger senses she is a ghost. Why?

8. What does Jack Wolfe's death signify?

9. The Amish kids came to the farm. What do you think the future holds for them there?

10. What is the goaty lesson?

11. Do you think Jesse ever opened the box?

12. Ginger's child's eye opens at the end of the book. Was Samuel there? What is the meaning of her vision?

Center Point Large Print
600 Brooks Road / PO Box 1
Thorndike, ME 04986-0001 USA

(207) 568-3717

**US & Canada:
1 800 929-9108**
www.centerpointlargeprint.com